KEELEY SAT IN SILENCE, THEN SAID, "SO WHY DID YOU COME?"

He sat on the edge of the desk and met her curious eyes, but didn't bother with his practiced smile. "I wanted to see you again." Gus let the words linger, undisturbed by the element of truth in them.

She frowned so deeply it looked painful; her expression darkened. "You're lying. Why?"

"Why would you think I'm lying?" He picked up a pencil from the desk, balanced the lead point of it on a paper block near the phone.

"It's in your face, behind those dark eyes of yours." Keeley stopped and seemed to consider her next words. "I get the impression you know exactly what you're about, Gus Hammond—and you keep it all to yourself." She took the pencil from his hand, put it down on the desk, and stood. "And, as I have no use for lies or liars . . ." She raised her eyes to his. They weren't angry eyes, more disappointed. ". . . I'll ask you to leave. I've got work to do."

When she moved to walk around him, he gripped her wrist, easily enfolding it in his hand. *Warm. Surprisingly delicate.* "You've also got trouble."

Novels by E.C. Sheedy

PERFECT EVIL

ROOM 33

KILLING BLISS

Novellas by E.C. Sheedy

Pure Ginger in BAD BOYS NEXT EXIT

In Good Hands in BAYOU BAD BOYS

E.C. SHEEDY

OVER
HER
DEAD
BODY

ZEBRA BOOKS
Kensington Publishing Corp.
www.kensingtonbooks.com

As always for Tim . . . first in my life, first in my heart.

And for my dearest friend and much-loved sister Pat Touchie, with whom I've shared so much of my life and dreams. You are singularly special to me.

And for the Red Door pen warriors. May there be many more Macaroni dinners to come. ☺

Dear Reader:

First up . . . I want to thank everyone who took the time to e-mail me regarding my last book, *Killing Bliss*. It is always wonderful, and an honor, to hear from readers. You are, after all, what writing is all about.

After reading *Killing Bliss*, many readers wrote and expressed their interest in a character in that story, Gus Vanelleto—a man with an assumed name, unknown past, and no fixed address. Gus's personal history is violent and tragic. As a youth, and as a man, he faced a perilous and uncertain future. But face it he did; perhaps not always making the best choices, perhaps not always in a socially acceptable way, and definitely not in a way that didn't leave lingering damage of its own.

Gus comes to *Over Her Dead Body* as Gus Hammond, dark, scarred, and deeply honorable—in his own way.

I hope you love him as much as I do.

E.C. Sheedy
www.ecsheedy.com

CHAPTER 1

Mary Weaver picked up the phone, scrunched her eyes tightly closed, and concentrated on her next move. What was it?

One more call to make. Yes, one more call.

Goodness, but her leg hurt. She looked down at it. All swollen up, like a fat blue-veined sausage, the stuffing inside too big for the skin holding it in.

I have to make things right. No time.

She rubbed her knee, looked around, and forced her brain to plod through the mist blurring its edges, threatening to curl inward, obscure everything.

Rain. There was rain beating on the old roof, wind hissing down the chimney. Not light. Not yet.

Where am I?

Why is it so dark? She should clean the windows. Yes. They were all fuzzy.

She shook her head until it throbbed, then blinked. No, the windows weren't fuzzy. She was.

Mary let the tears, frail and hot, run down her puffy cheeks and drip onto her stained nightgown.

She struggled to remember putting the gown on,

but couldn't. Buffeted by a new confusion, she sat stone still on the edge of the bed and clasped the gown's lace-edged collar, bunched it tight under her chin.

Naked. She'd been naked, dressed by a stranger. The grayness of shame colored the fog in her mind. So many strangers . . .

Maybe that woman . . . the one she didn't like. Hadn't she come yesterday? Last week?

Out of memory, out of time, panic closed her throat. Urgency clutched her heart. She had to make things right.

"Dear God, tell me, please . . . where am I?" she screamed into the empty room.

And, as if her scream were a wind blowing at it hard and fast, the fog receded, leaving the barest of clearings. Thoughts straight and sharp rose on the landscape.

Relief flooded her. "You're home, you mad old woman," she whispered and ran a hand over the mattress of the familiar bed she sat on. "Home," she repeated. "In Mayday House. Where you've always been." She closed her eyes. "You're here, in the now."

She brushed the moisture from her cheeks, firmed her will, and tightened her grip on the phone still in her hand.

"And the now won't last, so you'd best get on with things."

And she did.

Keeley Farrell's cab pulled up to Mayday House as two young men were rumbling a sheet-draped gurney toward the gaping doors of the County

Medical Examiner's van. Her heart shrank in her chest, then constricted painfully.

Oh, my God . . . I didn't make it!

She flung the cab door open, got out, and ran toward the van. Unable to speak, she held up a hand to halt the men set to slide a sheet-draped body into the vehicle's cavity. Several strands of long gray hair had escaped the shroud, straggling across the white cotton as if drawn in charcoal.

Keeley closed her eyes to hold back the flood of tears gathering there.

"Ma'am?" one of the men said. "You okay?"

She opened her eyes, took a breath and, ignoring his question and the concern in his curious gaze, placed her hand on the still, covered figure on the stretcher, near the heart. Mary's fine, good heart. Stopped now. Never to beat again.

"I'm too late," she murmured. "I'm sorry, Mary. So very sorry."

"We have to go, ma'am."

"I want to see her," she said.

"I don't know . . ."

While he hesitated, Keeley loosened the sheet and folded it back, exposing Mary from head to waist. She gasped.

Stringy gray hair framed a face so swollen and discolored that for a heart-stopping moment she had the crazy hope she was wrong, that this wasn't Mary. Wasn't the woman who'd raised her after the death of her mother, the woman who'd loved her. The woman who'd known her better than she knew herself. But of course it was.

Keeley reached for Mary's hand, turned it over in her own, and gripped it tight.

She pushed the hair from her forehead and bent to kiss it. "Godspeed, Grandmother. Godspeed," she whispered against the cold flesh, wishing with all her heart her prayers carried past her failed loyalties.

"Ma'am?" the attendant said again. "We've got to go."

She nodded, straightened away from the body and, swallowing hard, covered Mary's face.

The two men slid the body into the truck and closed the door. While one headed for the truck cab, the other gestured toward the house. "There's people up there if you have questions."

"Yes, thank you."

Keeley dealt with the waiting cabbie, then towed her rolling suitcase up the broken concrete path to its latest resting place, and with luck, its last—Mayday House.

Home.

Sort of.

She was met at the door by a tall, dark-haired woman.

"I'm Keeley Farrell," she said, attempting a smile.

"From your message to Mary, I expected you considerably earlier," the woman said, her tone cool, her eyes accusatory.

"Yes. I had travel problems." Understatement of the year, but about covering it. "What happened?"

"A better question would be, what didn't? Heart failure, dementia, edema. . . . Didn't have to happen, either."

"Why did it?"

"She became difficult, refused to take her medication." The woman's face had the stern grain of old lumber, and her voice dripped disapproval.

Keeley leveled her gaze on her. "Who are you, exactly?"

"Marion Truitt. I'm a private nurse with Barrker Contingent Home Care."

"Not much of one, by the look of things."

"I beg your pardon?" Her eyes widened; her mouth tightened.

"Mary's face was dirty, her nails were unclipped— also dirty. And her nightgown looked as if it hadn't been changed in weeks. If that's how bad she looked on the outside, my guess is you weren't doing much good for the inside, either."

"She wouldn't listen, I tried—"

"Get your coat and broomstick, Marion Truitt," Keeley said brusquely. Incompetence, it seemed, stalked the world—that and not giving a damn. She had no doubt Truitt epitomized both. "Your services—or lack of them—are no longer required. And if there's money owing, forget it. I write a convincing letter." She walked past the gaping woman into the house and didn't look back, even when the door slammed hard enough to shake the ancient rafters.

After propping her suitcase against the entryway table, she took a good look around.

The house looked as though it had been ransacked by a gang of bears on a honey hunt. Stuff— and there was no other word for it—was everywhere, a lot of it books, magazines, newspapers. A crusty layer of dust and grime stuck to every surface unfortunate enough to have missed the plop of the daily press. Through the open kitchen doorway she spotted the sink. It looked set to collapse under the weight of dirty dishes.

Oh, Mary . . .

Numb, she stood in the front hall, rubbed her face, then shoved her hair back, unable to ignore the stab of guilt poking her already seriously overloaded conscience. Mary should have told her she'd been having hard times, shouldn't have left her to hear it from some unknown female who'd left a whispery, virtually unintelligible message on the New York office's voice mail. It was miraculous it had even found its way to the hospital—or the tent that passed for a hospital—where she was working in Darfur, Sudan.

A day later and she'd have missed it entirely.

The loss of three aid workers during a brutal attack on a neighboring village had her team again decamping and awaiting instructions. Given the dangerous, unpredictable situation in Darfur, the directors of Medics-At-Large, MAL, the humanitarian organization she worked for, opted to pull Keeley's entire team. Some of the newer arrivals were redeployed; others, like Keeley—with problems—were sent home.

In the dark of her sleepless nights, she was secretly relieved the decision had been made for her. Something else to feel guilty about.

The call telling her she was needed at Mayday House, the chance to help Mary, couldn't have come at a better time. But she'd expected Mary to be here, for them to work together—

"Are you Keeley?"

Startled, her heart jerked in her chest, and she spun to face a young girl, early twenties maybe, standing on the stairs, her hand on the newel.

"That's me," Keeley said. "And you are . . . ?"

"Bridget. Bridget Garner." She hesitated. "I'm the one who called you. I hope that was okay."

"Better than okay and greatly appreciated. Thank

you. I'm sorry I didn't get here sooner." Keeley
gave her a quick scan. Short, blond, sickly thin, and
with nails chewed to the cuticle.

"Yeah . . . I guess I should have called sooner,
but . . . I didn't know she was going to—you know.
I'm sorry."

Keeley shook her head. "It's okay. But I did wonder
who exactly called. You didn't leave a name."

"Didn't I?" The girl frowned, brought her index
finger to her mouth. "I thought I did."

"It doesn't matter." Keeley forced a smile. "You're
one of Mary's girls, aren't you?"

"Not anymore, I guess. I was, though." She
touched her tummy with a splayed hand. "I lost my
baby. Seven months along. That was a while back. I
kind of . . . stayed on"—she lifted a bony shoulder,
then dropped it—"to help Mary."

*And because you had nowhere else to go, like so many of
Mary's sad and confused guests over the years.*

"I see." Keeley said. But from the look of the
place, she assumed Bridget's help didn't amount to
much. And from the look of the sad-eyed girl in front
of her, she assumed Mary wouldn't have expected
it. Unless things had changed in the years since
she'd left Mayday House, it would have been Mary
doing the helping.

"When she was . . . okay, Mary talked about you a lot."
Bridget started to cry. "She was the only one—"

Keeley went to her and put an arm around her
shoulder. "I know. Mary was the only one to help—
to love—a lot of people. Me included. I 'kind of
stayed on' with her, too."

"She said you were like"—she gulped a breath—
"her granddaughter or something."

"Yes." Keeley didn't say more, afraid the words would turn to a river of tears. At the moment, the fine line between granddaughter and goddaughter was too blurred to explain.

Bridget sniffed and rubbed her cheeks with both hands. "She didn't much like crying, did she?"

"'Tears are for silly boys and sissy girls.'" It was oddly comforting to repeat Mary's oft-used adage—always said with a grin. And empowering. Because as Keeley had learned so well in Africa, all the tears in the world, all the days and nights trying to stop your body quaking in pain and fear, didn't bring back the dead, or make things the way you wanted them to be. No. A person had to *do*, keep moving, make use of themselves. She'd come home to do exactly that.

Bridget smiled a bit. "Yeah."

"Now if I know Mary, there's bound to be a cup of tea or coffee around here somewhere."

Before following Bridget into the kitchen, Keeley took another look around at the sorry state of the house. One thing was obvious: if she planned to return Mayday House to Mary's vision, make it serve again, she was in for an awful lot of work.

A mingled sense of calm and excitement settled over her. Anticipation.

Because if it was true that hard work is good for the soul, she needed all she could get.

Gus Hammond paced the plush carpet in bare feet, his white linen slacks wrinkled from the heat, his black shirt still crisp from Rodina's meticulous ironing—his state of mind somewhere in between. He used both hands to shove his thick, sleek hair—

nearly as black as his shirt—behind his ears. When this was over, the first thing he'd do was get it cut. And buy some goddamned jeans. The *GQ* model look, always Dinah's choice, was history.

He poured himself a JD neat and walked to the window, a wall of glass twenty feet high and probably three times as long. He stared for a moment at the horizon, a sharp sunlit line where a diamond-bright ocean met a shimmering blue sky, a sky deepening slowly into early evening.

Gus glanced down at the view of South Beach far below, the old neon-lit hotels: the blue of the Colony, the hot pink of the Boulevard. Throngs of people cutting through the heat, out for a night of salsa and sex—the women wearing barely enough to stay legal. Miami Beach, where the perfect body hunted the perfect checkbook—and generally found one.

As he had.

From his vantage point, the street action was so far below, the scurrying people were ant-sized, too insignificant to matter. Exactly how Dinah liked them.

The penthouse, Dinah's latest acquisition and decorating work in process, boasted the best views in Miami. A guy could see forever. If there was anything out there he wanted to see.

He drank his whiskey slowly, thinking how he couldn't wait to leave this place behind, finally get back to Seattle where he could do what needed to be done. Hands on, goal in sight line. With the added bonus of having Josh close by again. Damn, he missed the kid.

"Mr. Hammond?"

He turned. "Uh-huh."

Rodina, the housekeeper, had taken a step or two

into the room and now stood silently with her hands clasped in front of her. "Mrs. Marsden is on her way up. She'd like a gin and tonic," Rodina said. "I'd do it, but she said—" She looked momentarily timid.

"She said, tell Gus to do it."

She nodded.

He moved automatically to the bar. "Thanks, Rodina."

She'd barely left the room when the elevator doors opened and Dinah Marsden entered. Tall, slender, and attractive in the high-toned, casually sophisticated way she favored, she looked at least a decade or two younger than her fifty-eight years, the feat a combination of good genes, a rigorous fitness regimen, and the best cosmetic surgery money could buy. In Dinah's case, her money bought a lot.

Oh, yeah, and sex. Dinah believed great sex, and lots of it, was the real fountain of youth.

The sex was Gus's contribution, or had been, until he'd developed a chronic headache.

Dinah dropped her tote and a couple of small logoed bags on the pure white leather sofa. The massive room had two colors, white and a blue so pale it barely registered as a contrast. The bags, one silver colored, the other black and gold, slid from the sofa to the carpet like a dark stain. Dinah ignored them and walked toward Gus.

Taking his face in her hands, she kissed him hungrily, and he let her, out of habit, enfolding her in his arms. She pulled back, touched his mouth with a long crimson nail. "I've missed you, baby," she whispered, running a finger along the jagged scar that ran from below his ear, along his jawline, almost to his chin.

He didn't bother mentioning it had been her

call to spend the whole goddamn day at the spa. No
doubt because she knew what was coming. He picked
up her G&T from the bar and handed it to her. "We
need to talk," he said, setting down his glass.

She immediately looked wary, then kicked off her
shoes and took a seat on the sofa. "I can think of other
things that are a lot more fun." She undid the top two
buttons of her shirt, stretched out her long tan legs,
and looked at him from under her lashes.

"Kittenish isn't your thing, Dinah."

"I know, but it was worth a try." She laughed then,
pulled her legs up under her, and took a sip of her
drink. "God, it's miserable out there today. Hades hot
and the humidity's thick enough to drown in." She
took another drink. "Thank God for air conditioning.
Did Peter call about the tapestry for the bedroom?"

"No idea. I didn't answer the phone."

"Why not?"

"I was busy." He took the chair across from her,
leaned back, and perched one ankle on the opposite knee. He gripped it tightly instead of gritting his
teeth at her latest attempt to divert the conversation,
escape the inevitable.

Any other day she would have asked, busy with
what? But not today. Today, Dinah's antennae were
up. She sensed trouble, and he was about to give her
some.

"I expected you hours ago," he said. "I wanted
to—"

"Freshen this, will you?" She held out her glass, still
half full.

He rose, crossed over to her, and took the glass—
for the fuckin' last time. And filled it. Poured a scotch
neat for himself.

"Where do you want to go for dinner tonight?" she asked.

"We're not going to dinner tonight. Tonight I'm getting on a plane. Which you damn well know. I waited for you to say good-bye."

"Gus!"

He stood over her and handed her the drink. "I've tried to talk to you about this for days. Hell, months. None of it should be a surprise. Did you think your not showing up would change things?"

She didn't answer; instead she put the G&T on the coffee table, picked up the black and gold bag, put her hand in, and pulled out a velvet box. "I bought you something."

"Jesus, you haven't heard a word I said." He let out all the damn breath in his lungs, slashed a hand through his hair.

"It's a Piaget. An Emperador something-or-other. Quite special, or so I'm told." She held it out to him. Ninety grand's worth of gold and diamond timekeeping.

He looked at it, then into her eyes, big, blue, and showing the barest trace of desperation. *Hell!* "I'm going, Dinah," he said as patiently, as softly as he could. Soft generally not being his thing. "Nothing's going to change that." He took the watch from her hand, set it on the table, and raised her fingertips to his mouth. "I don't want another watch, another car, or another Armani. What I want is for us to be straight with each other, and if possible, part as friends." He looked into her eyes. "I owe you, but I can't give you what you want anymore. I don't—"

She pulled her hand from his, holding it palm out to stop him from saying more. Then she closed her eyes, took a breath, and opened them. "You don't love me," she finished, her voice low and cool, "the way I love you."

Gus let her comment fall into the room's bright white void. If there was one thing he knew about women—and he'd learned a hell of a lot through the years—anytime the *L* word came into play, it was time to shift into reverse. Lately, with Dinah, the word had come up on a regular basis. "It's time for me to move on." *Years past time.*

She got up and walked to the window, keeping her back to him. "You're going to Josh. In Seattle."

"Yes." Only a piece of the truth. But enough.

She nodded, and he saw her straighten her shoulders before turning back to face him, pride and self-assurance intact. "I guess I shouldn't complain. We've had a good run."

"Better than most. You were there for me—and Josh—when no one else was. I won't forget that." And he wouldn't. Ever. This woman had saved his life—such as it was—and given him more than he damn well deserved, but he didn't owe her his future. The way he saw it, they were even—even if their relationship was damned complicated.

"Thank you for that." She walked to the coffee table and picked up her drink. "Give Josh a kiss for me, will you?" She gestured idly toward the abandoned watch, now gleaming hotly under the slanting rays of the afternoon sun. "Maybe he'd like it?"

Gus shook his head. "He's got a watch."

"Of course." She stopped. "When are you leaving?"

"In about an hour."

"I see." She took a step away, looked out the window, and took a sip of her G&T.

Gus knew she didn't see at all, would never see. If

Dinah Marsden was anything, it was stubborn. She liked things her way, and she didn't like to lose.

"Then you can save me a trip." She settled her gaze on him, this time speculatively.

"Pardon?" Her new tack caught him off guard.

"I need a favor. And I need discretion."

He watched her, the word *favor* ringing alarm bells.

"Who better than you to provide both?" A wily smile turned up her brightly colored lips. "That's what we're all about, isn't it, Gus, darling? Favors and discretion?"

CHAPTER 2

Gus should have seen it coming, should have been prepared. He knew Dinah well enough to know she didn't give up on anything she wanted—until she'd exhausted every hook she could come up with.

Shit! He eyed her, waiting.

"Someone I've known—and supported—for many years recently died. Her name was Mary Weaver. Yesterday I received a letter from a woman who says she's Mary's goddaughter, and who seems intent on taking over her affairs. She's requesting money. Quite a lot of money." She frowned. "Says she wants to continue Mary's good work."

"What kind of work?"

"Mary ran a sort of a private home for"—she stopped and seemed to search for words—"troubled women."

"You said 'sort of.'"

"It started out as a haven for unwed mothers, then grew into a shelter for abused women. Something like that. To be honest, I haven't kept up with her work—

her mission, she used to call it. I just lost track." She walked a few steps away and looked out the window.

Gus's interest was snagged, and he waited for her to go on. Dinah didn't *lose track* of anything, unless it suited her purpose.

She walked back to him. "The place is called Mayday House, and it's in Erinville, Washington, a couple of hours southeast of Seattle. The last time I spoke to Mary—had to be four, maybe five years ago now—she was talking about getting too old to run it, closing it down." She looked annoyed. "Obviously, she changed her mind and made other arrangements—without any consultation with me—shortly before she died, apparently assuming I'd continue my financial support." She shook her head, disgusted. "The whole idea of such a place is archaic. I should have stopped sending money years ago."

"Why didn't you?" It sure as hell wasn't like her to dole out cash, charitable or otherwise, unless there was a return, either in good publicity, or, as in his case, a more intimate payback.

Ignoring his question, she walked to a glass-topped desk in the corner, opened a drawer, and pulled out a letter. "I want you to go to Erinville, meet this Farrell woman, and tell her I have no intention of continuing my support for Mayday House. I expect when she hears that, she'll go along with what I want and move on."

"And that's what you want? For her to move on?" He was damn sure Dinah wasn't telling him everything, but shrugged it off. Her business.

"My loyalty was to Mary, not a creaky out-of-date refuge for women who let themselves be abused by men, or worse yet, don't know how to take a goddamn birth control pill. The place should be shut down. What I want is for you to assess this woman, then do whatever you have to do to get her out of that house." She gave him a thoughtful, amused look. "This might be a challenge for you, baby. Apparently Farrell is some kind of nun, so I doubt your particular talents"—she dropped her gaze to his crotch—"and generous attributes will help much."

Gus sucked up his anger, shot her a killing glance, and looked at his watch. Less than two hours and it would be bye-bye, Miami. Maybe, after thinking on it for ten years or so, he'd figure out how he'd come to actually like this woman—right now the reasons escaped him. "Why not answer the letter, tell her you won't be sending any more money? Suggest she move on. Sounds simple enough to me."

"Because I don't want trouble. And I don't want negative press. We all know how these do-gooder types are, crying 'poor me' to the media when they don't get what they want, making a public fuss. In the end I'd be the big bad wolf—or worse." She shook her head. "No. I want you to take a firsthand look, assess the woman. If it looks as though she'll be difficult, tell her I'll buy her out. That way she can set up shop somewhere else. I don't want to, but I'll pay over market if I must."

"Generous," he said. "And not normally the way you do business."

"I have my reasons."

"Yeah, you usually do." He finished off his drink, again glanced at his watch.

Dinah's expression hardened. "I want Mayday House closed. Boarded up. Or better yet, reduced to rubble. And I want it done as soon as possible."

She held the letter out to him. "Use your charm, your guile, or that intimidating scowl of yours to scare the woman to death. You're the chameleon, Gus. Hell, you've made it an art." She shook her head, irritated. "So just *be* what you need to be to get the job done— and get the Farrell woman out of there."

He looked at the letter in her hand—knew it represented a link between Dinah and himself he'd rather avoid. He also knew his reluctance was obvious.

Dinah, impatient now, waved the letter in front of him. "I'm entitled to a last request, Gus, considering how long you've been in my—Let me see, what would be the right word?" She tapped an index finger on her chin. "Service? Yes, that's it. My very *personal* service."

It was exactly the right word.

When he still didn't take the letter, she added, in a tone that was Oscar-award-winning sweet, "What was it you said, darling, about 'owing me'?"

"You might not make the grade as a kitten, Dinah, but you've got the bitch thing nailed."

She laughed.

Gus took the letter.

Keeley slumped into a kitchen chair and opened the bottled water she'd taken from the fridge. She drank deeply, set the bottle on the table, and rubbed her hands over her face.

A glance at the clock told her it was five minutes short of two A.M., which meant she'd been scrubbing and scouring since midnight. She felt like elephant droppings, beyond tired and into the realm of the living dead. But she knew she wouldn't sleep, that if she went to bed she'd see them coming across the flat, dry earth. Hear the gunfire, the screams.

When her hands started to shake, she flattened her palms on the tabletop and forced the memory into the black hole it had come from. Bad enough it haunted her when she tried to sleep; she didn't need it when she was trying to stay awake.

A limp smile turned up her mouth. She was definitely in a no-win situation—or at least a no-sleep situation.

Picking up the mop she'd propped against the table, she walked back to the bucket of hot soapy water. If nothing else, insomnia was productive. She'd done more in the last two hours than Bridget had accomplished in the last week. The girl made a snail look like a turbo-charged roadrunner, but Keeley knew depression dogged her, pulled her down. Losing a baby so close to term took a terrible emotional toll.

What now seemed like a thousand years of nursing and religion had taught her that much.

The phone rang, clattered into the room like dropped china, rattling her heart and sending a chill through her chest. Who would call at such an hour?

She went to the old phone leashed to the wall near the kitchen door. "If this is a wrong number, you're in trouble," she said, in no mood to dispense a cheery hello.

A man's voice curled into the room. "Am I talkin' to Keeley Farrell?"

"Yes, a very irritated Keeley Farrell."

"You're up late."

"So are you. Whoever you are." She didn't attempt to hide her annoyance.

"At two o'clock in the morning, names don't matter much, do they? Except maybe yours."

Keeley stilled. "If this is some kind of obscene phone call, you're wasting your sick breath, my friend. If you've got something to say, say it. You've got five seconds."

He laughed, and it came through the phone as mirthless as a hungry snake. "You're Mary Weaver's godchild or somethin'? Right?"

Who was this man and how did he know about her and Mary? "Four seconds," she said.

"Tough little cookie, huh?" He sounded amused now. "Well, guess what, sweet cakes, I've got all the time in the world. Not so sure about you, though."

"Is that a threat?" Keeley's sleep-deprived mind staggered to full alert.

"Nope. But a woman alone . . . in a big empty house makes a man think a certain way. Only natural."

Keeley's gaze, as wild and unfocused as her thoughts, scanned the room, looking for nothing, expecting anything.

Keep it together, Keeley. Keep it together.

Gripping the receiver tightly, and raising her voice over the thud of her heart, she said, "Well think about this: I don't frighten easily, and I'm not alone," she bluffed.

"Oh, yeah, the little blond parcel. A bit skinny, but usable."

His oily words squeezed her lungs like a pair of cold, clammy hands. "Look, gutter-mind, why don't you go get yourself some help before I get it for you—in the form of a police siren."

He laughed; then she heard his deep, raspy breathing coming down the line. His next words were lower, coarse and whispery. "I kinda like women with gumption. So much more fun than the dead kind." He stopped. "But those police you were talkin' about? A bad idea. A *really bad* idea. Won't do you any good anyway, because I won't be calling again. Besides, you wouldn't want them to find out about dear old Mary, would you?"

"What are you talking about?" Confusion mixed with the crazy flutter in her chest. "What do you know about Mary?"

"Everything I need to know and a lot you don't, sweetheart. And most of it ain't pretty." He paused, and she heard him breathing again. Heavy, as though he meant for her to hear. "Not as pretty as that bright red hair of yours. But I gotta say the yellow scarf you've got tied around it? That's a real bad color choice."

Click.

Keeley's hand flew to her head, the yellow scarf circling it, and at the same moment she heard the rumble of a car motor from the dark road beyond the fence. Her heart, wild as a dervish, danced up her throat.

She dropped the phone and rushed to the window in time to see the ruby of a car's taillights disappear around the corner.

"What the hell's the matter with you? All you had to do was confirm she was there, not set her running, for God's sake! . . . 'Having a little fun'? You're fucking crazy. Are you even sure you spoke to the right woman?"

Dolan looked down the darkened hall, saw the

sliver of light creeping from his father's room. He spoke in a low, tight voice, struggling to keep fear from rooting too deep in his chest.

"If you've botched this, Mace," he added, "neither of us will see a dime. . . . I know, I know, I owe you. Christ, you remind me of it often enough. But no more 'fun.' We need to be sure about this Farrell bitch and what she's doing there. And stop phoning this number. Call my damn cell like I told you to. You got that?"

He heard the rustle of newspaper coming from the room, and added quickly, "Gotta go. The old man's awake. Sit tight, will you? And for fuck's sake, leave her alone until I can figure out what to do. We don't want her calling in the damn police." He hit the OFF button, fought the urge to slam the phone into its cradle—or better yet, against the damn wall.

Jesus, it couldn't get any worse than having Mace Jacobs involved. The guy was a goddamn pervert! Unpredictable as hell. Not that Dolan had any choice. Owing a guy a couple of hundred thou kept him interested—and close. Trouble was the asshole thought he was calling the shots. Well, he was goddamn wrong!

"Who was that, calling at this ungodly hour?"

Shit!

Dolan James, still reeling from the phone call, didn't answer. His throat sand dry, and his mind dead numb, all he could do was grip the phone he'd just clicked off. If he'd had any doubts about the validity of Mary Weaver's call, Mace had laid them to rest.

Dolan dropped his head and rubbed hard at the back of his neck.

Jesus Christ! This couldn't be happening. Mayday House was for real. Just like the old woman said. And some woman named Farrell had moved in to run it.

"Dolan? Are you there?" His father's voice seeped into the hall along with the light from his bedside lamp.

The man never slept. No change there. Old William considered insomnia, whether he was working his ass off and running all over the world, or dying, as he was doing now—although too slowly for Dolan's taste—as added "productive time."

Dolan wanted to laugh but smiled instead. The good thing about successful workaholics is they never had time to spend their money—just died young and left it to those with nothing but time. At twenty-six, Dolan had time to spare.

"I'm here, Dad." He lifted his hand from the receiver he'd placed carefully back on the charger and tried to take his mind off Mace's call, sound as if his whole world hadn't hit an air pocket and dropped him ten thousand feet. "And the call was nothing. A wrong number."

Dolan brushed his straight, sandy-colored hair off his face and straightened his jacket. The suit hung on his thin five-ten frame as if tailored for a man twice his size, and his blue eyes felt dry, feverish. He blinked, forced himself to calm down before he took the few steps to his father's bedroom door.

"It's after two in the morning. Who would be calling anyone at this hour?" William James grumbled from his bed, the lines and hollows in his face looking like dismal smudges in the pale light from his lamp.

"Who knows?" he said, keeping his tone casual.

"But the teenage cell phone brigade never sleeps, so it was probably some kid." He assessed his father, an activity that since the diagnosis had become routine. Fortunately, every day he looked worse than the last. It wouldn't be long now. Hell, it couldn't be long, not after what Mace had told him. Plus Dolan was running short in the time and patience departments. The idea of Farrell nosing around in that house, finding out stuff, the chance of her getting to William—before he could get to her—scared the crap out of him. "And they're not the only ones who don't sleep. You should be lights out by now. You need your rest." He stopped at the foot of the bed, coiled his fingers around one of its four posts, and forced a smile.

"I'll be sleeping permanently soon enough." He settled his rheumy gaze on Dolan. "Where have you been, anyway?"

With a prostitute, big Daddy, two of them actually, getting it off, and getting the hell out of this hospital you call a home. "I took in a couple of movies."

"You sure that's all you took in?"

"I've been clean for more than a year, Dad. You know that." He sounded nicely sincere, which wasn't hard, because for once he was telling the truth, and he intended to stay clean until the son of a bitch was toes up and Dolan's name was on the bank account. He couldn't risk failing one of old William's random drug tests. Fuck, he hated those! But the old fart had made it clear: the barest sniff of drugs, and Dolan was out of the house and out of the will. His way of cleaning him up. Hah! "I wish you could trust me a little more." He put a trace of regret in his voice as an added touch.

The rheumy gaze shifted to sharp, and his father gave the barest shake of his head before turning his attention back to the book in his hands. Dolan didn't expect his father to trust him, or believe him, and he wasn't disappointed. It might have hurt him once; now he didn't give a shit. In a matter of weeks, maybe even days, according to the doc, old moneybags, William Daniel James, would be ten feet under, and it couldn't come soon enough to suit Dolan. Nor could the moneybags.

"You want anything?" he asked, pretending to care, when what he wanted to do was cut and run, have a drink, and figure out what to do about Mace's call.

"No. Go to bed. If I need anything, I'll ring the nurse." William's head lifted, then tilted to look more closely at him. Into my damn soul, Dolan thought, and as usual finding it—and him—wanting. After the scrutiny, the old man shifted his gaze back to his book, saying, "Looks like those 'movies' of yours took their toll."

Dolan, dismissed, sucked up his anger, quelled the urge to pick up a poker from the fireplace and end this father/son bonding farce right now. "See you in the morning then," he said. "Try to get some sleep." He left the room and closed the door behind him, the poker idea fresh meat in his mind. He chewed on it as he'd done for weeks now.

Hell, he'd be doing him a favor, save the old bastard his last round of pain before the grim reaper culled him. The only problem was, there was nothing in it for him—except trouble. And, on the brink of inheriting a fortune, he didn't intend to screw up. One wrong move and the cops would be all over him, and he hadn't spent the last year doing the reformed and penitent son gig to lose out now. No, old William had to die a natural death.

In his room he locked the door and poured himself a drink.

Mayday House.

Until a few days ago, he'd never heard of it—or an ancient bitch named Mary Weaver.

He gulped down his booze, smiling through his anger. Shit, either way you looked at it, he had to count himself lucky. If he hadn't intercepted the old woman's call, listened to her rant about forgiveness or some crap like that, he'd have been royally fucked. And there wouldn't be a damned thing he could do about it.

The more he thought about it, maybe it wasn't so bad Mace had put a scare into Farrell. Scared people were stupid people. They made mistakes. And while he might want to eliminate everything and everybody connected to that damn house, the smart thing to do was find out if there were loose ends and tie them up. Records, diaries, crap like that. Because when the time came, he didn't intend to leave a trace. Not a damn trace.

He turned it over in his mind, played the scenario through. It should look like an accident—the random act of some freako pervert. Mace qualified on that score. Hell, it'd be like tossing him a meaty bone. Dolan grinned. Looks like that rape and sexual assault record of his would come in handy yet.

Calmer now, he poured himself another shot and lifted his glass to the cavernous, luxurious bedroom. "Here's to ya, Mary Weaver. Thanks for the heads-up.

And don't worry, I'll keep my promise. Pass the message on to my dear Daddy—the day after his funeral."

Gus decided to use the Mayday House driveway, even though the amount of grass growing from the cracks in the cement told him it wasn't the norm.

A few yards in, he lowered his head, looked out the windshield, and studied the three-story Victorian house. On the left, a turret pointed skyward like a cumbersome rocket. It looked too big, too top-heavy for the delicate lines of the house, like some kind of architectural afterthought that would drop off its third-floor base given the smallest tremor.

The porch yawed like a half-sunken ship, and the whole place looked as though it hadn't been painted since the Great Depression.

Seriously ugly house, Gus decided. But he'd put this business off long enough, so the sooner he got this visit with Farrell over with, the better.

He pulled his new silver Jag to within a few feet of the front door. The early September day was a pearly gray from the light rain that had stopped a few minutes ago, but it was warm and surprisingly humid, so he tossed his leather jacket on the front seat before heading toward the six or eight steps leading to the porch and the front door.

He was halfway up when a voice came from behind. "Can I help you?"

He turned. A young girl was coming toward the house with a rake in her hand and towing a gigantic orange garbage bag behind her. Pretty, he registered, in a whitish blond kind of way. But much too thin.

"I'm looking for Keeley Farrell," he said, thinking he probably should have said the Sister bit.

"She's not here." She let go of the bag and a lungful of air at the same time, as if the dragging effort had exhausted her; then she planted the rake head at her front feet and rested both palms on the handle's tip. "You selling something?" She eyed his sleek car. "We already got a vacuum cleaner."

Gus damn near smiled. He'd been taken for a lot of things in his life—most of them uncomplimentary—but a vacuum cleaner salesman wasn't one of them. "No." He walked back down the stairs. "I'm not selling anything." He gestured to the orange bag. "Want some help?"

"Sure, thanks. Can you take it to the end of the driveway?"

"Done."

When he got back from his chore, he asked, "When will, uh, Sister Farrell be coming back?" Or maybe it was Sister Keeley. How the hell would he know? He hadn't been near anything religious since his grandmother baptized him from her deathbed. They'd been with her for a couple of years at the time. He remembered her praying, begging God to "take and keep" him and his little sister. For days after, he'd lived in terror God would do what she'd asked.

In the years following her death, he wished He had.

"Sister?" The girl frowned. "Oh, right, she said—There she comes now. She took some junk to the recycling station." She held out a hand. "My name's Bridget, by the way. Thanks for the help." She headed back up the driveway.

A pickup truck, in as bad a condition as the house, pulled up behind his Jag, and a woman got out and came toward him. While she eyed him as if he were a serial killer, he took a good look himself.

She had a yellow scarf tied around her hair, but it didn't stop coils of red curls from springing loose, some of them sticking to her flushed face—her dirty, flushed face.

As for the rest, his practiced male rating system said . . . a definite so-so. Average height, average face. Weight? Non-assessable, due to camoflage by a pair of jeans that gave new meaning to the word roomy. He glanced down and his eyebrows shot up. She was wearing thick gray sport socks—over her shoes. Gus had never seen anyone quite like her.

He met her eyes and saw her lips turn up into a quick, then-gone smile.

"I'm guessing you've figured out I'm not coming back from a shift at Hooters." Her eyes, an oddly dark shade of blue, were filled with wry humor. And challenge.

His gaze dropped to her feet. Hers followed.

"Most people wear socks under the shoe," he said.

She took a step back, lifted and turned a sock-encased foot. "The truck's got a north wind coming from the floor board somewhere. My toes were cold. The socks were handy."

"Ah." He nodded as if her explanation were completely rational.

"Besides, socks with sandals?" She bent to pull off the offending—but warming—footwear and revealed ten unpainted toenails. "Isn't that one of those crimes of fashion things?" She stuffed the socks in her jeans pockets, wiped her hand on her denim-clad thigh, and held it out. "Keeley Farrell. Who are you?" Her eyes settled on him, curious and alert. They were smart eyes, he noticed. Confident eyes. Eyes with stories behind them.

He took the hand. "Gus Hammond. And you're the strangest nun I've ever met."

One quick strong shake and their hands parted. She headed to the back of the truck, asking over her shoulder, "How many nuns have you met?"

She had him there. "None."

"Well, now there you go." She started tugging a chair from the back of the truck. Unsuccessfully.

He leaned in and grasped the other side. Between them, they pulled it out and set it on the ground. Sister Keeley pulled the scarf from her head and rubbed at the perspiration on her forehead. She looked at his chest, scanned his biceps, and sighed lustily—her expression completely lust free. "I hate to admit it, but those muscles men were endowed with do come in handy at times. Thanks."

"You're welcome." He looked at the wrecked chair. "Your girl told me you were getting rid of junk, not—" he stopped.

She arched a brow. "Collecting more?" She patted the chair back. "Nothing wrong with this a coat of paint and a bit of fabric won't fix." Leaving her hand on the chair, she said, "Now, what exactly are you doing here, Mr. Hammond? Give me the right answer, and I'll give you some lemonade." She raised a brow.

"I'm here on behalf of Dinah Marsden."

The brow stayed raised. "Ah, the Mayday House

patroness." She seemed to think a bit. "My letter, right?"

"Right."

"Lemonade it is, then, but I reserve the right to lace it with hemlock, if I don't like what you have to say."

She stepped in front of him and headed toward the house.

When he didn't immediately follow, she turned back and gave him a quizzical glance.

"Are you really a nun?"

"Ex-nun." A soft look came into her eyes. "Still crazy about the Man, but I took the habit off a few years ago."

"I see," he said, because he couldn't think of anything else to say.

"No, you don't." She eyed him and half smiled. "Now, how about that lemonade?"

CHAPTER 3

Gus trailed Keeley Farrell into the house.

The kitchen was a mess, a construction havoc, with paint, brushes, tarps, and displaced furniture creating a miserable tableau in a room that was floor-to-ceiling white. Gus had a flash of Miami, of Dinah Marsden.

"Primer," Keeley said. "I'm thinking orange or maybe lemon." Looking up, she let out a long sigh. "I haven't made it up there yet."

He followed her gaze to the high ceiling, where a rough yellowed surface was flecked with peeling gray paint; he said nothing.

"Sit there." She nodded toward a chair near the table. "It looks safe enough. Paintwise, I mean."

He took the seat and again glanced around at the chaos. "How long have you been here?"

"A couple of weeks," she said from behind the fridge door. "Just getting started on the place." She straightened and closed the door, picked a couple of glasses from the cupboard, and came toward him with a frosty jug of lemonade.

"Will you pour, please? I need to wash my hands."
She went to the sink and scrubbed, hands, face,
and arms, as if for surgery.

Gus poured. It was a job he was expert at. But he
didn't take his eyes off Keeley Farrell, and he had
no idea why. As average went, she'd get the gold.
Except for the odd red hair which didn't match
anything else about her. For one thing her complexion was too dark. Either that or her freckles had
formed a conglomerate—and her lashes were, if
not black, at least a dark brown. Nothing matched.
Nothing fit. Including her jeans. If they were any bag-
gier, a high wind would take her to Oz. As a woman,
Keeley Farrell blew the lid off the word ordinary—
except for the way she looked at him. Dead in the
eye, with what seemed unshakable self-reliance. He
sensed if the wind did take her to Oz, she'd be running the place within the week.

"Do you want some ice?" she asked.

"No, this is fine, thanks."

She pulled a chair up to the table, sat directly
across from him, and took a long drink of her
lemonade. Putting the glass down, she settled her
forthright gaze on him. "So, have you brought a
check, or do I go get the hemlock?" She smiled at
him, her eyes lighting with it, the curve of her lips
showing white, even teeth.

Her smile stilled him, sucker-punched him. His
chest tightened, and his focus shifted from words to
her lush mouth, then to her throat, the vee of warm
skin visible above the two undone buttons on her
outsized shirt. His out-of-nowhere reaction shocked
the hell out of him. Here, in this place, with a
woman like this, it made no sense.

"No check," he said, his tone sharper than he intended.

"You're kidding, right?" She eyed him, the smile ebbing slowly from her freshly scrubbed face. "You're not kidding."

"No, I'm not."

"And here I was hoping this was going to be easy. I don't know why, though, when anything to do with money never is."

"You're right about that."

Her expression was serious and puzzled when she said, "Why? Why won't Mrs. Marsden continue her support of Mayday House? According to Mary's records, she's been its most important patron since the seventies."

Good question, and until now Gus hadn't asked it, or given a damn, figuring it was another of Dinah's whims. Dinah gave and Dinah took away; it was what she did. Business as usual. "She didn't say. Just that she wants to close it down. Quietly."

Her eyes widened. "Close it down? This house has been operating as a haven for women for over forty years."

"So she said—and from what she told me, for most of those years, it's run on her dime." He stood, set his glass on the table. "It's her money, her call, Miss Farrell."

"Keeley," she said absently, adding, "Does she have financial problems, is that it?"

He damn near laughed. Dinah might have problems, but none of them had to do with money. "No."

"Then why?" She stood, going toe-to-toe with him, her eyes fixed on his as if she could see inside his brain.

He looked away, then back. A nun—even an ex-nun—had no business in his head. "She thinks Mayday House is irrelevant, that this kind of place is unnecessary. *Archaic* was the word she used."

"Archaic?" She puffed out a breath. "Does she think girls and women have stopped getting pregnant, stopped being abused, stopped needing help?" A frown gathered on her forehead. "I need to talk to her, make her understand."

"She doesn't want to talk. As for her reasons, they're not my business. Nor yours." He softened his tone, added, "I know Dinah Marsden. She's made up her mind. She won't be sending any more checks." He studied her face, her expression a combination of stricken and a near-painful concentration. "What she is prepared to do is buy the house and property, Miss Farrell—"

"Keeley," she corrected again, this time distractedly.

"Okay." He started again. "She's prepared to buy the house, *Keeley*, be generous enough that you can, as she put it, 'set up shop' somewhere else." He remembered Dinah's determination to close the house, and added, "And if you want my advice, I'd hold off a bit before I caved. It'll make for a bigger check."

She looked at him as if he'd taken the winner's podium after a stupid contest. "Why would you think I'd 'cave,' as you put it? This is my home. I was born here. I have no intention of abandoning it, or the services it provides. I'll *make* it work." She glared up at him. "With or without Mrs. Marsden's support."

"Have it your way. I'll call back in a few days. See if you want me to arrange that check for you." He headed for the back door off the kitchen.

Seeming rapt in her own thoughts, she let him go without a word.

At the door, he added, "If I were you, I'd take the money. Be easier all around."

Frowning, she looked up at him. "Money, Gus Hammond, is nothing but a huge pain in the behind and anything but 'easy.' Not to mention most of it goes to all the wrong places." Her frown deepened. "What I need to figure out is why—suddenly—everyone's turning against Mary and Mayday House."

He had no idea what she was talking about or who *everyone* was, and she didn't give him a chance to find out. The last message Keeley Farrell gave him was her back, walking through the open kitchen doorway and down a long hallway.

He let himself out.

Standing on the front porch, Keeley watched the beautiful car carry its scarred but even more beautiful man along the rutted Mayday House driveway, her heart as heavy as a lead ingot in her chest.

She might have sounded tough, but the truth was Dinah Marsden had been her best hope to save Mary Weaver's life's work. And that hope was gone.

She leaned a shoulder against the porch post and tried to think. She had enough money in the bank to last a month, maybe six weeks, if she raised miserly to high art, and lived on bread and beans.

Damn, damn, damn!

But worse than anything was the sinking feeling she was failing Mary, not living up to the faith she'd placed in her, and the growing fear that under her stewardship Mayday House would falter—maybe close forever.

She closed her eyes, shook her head, and clenched her teeth.

She *would not* let that happen. She'd make things right again. She owed it to Mary and she owed it to herself.

Get your butt in gear, Farrell, and start figuring out what's happening here, and what you're going to do about it.

She walked to the far end of the porch, unclenching her hands which had somehow turned themselves into fists, and tried to make sense of things.

Mary was dead, and suddenly the main supporters of Mayday House, someone named Christiana Fordham, and now Dinah Marsden, wanted no part of it. Or so Gus Hammond had said. And she had no reason not to believe him.

Keeley took in a deep breath, then let it out. She'd never met anyone like him before, everything about him so dark, so intense. When he'd taken his eyes off her ridiculous socks and looked at her—really looked at her—her knees had wobbled, for heaven's sake, went as weak as a schoolgirl's. Crazy!

At least Dinah Marsden had sent someone to give her the bad news. Christiana Fordham had simply ignored her letter and refused to take her calls.

And there was that weird phone call last week. Thank God, there'd been none since, but when she finally fell exhausted into her bed at night, she lay there convinced there was a bogeyman underneath it. Wracked nerves, that's what she had, which did her no good at all.

Those same nerves used to work for her, push her to do what needed to be done in the face of hunger, sickness, bombs, and gunfire. Now all they did was rattle her, confuse her—and too often get the better of her.

She pulled the yellow scarf from her hair, gripped the porch railing, and dropped her head. Before Mr. Slick-And-Beautiful showed his damaged face again, she had to have a plan. If she didn't, she'd be forced to take his offer.

That plan meant fund-raising and information gathering. Keeley straightened away from the railing and headed back into the house.

The rats were deserting Mayday House, which meant that somewhere along the line, something had to have gone terribly wrong. She needed to find out exactly what that something was.

Christiana Fordham tossed the letter on top of her new pile of fan mail. She'd already read it a half dozen times. She'd hoped that when Mary Weaver died, she could forget her phone call, pretend it never happened. But no. Now this Keeley person had arrived and taken charge at Mayday House. God only knew what she'd find out, what Mary had told her.

"Christiana, they're waiting for you."

"I'm coming, darling. Five minutes. I want to freshen my makeup." She picked up a puff from the dresser and dabbed at her made-for-TV face. She had so much makeup on she could barely hold her head up.

Duke Thomas came up behind her and their eyes met in the mirror. He rested his hands on her shoulders, kissed the top of her blond head. "Your makeup is perfect. You're just nervous." He massaged her neck, and it felt so good, she leaned back into his masterful hands. "Everything will be fine," he added, close to her ear. "You'll be wonderful. Don't worry."

"I'm going to be the best thing that's happened to daytime TV since Oprah, right?" She forced herself to smile up at him. "Isn't that what the *Times* said?"

"That's what they said—and the *Times* is never wrong." He chuckled.

She couldn't hold the smile. "Then why do I feel like the biggest fraud ever to set foot in New York?" She tossed the puff. It dusted the dresser and scudded to the floor. She ignored it.

"You're not a fraud, baby." His lean, handsome face took on a look of concern. When he looked at her like that, she could barely take her eyes off him—even when she distrusted him. "Not only have you spent years in the trenches," he went on. "I've worked like a dog getting you to this point. You deserve this."

"I spent years listening to sob stories for a backwater station in Oregon, for God's sake. This is New York. This is NBC!"

This is what I've wanted all my life!

"Chris, for God's sake!" A look of consternation laced with irritation crossed his face.

Now she'd made him angry. She hated when she did that, hated the way it made her stomach contract, old insecurities well up like sludge from the bottom of a well.

Her eyes went to the letter, and it was all she could do not to pick it up and tear it to shreds. "The truth is I'm a small-town psychologist, with a second-rate degree from a mediocre college, who photographs well. You know it and I know it."

"What I know"—Duke's strong hands gripped her shoulders, tightened, and his voice went down an octave—"is that you need to get it together. This is prime time—and most importantly, it's *our* time. Keep talking like that, and you'll blow the interview. And remember, the contract isn't finalized, and until it is, we've got to be on top of our game." He kneaded her shoulders. "I shouldn't have to tell you the danger of negative thinking. And that small-town psychologist thing you mentioned? Forget it. They want you because you're more than that. To quote the *Times* again, 'Christiana Fordham provides common sense, wisdom, and more important, a workable morality in immoral times.'"

She took a breath and sealed her eyes closed, careful not to smudge her eyeliner. He was right. Duke was always right. Standing to face him, she tried to find her smile again but couldn't. She did manage to lighten her tone when she looked up at him and asked, "That 'workable morality' line . . . Do you have any idea what it means?" She ran her hand over his silk-clad chest and felt the rough hair beneath his shirt.

"Not a clue, but it sure makes a good sound bite." He took her hand and kissed her knuckles. "But when I look at you, baby, morality is the last thing on my mind."

When he drew her into his arms, she went willingly, hungrily took his mouth, and was instantly on fire. It was always like this with Duke, a terrible blistering heat, crazy and frightening, his slightest touch a lit match on kerosene.

He set her back from him and his dark green eyes narrowed. Holding her chin, he turned her face, warmed from his deep kiss, left, then right, studying it carefully. "Perfect. You look perfect." He nudged her chin higher and rubbed his thumb over her lips. "If a kiss does this, maybe we should try something even more stimulating the next time around." He stepped back and smiled. "Now get that sweet ass of yours downstairs, Dr. Fordham; the world is waiting."

Feeling surer of herself now, she nodded and turned for one last check in the mirror, but she couldn't stop her gaze from skittering across the letter. She wanted to burn it, tear it into a million pieces—or at least put it out of sight in the drawer. But doing anything at all right now would attract attention, make Duke curious.

Oh, God, I wish you'd never called me, Mary Weaver— and I wish Mayday House with all its dangerous secrets didn't exist—had never existed.

But wishes weren't worth the breeze they drifted in on, and having Duke, or anyone else, discover the truth about Dr. Christiana Fordham would ruin everything. The more she thought about it, the more certain she became. The Farrell woman at Mayday House was a problem, a problem Christiana had to handle herself.

Just as soon as she figured out how.

Gus Hammond took one last look around his condo. Not exactly Miami, but all his own—including an empty bed. If he knew how to be happy, he was pretty sure being back in Seattle brought him damn close to it. Okay, maybe the neighborhood had its share of sleaze and grit when you turned the corner, but it worked for him. A transitional area, the real estate agent had said when he'd shown him the place and pointed to the new construction across the street.

Good word, transition, for the neighborhood and him.

He'd spent the first few years of his life within a few blocks of here. Back then the operative word would've been regression: dirty alleys, dangerous even at high noon; crack havens tucked into the ancient apartments; rows of crappy shops with even crappier rooms above them, each with a single light bulb hanging from a bare wire. And sirens. Endless screaming sirens.

The sirens had always made April cry. She'd put her hands over her ears, and he'd put his hands over hers . . .

He cut off that line of thought; it was too soon to think about April, to go where he'd been so many times before and always come up empty. He wasn't ready for the simmering rage to boil again, wasn't ready for the obsession to take hold, start eating its way through his raw gut.

He headed for the kitchen and got himself a beer from the fridge. Other than a six-pack—now dwindled to a four-pack—of beer, some cheese, milk, and a half-dozen fresh eggs, the fridge was an empty white cavern.

He'd stuff it to overflow mode before Josh got here for his Christmas break; that kid ate enough for an army unit. As for Gus, this close to the Pike Market, the restaurant pickings were good.

And tomorrow, if his luck held, he'd have his first

contract. He didn't need the money, but he sure as hell needed the work. There was only so much sitting on his ass a man could tolerate. He already had some lines out for April, but God knew when there'd be something worth reeling in.

Beer in hand, he sat on the sofa and pulled today's *Seattle Times* toward him on the coffee table. When the phone rang, he glanced at the call display. Nil. Or blocked.

So far Dinah hadn't tried disguising her calls, and he'd been out so much he'd avoided most of them anyway. He knew she'd be impatient to hear about his *mission*, but he'd already told her about his visit to Mayday House; he figured that was enough. Small talk wasn't an option. They needed some time between them, a little perspective. He'd go for the let's-be-friends arrangement, but he doubted Dinah would be up for that.

On the third ring, he picked up the phone and gave a standard hello.

"Am I speaking to Gus Hammond?" a female voice said.

"Depends on whether or not you're selling something." He turned his attention back to the paper.

"No, I'm not." A pause. "Actually I'm, uh, wanting to buy. Dinah gave me your name. She said you might be . . . available." Now she sounded nervous.

Shit! He leaned back on the sofa and tossed another silent curse toward the ceiling.

When he said nothing, the voice rushed on, "I need an escort for next week. The opera? She said a thousand—Sorry, I guess I shouldn't say the money up front, but—" She stopped. "I'm sorry, I'm babbling. I guess you can tell I've never done this before, but Dinah told me—"

"Whatever Dinah told you," Gus said, sitting up and shoving the newspaper aside, "it was wrong. I'm not available for stud at the moment."

"*Stud?* Oh, no. I don't want sex from you."

"Of course you don't." *That's what they all said.* "All you want is a monkey in a tux, right? Until the monkey takes you home."

"No, really . . . Oh, my God! I feel so stupid."

Definitely her first time. "Not stupid, baby. Duped. You're Dinah's way of reminding me of my not-so-illustrious past." *And probably testing my future.*

He hung up. When his being-pissed-off-at-Dinah mood passed, he damn near laughed. He'd turned down an easy grand, which made him something like a drunk turning down a cold beer in the Sahara.

Things were definitely looking up. Now if that peculiar ex-nun would answer his calls, tell him she was going to take the money and run, Dinah would be history. Gus could get on with his life, which meant going back to work and getting this security contract he was working on and—he rubbed his brow—finding April.

But before that happened, there was this business with Mayday House and the nun . . . the ex-nun.

Keeley Farrell had to be the oddest woman he'd ever met. And he'd met more than his share. He couldn't figure out what it was about her that got to him and wouldn't let go. Maybe because she looked at him as if he weren't there. It was as if she'd given him one piercing look, decided he was empty, and didn't bother looking again. A new experience for a guy used to being paraded around like a stallion up for bids.

God, how he'd hated that—particularly early in the game, when Dinah's friends would look up at him, smile and stroke his bicep, then squeeze it to feel his muscle. Or worse, run a finger along the scar that disfigured his jaw, and say, "Poor baby, whatever happened?"

Christ, he couldn't remember how many of them had offered to pay for surgery to "get it fixed."

It was a relief when Dinah quit passing him around to her friends, amusing to see her become possessive and insist on an exclusive arrangement. He'd been twenty-two then and smart enough and desperate enough to see a brass ring when one dropped around his neck. A tarnished brass ring, but good enough to form a circle of safety around Josh, get him settled in school. Back then it was all about food, clothes, and a roof over the head—and steering clear of an outstanding murder charge.

"My friends have had their fair share of you, Gus," she'd said after an afternoon of sex. "From now on you're mine. All mine. I'll take care of you and I'll take care of Josh—"

"No one takes care of Josh, except me."

"And my money, darling. Don't forget that."

"As if you'd ever let me." He'd leaned to kiss her, which he hadn't minded doing in those days, because he was either a little bit in love with the woman or had convinced himself he was. Or maybe it was just a young man's volcanic sex drive coupled with readily available sex with a woman who was white-hot in bed.

His phone rang again.

"Gus Hammond?"

"Uh-huh."

A man's voice said without preamble, "I've been called to a meeting which means flying out of town in the morning. I'd like to reschedule tomorrow's meeting, move it forward."

The potential security client. Gus reached for a pen. "Where and what time?"

"Right now, if you're free. An early dinner at Malta's suit you?"

"I'll be there."

"You have Malta's address?"

"Yes. What I don't have is your name."

"Let's hold off on that until the face and name come together. I'll leave your name at the desk. Rick will bring you to me."

"Works for me."

Gus grabbed his jacket and car keys and headed for the door, unconcerned with not knowing who he was about to meet. That bit about the rich being different from "you and me" was dead-on. Most put a high premium on their personal privacy, and Gus had no problem with that.

Hell, he hadn't used his own name since he'd hit the streets at twelve. Sure as hell didn't use it when the cops were on his ass for the murder of his and Josh's foster mother.

He wasn't using it now.

CHAPTER 4

Disgusted, Keeley tossed the papers on the desk. She was exhausted, as usual, and completely flummoxed. She'd always loved that word, but until now had never had reason to apply it to herself.

But flummoxed she was.

Neither Dinah Marsden nor the always-elusive Christiana Fordham would take her calls. So her idea of a last-ditch personal plea for help—and maybe getting a few questions answered about their changed attitudes toward Mayday House—was a non-starter. Good thing she didn't plan on a career as a telemarketer.

She leaned back in Mary's rickety desk chair and reviewed her dismal attempt at sleuthing and fundraising. She had no trouble begging. Her time in Africa ended that bias, but you couldn't beg if no one would listen. No one's fault, really. There were so many worthwhile causes in the world, so many hands out for help, it was overwhelming. Most people were good-hearted, but hearts—and wallets—stretched only so far. If the ladies, Marsden and

Fordham, didn't want to support Mayday House, she had to accept it and find another way.

Which did nothing for her current predicament.

She needed money for the mortgage, and she needed it yesterday. And food? That would be good. If she were on her own, no problem, but she wasn't. She had Bridget to consider.

She twirled a straggly bit of hair at her neck. Bridget was eating more these days, and Keeley was glad to see it. Glad, too, that the girl's spirits had picked up a notch. Not much of a notch, but right now Keeley would settle for it, because if things kept up the way they were going, she'd try talking to her again. Maybe this time they'd get past the tears and silence and into what, if any, plans the girl had. As far as Keeley was concerned, she could stay for as long as she liked, certainly until she felt strong again, but the mystery of Bridget—her dark silences about her family, the father of her lost baby, where she came from—was wearing thin.

Leaning forward in the chair, Keeley rested her elbows on the desk, cupped her face, and huffed out a frustrated breath.

Enough about Bridget, Keeley Farrell, you have high finance to think about. She frowned so deeply her head hurt.

Maybe a yard sale—

"Keeley?"

"Hi, Bridget." *I could check the attic, maybe sell that old loveseat in the turret, and . . .*

"There's someone at the door. She says her name's Erica."

"I don't know anyone named Erica," she said, her mind caught in the gridlock of financial chaos. *A nice little miracle might help, too, but the Man upstairs wasn't exactly in her corner these days. Not that she blamed Him.*

"She said Mary was expecting her." Even Bridget, not the most expressive of souls, indicated disbelief upon uttering that statement.

"There's nothing here." Keeley waved a hand over the surface of the ancient rolltop desk, laden with bank statements, stacks of manila files, and a dog-eared schedule with a missing cover. Not that she could visualize Mary writing anything down, particularly in the last few months, when she'd been floating in and out of dementia.

Bridget glanced at the hurricane of paper, then at Keeley. "She's knocked up, I think."

Keeley grimaced. "Ugh, don't say that. It sounds so abusive. And 'bun in the oven' isn't any better."

Bridget shrugged, apparently unaffected by semantics. "She's pregnant, then. Shall I bring her in?"

Another mouth to feed; her heart sank. She hadn't planned on taking anyone in until the place was back in order. Mary's health—so she'd learned—had been in free fall for over a year, and along with it the maintenance and financing of an old house that had been in desperate straits long before that. So here she was, intent on nurturing Mary's legacy, and her first act would be turning away someone needing help.

"Keeley? You okay?" Bridget asked. "Shall I go get her or what?"

"I'm fine, but it's a mess in here." She pushed the chair away from the desk and stood. "I'll see her in the front hall."

"Forget the mess. You can see me right here."

Keeley looked up to see a tall brunette step into the

room. She was probably closer to forty than the fourteen she'd expected, and one of the most spectacularly beautiful women she'd ever seen. Vivid was the word that jumped to mind. That and . . . sumptuous. Her eyes, wary and sharp, observed Keeley with a degree of studious detachment, as if she were in need of a personal makeover or was a stooge in a police lineup.

What she was sure about was that the woman looked one labor pain away from giving birth.

"Are you Keeley Farrell?" she asked.

Keeley crossed to where the woman, dressed in designer maternity wear and gripping an expensive leather bag, stood straight as a spar; she held out her hand. "That's me."

"Erica Stark." She set the bag down and shook Keeley's outstretched hand.

Keeley gestured toward a cracked leather chair beside the rolltop desk. "Sit," she instructed. "You look exhausted."

"Thanks." She flicked her long hair back, gave the chair a distrustful glance, and sat carefully on its edge.

"Bridget, would you get us some tea or—" She looked at her unusual guest questioningly.

"Water would be fine," she said to Bridget, who nodded and left the room, leaving the door open.

Keeley took the seat she'd just vacated and studied the striking woman in the chair across from her. "I'll say this right off. You do not look like the kind of woman who needs the services of Mayday House."

"I suppose not. But here I am," she said, her

expression tight, guarded, or maybe embarrassed. Keeley couldn't be sure.

"How did you find us?"

"From a friend. I remembered her telling me how, uh, out of the way Mayday House is. So when I got myself into this ridiculous situation"—she rolled her eyes, patted her stomach—"I talked to her, and she put me on to Mary Weaver. I called, she asked me a few questions—mostly about the pregnancy—I answered them, and here I am." She paused. "I was sorry to hear she passed on. The girl"—she gestured toward the door Bridget had gone through—"says you're running things now."

"Yes," Keeley said, nodding, then added, "When was it, exactly, that you talked to Mary?"

"A month ago, maybe."

"And she sounded . . . all right?"

"All right? I'm not sure what you mean by that."

"Mary had been ill and toward the end she often got confused."

Erica Stark studied a fingernail, looking bored. "She did ramble on a bit, but I'd say she sounded okay. We talked for fifteen, twenty minutes, I made the booking, and here I am."

"I see." And she did. A month ago, according to Bridget, Mary was barely able to remember where she was most days, and her lucid times were becoming further and further apart. Erica must have called at exactly the right moment—or wrong one, considering the perilous state of Keeley's finances.

She picked up the pencil she'd been figuring with minutes before and rolled it between her fingers while she tried to come up with a way to let Erica Stark down easy. "Mayday House is pretty basic accommodation, as you can easily see, Erica, and most of Mary's guests were without resources. Often without family. In need, both financially and emotionally."

Erica nodded, looked away for a second. When she turned back, her gaze was unflinching. "Look, all I need is a place to be alone, a place to disappear for a while and think a few things through." She shifted back in the chair, placed a hand on her distended abdomen, and glanced around the room, her expression weary. "And frankly, Mayday House is perfect."

Everything in Keeley wanted to help. There had to be a way. All she had to do was find it. "How far along are you?"

"Going into my seventh month." She paused before adding, "Twins."

"Congratulations."

"Thanks."

"And the father?"

Erica took in a breath, then glanced away. "Out of the picture." She got to her feet, placed both hands on her lower back, and looked down at Keeley. "Look, I'm exhausted, so if we can continue this interview later, I'd appreciate it. I need to lie down. And for your information—and as I explained to Mary—you don't have to worry, medically speaking. I've had regular checkups, and I'll be gone before my due date. I've already arranged for the delivery, and I'm healthy as a horse. My doctor, one of the best in Seattle, by the way, says my pregnancy is normal given my age—"

"Which is?"

"Forty-five." Her expression was challenging.

Keeley raised her hands, tried to look innocent instead of shocked. "You look a lot younger."

Her face softened somewhat. "Thank you for that, but right about now I feel like a hundred." She rubbed her back again. "Now can I fill you in on the intriguing details of my late-in-life pregnancy tomorrow? Right now I need that bed. If you'll just tell me how much, we're in business." She picked up the tote she'd placed beside her chair when she sat down, and withdrew a checkbook.

How much? Keeley's mind stumbled. Erica Stark wanted to pay! "We don't actually have rates. Mayday House is a women's refuge. It's always been privately sponsored," she said, sounding as stiff as a besieged bureaucrat. "But we are willing to accept donations."

Erica smiled thinly. "I'll bet." She scribbled out a check. "Will this do?"

Keeley gulped once, hoped it didn't show, and looked up into the tired face of Erica Stark. "How long are you wanting to stay?"

"A week . . . a month." Erica walked to the door and, for the first time, let her shoulders sag.

"I still don't understand why. Why Mayday House?"

"Because I needed to get away, and I need time."

"Time for what?"

"To make a choice."

"Between?"

She hesitated, pursing her lips. "Becoming a midlife mother of twins or putting them up for adoption."

"That's some decision."

"Not one an ex-nun could fathom, I'm guessing."

"How did you know about that?"

"Like I said, Mary did ramble a bit. She mentioned it. It's the kind of information that sticks." She walked to the door, almost colliding with the slow-moving Bridget who'd finally arrived with the water. Erica turned and looked back, her expression curious. "Mary said you worked in Africa. I'd like to hear about it sometime."

And it was the last thing in the world Keeley wanted to talk about.

She gestured to Erica's bag. "Bridget," she said. "Will you take Miss Stark upstairs, please. Either of the freshly painted rooms should do. They're well aired by now. I'll get some clean linens and be right up to help her get settled."

When Bridget and Erica were gone, she looked at the check again. "Two thousand dollars." She looked up and whispered the sum like a prayer, then silently mouthed the words *thank you* and closed her eyes.

Mayday House was safe . . . for now.

Upstairs, the door closed behind her, Erica sat heavily on the edge of the bed. She rubbed her face, took a couple of deep breaths, then rifled in her bag, first pulling out a 9mm Glock, then a cell phone.

She dialed, waited until the familiar voice came across the line, and said, "I'm in." She immediately disconnected from the call.

Gus walked into Malta's Bar and Grill. Its casual name belied its expensive and classy interior. Definitely upscale. Exactly where he'd expect to meet a client looking for personal security.

The host, busy reorganizing poster-sized menus, looked up when he approached the front desk.

"Gus Hammond," he said. "I'm expected."

"Yes, of course, Mr. Hammond. Follow me."

He did and was led to a table in the back, not quite a booth, but made private by being enclosed in pony walls, surrounded by greenery, and placed a discreet distance from the other tables.

As to the occupier of the table, Gus saw only his back until he stepped closer. He started to offer his hand, but dropped it immediately when he recognized the man in the chair.

Gus usually rallied fast, but Hagan Marsden—here—was a real ass kick. It had been six years since he'd seen him. He'd tried to make it his last.

Hagan didn't bother standing, nor did he offer a handshake. What he did was scan Gus from his ankles to his face. "Looks like the male whoring business is treating you all right, Hammond." He did another scan. "Maybe I took a wrong turn in the road, working for a living instead of fucking for one."

Gus considered his options: walk away, slam a fist in the bastard's mouth, or take a seat.

He sat. "From what Dinah told me, you'd never have made it. Best you stick to your paper clips or whatever the hell it is you get for a penny offshore and sell at a thousand percent markup." He was about to signal a waiter when one arrived at his shoulder. "Vodka, lots of ice," he said.

"Brand, sir?"

"The best you've got." The waiter gone, he turned back to Hagan. "If this is about Dinah, you're wasting your time. She's in Miami. I'm in Seattle. That should answer all your questions."

"I know all that. It's one of the reasons I set this meeting up. And as to the bitch of the century, I don't give a fuck where she is."

"Hm-m, that's a switch from a few years ago, when you tried to throw me off a twenty-story balcony."

"I was seeing a little red that day. Watching Barracuda Woman living the high life—with a piece of male ass young enough to be our son—and me so goddamn broke, I—Forget it." He glanced away, his expression sour. "Bitch doesn't describe that woman. More like miserable cu—"

"Don't go there, Hagan." Gus picked up a knife, made circles with its point on the white tablecloth. "The way I see it, Dinah might have been a whole lot friendlier if you'd kept your fists in your pockets instead of using them on her face."

Hagan's voice dropped an octave. "That's a goddamn lie. One of her lousy ploys to get sympathy and pump up the settlement."

"Right," Gus said, letting his tone drip with disbelief and balancing eight inches of knife between tabletop and index finger. "Still . . . that's no way to talk about your wife."

"Ex-wife." He took a drink of what looked like single-malt scotch. "And as it turned out, getting rid of that woman was the best thing that ever happened to me." He shook his head and pursed his lips. "Even if it did take the next ten years to get back a quarter of what she took from me."

"Her and those unsavory business partners of yours."

Hagan shrugged, but the gesture was more defensive than nonchalant. "I owed people. When they saw that Dinah was going to clean me out, they wanted their pound of flesh while there was still some on the bone."

"Either way, it looks like you've survived." But from the looks of him, the survival had come at a price. Hagan Marsden looked a hell of a lot older than his sixty-odd years. Every fiber and weave covering his body might be the best money could buy, but his hair was a muddy gray, and his face was lined and pale. But his eyes were the same, still feral sharp, and at the moment, gleaming with intent. The intent to what, Gus couldn't yet figure out.

"Survived and prospered, Hammond. Survived and prospered." He looked at the knife Gus fooled with on the table. "Still playing with your toys, huh? You're damn good with those things, as I recall." He touched a thin, white scar under his ear, a souvenir Gus had left him from the balcony episode.

"Good enough." Gus set the knife back on the table. "What am I doing here, Hagan?"

"Applying for a job."

"I don't think so. You know damn well if I'd known who I was supposed to meet today, I'd have been on the other side of town." Gus made to stand. To hell with the damn drink—this guy made his skin crawl.

Hagan's hand shot out and clasped his wrist. "I don't think so. Not when you hear what I have to say."

Gus looked at the knuckles whitening from their grip on his arm, then hard into the eyes of the man they belonged to. "Let go. Now."

Hagan released his grip and lifted his two hands in the air, palms facing Gus. "There, you see how agreeable I am." He paused, and the lines in his face firmed and set. "Now, if that nice little nun will be half as agreeable, we'll all be happy. What was her name again? Something Irish sounding, wasn't it? Oh, yes . . . Sister Keeley Farrell."

Gus reined in his shock just as the waiter showed up.

"Your vodka, sir?" The server stood over them, tray in hand, his gaze darting between him and Hagan.

"No point in letting a perfectly good drink go to waste," Hagan said, nodding at the tray, then settling back in his seat. "And bring some menus, will you? I'm hungry as a starved dog." He glanced at Gus. "Plus we've got a lot of ground to cover."

"How do you know Farrell?"

"I don't. What I do know is that Dinah has been sending money—my money—to support that house she's living in for over thirty years."

"And you know this how?"

"Divorce has a way of exposing things—especially ugly divorces."

"Then my next question is, so what? It isn't the only charity Dinah supports."

Hagan snorted. "It's the only one she keeps quiet about. All the others are strictly for PR and name-dropping privileges." He snorted again. "You honestly believe Dinah gives a shit about kids starving in some godforsaken African village, whether or not some poor schmuck knows how to read, or some fag somewhere is dying of AIDS?" He shook his head. "No way. All Dinah cares about is Dinah getting lots of good press."

Gus couldn't argue with that. "Same question. So?"

"So I want to know why she's paid out thousands over the years to support a women's halfway house, or whatever the hell it is, in the middle of nowhere."

He paused. "And why she *quit* paying the minute Mary Weaver went toes up."

"For a longtime ex, you've got a lot of current information."

Hagan eyed him coldly. "Dinah is the mother of my son. I make sure I keep up. Make sure his interests are protected."

"Perry is thirty years old. He can look out for himself."

"She's threatening to cut him out of the will. When every fucking dime she has is mine—and Perry's. I won't let her do that." The feral glint in his pale eyes set diamond hard.

"First off Dinah *won't* do that, and you damn well know it. And even if she did, Perry wouldn't give a damn." But Gus didn't put it past Hagan to use Perry as an excuse to get back at Dinah, stir the old resentment pot. Because if ever two people had raised marital discord and outright hatred to high art, Dinah and Hagan Marsden had. No doubt whatever Hagan had in mind, it had more to do with vengeance against Dinah than concern for Perry's financial well-being. Because unless things had changed, Perry was still living in a drafty apartment in Tribeca, doing the starving artist routine and staying as far away from Dinah and hostile Hagan here as the planet allowed.

"He doesn't give a damn. But I do," Hagan grumbled. "That money is his. And I won't let that bitch screw him like she did me."

Gus picked up his drink, swirled the glass, listened to the ice clink against its sides, then took a drink. No way did he intend to get involved in Dinah and Hagan's endless dispute over which one of the two was the most hard done by during the divorce; Dinah because Hagan was an abusive, egotistical jerk, or Hagan because Dinah was a greedy, self-centered money grabber. The way he saw it, their son had the right idea, take off and never look back. Gus looked at his watch. "This is fascinating stuff, Marsden," he said, "but I've got a late date." He tossed some bills on the table.

Before he could stand, Hagan leaned forward, his expression hard. "I know Dinah asked you to come down here and buy off the Farrell woman. That she wants that Mayday House place shut down for good. She's hiding something, and I want to know what it is, Hammond, and I'm willing to be generous to the person who finds out."

"Not interested. Not only do I not give a damn. I'm not inclined to work against my former employer." Gus sat back in his chair, puzzled and more than a little interested. "But I'm interested in how the hell you know so much about Dinah's plans."

Hagan said nothing but managed to look smug as hell all the same.

An errant thought bumped against Gus's logic. "Can't be," he muttered, more to himself than Hagan. But, damn it, he couldn't see any other way for Hagan to have access to this kind of information. "You're paying off Cassie, aren't you?" He should have guessed. It was a typical Hagan maneuver. Cassie was Dinah's manager, bookkeeper, secretary, and any other thing Dinah wanted her to be. She was a twenty-four/seven employee, quiet as a unplugged radio, and was—or so Gus had thought—as loyal as a hound. She'd also been endlessly good to Josh, who was nearly the same age as her daughter when Gus first went to live with Dinah.

"A no-brainer. The woman's a single mother. Wants to put her kid in college. Dinah treats her like shit and pays her the same."

"She'll be making less than shit when Dinah hears about your cozy relationship."

"Dinah's not going to hear about it. Because you're not going to tell her."

"Yeah? Why's that?"

"Because if you do, there's a good chance that nun will get herself roughed up, good and proper."

"What the hell are you talking about, Marsden?" Visions of out-sized jeans, bright red hair, and those oddly dark take-no-prisoner blue eyes flashed across his mind.

"I'm talking about Dinah's goddamn secret, that's what. Something my hellish ex-wife will do anything to protect. Hell, there's nothing that bitch won't do to get her way. If that nun doesn't oblige—" he picked up the knife Gus had been toying with and dragged the point of it along the stiff white tablecloth, leaving a clear, straight rut in the linen. "Shame to see the woman hurt." He eyed Gus carefully. "You want to be responsible for that?"

Gus eyeballed him back but said nothing. Dinah was forceful, stubborn, and calculating, yes, but capable of violence? Okay, the woman had her dark side, but that was mostly sexual—and consensual. *Dinah physically hurting someone?* The idea wouldn't process. "And you want this information, so you can hold it—whatever the hell *it* is—over Dinah's head." He smiled thinly. "You can't tell me you give a shit about Keeley Farrell."

"Oh, I give a shit, all right, and so should you. Farrell's the keeper of the keys, born and grew up in that house. If anybody knows anything about anything, it's gotta be her. And if the little lady crosses Dinah . . . well, then I'd like to be the beneficiary on her insurance policy. You understand what I'm saying?"

"I understand you're talking about blackmail."

"Better a little all-in-the family blackmail—and one live nun—than the alternative."

"And if I do find out what's going on, why the hell would I tell you and not Dinah?" He'd done a lot of things in his time, but he'd never knifed someone in the back, figuratively or otherwise. He didn't intend to start now. "Your IQ is even lower than I thought, Hagan."

"Is that so? Then maybe this will take it up a notch." He leaned forward. "Because if you don't do what I want, I'll get someone who will, and it's you who'll be the loser, Hammond. Big time."

"I don't want your fucking money, Marsden. You got that?"

"Good, because I wasn't planning on giving you any. What I'm after is a trade. Your services for a little information." He settled back in his seat, looking like a tomcat about to down a rat steak. "That sister you've been looking for? What's her name again? April, right?"

Gus fused to the chair. *What the hell . . .*

Hagan dropped the tight smile. "Cute, those parents of yours naming you and her for your birth months." Smoothing his red silk tie down his chest, his voice flat as dank water, he added, "The thing is, I know where April is, and if you're a good little whore-boy, and get up close and personal with that Mayday House woman—get me the information I want—I'll drop her address on you." He snickered and leaned back in his chair, enjoying himself. "Hell, you've fucked for money before, Hammond, all I'm asking is you do the same for information. Farrell, being an ex-nun and all, is probably panting for it. With your creds . . . should be no problem at all."

CHAPTER 5

Keeley headed out at first light.

With the house so quiet—neither Bridget nor her new guest had a fondness for mornings—she had the next couple of hours to herself.

The graveyard called, and until now she hadn't had time for a proper visit.

Now that's a whopper, Keeley Farrell. You've been putting it off because you're afraid you'll start crying and won't be able to stop.

She went out the back door of Mayday House, careful to close the screen door soundlessly, not because she thought anything short of a semi ramming the house would wake her sleepers, but from force of habit. Plus she reveled in the clear, soft stillness of the morning air, the scent of last night's light rain clinging to it like an exotic fragrance, and the deep silence surrounding the stirring of birds in the trees. She had no wish to disturb it.

She crossed the backyard, the grass squishy under her feet, and went past the garden shed and the lumpy old sandbox. When she got to the tangles of the overgrown, misshapen cedar hedge, she stopped, uncertain if she was in the right spot. There was a chance it had grown over, that her "peephole to heaven," as Mary and her mother had called it, had closed up. Brushing aside some wet leaves and branches, she realized she was still a few feet off. A couple more steps, a bit of pushing and pulling of sodden branches, and she was there; the secret passage had grown over, but with effort she pushed through the grasping shrubbery to the graveyard beyond.

A torn shirt was a small price to pay for entry to St. Ivan's Churchyard, the final resting place for over three hundred of St. Ivan's early parishioners—her mother being among the last of them.

Keeley stepped carefully around the gravesites with their old sod and aging markers, some wood, some granite, and some merely iron plaques embedded in the grass.

Her mother's grave was two rows in; its headstone, a simple stone marker in the shape of a Celtic cross, stood straight and strong, as had the woman now lying beneath it. The words on the stone were simple. *This is my Mom, who I will love forever. God keep you.*

Keeley swallowed, remembering Mary coming to her, asking her for the words, telling her she was the only one who knew exactly what to say.

She ran her hand slowly over the epitaph. "I still mean it, Mom." She choked up. *Oh, God, she was going to weep buckets. For Mom, for Mary, for everything.* "And I still miss you," she whispered.

"Are you here for the morning service?"

The soft voice came from behind her, a few feet away, and she turned, rubbing at her nose, to see a balding man, probably ten or so years older than her own thirty-five, approaching her. He wore jeans and a sweater that appeared to be two sizes too large for his tall, thin frame.

"No," she said with a sniff. "I'm visiting my mother."

He came up to her and put out his hand. "Glen Barton. Father Barton if you're of the faith." He smiled.

His hand was big and warm and their greeting brief. "Keeley Farrell. I live behind the hedge." She gestured to the high shrubs and cedar trees at the edge of the churchyard.

"Ah, Mary's . . . what? Godchild?"

She smiled. "Yes, I suppose that's right." Grandchild was more how she saw it.

"And a nun?"

"Ex-nun, Father." She looked him in the eye, beat back the vaguely uncomfortable feeling that came with any conversation with people of the cloth. "A few years now."

"But still a believer, I hope." He tilted his head.

She eyed him. "You looking to make a new convert— or an old convert new again?"

He laughed and his eyes crinkled as if they were used to it. "No. I'm getting too old for the arduous work of changing minds. From here on I'm counting solely on my charm."

"Smart," she said.

"Lazy," he replied. "Charm takes much less energy." He glanced at the headstone where Keeley still rested her hand. "Your mother?"

"Yes. She was almost the last person buried here." She gave the stone one final caress and pulled her hand back. "Twenty-four years ago now. I was eleven when she died."

"That would have been Father Randall's time, I think," Father Barton said. "He went to God a couple of years ago."

"Yes, I remember him." She paused, her chest thick and tight again. "He was kind to my mother, to Mary, and me. A good man." It was Father Randall who'd arranged it so she could stay with Mary. And it was Father Randall who'd assured her that her mother was "happy and healthy again in paradise," a thought she'd clung to with the passion and heart-wrenching need of a little girl who'd lost her mother, her only family, far too young.

As if sensing her pensive mood, Father Barton said, "I'll leave you to your privacy now, but perhaps we'll meet another time." He raised both brows and smiled down at her. "Sunday Mass, perhaps?"

"Be careful, Father. It wouldn't be smart to use up all that charm of yours the first time out."

He laughed again. "If nothing else, you'll make an interesting neighbor, Keeley Farrell."

When the priest left, Keeley knelt beside her mother's grave. It had been too long since she'd been here—far too long—and it was comforting in some strange way to think of her mother resting beside the church she'd loved and attended so faithfully, only a few yards from the only home she and Keeley had ever known together.

She scanned the gravesite. At first, it had been raised, a soft grassy hump in the earth, but time had flattened it, leveled it to the rut of the path winding through the graveyard. She ran a hand over the plot, carefully and with intent, pressing her palm into the damp earth, stopping when the familiar rough lines of the stones touched her palms.

They were still here . . .

As Mary had promised they'd be. "The grass will grow around them, Keeley, darlin', and protect them. They'll be with her forever. Like our love for her."

Keeley traced the carefully set pattern, the stone daisies she and Mary had formed, then pushed deep into the soft sod during one of their early visits to the grave.

Mary had been right . . . about so many things.

In the days before she'd left the Sudan, Keeley had come across a mother burying the last of her children in a shallow, dusty grave beside the road leading out of Darfur. Keeley closed her eyes against the pain of remembering.

So many dead, and with them gone, so much lost: the innocence and joy of children, the love and nurturing of women, the lore and stories of the aged.

So much killing . . .

Mothers left with no time to grieve. Or with no grief left in a soul battered by it. Children, women, the elders: in the Sudan, they were fresh meat to the brutal Janjaweed militia who arrived without warning and slaughtered without cause.

With only minutes to spare before forced relocation, the child's burial was a hasty roadside affair lacking ritual or tradition, attended by only a small group of people whose homes and hearts were too damaged and shocked by the raid—and their own loses—to speak.

Keeley had knelt beside that mother—as she was kneeling now beside her mother's grave—her psyche numbed by the hunger, pain, and horrific violence of her final weeks in Africa. She'd picked up a handful of stones, and while the mother watched vacantly, she formed a stone daisy over the child's grave.

Another woman, then another joined to form a silent circle around the tiny grave. Each made a flower, each touched the shoulder of the grieving mother. Each then shuffled toward the dust of the road and an unknown future.

Keeley knelt in the silent graveyard, bowed her head, and prayed, first for the mothers of Darfur, then for the nameless child by the side of the road.

She should have done more, so much more, instead she'd been weak, sabotaged by her own nerves—made useless, then told to go home. A right decision, but her failure all the same.

She stood and looked down at the grave.

In the past, Keeley Farrell, that's all in the past.

Her life was here now, doing Mary's work, helping one person at a time, loving one person at a time, and making sure the doors of Mayday House remained open to the women who needed it.

It might be a small thing, but it was her calling, and she'd give it everything she had in her to give.

Gus strode out of the bank, enough cash in his jeans to tide him over while he was in Erinville—which he hoped wouldn't be too long.

As usual the amount of money in the account made him uneasy. Over a million and a half. Hell, he might as well stuff the cash under his mattress for all the thought he gave it. He'd worked his butt off—literally—for years to get it, and now he had no idea what to do with it. In the beginning it was for Josh.

And to pave the way to April.

If there was even a chance Hagan knew anything about his sister, Gus had no choice; he had to act on it. The last time he'd seen her she was nine; he was eleven. Since then, no matter how much time he put in, how much money he spent, he'd found no trace of her.

How the hell Hagan had learned about his missing sister was anybody's guess, but he'd put his money on Cassie. She'd probably been through his bank statements, picked up on the funds funneled to PIs through the years when he couldn't risk returning to Seattle to do the legwork himself. No giant leap for Hagan to take it from there.

Gus's stomach clenched. If that son of a bitch was lying about what he knew, he was a bigger fool than Gus pegged him for—and he'd made the biggest mistake of his life.

When Gus stopped being Dinah's paid plaything a while back, and went into the personal security business, he'd made more money than he'd ever figured he would. It seemed the rich were willing to pay plenty for a bodyguard who looked good in a tux and could take out a man's eye with a knife from fifty feet. Yeah, he'd made more than enough for himself and Josh. Enough to hire the best of the best to start looking for April—which had netted him zero. A debit account that made him more than uneasy; it made him coldly furious and dangerously frustrated, feelings that had deepened since his return to Seattle. Distance made it easier to forget. Here, the memories roared back.

Pushing thoughts of his failure aside, he walked out of the bank into a cool misty day and headed up the street to where he'd parked his Jag.

He wasn't too happy about getting tangled up in Dinah's life again, either, even if it was to save her sophisticated ass.

But if she was in trouble . . .

He cursed himself, pushed thoughts of Dinah aside.

Damn it, this job wasn't about her, it was about finding April. He unlocked his Jag, got in, and shoved the bank book into the duffel bag in the back seat of the car.

Fifteen minutes later he was heading southeast on the road to Erinville.

Lightly scratching the scar on his jaw, Gus turned his mind to the problem at hand which was how to find out what was going on at Mayday House, while lying through his teeth to a woman who had a pair of lie detectors for eyes.

Dinah was right about one thing: his male "attributes" weren't going to help with Farrell. Which didn't mean he wouldn't give them a try.

Even if he wouldn't touch that nun with a barge pole.

Dinah Marsden drank the last of her morning coffee, her thoughts divided between the unceasing ache left by Gus's absence and the drone of Cassie's voice telling her about her day.

". . . the opera tonight with the Smythes and the Uriens—"

"Who in hell are the Uriens?" Dinah snapped, forcing herself to the matter at hand.

Cassie, sitting across from her at the breakfast table, flipped through Dinah's schedule. "Friends of the Smythes and the Connellys. You met them at the AIDS fund-raiser in March?" Cassie looked at her in that irritatingly quizzical way she used when she knew damn well Dinah had no idea what she was talking about—but should! It was an expression she used more and more of late.

Dinah made an impatient hand-it-over gesture with her hand, and Cassie shoved the schedule across the table.

Dinah read, then shook her head. "I have no idea who these people are." And it made her nervous. People made jokes about senior moments. Although what was funny about forgetting things, forgetting seriously important people, she'd never know. One thing was obvious: all the cosmetic surgery in the world didn't stop brain seepage. She pushed the book back across the glass-topped table toward Cassie. "Check them out, will you?"

When Cassie nodded, took a bite from her toast, and picked up the novel she'd set beside her plate, Dinah added, "Now, Cassie."

She dabbed her mouth with her napkin. "Of course," she said and gave Dinah her dead-fish look that said nothing and everything. She started to get up.

Dinah shot out a hand and closed it over hers. "Oh, God, I'm sorry, Cassie. Sit down. Finish your breakfast." She forced a smile, tamping down her edgy impatience, a feeling that dogged her more and more of late. "The Urine can wait."

"It's Urien, Dinah."

"What a difference an E makes!" she quipped, receiving only a faint smile in response.

Rodina came in and filled both their coffee cups.

"Oh. . . I remember now," Dinah said, relieved.
"Miles and Bunny Urien. Construction. He's building the Balustrada Towers at the other end of South
Beach. She's director of the Canterby Foundation.
Something to do with illiteracy." Both of them worth
knowing. She sighed. Which didn't change the fact
that she hated opera, or that she hated her life—
since Gus had walked out of it.

I wonder who he's fucking. . . .

Her stomach curled, and the hand she used to
reach for her coffee shook. No! She wouldn't think
about that, couldn't bear it. Christ! What a fool she
was, letting him go.

He'd called only once, and typical Gus, the message left with Rodina was terse: he'd seen the nun
"with no results." And he'd see her again when he
could. The "when he could" part pissed her off. But
then he didn't know that every day that nun spent
in Mayday House brought Dinah closer to disaster,
and she didn't intend to tell him.

She cursed herself for the stupid whim that had
caused her to involve him in this nasty bit of business
in the first place, but looking back, why she did it was
pathetically clear. It was rich-bitch Dinah Marsden's
twist on the old I-forgot-my-sweater trick, concoct-
ing a reason to contact him again, because she'd
been terrified that when he left Miami, she'd lose
him forever.

A man that to this day she knew absolutely nothing about—other than how marvelous he was in
bed. From day one her questions about his past
met with rigid, unyielding silence and, truth be
told, she hadn't much cared. Pasts, as she well knew,
often deserved to be forgotten—certainly hers did.

Then a couple of months after he'd come to live with her, he'd told her he needed new names and birth certificates for him and Josh, his little brother. It was the first of only two times he'd asked her for anything, and she'd complied, no questions asked. Not that asking would have done any good. Gus kept to Gus. Had in the beginning and had in the end.

Which made her even more of a fool for trusting him with Mayday House: something so critical, something that could destroy her life.

She hadn't started out being a fool for him, had simply thought she'd procured a young, energetic lover, a plaything, someone she could control. Then one day everything changed; Gus changed—like all self-protective chameleons do. It amused her now to think she'd ever thought she could control Gus Hammond.

She remembered the exact day. . . . It was the day that stupid bitch, Idona, had asked to borrow him—for the fifth time. Dinah had said yes, afraid even then to admit her growing feelings for him—but, God, he was so beautiful, so maddeningly detached, so deliciously fuckable, yet always filled with that strange dark pride, that incredible inner assurance. Like a tall young king he was—even when she began sharing him with her friends. At first it was a lark, a way of proving she didn't care, and a means of attacking that frustrating, untouchable pride of his that drove her crazy.

When she'd make a date for him, he'd give her one of his cool dark looks, and say, "Where and when?" Never who, because the who didn't matter.

Until Idona. Twice as wealthy as Dinah and ten years younger, she'd wanted to keep Gus, had asked him to move in with her, promised him the moon, and a few million stars to match. Dinah pulled in a breath; even now that moment of truth paralyzed her. When she'd confronted Gus, accused him of disloyalty, he'd looked at her, his eyes cold and unforgiving. "You're the one with all the hot friends, Dinah. Me? I go along for the ride. Or should I say rides? You want exclusive, say so."

She'd said "so" and he'd set out his conditions. No sex unless they both wanted it. A college fund for Josh, and night school classes for him—college after that. And no hassles when he chose to leave.

That was the day she'd fallen hopelessly, helplessly in love with Gus Hammond.

And if she was going to get him back, she'd have to take care of the nun and Mayday House herself—or at least help things along. She had a hunch who the nun was, but who the hell would have thought she'd show up now, at the worst possible time, in the worst possible place—that horrible old house.

Taking in another breath, she decided not to dwell on it, or the nun.

Gus wasn't so easy to put out of her mind. At least he hadn't taken the escort job she'd sent his way. Okay, maybe she had been testing him, but dear God, she was happy he'd passed.

He'd been gone over two weeks, and it was like missing every second beat of her heart. She'd sworn she wouldn't call, that she'd have more pride than that—but she had called. Hadn't connected either time. And now here she was, a busy day to be scheduled, and all she could think about was Gus.

She was suddenly, abruptly, and absolutely goddamn tired of thinking.

"Cassie, get Gus on the phone, will you?"

Cassie, her nose, as usual, buried in one of her paperbacks, lifted her head and gave her another fish-eyed stare, thick with disapproval. "You sure?"

"Sure about what? Whether my pride can take it when he tells me to get lost?"

At first Cassie didn't answer, her tight expression saying it all; then she said, "He's all wrong for you, Dinah. You know that. He's across the country. Let him be."

Cassie was right, of course. Gus was the last man on earth she should care about. For one thing there was the age difference. Twenty-four years was twenty-four years no matter how many times she went under the knife. She was old enough to be his mother, Josh's grandmother. Fuck!

"Just get him on the phone, will you?" *Because if I don't hear the sound of his voice, I'm going to go crazy.*

"Okay, if that's what you want." Cassie sighed, put down her book, and picked up the phone.

Dinah waited, tried to be cool, tried not to count the seconds until the call went through.

After what seemed forever, Cassie clicked off. "Well?"

"There's a message on his home voice mail, says he'll be gone a week, maybe more."

A week or more. No message. Nothing!

"Check my schedule, see when I have a few days free. And if you can't find any, make some," she said, getting to her feet.

"Dinah . . . don't." Cassie's face managed to look sympathetic and disapproving at the same time.

"Don't what? Follow the man I love like some kind of aging rock groupie?" *Don't hurt like a young girl who's lost her first love? Don't be a foolish old woman who can't accept an "I don't love you" as final?*

"No, that's not what I was going to say." She clasped Dinah's wrist. "We used to be friends, Dinah, and I . . . hate seeing you like this."

Dinah put her hand over Cassie's, meaning to yank it off. Instead she squeezed it. *My God, I'm going to cry. I never cry . . . except over Gus.*

She coughed, pulled her hand back, and brushed at her cheeks. "Deal with my schedule, Cassie. And get us tickets to Seattle."

She walked out of the room. In fact, her decision to go to Seattle was perfect. She might be in love with Gus for all the wrong reasons, but she'd get him back, one way or another.

While she was at it, she'd do her part in getting rid of the nun and getting that filthy old mausoleum shut down for good.

CHAPTER 6

"Duke, what are you looking for?" Christiana, wearing running shorts, a high-cut tank top, and carrying a bottle of water, stepped into her home office just as Duke Thomas was closing the top drawer of her desk.

He turned from the task immediately and stepped toward her. "I was looking for that bottle of brandy the local station gave us." His green eyes rested hotly on her bared legs, then her naked midriff. He hooked a finger in the elastic waist of her shorts. "Now, I'm looking for a little pussy."

Christiana took a drink from her bottle of water and set it on her desk. "You won't find either one in my top drawer."

"How about this one?" He tugged on her waistband until it gaped, raised an eyebrow, and looked inside her cotton pants. "Looks like pussy to me. Nice soft pussy." Smiling then, he took her in his arms and nuzzled her hair. "You smell fabulous."

She knew he'd detoured from her question, but didn't much care. When she got this close to him,

she didn't much care about anything other than getting closer yet—and she had an hour before her
magazine interview. Plenty of time. She pressed her
body to his, rested her head on his shoulder, and put
her nose to his neck and breathed him in. He
smelled . . . expensive. "You're the one who smells
good. Me? I smell like a rain-drenched dog. I need
a shower." She kissed his neck, then pulled back,
again stabbed by curiosity. "And you know darn
well I don't keep brandy in my desk."

He raised his hands in surrender, arched a brow,
and smiled. "I wanted to surprise you."

Christiana frowned and smiled at the same time.
"What are you up to, Duke Thomas?" Her heart
fluttered. Expectation unfurled.

He gestured toward her desk, the drawer he'd
had open when she walked in.

Walking toward it, she glanced at him from over
her shoulder. He looked exceedingly pleased with
himself.

She opened the drawer and discovered a box,
about eight inches long and covered in velvet. She
ran an index finger along the long—wrong—form
of the box, and the fluttering in her heart stopped,
leaving it to sink. Inside the box, resting on black
satin, was a double string of pearls. She hated pearls.

Pearls are for tears. . . . That's what her mother
always used to say. "They're beautiful, Duke," she said,
infusing her voice with false sincerity. "Thank you."

"I saw them last week, at a jeweler's near the station. They seemed right for you." If he noticed her
lack of enthusiasm, it didn't show. His pleased expression held.

"Yes, they're perfect." She looped them back onto

their satin sheet and returned them to in the drawer. "I'll wear them with my navy blue dress." *And look like somebody's spinster aunt fresh out of mothballs.*

"Now that's amazing," he said. "That's exactly the dress I had in mind when I bought them." He stopped. "Although they'll be great on your black silk, too. Isn't that what you're wearing for *The Benny Catz Show?*"

The Catz show was two weeks away, and Duke was already focused on it. She should have guessed. "The Catz show is more of a twenty-something show, Duke, and black silk and pearls aren't exactly cutting-edge fashion. I'll look as if I'm attending an Italian funeral." She'd been down this road with Duke before, so he knew she hated it when he did his Svengali routine, telling her what to wear, what to say.

"Which is why it's so perfect," he argued. "The pearls, the carefully arranged hair, the conservative clothing, they're all about class, real substance—an image of a better time. It's what you're all about." He gripped her shoulders and looked deep into her eyes. "Plus, it's the real you, baby."

The real you . . . Christiana didn't think so, but then she'd been so out of touch with what she was for so long, she didn't remember. She'd been too busy recreating herself—the way Duke wanted her to be.

He kissed her then, brushing his lips over hers so softly he took her breath away.

Her heart thumped wildly, and she closed her eyes, placed her hands on his sides above his belt. The cords of his muscles were taut and hard. She ran her hands up, around his back, splayed them across his shoulders, and pulled him closer.

He deepened the kiss, slipping his tongue inside to taste and tease, then bringing his hands up to cover her breasts. "And while we're speaking of substance . . ." He kneaded her breasts, catching her hard nipples in the space between his index and middle fingers, compressing gently.

Christiana drifted into the first simmer of need, the sensual fog that surrounded her when Duke touched her. She took his face in her hands, kissed him, long and hard, then pulled back. The kiss still burning her mouth, her lips moist from his tongue, her voice stumbled when she muttered, "I need that shower—"

He urged her down to the floor, then stood over her. "What you need is your pants off—and this." He undid his belt, unzipped himself, and exposed his engorged penis. It was fully erect, emerging from his expensive slacks with a bravado earned inch by extended inch.

Her breath lumped in her throat and she gasped for air before reaching up to touch, then kiss the silken tip of him.

"Oh, that's good. I'll take all of that you want to give." He put his big hands on her head.

She took him in her mouth, played with him. He groaned and shuddered, and she worked him more, took him to the edge—but only the edge. When she felt his pelvis thrust, the shudder in his thighs, she quickly pulled off her shorts, stretched out on the floor, and spread her quivering legs wide. The lips of her labia were already moist and hungry for him, rabid for him.

"Just a tease, huh?" He ran his tongue over his lower lip and smiled. "Can't wait, baby?" Of course, he knew he was right, knew the depth of her need, the harshness of her obsession for him. Her impatience to have him inside her, filling her with his thick, hard length.

When she didn't answer, he chuckled, then knelt and lowered his body to hers. Bracing a hand on either side of her head, he plunged inside her, the stroke so powerful it shifted her up the carpet.

"Oh, God . . . yes," she moaned. "More, Duke, more." He thrust again, and again . . .

Christiana tried to restrain the wave of her release, make the moment last—make Duke last. Then his thumb found her clitoris, rubbed and circled it. "Come on, baby. Come on . . ." He shifted his body, increased the friction, and rocked into her, deep, then deeper still, his moves hot, rhythmic, and demanding.

"Oh, God." She clenched her eyelids tight, struggled to hold back, savor the anticipation, but it was useless. She came in the usual heart-pounding, mind-numbing rush that left her weak to the bone. One thrust later and Duke released in her on a long satisfied moan.

She lay back, her body slack, tired, sated and deprived all at once.

Duke, heavy on her breasts, groaned, then muttered hoarsely in her ear, "Jesus, Chris, you're the best fuck I've ever had."

Christiana turned her head, feeling the moisture fill, then seep, from the corner of her eye.

Pearls are for tears . . .

She wondered if he said the same thing to his wife.

* * *

The knock on Mayday's front door was quick, sharp, and loud.

"Get that, Bridget, will you?" Keeley called over her shoulder, from the top step of the ladder, nearly knocking over her paint can in the process. She wanted to curse. She would have if she hadn't decided to pull back on her use of bad language, which seemed to have increased with each mishap that came with home renovating.

"Okay," Bridget said, looking momentously relieved to abandon the task of emptying out the kitchen cupboards to ready them for Keeley's unstoppable paintbrush.

She was back in seconds.

"Who was it?" Keeley carefully ran a putty knife over the fill she'd smeared over a gash in the wall.

"No one was there. Just this," Bridget said, holding up a small package. "It's addressed to you."

Keeley did another careful drag over the fill in the wounded wall and descended the ladder. "Let's see."

She wiped her hands on the front of her coveralls and took the package from Bridget. Plain brown paper. Carelessly wrapped. No postage or shipping labels. Address printed in bold black ink. She turned it over. No return address.

Feeling her stomach flip uncomfortably, Keeley tightened her grip on the package and glanced at Bridget. "You didn't see anyone?" She moistened her lower lip.

"Nope. It was propped against the door."

The package seemed to heat up in Keeley's hand.

Bridget went back to her cupboard cleaning. "Probably something from a neighbor. Mrs. O'Neil down the road, maybe. She was always dropping off baked stuff."

Keeley nodded, telling herself she was being foolish, spooked by a plain brown wrapper. No doubt Bridget was right. She tore the tape off one end of the package and pulled back the wrapping.

"It's a book," she announced, feeling stupidly relieved. She was reminded again of the way that strange phone call during her first few days in the house had put her on edge. Then she looked at the cover, a lurid near-photographic depiction of a woman tied to a chair with a man behind her holding a knife to her throat. Dripping from the knife, and raised by embossing, were drops of blood so deeply red they bordered on black. *HOLY MURDER!*, the title of the book, was slashed diagonally across the cover in the same dark crimson.

A string dangled from the pages. A page marker. Something jittered along Keeley's nape as she opened the book to where the string rested. Page 186. Some paragraphs were highlighted in yellow:

"What goes on here is my business," he snarled. "And you'd be smart to remember that. So do what you're told—and stay away from the cops."

She glared at him, challenged him. "I'll do what I want when I want. You don't control me. You never did."

He lifted her chin using the barrel of his gun. "I don't want to control you, sweetheart," he said, his lips curling, his words soft with threat. "I don't have time for that. What I want is for you to clear out. Out of my life. And out of this town."

"And if I don't?"

His trained eyes saw the beginning of uncertainty in hers. Finally. "If you don't, bitch, someone is going to get hurt. Really hurt. And it won't necessarily be you."

Under the paragraphs, and written over the following text in the same heavy ink that was on the envelope, was some rough, childlike printing:

Don't be stupid and don't be brave. Get out now. Mayday House is not worth dying for.

Keeley closed the book, placed it on the table, and wiped her suddenly damp palms over the paint-spattered fabric covering her thighs. Her breath crowded her lungs. Her brain grasped for a sense of things. For meaning.

The police. She'd call the police. They'd know what to do.

She pressed a hand to her heart, willing it to settle, stop its arrhythmic, painful thumping against her ribs. But it was words that settled like lead knots at the bottom of her mind.

. . . stay away from the cops.

. . . someone is going to get hurt.

. . . not necessarily you.

As warnings went, this one was siren clear. She clenched her jaw.

"Keeley, what's wrong? You're the color of this plate." Bridget held up the white dinner platter she'd pulled from the cupboard.

"Nothing. I was wondering who sent this." She cleared her throat and closed the book, her nerves warring with her growing outrage. Fear and threat, the tools of the mad and the impotent. Terror, the tool of the ignorant and cowardly. She'd thought she'd left them all behind, doing their evil work in the dust of Africa. She'd been wrong.

Bridget gave her a bored look. "Like I said, probably a neighbor. Mary had lots of friends."

Keeley frowned. Mary might have had a lot of friends, but she'd obviously also accumulated some enemies. First the late-night call, now this package. They had to be connected, but how? The voice on the phone hadn't told her to get out of Mayday House, and any threat had been more of a sexual nature, but whoever sent this—she looked at the lurid paperback in her hand—definitely wanted her gone.

Which was not going to happen.

Mayday was her home and short of a full-scale invasion by an armored tank unit, she wasn't leaving it.

Needing time to think things through, she took the book into her office and put it in the bottom drawer. She *would* call the police, when she was sure no one else was at risk, and she had something more substantial to give them than an ambiguous phone call and a highlighted passage in a bad novel.

Gus stopped at the first motel he came to in Erinville, the Jasper Inn. It wasn't much, but it was clean, convenient, and far enough off the highway bypassing the town that he wouldn't hear the road noise.

Besides, he didn't plan on staying long, not that Mayday House accommodations promised much better.

As distasteful jobs went, this one took first place, but if he played it right—played Keeley Farrell right—he'd be out of here in a few days, tops. But to do that he needed to get close to her and stay there. Twenty-four/seven.

He tossed his leather duffel bag on the second bed in the room, then picked up the phone and punched in Mayday's number.

"Mayday House, Keeley here."

"Ms—" He stopped himself. "Keeley, this is Gus Hammond. We talked a few days ago?"

"Oh, yes, the man with the muscles."

Gus let that one go. "Have you had a chance to think over Dinah Marsden's offer to buy your property?"

"Actually, I haven't thought about it at all—and don't plan to."

"You intend to keep the house open, then?"

"I do."

It was the answer he had expected and he paused, gathering words for a workable lie. He had to get into that house. "I'd like to come and—"

"Where are you? Right now, I mean," she interrupted.

"At the Jasper Inn on the edge of town."

"Look, I'm a bit rushed at the moment. I've got a paintbrush in one hand and a soup ladle in the other, so why don't I—" She stopped abruptly. "No. Why don't *you* come for dinner? It's roast beef . . . say in an hour?"

The invitation caught him off guard. "Sure, I—"

"Perfect! I'll see you then. I've got papers for you to take back to Mrs. Marsden. Some kind of tax receipts I found when I was cleaning out the office. She might need them." He heard the phone drop, a muttered "Damn it!" and she hung up.

Gus was left holding the old motel phone receiver and staring at it. He'd expected problems getting back into Mayday House, not an invitation to a roast beef dinner.

He put the phone down.

Now all he had to do was figure out how to move in.

When Gus spotted the display of cut flowers outside the corner store, he swerved to the curb and jumped out. Roses were overkill, he thought, so he opted for a handful of white daisies wrapped in gaudy purple paper. Fifteen minutes later he was at the front door of Mayday House.

The door opened the second he poised his finger over the bell.

Keeley Farrell looked at his raised hand. "It doesn't work anyway. Come in." She caught sight of the flowers then and her eyes widened, their expression a mixture of surprise and confusion. "For me?" she said, staring at the small bouquet as if it were a handful of diamonds.

He'd planned to smile, but he was too taken by the sight of her coppery hair, which seemed on fire under the too-bright entry hall light, then the true shape of her, this time visible under a blue T-shirt and jeans that came damn close to fitting. She was thinner than he'd first thought, with a surprisingly small waist, and she had freckles on her arms. But damn, she had curves, and in all the right places. Feeling oddly juvenile, given the direction of his thoughts, he held out the flowers. "They won't do much for a second-rate motel room in Erinville."

"Thank you." She took them, then tilted her head and smiled up at him. "Tell your mother she raised a very nice boy."

"I will." *When I see her in hell.*

She stepped aside and he walked in. The place didn't look any better than when he had been here three days before. "You're making progress," he said.

"And you're a good liar."

This time he almost did smile. This woman gave no quarter. He'd have to remember that. "You're wearing new jeans. They damn near fit."

Her lips twitched.

Bridget came down the stairs then, also wearing jeans but with a bright red T-shirt. Neither hid her painful thinness. Her eyes met Gus's and slid away shyly. "Hi," she said. "Gus, right?"

"Uh-huh. And hi back."

"Dinner ready?" Another woman followed Bridget down the stairs. A beautiful woman, dark hair, tall, straight, and big as a goddamn house. Expensively dressed. Other than the big-as-a-house thing, she was a darker version of Dinah. Stopping on the bottom stair, she gave Gus a slow once-over with an edge of sexuality. "And who do we have here?" She kept her eyes fixed on him and moistened her lower lip. It was the kind of assessing, check-him-out look he used to get from Dinah's friends.

"Gus Hammond." He offered his hand. "I'm a last-minute dinner guest." *And when I get some time, I'll do some checking of my own.* Somehow she didn't look like a woman who needed a refuge—from anything. She looked tough as sheet metal.

"Erica Stark." She took his hand and held it too long. "Somehow I didn't think you were a new live-in. Too bad."

"Shall we eat now?" Keeley said. "If we're lucky, I kept the paintbrush out of the soup pot and the ladle out of the paint can." She looked at each them and frowned. "But I can't guarantee that."

She led the way into the big kitchen, where mismatched dishes were set neatly in four place settings. Unlike the entrance hall, there'd been some progress in the kitchen. Two walls were painted yellow, not a screaming yellow, more like the color of bananas, and most of the junk was gone. And it smelled good enough to make his stomach take notice. He couldn't remember the last time he'd sat at a kitchen table for dinner. Probably because he never had.

"Sit," Keeley instructed them all.

When they'd each taken a seat, she ladled soup, something made with squash and coconut, into their bowls, then, with Bridget's help, set steaming dishes of roast beef, potatoes, and mixed vegetables in the center of the table.

"Camp style," she said. "Easier this way."

Also delicious, Gus thought, taking his first spoonful of soup.

"Any paint taste?" Keeley asked, a brow raised, her mouth quirked.

Gus shook his head and took another spoonful. "A bit of turps, though. Really kicks it up."

She laughed.

He liked her laugh, liked her no-nonsense style, too. He couldn't imagine anyone wanting to harm this woman. Certainly not Dinah.

"Speaking of camps," Erica said, reaching for a warm bun and looking at Keeley, "how long were you in Africa?"

The remnants of humor seemed to rearrange themselves on her face. "The last time? Two years."

"Where, exactly?"

"Darfur. Sudan. I was a nurse working for MAL, Medics At Large." That said, she bent her head and gave her full attention to the roast beef she'd put on her plate. The woman liked to eat.

"That must have been hell."

Keeley raised her head and met Erica's curious gaze dead-on. "Hell enough that I don't like to talk about it."

Erica studied her a moment, then shrugged. "I guess we all have things we don't like to talk about," she said, then turned her attention to Gus. "Like good-lookin' here, I'll bet he's got more than most."

He raised his hands and met her speculative gaze. "Me? I'm an open book." No need to tell her the book was pure fiction.

"Right, and I'm Tinkerbell." She snorted. "Well, Mister Open Book, would you please pass the potatoes?"

CHAPTER 7

"They're in there." Keeley, who'd taken the last of the garbage out after dinner and shooed both Bridget and Erica up to their beds, arrived back in the room and pointed to a door off the hall directly outside the kitchen.

"Excuse me?" Gus said, not getting it.

"Those papers I mentioned? She probably won't want most of them, but there's definitely some receipts she'll need for tax reasons."

"Right." Gus tossed the towel he'd been handed after dinner with a terse you-can-dry instruction on the counter. Among a million other things, this place could use a new dishwasher, one that worked. "Let's have a look."

The office rivaled a recently excavated landfill site. Keeley went to a battered three-drawer metal cabinet behind a wooden desk and tugged on a stubborn bottom drawer, pulling it far enough out for her to reach the back end.

She removed a bulging hanging file and put it on her desk. After ferreting through it, she pulled out several sheets of paper. "Here they are." She handed them to him. "I don't know how Mary did things, exactly, because I haven't had much time to dig around in here, but you might as well take these back with you, considering there won't be any more payments this year. It'll save me a stamp."

When he took the papers, she smiled, then glanced at her watch.

Gus felt dismissed and vaguely embarrassed, both new sensations. Hagan really was stupid; there was nothing "easy" about Keeley Farrell. He was used to getting what he wanted from women using well-honed charm and what they considered his good looks. Farrell, it seemed, was immune to both, which would be refreshing if it weren't so inconvenient, although it was nothing he couldn't handle.

He turned his attention to the papers and did a quick tally. Jesus, based on these numbers, Dinah had been forking out over a hundred grand a year to Mayday House. There had to be a reason, and chances were, some clue to it was in that fat, sloppy file Farrell had left open on her desk. He tossed the papers back on the desk. "I'm not going back."

Her brow furrowed. "But I thought . . . That's why you came tonight, to pick up the papers. You didn't say—"

"You didn't give me a chance to say anything. You hung up on me, remember?"

She grimaced. "You're right, I'm sorry. I get, uh, overly focused at times." She sat in silence, then said, "So why did you come?"

He sat on the edge of the desk and met her curious eyes, but didn't bother with his practiced smile. "I wanted to see you again." He let the words linger, undisturbed by the element of truth in them, and watched her carefully before adding, "Plus there was the home-cooking aspect of things."

As he'd intended, her attention caught on the first reason rather than the second. Farrell might have been a nun for a few years, but she'd been a woman all her life. And women were his area of expertise, them and cold steel. All he needed to do was concentrate.

She frowned so deeply it looked painful; her expression darkened. "You're lying. Why?"

"Why would you think I'm lying?" He picked up a pencil from the desk, balanced the lead point of it on a paper block near the phone.

"It's in your face, behind those dark eyes of yours." She stopped and seemed to consider her next words. "I get the impression you know exactly what you're about, Gus Hammond—and you keep it all to yourself." She took the pencil from his hand, put it down on the desk, and stood. "And, as I have no use for lies or liars . . ." She raised her eyes to his. They weren't angry eyes, more disappointed. ". . . I'll ask you to leave. I've got work to do."

When she moved to walk around him, he gripped her wrist, easily enfolding it in his hand. *Warm. Surprisingly delicate.* "You've also got trouble, Sister Farrell. And I think a good part of it is in that file." He gestured to the sheaf of papers spilling onto her desk.

When she tugged her arm from his grasp, he let her go. "The obvious response to that statement," she said, "is what business is that of yours?" Rubbing her wrist, she leveled her gaze on him with the dead-eye focus of a sphinx.

At least she didn't deny it. "Because someone wants

me to make it my business." He saw no reason not to use the truth when the truth served his purpose.

She leaned a hip against the desk and crossed her arms under her breasts. Gus was pretty damn sure that if she could have turned him into stone, she'd have done it in a heartbeat. "And why would they do that?"

"That's the million-dollar question. Why don't you tell me?" Not much chance she'd start spewing Mayday's dark secrets, but it was worth a shot.

She studied him for a long time, the rise of anger in her eyes giving way to consternation. She started to circle the office, stopping at the high undraped window facing the front yard. The room was quiet except for the sound of rain on the porch roof and the occasional clanking of old pipes from somewhere overhead. She turned and again folded her arms across her breasts. "Who hired you, Mr. Hammond?"

So it was "mister" now. "Hagan Marsden. Dinah Marsden's ex-husband." Gus shifted away from the desk, walked the eight feet between them, and stood directly in front of her.

"And why you?" she asked. "Don't you work for Dinah?"

"Past tense. And he hired me because my business is security." He pulled out his wallet and gave her a card.

"August Hammond, Personal Protection," she read, then looked at him, her eyes no less wary, no less distrustful. "That makes you what? Some kind of bodyguard?"

"Among other things, but in this case that's as good a description as any."

"My most valued patron's ex-husband sends *me* a bodyguard. Here's the obvious question. Why?"

"He wants you, and this house, to stay safe," he said, amazed his lie didn't lodge in his throat and cut off his air.

"Considering your Mister Marsden doesn't even know me, how about trying again? The altruistic ring in those words was like a lead ball hitting a mattress."

Gus ran a knuckle along his scar. "Okay, how about this? Hagan Marsden is a mean bastard. His and Dinah's divorce made headlines a few years ago, as ugly as they come. Dinah cleaned him out. He hates her and the feeling is mutual. Hagan sees a chance to get his pound of flesh, which to him means as much of his money back as he can get. To do that he needs something to use against her. He believes that '*something*' is here—in Mayday House."

She frowned. "If I've got this straight, you're telling me Dinah Marsden's ex-husband hired you to protect me from her, while you dig up the information he needs to blackmail her?"

"That's about it."

"And you're going along with it—this blackmail scheme. What kind of a man are you?" She looked at him as if she knew exactly what kind of man he was, the dirtbag kind.

"If I was going along with it, would I tell you?"

"Why *are* you telling me?"

"Because you need to know the truth. First off, if you and your precious Mayday House have fallen between the Hagan/Dinah firing lines—you *are* in danger. Hagan, and Dinah, if she senses a threat, will tear this place apart if they don't get what they want. Dinah's already played her first hand, trying to buy you out. She's capable of more—and Hagan even worse. That said, Dinah and I have"—he stopped, thought a second—"a history. I owe her. I don't owe Hagan. If there is something here she wants kept secret, it stays that way. Hagan gets zero." Gus wanted that to be true, but his gut rolled all the same. In the end everybody did what they had to for their own ends. He was no different. Especially if it meant finding April.

"And you suspect what? The bones of Dinah's illegitimate baby hidden in the attic?" Her expression ran short of a sneer. Barely.

"Something like that. Considering this place has seen its share of unwed mothers for the past forty-odd years, it's no stretch to think in terms of an abandoned kid."

She gave him a dark look. "Putting a child up for adoption after an unplanned pregnancy is not abandonment, Mr. Hammond. And neither is it a felony if a woman chooses to keep that information to herself. Nor should it provide grist for blackmail."

"The name is Gus," he said. "And semantics aside, what you can't fudge is the fact that for more than thirty of Mayday's years—judging from those papers you showed me—Dinah has donated over three million dollars to Mayday. That pays for a lot more than an illegitimate birth."

That made her eyes widen. Obviously this was not a woman who did the math. But they narrowed quickly when she said, "So? If she was here at one time, and I don't know if she was, maybe it was her way of saying thank you for the help. Wealthy people are often generous."

"That's a hell of a thank you. And as to the generous part, that's not Dinah's style," he said, his tone flat. "Unless there's a damn good reason. That's the way Hagan sees it. And he's right."

"Perhaps Mary and Dinah were friends," she insisted. "Maybe that was it."

"Nobody's that friendly."

"You're cynical."

"And you're stubborn." He ran a hand through his hair. "Look, none of this matters. What matters is keeping you and this house safe until I can figure out what the hell's going on around here."

Her eyes snapped to alert—and direct. "Add presumptuous to cynical. I can take care of myself and Mayday."

Gus left the room to silence for a time, decided what card to play. "Can you also take care of those two women we had dinner with—one of which looks about twelve months pregnant?" He pushed his point. "Can you keep them safe from some creep hired by Marsden who does his best work after midnight? And is that a chance you're willing to take?"

"You're being dramatic."

"I'm being honest."

"And why should I trust you, a man hired to get dirt for a blackmailer?"

"Truth? I don't want to be here any more than you want me here, but Hagan Marsden is a determined man who's damned short in the scruples department. If I'd turned him down, he'd hire someone else. Then someone else." He met her eyes. "In the end he'd get what he wanted, any way he had to. Dinah would go down, and this place right along with her. He'd make sure of that. Like it or not, you've got trouble, Farrell. Big trouble." He stopped. "So, make your choice, me or brand X."

He expected an argument; instead Keeley glared at him, then turned her back and walked to the window. She stood in front of it, staring into the rain, her back plumb-line straight, and said nothing.

Her silence finally spoke to him, so he took the few steps to reach her and stood behind her. "You've already had some trouble, am I right?"

She smelled like cloves and lemon . . . and woman. And her hair, a crazy mop of red, needed a brush—or his fingers.

Shit! He shoved the thoughts aside, took a step back.

When she turned to face him, her expression was grim. "Yes, there's been some situations. But we'll talk about that in the morning. For now I'd suggest you go back to the Jasper Inn and get your things. There's an empty room across from mine, here on the main floor. The best place for you, I think. It used to be Mary's room. She said she liked it because she could hear every noise in the house." She was all business now.

And so was he. "Sounds fine. Tomorrow, I'd like a complete tour of the place—but maybe you can give me a quick verbal sketch. I need to know exactly where everyone sleeps."

She nodded, the gesture curt. "You've seen most of the main floor. All the usual: entry hall, kitchen, dining room, living room, this office—once a music room. Other than that there are nine bedrooms in Mayday, three on the main floor, five on the second, and one in the turret, but it hasn't been used in years. Mostly storage now. Erica and Bridget are both on the second floor."

"Anything else?"

"An attic"—she made a wry face—"where the bones are kept. And a cellar."

"Outbuildings?"

"A couple of sheds for storage, gardening tools, that sort of thing. The house sits on a couple of acres, maybe more. It used to have a big garden. St. Ivan's church is on the other side of the back hedge." She glanced away, for the first time looking worried. "I was born in Mayday, lived here until I was almost seventeen. I can't imagine what this . . . threat is all about."

"With luck we'll find out before anyone gets hurt. For now I'll get my stuff. Should be back in under an hour." Gus headed to the door. He didn't want her to leave the door unlocked for him, and it was getting late. His hand was turning the old crystal knob when she said his name. He turned.

"I'm still not sure about this whole thing, but there is one rule for as long as you're here. And it is *absolute*." The worry was gone from her face, replaced by a fierce doggedness.

He cocked his head, waited.

"You will not—under any circumstances—bring a gun into this house." She took a step toward him, never taking her eyes from his.

"Fair enough. No guns."

She eyed him a second or two longer. He figured his quick agreement had raised more suspicion than it had allayed.

After a second or so, she gave him a quick nod, then walked past him through the open door. "I'll make up your bed."

CHAPTER 8

Christiana stared at the contracts on her desk, pushed aside the vase containing a single blood-red rose, and centered the paper carefully in front of her. Duke had insisted she didn't need to read them, that he'd taken care of everything, but she should at least take a look.

At the first *whereas* and *hitherto* her mind wandered, and she pushed the papers aside.

Minutes later, she stood staring into the dying embers of the fire she'd built earlier, now sputtering down to sparks and small bursts of heat and light. Only a trace of its warmth remained.

The Oregon night was cool, so she prodded the weak flames to renewed life and put on another log. One of the joys of working at home was her office. She felt more comfortable here than in any other room in the house. It was here she made a difference, helped people. And it was here where her first show for local cable was filmed.

She remembered that day—the nerves, the excitement, the sense of accomplishment. The feeling of doing something worthwhile. She'd worked like a dog, true, but she'd felt so energized, so . . . new, the recognition for her work both fresh and satisfying.

Then she'd met Duke.

And now, two years later, barely a trace of that person remained. Now all she thought about was Duke. Her obsession.

When he was with her, he filled her mind, stoked her ambition—owned her body. Christiana swallowed, ran a hand across her breasts. She raised her hand then, idly stroked, then turned one of the blue votive candles on the mantel.

Her sexual need for Duke had begun to frighten her. Relentless and constant, it was a shimmering heat beneath her skin waiting for his touch. When she was with him, that heat made her feel alive, vibrant, wanted. When she wasn't with him—like tonight— she felt arid, itchy, and strangely frail, like a dried flower, dulled by too much heat and held too tight.

Everything about her and Duke was wrong, had been from the beginning.

Her body flushed.

The beginning . . . when he'd taken her against the wall of this office, hastily, roughly, with neither finesse nor tenderness. And she'd loved it, come alive under his hands in a way she'd never done before.

A week later he became her manager.

Stupid, stupid woman, falling in love with a married man. So stereotypical, so hypocritical, and now, faced with the light of impending public exposure, incredibly dangerous. It could ruin her career.

Duke told her not to worry, to work hard and keep what was between them quiet. No one would find out, he assured her, as if saying the words repeatedly made them true. He'd get his divorce, they'd get married, with no one being the wiser. And by then, she'd be such a big star, if some bad press did develop, she'd easily survive it.

At first she'd believed him, wanted desperately to believe him, but two years later, Duke was still with his wife; nothing had changed. Except her guilt at being the worst kind of fraud, and the nagging fear that her obsession with him would ruin everything.

He was another woman's husband.

She was dancing on the edge of a razor.

Pacing her office, she wrapped her arms around her middle, then straightened her shoulders. Her damn head hurt as much as her aching heart.

Something else happened when Duke wasn't around: her brain switched on, told her to end it, say good-bye, and get on with the life she'd planned, a life of discipline, honesty, and professionalism— the perfect public image, like the one she'd had before falling in lust with Duke.

Television, her new talk show, *Christiana*, with the tag line, *How to live a life of love, honor and compassion*, would finally give her the forum to reach people, motivate them to become more than they'd ever thought they'd be. She wanted that, believed in that.

She rested an arm, then her head against the fireplace mantel, and let the new bright flames send their heat to her face.

It was crazy. She owed Duke for getting her to this point in her career, and yet it was Duke who imperiled everything.

Her relationship with Duke wasn't her only problem. Another lurked somewhere in the dusty files of Mayday House. Even in her frantic state, she saw the bizarre humor in the relationship of the two. Jeans and genes. Duke in one, Mayday House in the other. Somehow she had to shake loose from both of them.

"Christiana?"

She turned to see her assistant standing in the door with her coat over her arm. "I thought you'd left, Terry," Christiana said.

"I was on my way when the phone rang, and I hadn't switched you over yet," she replied. Christiana kept her phone ringer off during the day while she was in sessions, leaving Terry to take her calls. Unless the world was coming to an end, or Duke called, she never interrupted. "It's Duke. About the setup for the Seattle tapings."

Christiana went to her desk. "Thanks. Now get out of here." She smiled along with the order and made a shooing motion with her hand. "That new husband of yours will be waiting."

The young, trim girl put on her coat, grinned, and flicked her long hair from under her collar. "Color me gone. And good luck tomorrow."

"Thanks." Christiana waved as she picked up the phone.

"Hi, lover." Duke's silky voice poured down the line, pulling strings that, until he'd come into her life, Christiana hadn't known were there. "Are you missing me?"

She was, damn it, she was! She swallowed, hoping it wasn't her meager pride. "I always miss you, Duke," she said, adding quickly, "Is everything ready for tomorrow?" She walked back toward the fireplace where the flames were again snapping brightly.

"Everything's set. KVOS at ten. KING5 at noon, and a visit to Evestwood High at two. They're planning a full assembly. KING says it will cover, but because we can't count on it, I've hired an independent for some video."

"Sounds good." Her stomach curled, half in excitement, half in early stage fright. Kids, she loved talking to kids, but they were always a tough audience.

"I think the high school thing is particularly good. You can't have enough of that kind of PR."

"Yes. It's very good."

Silence dripped down the line.

"Chris, what's wrong? You don't sound excited at all. Hell, I've been working on this Seattle thing for weeks." Irritation spiked his tone.

"Of course, I'm excited." It wouldn't do her or him any good to talk about the nervousness that preceded these kinds of appearances—or her confused thoughts about their relationship. "I'm tired, I guess, and still anxious about the first taping. New York still rattles me."

"They're airing it next week, by the way. And stop worrying, will you? I'm with you every step of the way." He still sounded annoyed as if he were exhausted by the sound of his own voice giving her support.

"You're right . . . as always. Like I said, I'm tired. I'll see you tomorrow. I should be there at least an hour before the first interview."

"Why not come tonight, baby?" His tone lowered again. "It's barely a three-hour drive. If you left right away, you'd be here before ten." He paused. "We'd have the night together—and you know we'd make good use of it."

She felt his smile, the draw of him, and her mouth went dry. "I don't think so, Duke." She looked at the contract, the lump of files on her desk, uncharacteristically askew—exactly like her brain cells. "I'll be in my office until at least midnight."

"My loss, sweetheart."

If only you meant that.

"Mine, too, darling. See you tomorrow." Christiana hung up the phone, hesitated, then picked it up again. She took the deepest breath of her life and dialed.

The voice that answered was soft and sounded young. "Mayday House. Can I help you?"

If you can't, I have no idea who will.

It was after one A.M. when Keeley took the first step leading to the cellar. Lord, it was like stepping into a tar pit. And what the heck she'd do once she got down there, she had no idea, but she had to start somewhere, and the cellar seemed as good a place as any.

It would've helped if Mary had put something higher than a twenty-five-watt bulb down here. She'd take care of that tomorrow, and next time she came, she'd bring a flashlight.

Through the gloom, she saw the stacks of boxes she'd spotted during her quick tour of the house the first week she was here. On that day, they were merely another acre of chaos to be dealt with when she got to it, and easily forgotten in the needs of the upper floors. Unfortunately there were this many cartons again in the attic.

She scanned the stacks of boxes, most of which were crumpled old cardboard, but somewhere along the line Mary had gone high-tech and bought some newer ones, clear plastic storage bins with lids, probably from the Wal-Mart in the next town. Most of the plastic ones were on the top, and a lot of them—at least thirty or more—were propped against the wall farthest from the ancient furnace.

She raised her eyes. "Dear God, Mary, I hope you at least marked them by year." She said the prayer aloud, but she didn't hold much hope that Mary's administrative skills, always horrendous, would yield that kind of order.

Two minutes later, discovering she was right, she let out a long sigh. No neat labels written in black felt pen marked either the year or the contents of the boxes. Not one of them was labeled. Keeley's next hope was that their order would provide a chronological clue, by running up from the floor, oldest to newest.

She decided to test her theory and started to move the plastic boxes that formed most of the top tier to the floor to get at the cardboard boxes on the floor.

As she shifted the third box, the wall of cartons started to wobble—along with her nerves. She covered her head, sure she was about to be engulfed in a semi-load of cardboard and plastic. "Darn it, Mary!"

A big hand came from behind her and averted the avalanche.

"What are you doing down here?" Gus said, his voice low, his palm flattened against a plastic container to hold it in place against the wall. "It's the middle of the night." He sounded annoyed.

Keeley, not over her surprise at his being here, wearing nothing but low-riding sweat pants and chest hair, glanced away and said, "Or very early morning, depending on your point of view." She got to work, and using her foot, she shoved aside one of the boxes she'd taken from the stack. "Don't let go for a minute," she said, then pulled out a mashed cardboard box from the bottom and shoved a plastic one in its place. The stack stabilized. "Thanks." She risked another quick glance at him before kneeling in front of her quarry and opening the flaps. Oddly, she didn't want to look at him, ridiculously unnerved by being in the dark with a half-dressed man—in particular this half-dressed man who currently resided in the room next to hers.

"You're welcome. Even if you are crazy." He brushed some dust from his hands and gave the box she'd opened a curious look. "What is that?" Looming over her, he put his hands on his hips, utterly relaxed and seemingly unaware of his almost-nakedness.

"Records, I hope." She coughed, blamed it on the dust, and turned her attention to the overworked file tabs in the box at her knees.

"You're kidding," he said.

"About what?"

"Going through these boxes . . . tonight. It's a hell of a good idea but"—he waved a hand around the room—"not in the middle of the night."

"Or very—"

"—early morning depending on your point of view." He gave her a speculative look. "You don't sleep."

"Highly overrated, sleep." She lifted a file toward the miserable light. "Most of the records in this box are nineteen sixty-seven. Too early, I think. Dinah's contributions started in late nineteen seventy—the same year I was born."

"Get up."

"Excuse me." She looked up at him, just as he

gripped her upper arms and dragged her to her feet. He tried to maneuver her toward the cellar stairs, but she dug her heels in. "What in hell do you think you're doing?"

"Sleep may be overrated but going blind isn't. You could grow mushroom crops down here. The files can wait." They faced off, and she caught the hint of a boyish frown. "You said hell. I didn't think nuns used that kind of language."

The man, standing there looking like the devil himself with his black hair, his mysterious scar, and his dark-eyed intensity, appeared genuinely surprised.

"I haven't been a nun for years now, as I've already told you." She looked pointedly at his hands, still grasping her arms. "What I am is a woman who doesn't react well to orders. And if you think hell is *naughty*, try giving me another one."

His lips barely moved, the smile so slight and gone so fast, she thought she'd imagined it. But when his gaze trailed hers to where his fingers wrapped around her poor excuse for biceps, he immediately let her go. "Sorry," he mumbled, and for a moment that rivaled his smile for brevity, he looked awkward.

Keeley didn't know why that word sprung to her mind, but it was the only one that fit, because even though she didn't know Gus Hammond very well— if at all—she was somehow certain being awkward was a distant memory for this purposeful, unnervingly handsome, too-confident man. The idea piqued her curiosity.

She rubbed at her upper arms, looked up at him. "I make you uncomfortable."

He was standing under the low-wattage bulb that

dangled from a short cord attached to the low ceiling. It was barely an inch above his head, and its position cast long shadows over his angular perfect features and blackened his scar. "What makes you say that?"

"Ah, a question for a question. I'll take that as a yes."

He was silent for a second or two, then finally nodded. "Yeah, you do. Make me uncomfortable. I'm not used to dealing with . . . righteous women."

"What kind of women are you used to dealing with?"

The look he gave her was unreadable. "The kind who don't ask questions, the kind who—"

"—who aren't around for coffee and donuts the morning after?"

His gaze didn't shift, but something in it did, darkening to anger. "That about sums it up, Sister." His gaze was steady, his emphasis on the word *sister*. "Now unless you want to start right in saving my soul, I suggest you get your holy butt up those stairs. We've got a lot of work to do tomorrow. It would be best if we were both awake for it."

"I'll go, but for the last time, I am *not* a nun, a sister, or any other religious manifestation your mind wants to dream up." She paused. "If you must know, I'm a widow." She had no idea why she told him that, why it was suddenly important that he see her as a woman instead of an . . . untouchable. The minute the words were out of her mouth, she wished them back. She never spoke about her marriage, mainly because there was so little to say. Tragically short, it was easier to forget her time with Marc, accept it as God's inscrutable hand at work, and let it go. With sadness, yes, but no more tears.

Surprise lifted his eyebrows, and for a moment he

said nothing. Then he ran a hand through his thick hair, accidentally touched the light bulb, and set it swinging, causing shadows to writhe along the wall of boxes and the tin side of the ancient furnace. "What happened?"

"His name was Marc. Marc Lasalle. He was a doctor, a pediatrician. He headed up the aid group I was attached to at the time." She stopped, took a breath. "He stepped on a land mine a month after we were married." She didn't add she'd been barely ten feet behind him when it happened.

"Jesus! When?"

"Five years ago. In Beida, a small village in the Sudan. We were setting up a clinic."

"Hell of a honeymoon." He studied her for what seemed forever. "I'm sorry," he said.

She had the sudden urge to back away, hide behind a leather face, a stone heart. "What for?" she asked abruptly, again wishing she'd never brought up the subject of her marriage. "You didn't know him."

"No. But I know you," he said. "And I know about losing someone you care about." Again leveling his gaze to meet hers, he added, "So I repeat. I'm sorry."

She opened her mouth to say . . . God knew what, something about how she'd accepted Marc's death, had canonized him in her mind and moved on because moving on, in the Sudan where the need was so immense, was the only choice. She settled for a simple, "Thanks."

"Now can we go to bed?" he said, then immediately scrunched his face into a grimace, making him look boyish and uncomfortable.

His discomfort made her smile and tripped her heart. "Yes, Gus. We can go to bed now." She started up the stairs, her silent, once-again-awkward house-guest trailing behind her.

Dinah tossed down the book she was reading and walked to the window. The view wasn't much, primarily other tall buildings, most of them offices with their drones toiling away behind vast sheets of glass, with glimpses of water and the Seattle Space Needle somewhat to the north. So gray, so cold, compared to Miami, and home to so many dismal memories. She pushed them aside and turned back to Cassie, who was on the phone—again. No doubt with that tiresome teenage daughter of hers.

Dinah chewed back her annoyance and decided to leave her to it. She turned to look again at the lifeless wall of office towers outside her luxurious suite. She hated Seattle, and if it weren't for Gus being here, and the confusion surrounding Mayday House, she'd never have set foot on its sidewalks again. Two days here, living like a recluse, and she was going mad.

Damn it, Mary, why didn't you keep your promise, leave Mayday to me like we agreed? I kept my part of the bargain, why in hell didn't you keep yours? Why put my life at risk after all these years?

Dinah hoped she'd kept her other promise and destroyed all the records—if there were any—because if she'd left one link to Dinah . . .

Her heart was beating too fast; she took a breath. Odd how coming back to Seattle had initiated a panic she hadn't felt in the Miami sun. And stupid. Getting upset would accomplish nothing. No need for it. So far everything was under control. Although it would help if Gus called, told her he had the Farrell woman's agreement to sell. She had no doubt her plan to remove the woman from Mayday House would work eventually. Money always worked—especially when it came with a touch of fear.

Finally she heard Cassie say, "Good-bye" and hang up the phone.

"Try Gus's number again, Cassie," Dinah said. "Then order us some lunch, would you?" Dinah worked to sound cool, to ignore the soft flutter in her stomach that came with even the possibility she'd hear Gus's deep voice.

Cassie nodded, but before her hand touched the phone, it rang. She picked it up. "Hello."

Dinah could see her grip on the phone tighten from ten feet away.

"I'll see if she's in." She looked directly at Dinah and put her hand over the phone. "It's Hagan."

"How in hell did he know I was here?" Her ex-husband.

Jesus, talk about bad Seattle memories!

"I have no idea," Cassie said, adding in a whisper, "What do you want me to do?"

Dinah made a quick gesture with her hand toward the phone. "Give it to me." She took the phone and held it to her chest. "And make yourself scarce, will you?"

"Not a problem," Cassie said. Looking relieved, she quickly left the room.

Dinah took a deep breath and settled the phone near her ear. "Hagan, darling, how wonderful to hear from you—after all this time." She oozed the insincerity over the phone, keeping her voice low and flat. God, how she hated this man.

"Yeah, I can tell you're overjoyed."

"I was on my way out. What do you want?"

"Other than you giving me all my money back? Absolutely nothing—except maybe getting your expensive ass out of my town."

She heard him take a drink.

"You'll be happy to know," she said, "that I'll be leaving 'your town' at the first opportunity. And as to the money issue, I believe we've settled that." *About fifty million times.* Somewhere along the line jousting with Hagan had stopped being fun. "And so did the courts, as I recall—in my favor." Suddenly anxious to get him off the phone, close the line that seeped his terrible voice into her ear, she said sharply, "I repeat. What do you want?"

"Being friendly, darlin', that's all."

"Good thing you're not in the room, then, because if I remember correctly, the friendliest thing about you was the fist you used on my face."

"Ah . . . those were the days."

"You're a son of a bitch, Hagan, and the worst thing that ever happened to me," she said, keeping her voice cool and level.

He laughed. "Says she who is happily situated in the best hotel suite in Seattle, courtesy of my money."

"Your money was the best thing about you, Hagan. It sure as hell wasn't that poor excuse for a cock you've got between your legs."

No laughter now. Dinah could feel the venom slithering through the line. "On the subject of cock, bitch, you want to tell me which one sent you running to Mayday House?"

"Mayday House?" Her bones locked and froze. "I don't understand."

Hagan spoke softly now. Too softly. Threateningly soft. "Oh, you understand well enough. It's me who's in the dark. But not for long." He stopped. "I hired a mutual friend of ours."

"We don't have any mutual friends." Dinah put a hand to her throat, rubbed the knot holding back her breathing.

"We do now. And this time he's all mine. Bought and paid for."

"What are you talking about?" She forced herself to show anger, impatience—anything but the sick dread bunching low in her belly.

"Not what, who. I hired myself your boy toy, bitch. Gus Hammond works for me now. I guess he got tired of crawling over those skinny old bones of yours and set his eye on the main chance." The guttural laugh coming down the line was a sneer. "And that's me. I hold all the cards, including your fuck jock. You'll be hearing from me." He hung up.

Dinah couldn't move, couldn't think, couldn't blink.

Gus's disloyalty was a knife in her heart, unbearable. She closed her eyes, and her mind filled with the vision of Gus and Hagan, together, against her. Then it shifted to Mary Weaver in her blood-soaked nightgown running down the long dark hall of Mayday House, halls Dinah swore never to walk again.

She replaced the receiver in its cradle, slowly, carefully, as if it were the most fragile of crystal, her mind hovering, then locking on the grisly secret that could destroy her life.

If she let it . . .

CHAPTER 9

When Gus stepped into the kitchen, it was nearly ten. He'd been up since seven. Determined to get a good feel for the place, he'd already checked the outbuildings, walked the property, and the surrounding neighborhood, mostly houses like Mayday, timeworn Victorian-style farmhouses, set on acreages about eight miles from the town of Erinville.

Keeley sat at the table with a piece of toast, largely ignored by the look of it, in one hand and a pen in the other. She was scribbling into a blue notebook. An empty coffee mug sat to her right.

When he walked in, she barely glanced at him. "There's coffee in the pot," she said, turning her attention back to her note-making.

He poured himself one, filled her mug, and returned the pot to its home unit. She muttered a thanks, then glanced up at him and frowned in what appeared to be annoyance. "You always look so good? Smell so good?"

As morning conversation, it wasn't what he expected, nor did it look as if she were waiting for an answer. He leaned against the counter and drank some coffee. "What are you doing?"

"Making a to-do list." She studied him again. "And I came up with another chore."

"Which is?"

"Get you some painting clothes. You can't work in those . . . Calvin's or whatever."

Gus had never held a paint brush in his life; he didn't intend to start now. "I don't paint."

"You do if you intend to stay here. Be a sin to let those muscles of yours go to waste, when there's so much that needs doing around here."

He set his coffee mug down. "I don't paint," he said again.

"Then how do you expect to earn your keep?"

"My keep?" He was hunkered down with a crazy woman.

"I'm not giving you bed and board for nothing."

He pulled his wallet from the back pocket of his jeans, dropped five one-hundred-dollar bills on the table. "This cover it?" Putting his wallet back in his pocket, he added, "When that runs out, let me know."

She stared at the cash a moment, then picked it up and stuffed it in her pocket. "At the moment, Mayday House needs your energy more than your money." She gave him the look of a disapproving schoolteacher. "But as the House can use a little help with financing right now, I gratefully accept your donation," she said. "And if you want to sit around all day doing nothing, that's fine by me. If you don't, you'll find some old coveralls by the back door."

Before he could answer, Erica walked into the kitchen. "Morning." She covered a yawn with her hand and headed directly for the coffeepot.

Gus's glance in her direction had him thinking it was Erica Stark, wearing the legal minimum in night-clothes, who needed the damned coveralls. He didn't miss that Keeley shot her the same disapproving look she'd just flayed him with.

"You should take it easy on the coffee, Erica," Keeley said. "Too much caffeine isn't good for the babies."

Erica shot her an annoyed look. "I'll remember that." When she turned, coffee in hand, and spotted him leaning against the counter, her eyebrows damn near hit her hairline. Her shocked gaze bounced between him and Keeley. He knew what she was thinking—that he and Keeley . . .

Shit! It shouldn't have bothered him, but it did.

Keeley obviously caught her whiff of suspicion, too, but all she did was smile, a little too sweetly for his taste. "No, Erica. Gus and I did not spend the night together."

"Hey," Erica said, rubbing her tummy with one hand and drinking coffee with the other. "I'm not the one to talk about who sleeps with who. Sex makes the world go 'round, after all."

"That's *love*, Erica." Keeley frowned at her.

"Whatever."

"I repeat, we did not spend the night together." She glanced at Gus. "But he will be staying with us for a time. He's trying to buy a property in Erinville, so he'll be in town for a while. I've offered him a room, in exchange for his kind offer to help with the Mayday renovations." Her look turned devilish. "He tells me he's quite a skilled handyman. Isn't that right, Gus?"

Gus took his time studying her. She was trying to

snooker him. He pulled up a smile and sent it her way, not taking his eyes off her. "Very skilled," he said. "Depending on the job . . . This is a great old house, but she's been alone a long time. Needs plenty of TLC. But with the proper handling and a few strokes in the right places, she'll come . . . back to her old glory." He paused, slanted another long gaze her way. "It will be fun to work on her."

Keeley looked away first.

Erica, who'd followed the exchange avidly, refilled her coffee mug and looked at each of them in turn before settling her eyes on Gus. "You're my kind of handyman, Hammond." She looked at Keeley then and shook her head before adding, "That TLC he's talking about? I'd go for it, if I were you." She set down her mug. "I'm going into town this morning. If you need anything, let me know, and I'll pick it up. Have fun, you two." She walked out of the room.

Gus dumped the last of his coffee in the sink. "We need to talk."

Keeley, her face nearly as red as her hair, closed her spiral-bound notebook. "Yes, we do." She stood. "And it's best we do it in the office, where we won't be interrupted."

"Lead on."

When they were in the office, she took the seat behind the desk, he the one in front.

"First"—she took a deep breath, clasped her hands together, and rested them on the desk—"I apologize for being so pushy." She rushed the words into the room as if she couldn't rid herself of them fast enough. "Sometimes, I forget that I don't rule the world. I'm sorry. Of course you don't have to paint, or do anything else that you don't want to do." She stopped as abruptly as she'd started, her discomfort painfully apparent.

"And I apologize for the innuendo. Sometimes I do a little forgetting of my own."

She nodded, her expression sober, then took another breath. "That being said, we need to talk about Mayday House."

Gus rose from the chair. "Yes, we do." He went to the window, turned and looked back at her. "Tell me what's happened so far."

"There's been a . . . delivery."

"Explain."

Before she could answer, there was a knock on the office door. "Keeley? You in there?" a voice called from the other side.

"Bridget," Keeley said to Gus. "Come in," she said to the door.

Bridget opened the door a few inches and poked her head in. "Sorry, but this"—her hand came through holding a package—"says URGENT."

Keeley got up, went around the desk, and walked to the door. "Thanks, Bridget." She took the parcel.

"I'm going into town with Erica," Bridget said. "See you later."

"Yes, see you," she said, unable to take her eyes off the package.

When the door was closed, she looked closely at the address label and muttered, "No stamp." She tore open the package. It was a paperback novel; a string dangled from the pages. Keeley opened it to the twine-marked page, read quickly, then handed the book to him, her face strained and tight. Angry.

"That delivery I mentioned? You're holding its twin. The first came a couple of days ago." She nodded at the book now in his hands. "Read the highlighted part."

"You're not listening to me," he said, pulling the twine tighter around her wrists, tighter again until it rutted deep in her delicate skin.

She ignored the burn of the rope, the pain shooting up her arm. "You hurt Trisha. You shouldn't have done that. She had nothing to do with any of this. You're a sick, evil bastard!"

He grabbed her hair, yanked her head back, and put his face so close to hers his hot breath seared her nostrils. "And you're the same stupid bitch you were when we started this game." He gave her hair another quick, hard yank. Her eyes watered. "And the game is over, baby. You've got one last chance. Like they say, three strikes and you're out."

"Let me see the packaging," Gus said. She handed it to him. He expected nothing and that's what he got: brown wrapping paper from Anywhere, USA, Keeley Farrell written in bold black print, no return address, no postage. The package was hand delivered, which meant whoever was behind it was close by or knew someone who was.

He handed the book and wrapping back to her. "Anything else?"

"No. Just another like this and a phone call. A few nights back, not long after I got here."

"Same get-out-of-town message?"

She hesitated. "No, that's the strange thing. It was nothing like that. It was more like he wanted to confirm who I was."

"A man."

"Yes. It was late, and I was still cleaning, but whoever he was, he was nearby." She touched her hair idly. "He knew I was wearing a yellow scarf."

Gus's gut knotted and he tugged on his earlobe. "Inconsistent."

"What do you mean?"

He went to the window, watched Erica and Bridget get into a platinum Altima. "These creeps generally follow a pattern, stick to one means of communication. Big difference between a phone call and highlighted passages in a book."

"What are you saying?"

"I'm saying they aren't the same person."

It was damned awkward, Erica thought, the girl latching on to her, because what she had to do, she had to do alone. So when Bridget said she wanted to buy Keeley some tulip bulbs, Erica seized the moment and lost her in the local weed-and-feed store. Telling her she needed some shampoo, she promised to meet her at the drugstore in half an hour. As if Erica Stark would use drugstore shampoo. Not in this lifetime.

God, this place was a burg!

When she reached the Jasper Inn, she spotted his rental car immediately, directly outside room eleven. She rapped sharply on the door, then turned her key in the lock.

She stepped in.

The day outside wasn't bright, but still the dimness of the motel room took the shape of a dark tunnel. When her eyes adjusted, she saw him sitting on the edge of the bed, the room neat as a pin, his bag stowed on the stand near the blank television, a book open on the bed beside him.

"You doing okay?" He walked to her and they embraced.

"I've been better."

"Sit down, you look tired."

She nodded and sat heavily in the chair near the door, grateful to be off her feet. "I'm too damn old for all this spy crap and much too pregnant." She sighed as she settled back into the chair.

"What's your sense of things so far?" he asked. "Do you think she knows anything?"

Erica had asked herself the same question, over and over. "Too early to tell but I'm guessing no. Not yet."

"Christ, Erica, all this time and you're still guessing?" His annoyance hit the room like a slap, and he started to pace. When he came back to stand over her, she knew he was holding back his temper. He always did.

For Paul, taking over their father's business was one thing—and bad enough by his standards—but taking on his rages and violent outbursts was another, and completely unacceptable. Her brother, although smart as a sitting judge, worried nonstop and had enough tension bottled up inside that if you shook him, he'd shatter. "Sorry," he finally muttered, then added, "Are you going to tough it out?" He stepped behind her and kneaded her shoulders, his touch surprisingly gentle, considering the stress he was under—they were both under.

Erica thought that question would be better

directed at him, but she didn't go there. "You even have to ask?"

She heard him let out a breath, a long, resigned breath. "No, I suppose not."

Straightening away from his comforting hands, she said, "But we've got trouble."

"What kind of trouble?"

"The worst kind." She patted her tummy, smiled thinly. "Man trouble. A guy named Gus Hammond has moved into Mayday House. And unless pregnancy is making me dumb as well as fat, I'm betting he's after the same thing we are."

Paul's eyes widened. "Why? Who the hell would care, after all these years—other than us?"

She wanted to laugh out loud. Paul was so naïve—which was amazing considering the business they were in. "Same reason as us, I suspect. There's always money to be made from sex and murder, darling brother. You, of all people, should know that."

"What are you going to do about him?"

"There's nothing I can do—for now—except keep an eye on him." Which isn't the worst job in the world, she thought, when those sinfully deep eyes and his made-for-between-the-sheets body jumped to mind. "If I have to, I'll take care of him."

"Which is exactly where it gets dangerous." He gripped the back of his neck with one hand, pulled his head forward, and resumed pacing. "The more I think about it—particularly now this Hammond guy has shown up—the more I think you should get out of there. This could get rough. We agreed, didn't we?"—he stared at her, his expression determined—"we *do not* want anyone hurt."

Erica ignored the last of his spiel, stood, and

walked over to him. "No one will get hurt, but I'm staying until we find out what the hell happened in that house. Until we get what we need." She shuddered theatrically. "Even if the ramshackle old place does creep me out."

As to the not-wanting-anyone-hurt plan, that would depend on how things went. What they got out of the deal. She touched her tummy. Thanks to the asshole father being a useless, no-good lying bastard, and Paul being so adamant about her not giving up the kids—the hope for a new family line, he called them—she'd have a couple of brats to raise. She sure as hell didn't intend to do it without nannies—twenty-four/seven. And that meant saving the family business, using any means available. There was a golden egg tucked away in Mayday House, she was sure of it, and one way or another, she'd find it. "Just a few more days. That's all I need."

"You sure?"

"I'm sure."

"But the babies—"

She restrained from puffing out her annoyance. The man never stopped fussing about them. "The babies will be fine. I'll be fine. And I'll make sure we stay *fine*." She went back to the chair and eased herself into it. "If what that old woman told you was true, there's money to made—and it belongs to us."

"We're not sure, Erica. The woman sounded half crazy, going on about forgiveness, yammering on about a bunch of religious stuff." Paul didn't look convinced, but then Paul never looked convinced. She adored her brother, but he was one cautious cowboy.

"We're sure enough to keep digging." When her

frustration rose, she tamped it back. "But damn it, there's enough paper and files in that Victorian nightmare to sink an aircraft carrier. Stacks of them from the attic to the cellar. I've already sneezed my way through a barge load and come up empty. If we do have a sister, courtesy of Mayday House, it's not going to be easy finding her." Or her goddamn mother. And the way she saw it, the mother was the golden goose.

"I thought you said you didn't care about our sister," Paul said, eyeing her with renewed interest.

"I don't."

"You're not even curious?"

"No." She shook her head, hoping Paul wouldn't launch into one of his family-is-everything lectures. Considering their own upbringing—or lack of it—his family fixation was ludicrous. And how the hell he managed to separate what they *did* for a living from what they *were*, was amazing. She wished she could compartmentalize her life as easily.

"Just the mother, then?" He looked disapproving, but Erica didn't care. Paul would go along. Paul always went along—except about her getting rid of the babies. The idea of that made him crazy.

"The *mother lode*," Erica corrected. "And the end to all our problems."

"So you keep insisting," he said, letting out a breath. "But if there's no sister to be found, no proof, no record of adoption . . ."

The smile dropped from Erica's lips, and she tightened them. "It's there. I know it. The Weaver woman kept receipts for light bulbs bought in the sixties, for God's sake." She paused, refusing to let doubt cloud her vision of salvation—money enough to save both their asses. "It would be easier if I didn't have to sneak around, but the girl Bridget follows me around like a puppy and Farrell never leaves the house—and now I've got Hammond to deal with." She breathed out to ease her tension, tired of her brother's endless second-guessing and a Mayday situation she couldn't control. Erica liked control. "You're absolutely certain about the year of birth?" she asked, desperate to limit her time shuffling through the endless files.

"Nineteen seventy. That's what she said."

"At least that narrows it down somewhat. Now, tell me again exactly what the recently departed, and oh-so-saintly Mary Weaver wanted her precious 'forgiveness' for. Word for word."

Christiana pulled her tidy, compact station wagon off the road, about a quarter mile from Mayday House. She turned the car off, leaned her head back, and pressed her hand to her thumping heart, the depth of her fear her biggest surprise. But she had to do this. Had to find the truth before she took another step into the future she'd so carefully planned.

For the millionth time she wished she'd never picked up the phone that night, never listened to Mary's ramblings, her begging for forgiveness while Christiana's head reeled under the weight of her confession.

A confession slamming into her carefully constructed life with the impact of a wrecking ball.

Christiana clung to the hope that Mary was confused, had mixed her up with someone else, but that thread of hope was too fragile to build a life on— and far too risky.

If she were one of her own patients, she'd urge him or her to seek the truth, not attempt to build a life on lies or deceits. It was time to take her own advice.

She put the car in gear and drove slowly forward until Mayday House came into view. She remembered it from her one visit years ago, when she'd come looking for her birth parents. Mary had lied then, but then she wasn't dying, wasn't begging Christiana for her forgiveness, wasn't, as she'd said the night of her call, going to meet her Maker and wanting to leave her "black deeds behind."

Black indeed . . .

The house rose in the gathering darkness, tall and gray. Yellow light filtered from the main floor windows and from one on the second floor. The third floor was dark. A large construction refuse container sat at the end of the driveway with some broken furniture propped against it. A pickup was nosed up to it. Behind the pickup, a rising moon cast its light on a highly polished silver Jaguar. A path led from the road to the house: on one side of it, the lawn was mowed; on the other the grass looked a foot tall with weeds reaching even higher. The porch lurched to the left and had missing posts under the railings.

She pulled in behind the Jaguar, got out of the car, and checked her slim gold watch. Almost seven. She told herself nervously, they'd be at dinner, and she'd be interrupting. She should wait. Do this tomorrow.

While she dithered, the front door opened and a woman stood framed in the light of the doorway. Christiana took a deep breath for courage. She had no choice but to move forward now, because there was no way the woman hadn't seen her.

She got out of the car and made her way toward the steps, gathered what resolve she could with each step. Dear God, she'd spent the day in front of cameras, talked to a room full of boisterous high school students. She could do this.

The woman on the porch stood at the broken railing and watched her approach. When she reached her, Christiana put out her hand. "I'm Christiana Fordham," she said, sounding surprisingly normal, considering the swirling and jumping in her stomach. "I called, made an appointment to see Keeley Farrell."

"I'm Keeley." The woman, whose face she couldn't see clearly in the porch shadows, took her hand and said, "Bridget told me you called, but she didn't tell me exactly when you were coming. It's always nice to meet a Mayday House patron. One I wrote several letters to if I remember right. Requesting donations—as usual."

Christiana sensed her smile through the darkness. "Yes, you did, and I'm sorry I didn't reply, but I've been terribly busy." She lifted a hand and waved it awkwardly. "But I'm in the neighborhood, so—"

"Good, come on in. We're about to have coffee and apple pie. Not very good pie"—she shrugged—"I made it. But at least the fruit won't let us down."

"Thank you." Christiana followed her into the house. The house where she was born. The house that held the secret to a past, that if brought to light, would destroy her future.

"You've been here before, haven't you?" Keeley said when they were in the roomy kitchen.

"Yes. Once. I came to see Mary, and—" she

stopped when she noticed the man sitting at the table, drinking coffee and turning the pages of a newspaper. When he looked up and saw her, he stood.

Except for the scar running along his strong jaw, he was as physically perfect a man as she'd ever seen, maybe six-two, dark hair, lean muscled body, smooth tan skin, and deep golden brown eyes shadowed by eyelashes that made women weep with jealousy. And desire.

He was exactly the kind of male she'd lusted after in high school, when she'd been trapped behind braces, glasses, and severe acne. Although those years were long behind her, men like Gus reloaded all her insecurities, both the pain of youthful yearning and the awful tide of confusion and distress that came with being invisible. A teenage ghost.

"Gus Hammond," he said, offering his hand, then enclosing hers. Not quite a handshake, not quite a caress, but sustaining the hand/eye connection just long enough to be intriguing. To be flattering.

Keeley handed her a coffee and said, "Be nice to Christiana, Gus: she's been a generous patron to Mayday through the years."

"I'll try," he said, and when he tilted his head and half smiled at her, Christiana sensed Gus could be *extremely* nice—if he set his mind to it.

Keeley gestured toward the table Gus had risen from. "Take a seat; I'll get the pie." She went to the counter. "You're a long way from Portland. What brings you our way?"

She was about to answer when Gus said, "If I've got it right, it was a TV spot." He studied her until she blushed. "When you walked in I thought I'd seen you before. The early news, right? Speaking at a high school? You're a psychologist." He rested his liquid brown eyes on her and her stomach fluttered.

"Yes, my own show will be airing in the new year—if all goes well. The high school in Seattle was a PR stop . . . of sorts." She sounded vague, apologetic. That had to stop.

"Ah," he said, not taking his eyes off her. "Sounds like a lot of work."

"Yes . . . but rewarding."

"Teenagers are a tough crowd."

"The toughest." She smiled at him.

He didn't smile back, but somehow managed to intensify his gaze, as if he'd switched on a light behind his eyes.

"So, what brings you to Erinville?" Keeley, carrying two plates of pie, took a chair beside her.

Christiana glanced at Gus, then back to Keeley. "I, uh, have some questions. But I, uh . . ." She glanced at Gus. The conversation with Keeley Farrell would be hard enough; talking in front of a man she'd met only moments before and knew nothing about would be impossible.

He stood immediately. "I'm going for some fresh air." He looked at his watch, then said to Keeley. "I won't be long—or far."

She rolled her eyes, and he gave her an annoyed look. Christiana couldn't figure out whether they liked each other or there was some kind of subtext between them she couldn't read. Interesting.

When he'd left the room, Keeley said, "Don't mind Gus, he's just doing his job."

"His job?"

She hesitated. "He's . . . security. We've had some problems around here lately."

"What kind of problems?"

"Nothing to worry about—especially if you're here to do what I hope you are and kick-start your donations to Mayday House."

She'd smiled along with the obvious charitable plea, but to Christiana's eye, the smile was forced, tense. Like someone required to conduct business as usual as chaos reigned behind the scenes. She knew the feeling well, especially lately. "That's not why I'm here," she said. "It's something else entirely. Something . . . unsettling."

"Not the answer I was hoping for, but . . ." She sat back and lifted her coffee to her lips, looking calm, politely interested. "I'm listening."

Christiana swallowed hard, tried to peel away the fear lining her mouth, and took a deep breath. "I'm here to find out who my father was and why Mary Weaver killed him."

CHAPTER 10

With the barest of tremors, Keeley set her coffee mug on the table. "I don't think I heard you right."

Christiana knew she was shocked, but no more than she herself had been during Mary's midnight phone call. "You'll want to hear it from the beginning."

"Yes." Keeley sat forward in her chair and nodded. "The very beginning."

"Okay." She picked up her unused pie fork and held it between her hands. "I was born here. September, nineteen seventy. Adopted that same month."

"Go on."

"I wasn't told I was adopted until ten years ago. My mother told me just before she died. She said it had been a private adoption—" She stopped. "Which I took to mean the legalities weren't observed. It turned out I was right. My mother said that my father's poor health—he died when I was nine—coupled with the fact that they were older than the norm, made adopting through regular channels impossible. Then they found Mayday House and Mary Weaver. It was Mary, to quote my mother, who made it happen." She smoothed some stray hair behind her ears. "So here I am."

"Do you have proof? Of any of this?"

"I have a letter from my mother. When I showed it to Mary, she got terribly upset, but she didn't deny it."

"When was that?" she asked.

"A few months after my mother died," Christiana said. "I came here"—she waved a hand—"to find out what I could about my birth parents."

"And did you? Find out anything, I mean?"

"No. Mary told me they were both dead. She said my father, a businessman of some kind, had died during my mother's pregnancy, and my mother was killed in a car accident a year after I was born. Apparently she'd been an aspiring actress. When I pressed her for more information—anything at all— she said she didn't remember, and she didn't have any records because they'd been lost in the fire."

"The fire?" Keeley looked confused. "She said there was a fire, you're sure?"

Again Christiana nodded, but she didn't say anything, deciding she'd let the next question lead the way.

Keeley took her time framing it. "What did you do then?"

"I left. I know this sounds awful, but to be honest I think I was relieved to hear they were dead, that I didn't have to take things any further." She closed her eyes briefly and opened them to see Keeley staring at her, judging her. "You think I'm strange, don't you, to come all this way, then let things drop?"

"No. I don't." She got up, walked to the sink, and placed her mug in it. "I think relief is a natural reaction under the circumstances. There are times the unknown is better left . . . unknown." She looked back at Christiana. "But you're here now. And you're accusing Mary Weaver of killing your birth father. I don't understand."

Whatever shock Christiana had seen registered on Keeley Farrell's face was gone now, replaced by cool speculation.

"Accusing?" she echoed. "I'm not sure that's the right word. I'm here looking for the truth." She paused before continuing, because what was to come was the most difficult to explain. "About a month ago, shortly after one in the morning, I received a call from Mary. To say she was . . . over-wrought would be an understatement. And the conversation was quite scattered. At first all she did was ramble about all her girls, how important her work was, then she went on about what tools and appliances Mayday House needed updated—" she stopped and smiled briefly. "A lot of accolades about you, your work in Africa, how you were going to carry on for her. The conversation—if you could call it that—veered this way and that, not making too much sense, but I didn't want to hang up on her. I knew she was troubled, so I listened—all the while wondering why she was calling *me*. I barely knew the woman."

She paused, then pushed her uneaten pie toward the table's center, while Keeley stood woodenly across the room.

"I'd made some donations to the house from time to time after our one meeting," Christiana went on. "But always by mail. It had been ten years since my visit." She rubbed the lines gathering in her forehead. "But because, in my profession, phone calls like Mary's—cries for help—aren't unusual, I did what I could, which—given the time of night and the miles between us—was listen and try to soothe her. Just when I thought I'd be on the phone all night, she calmed down. Then, almost formally—and very, very clearly—she said she'd killed my father, and she begged for my forgiveness."

Keeley walked to the table and took the chair she'd left minutes before. Christiana knew that no matter how relaxed she might look, chances were her knees were as rubbery as her own. After a moment sitting quietly, Keeley asked, "Forgiveness? That was the actual word she used?"

Christiana nodded. "Yes. She said the killing was an accident, that she hadn't intended it to happen, that she'd done the right thing by him—whatever that meant—but that she couldn't leave with—" She wanted the exact words, found them. "A lie's blood on her soul."

Keeley swallowed visibly. "What did you say?"

"A woman I barely knew had called me in the middle of the night to tell me she killed my birth father," she said. "I didn't know what to say, how to react. And I think my silence upset her, because she hung up on me. When I'd rallied a few mental resources, I called back. There was no answer. I called again the next morning. Spoke to a woman named Truitt. She told me Mary had died in her sleep." She shivered and rubbed her arms. "I think it must have happened within minutes of her hanging up the phone from me."

"Nothing else? No details? Nothing more about your mother, other than she was an actress?"

"Nothing. You know everything I know." Christiana

let go of the fork she'd been twisting and folded her hands in front of her on the table. "I tried to forget about it, put Mayday House, Mary Weaver, all of it, out of my mind . . . I thought it was the smart thing to do."

"Why?"

Christiana had trouble meeting the straightforward, questioning eyes now meeting hers. A gaze that said a lie wouldn't be acceptable. Each of her hands nearly strangled the other in the tight lock they formed on the table in front of her. She loosened them. "Earlier, I mentioned my television show. It's important to me, I've worked hard to get this chance, and its success depends on my having the right image."

"Meaning?"

"So far my life—small-town girl, solid West Coast family, widowed mother, worthy community service record—is an open book. I wanted to keep it that way. If that sounds selfish, so be it. But the fact is that suddenly—and publicly—becoming the daughter of unknown birth parents whose father was killed in a women's refuge won't do much for my career. A career I've worked years to build."

Keeley eyed her. "You're right. It does sound selfish."

Christiana felt her face redden but said nothing.

"But you're here now," Keeley said. "Which means you've changed your mind. Why?"

"I didn't change my mind, but I can't keep doing what I'm doing without knowing the truth." *Because if I know the truth, there's a chance I can control it.* She kept the last to herself because in her heart she knew it was more dumb hope than grand plan.

"It also sounds as if you're scared." Keeley reached across and touched her clasped hands. "And I don't think you should be. In the last few months before

Mary died, she suffered from dementia and toward the end it was severe." She pulled her hand back from Christiana's. "Mary Weaver was the kindest, gentlest woman I've ever known and the grandmother I never had." She stopped. "Like you, I was born in this house. Unlike you, I never left. After my mother had me, she had nowhere to go, so Mary let her stay on, help her run Mayday. Mom died in this house a week after I turned eleven. And from then on it was Mary who raised me, loved me." She paused. "And tried to teach me—with limited success—to always 'care for something bigger than my wee self.'" A smile came with the memory and hovered briefly over her lips. "I can still hear her . . . 'The world is short on mercy and long on need, girl, so you make sure your life's work goes on the right side of the ledger.'"

The look she gave Christiana was deep with conviction, when she added, "Does that sound like someone who could kill another human being?"

Christiana prayed Keeley was right, but she couldn't get Mary's rambling, crazy phone call out of her mind. "No, but—"

"Anyone can kill—given the right set of circumstances."

Both women turned to see Gus Hammond standing in the doorway.

Keeley, after glancing at the woman who'd just made such startling accusations about Mary, and who now looked as if she'd been turned to stone where she sat, stared at Gus. "How long have you been there?" she asked.

"Long enough."

Christiana shot to her feet. "This was a private conversation. You had no right—"

"I had every right. My job is to look out for this place"—he gestured with his chin toward Keeley—"for this woman. And I make the decisions on how to do that job." He crossed his arms over his chest and stood dead still in the doorway. "And if there's one thing always in short supply in the protection business, it's information." His interested gaze slid to Christiana. "Yours is A-1."

Keeley stood, and the two women faced him. Keeley thought *faced off* might be a better expression. With the electricity in the air, they were like a pair of cats bristling at a marauding dog. "Mary Weaver didn't kill anyone," she repeated, wanting there to be no mistake. "Before she died she was bedridden, in pain, and confused—very confused. God, she was probably dreaming."

"Some dream," he said.

"I'm telling you Mary didn't—"

"Didn't kill anyone. I know." He pushed away from the door and came toward them. "But one thing's clear." Standing in front of them, hands on hips, he gave Keeley a measured look. "*Something* went on in this house, and more than one person isn't too happy about it."

Keeley opened her mouth, then sealed it shut. If she lived to be a thousand and turned this conversation over in her mind every minute of every day, she'd still never believe Mary would kill. *Could* kill. Ever! Some might call it denial. She called it faith. "Mayday House is a women's refuge. Lots of things 'went on' here. But they didn't involve killing anyone."

"You don't know that, Keeley. Not for certain."
Christiana spoke quietly but with a natural authority.
"When Mary called me, she was distraught, full of re-
pentance, and terrified of dying without forgiveness.
Maybe she was simply confused, but you can't leave
it there. I know I can't. Not anymore." She paused and
looked at Gus, standing in front of them silent as a
church, then at Keeley. "If nothing else, you owe it to
Mary to find out the truth."

Keeley wanted to ignore Christiana's sound logic—
her down-home common sense—but she couldn't.
Neither could she face the prospect of digging
around in Mary's good and honest life, a life that had
been the model for her own. A life she'd failed at.
First her church, then her husband . . . then Africa.
Mary had given her the gift of Mayday House, the
chance to start over, make things right. The idea of
making them right at the risk of her good name
smacked of betrayal and disloyalty. She didn't know
if she could do it.

She didn't know if she couldn't . . .

Silence filtered into the kitchen, rested among the
three of them like a chilled mist.

"I owe it to Mary to protect this house and everyone in it," Keeley said. *Including myself, my chance to
start over and leave the fear and evil behind. Oh, Keeley,
you selfish, selfish woman.* On that thought, her face
heated, and she turned her back on both of them and
walked toward the kitchen door. When she had it
open, she looked back at the two people in her
kitchen, both of them watching her, Christiana with
concern, Gus with his usual detached speculation. "I
need to clear my head," she announced, her voice
finding a level of firmness. "I'm going for a walk."

"It's hell-black out there," Gus said. "I'll come with you." He took a step toward her.

"No." She lifted a hand. "At the risk of sounding melodramatic, I want to be alone."

"I don't think that's a good idea," he said.

A surge of irrational anger boiled up in her belly. "Whether it's a good idea or a bad idea is irrelevant. It's *my* idea." She stomped out.

Gus was right, it was hell-black. Although Keeley had generally thought of hell as a hot fiery orange, this night with its chilling wind, groaning tree branches, and sinister clouds thick with rain, and offering only glimpses of a spectral moon, came a close second.

Thank God, she'd thought to bring a flashlight, because without it she'd have had trouble even finding the passage through the hedge.

In seconds she was in the churchyard arcing light over the graves to find the path. She glanced up, afraid the lights in Father Barton's house, adjacent to the church, would suddenly come on. They didn't. She enjoyed Father Barton's company, but not tonight.

She stopped a moment, made the sign of the cross at her mother's grave, then walked around the side of the stone church to the heavy, planked, double doors leading into the church.

It was locked, as she knew it would be, but unless Father Barton had changed the rules, a key would wait behind the marble cross to the right of the door.

According to Mary, they'd started locking St. Ivan's in the late sixties after a spate of vandalism, but the idea of a locked church didn't sit well with Father Randall, so he'd found a place for a key and told St. Ivan's faithful where they'd always find it, saying, "Moments of need too often arrive after midnight." Mary said the key was his way of putting a candle in the window for lost or troubled souls.

With a silent thank you for Father Randall's foresight and Father Barton's willingness to honor the tradition, Keeley stepped into the narrow vestibule and closed the huge doors behind her, careful to do it as soundlessly as possible.

In the nave of the church, she took a seat in the last row. St. Ivan's was a small church, sitting proudly on land donated by Mary's forebearers over a hundred years ago. To Mary that donation was a deep source of pride.

St. Ivan's builders had been ambitious, giving it a touch of Gothic by including delicate pointed arches and a high ceiling. The floor was oak, rutted and scarred by the endless shuffle of the faithful along its aisles and between its benches. From where Keeley sat in the last pew, the tiered row of amber and red votive candles to the right of the altar were a soft colorful blur, glinting off the polished altar rail and spilling, flickering, to the floor.

On either side of the altar two tall cream-colored candles burned, lending a shadowy glow to the apse housing the linen-draped altar. A brass sanctuary lamp added its dim red glow. When Keeley's eyes adjusted to the low light level, the broad outlines of the church, the stations of the cross, the confessional, and rows of sturdy benches emerged from the gloom, colorless, architectural ghosts from the darkness.

The church was the same.

But she was not.

She clasped her hands together in a ball and

ground her palms together, then released them to rub the coil twisting in her stomach. She reminded herself she wasn't here to pray, to ask for help; she was here to calm down, to think.

But memories came in the somber darkness. . . .

Memories of the Sundays she'd come here with Mary and her mother, early so they'd get a front pew, neither woman wanting to miss a word of Father Randall's gentle sermons; the countless hours they'd spent working for St. Ivan's: the bake sale, the annual church bazaar, visits to "those less fortunate."

Keeley listened enrapt when her mother told her how, as a young girl in Ireland, she'd been called to be a good sister, but had ignored the call—ignored God's plan for her—until it was too late. The story was always told in urgent whispers and followed by the plea for Keeley to listen hard, should that call come to her. And if it did, to respond with her whole heart and soul.

Keeley thought it had, but she'd been wrong—and Mary had been right. After a year of nursing, Keeley told Mary of her plans to become a missionary nun. Her response was unexpected. She'd said, "I know you'd like to do this for your mother, Keeley, and I admire our holy nuns, I truly do, but I can't see you being one of them." It was a remarkable admission coming from her devout godmother, but Keeley, convinced she was wrong, became a postulant, and three years later she took her vows. Five years later, in an African mission hospital, she'd met Marc Lasalle—

I shouldn't be here. I don't belong.

She'd come here to think about Mary, about the awfulness of the accusations against her, but she'd made a mistake. The truth wasn't in this church: it was in her heart. Mary didn't kill anyone, and to believe it for a moment was insane.

Disloyal.

Smothered, boxed in by stone walls, crosses, burning candles, and broken vows, she stood abruptly. Her heart pounding—aching—in her chest, her throat painfully tight from the effort to hold back the tears, her soul stung by the lash of guilt, she left the pew and genuflected perfunctorily. Ignoring the holy water, she pushed through the two sets of doors to the rain-slicked darkness of the night outside.

Stopping in the dimly lit alcove outside the doors, she filled her lungs with clean chilled air—rid herself of her treacherous thoughts.

"You okay?"

The voice came from beside the church door and, low as it was, she started, then placed a hand on her leaping heart. "What are you doing here? I told you I wanted to be alone."

"You were alone." Gus pushed away from his casual stance of leaning against the old stone wall. "I'll walk you home."

She rubbed at her eyes and sniffed away the last of the telltale moisture. Tears were for sissies, and sissies were lousy problem solvers. Gus's being here reminded her she had more pressing problems than her own botched life: Mary's name and the safety of everyone at Mayday House, for starters.

Keeley focused her attention on Gus, which seemed to be getting easier every day. Her stomach knotted. Not only was she a crybaby, she was indulging in a few too many foolishly female thoughts about her houseguest. "You take this protection stuff seriously, don't you?"

"Yes."

"Why?" she asked, curious, but also determined to keep her thoughts out of her own cage of demons for a time. "What's in it for you?" she asked.

"I told you. I owe Dinah." He crossed his arms, settled back into an easy, deep coolness.

She studied him. He was no more than a shadow beyond the low overhead light in the alcove, his face indistinct, his eyes unreadable. "I don't think that's all of it," she said. "I think you've got reasons of your own for being here."

"Yeah? And what would those reasons be?"

She thought a minute. "Money, maybe," she said, then immediately shook her head, answering her own question. "No. Not money. You don't strike me as a man who can be bought."

He stepped toward her then, his face set in hard, deep lines, his eyes shot with anger. "And you don't strike me as a naïve woman." He took her arm, led her toward the three steps that led down from the church entrance. "And it's not getting any drier out there, so if you're finished your praying, we'd best get back to the house."

She held her ground. Unduly conscious of his strong hand on her forearm, she pulled it from his grasp.

He looked down at her, unmoved. "Fine. You want to stay. We'll stay."

"We'll stay until I know a lot more about the man who's living in my house—a bedroom door away from mine."

"A little late for second-guessing the room and board arrangement, isn't it?"

She ignored his question. "What kind of man are

you, Gus Hammond?" She'd been stupid not to ask
this question sooner, not to have checked him out
more carefully. Well, the stupid bit was over. She was
more determined than ever to find out about everything and everyone connected with Mary and
Mayday House. Past and present. "And make it the
truth. Like I said, I don't have time for lies or liars."

Gus didn't speak for what seemed forever. Then,
watching her face intently, he said, "I'm the kind of
man who makes women happy."

She frowned, irritated by his sarcastic reply. "You're
not making me happy."

"You're not paying me."

Her breath snagged in her throat. "Are you saying
what I think you're saying?"

He briefly looked amused. "Probably."

"You're saying you, uh, have . . ." *Sex for money!*

He nodded, all trace of amusement masked by an
expression of flat indifference.

Keeley turned his non-reply over in her mind,
no longer shocked, not even repulsed, just confused. Trying to look into his dark eyes was useless,
they gave away nothing. It seemed Gus Hammond
was as adept at caging his demons as she was hers.

"Now can we go?" he asked.

"Dinah Marsden," she said. "Was she one of the
women who . . . paid you?"

"Yes."

"Is she still?"

"No."

Keeley took a step away from him and wrapped her
arms around herself. "Let me get this straight. You
were Dinah Marsden's lover, yet her ex-husband
felt fine about calling you to work against her." She

paused, for the first time feeling uncomfortable with Gus's revelation. "Cozy."

"Dinah's lover, past tense. Now the personal security business—and there's nothing cozy about it. Just like there's nothing cozy about that Victorian nightmare of a house you're so fond of."

"What are you saying?"

"I'm saying, if the woman waiting for you in your kitchen is right, there's a body buried somewhere in that mausoleum. And from what you've told me about the late-night phone call and the book deliveries, I'd say we're not the only ones out to find it— and use it."

"Mary didn't kill anyone," she repeated stubbornly, her heart starting to race. "And there are no dead people buried in Mayday House."

He gave her an impatient glare. "Good. Then all we have to do is prove it. Then we'll watch the bad guys put their forked tails between their legs and hoof themselves away."

"Ah, a little religious irony. How clever."

She heard him expel a breath. "What I'm doing is trying to get your attention—and shove that sharp brain of yours into a forward gear. Fordham says she was adopted out by Mary in nineteen seventy— illegally—the same year Dinah started donating to Mayday. Body or no body, there has to be a connection."

"You think Christiana Fordham is Dinah's daughter."

"Could be, but if she is, it's unlikely Dinah is going to willingly let some medic swab for DNA, so those house records of yours are all we've got."

"And you think Mary Weaver killed her father?"

Her throat closed over the question as if trying to pull it back.

He hesitated, ran a hand though his hair. "Don't know. But either we find out what went on here, or we play a game of let's-pretend, and hope like hell no one gets hurt. Your choice."

She worried her lower lip a moment, then started down St. Ivan's church steps. The first drops of rain cooled her face and the wind lifted her hair as she turned to look back at Gus. He was following her down, pulling up the collar on his expensive leather jacket.

When he caught up to her, she faced him, less than a foot separating them. "Before I agree to help you, before I do *anything*, I want a promise from you."

"I'm listening."

"You agree to work for me, not Dinah, not Hagan. I want what's best for Mayday House, and whatever went on here—if anything at all—stays here. I won't have Mary's name destroyed because of some marital vendetta." She looked up at him. "I want your promise you'll respect her life, and not use what happened here for anyone's gain."

They stood in the rain, the silence between them louder than the wind swirling the leaves around their feet. Keeley swore she could hear the wary gears in his mind turning.

"Why would I promise you that?" he said at last. "And why would you trust me if I did?"

"Because I asked you to and"—she stared into his dark, impenetrable face—"because if you don't promise, you can walk back to the house with me, pack your bags, and get out of Mayday House."

CHAPTER 11

Gus ran his knuckles along the scar on his jaw, then shifted his gaze from Keeley's upturned face to the blackness beyond St. Ivan's gate. Christ! No way could he promise what she asked. The stakes were too high for him and his sister. He might not plan on giving up Dinah to Hagan Marsden, but if he ran out of options, if that's what it took to find April . . . Hell!

"Well?" she urged.

He swallowed the bile that came with his lie and said, "You have my promise."

"Good." She turned toward home.

"So with those few words, you trust me?" he said from behind her, his question stopping her—and surprising him. For a time she kept her back to him.

When she looked back, he could barely make out her face through the sheeting rain, but he heard her sigh, then watched her straighten to meet his gaze, even though he was sure she couldn't see his eyes. "Have you ever broken a promise to me before?"

"I haven't made one."

"Exactly."

"Cute." He stepped in front of her, grasped both her arms. "But not good enough."

"Okay, how about this?" She pulled from his hold and rubbed where his hands had been. "I'm trusting you, Gus Hammond, because I want to, and because"—she stopped, as if uncertain of the personal territory her instincts had led her into— "I think we have something in common."

"Go on."

She continued to rub her arms, then took a deep breath. "I think we both want to start over. Leave the . . . sins of the past behind us."

"Sins." He knew his cold skepticism showed in his face. "Not a concept I'm familiar with."

"Mistakes, then, if that word works better for you." She walked a step, then turned back. "Whatever you call it, I think both of us are tired of being what we were, tired of—"

"Fucking up?" He used the word to shock, jolt her into reality, make her see the difference between the convent-bred young girl and the street-hardened tough. Hell, for him 'fucking up' didn't come close to describing his mistakes. She looked unfazed by his crude word.

"Yes." She nodded her head firmly. "Exactly. Now let's go."

He watched her walk away from him and worked to settle the complex skew of emotions this unusual woman had set bulleting around in his head. Keeley Farrell had a way of getting to the bones of things. He'd have to make sure that's as far as she got, because his goddamn black soul was his own business.

* * *

When they got to the house, Christiana was in the front hall preparing to leave, her coat in hand.

"I wasn't sure when you'd be back," she said, glancing at Gus. "So I thought I'd better get going. I'll come again . . . when we've both had time to think about things."

Keeley took the coat from Christiana's hands and hung it on the coatrack near the front door. "You'll stay the night," she said, her tone brooking no argument. "The weather's miserable, and we have plenty of rooms." When Christiana hesitated, she added, "And I think we need to talk more—but in the morning after we've had time to think."

Gus studied both women: same height, same complexion; oddly dark tan complexion, for either a blonde or redhead. If Christiana was Dinah's daughter, the resemblance was superficial and all about being tall and blond. And he knew firsthand Dinah's color came courtesy of Miami's most expensive salon.

Keeley looked exhausted but determined. Fordham just looked exhausted, but still she waffled. "I don't know . . ."

"Well, I do." Keeley said. "Come with me. I'll find you something to sleep in. It won't be fashionable, but it will do."

Fordham caved. "That won't be necessary. My bag's in the car. I went right to the station for my interview, so I didn't get around to checking into the hotel." She looked at Gus. "It's just an overnight bag."

"I'll get it," he said.

Ten minutes later, after she'd settled Christiana in a room, Keeley came back down the stairs. "I'm for bed," she said. Glancing up the stairs she'd come down, she grimaced. "It looks like tomorrow is going to be an interesting day."

"Erica and Bridget, where are they?" Gus asked.

"Erica's in her room. Bridget's gone to a movie. She has a key."

"Hm." Gus planned to check the house and grounds before turning in, but walked the few paces down the hall with her.

At her door, she stopped and looked up at him. "That promise I asked you for?" she said, her eyes fierce and squarely set on his.

"Uh-huh."

"I expect you to keep it." With that she turned away from him, walked into her room, and closed the door.

She might as well have shoved one of his own knives into his frozen heart.

Dolan James ordered another beer and cast a moody glance around the gloomy no-name Seattle tavern. This meet with Mace was necessary but not welcome. He couldn't wait to get back to San Francisco, but he didn't like what Mace was telling him. There were now five people in that fucking house.

"Who the hell is this one?"

"Don't know. Oregon plates. And I don't think she's staying—the guy just brought in one of those overnight bags. If she hangs around, I'll check her out."

Dolan let his breath hiss through his teeth. "Christ, what the hell is the woman running, a damn motel?"

Mace sat across from him in the high-backed booth and stirred his scotch on the rocks with his index finger. "Looks like it." He licked his alcohol-slicked finger and watched the waitress's ass through narrowed eyes.

Dolan couldn't believe he was tied to this lowlife. Shit! When the old man kicked off, and he got his hands on some real money, it was *sayonara* for sure. He took another look at the big man opposite him. One more pumped-up bicep and the guy would bust the seams on that silk suit he was so fond of wearing. Mace Jacobs was all muscle—as Dolan had found out the one time he'd tried to stiff him on a drug deal. Dolan ran a hand roughly through his fair hair. "This is getting complicated. Maybe we should just knock her off and be done with it."

"I don't think so." Mace's eyes came back to meet his, shrewd and hard.

"Why the hell not? It's what we planned in the first place." And Dolan hadn't flown up from San Francisco for a one-hour meeting to maintain the status quo. "Think about it, we get rid of her, empty the house out, search it from top to bottom." He brightened, lit by his own idea. "Or better yet, burn the sucker to the ground."

Mace gave him a searing look. "You really are a stupid bastard, Dolan. No wonder your old man hates your guts."

Something inside Dolan twisted. Hurt. Maybe what Mace said was true, but he didn't like hearing it from what amounted to a hired hand. Not that Mace saw himself that way. Mace saw himself as the center of the universe. A misconception Dolan would fix when the time was right. "If he hated my guts, I wouldn't be living in his house, and I sure as hell wouldn't be in his will."

"You wouldn't be within signature distance of

that fuckin' will, if I hadn't got you straight and sent you home." He shook his head. "You being too cracked up and dumbass to figure things out on your own, even with a sick daddy worth millions."

Dolan looked at his ex-dealer sourly. He owed him, all right, and he'd damn sure get what he had coming.

Again Mace shook his head. "Surprised the man didn't put you down at birth." He took another drink and turned his eyes back to the waitress's butt.

"You're a son of a bitch, Mace."

Mace shifted lazy eyes to his, smiled thinly. "You maligning my mother?"

Dolan, uncomfortable with the look in Mace's eyes, looked away, said nothing, then muttered, "If you don't want to get rid of the woman, what do you want to do?"

"I'll get rid of her, all right, I've just got to pick my time is all. But considering all the company she's in, it's gonna have to wait." He rubbed the side of his nose and seemed to think a bit. "The thing is some of the company's damned interesting."

"Like?"

"Erica Stark, for one."

The name meant nothing to Dolan.

"Starrier Productions?" Mace raised a brow.

Dolan shook his head.

"You ever see a movie called *Getting A Long*?"

Dolan shook again. What the hell was the muscle-bound idiot talking about movies for?

"Porn, one of the greats. Made a ton of money a few years back. Kind of a baby *Deep Throat*, ya know." He rubbed the side of his nose again. Dolan figured he did it to warm up his brain. Mace went on, "Starrier's been in the biz for years. Their daddy, Jimmy, started it, and when he ran off, their mommy took over. Used to be a customer of my uncle. Sure did like her snow. Saw her once. I was just a kid, though."

"You getting to some kind of point here?"

Mace made like he didn't hear him and rambled on. "Erica and her brother jumped in when mommy died a few years back"—his look turned mean, bitter—"some of you bastards sure are lucky in the daddy department. Me? I had a weeping alky who ended up with his nose pressed into back alley pavement in the asshole of Seattle. He had nothin', and when his liver finally rotted out, I got nothin'. Not like the Starks—or you. You all get a platter full of cash you didn't do squat for, while I'm the one doing all the work." He paused, his expression sour. "Ain't fair."

"What's a porn producer got to do with the Farrell woman?" Dolan ignored the poor-me crap, determined to bring him back on point.

"No idea. But I'm gonna find out." He signaled the waitress. "All I know is that the Stark kids have damn near busted Starrier. They owe some big, bad people some serious cash. So if they're hanging around, they've got a reason." He chuckled. "And it's likely not good works. Paul's nothing, but Erica? Now that's one serious bitch."

"What are you saying?"

Mace rolled his eyes. "I'm saying, *slo-mo*, that maybe your daddy wasn't the only person the Weaver dame called."

Dolan's blood chilled in his veins. "You think they know?"

The waitress arrived and dropped the tab in front of Mace. He eyed her as if she were naked on a buffet table, then shoved the bill toward Dolan. "I'm thinkin' Mayday is gettin' to be a real interesting place." His eyes burned into Dolan's. "And I don't intend to do nothing until I know what's in it for me."

"Don't start messing with things, Mace. We have a deal," Dolan said, panic overwhelming his common sense. "You don't come through, I'll get someone who will." The minute the words were out of his mouth, his mistake took hold.

Mace's hammy hand shot across the table, grabbed his wrist, and twisted hard. "You call someone else, I call your daddy. Have a little chat with him about what you're up to." He bent Dolan's wrist to snapping point. The pain shot to his brain. "You got that?" he snarled.

"Ye-s. I've got it."

"Good." Mace let him go. "Maybe you're not so stupid after all."

He stood then, planted both his hands on the table, knuckles down, and leaned in; he put his face six inches from Dolan's. "And as to our deal you're so worried about, I'll see it done. When the time's right, the woman's as good as dead. You get your money, I get what you owe me—with interest." Dolan rubbed his wrists and smelled Mace's scotch-laden breath when he smiled. "The thing is, that's break-even for me, Dolan, buddy. The Starks? Now that could be pure profit." He straightened. "Hell, maybe they'll even put me in one of their movies." He cupped his cock, smirked. "They get a load of this baby, they'll shit themselves. Make me a star."

Watching him walk away, and still massaging his aching wrist, Dolan was freaking. Every nerve in his body was jigging, and he had no idea what he should do.

Mace, if he messed with those people, would screw everything.

He had to get rid of him, take care of things himself. His stomach clenched as if punched, and he swallowed a clump of nerves lodged in his throat. Doing things himself wasn't in the plan. He rubbed his knuckles, then took a long swig of beer.

The tip of an idea poked up from his gray matter, a bit crooked and uncertain yet, but he decided to stay in Seattle until he worked it all the way out.

The next morning Gus left Keeley in the cellar going through box number three million—and it wasn't eight A.M. yet. Okay, maybe his count was inflated, but with nearly a half century of unlabeled boxes to slog through, it damn well felt like millions. Hell, the woman had even kept her parents' farm records. Keeley had been at it since well before six. He knew she hoped she'd find something before seeing Christiana again this morning, but so far she'd come up empty, which put a fresh cup of coffee on his agenda and a quick check to see if the Fordham woman was stirring yet.

She was. Sitting quietly at the kitchen table, she glanced up at him when he came in. "Good morning," she said and gave him a bare-bones smile. She was dressed in beige slacks and a dark brown sweater; a blue cell phone rested on the newspapers scattered in front of her. She was either planning on making a call or waiting for one.

He jerked his chin toward the coffee mug she choked between her hands. "You want a refill?"

She glanced at the mug as if seeing it for the first time. "Yes, thanks."

Gus walked over and filled it for her. The woman was tense, damn near strangling her cup. When her cell phone rang, she picked it up with such haste she bumped her coffee mug, and some of the dark brew slopped onto the table. She winced at Gus, said "hello" into the phone, and after another quick glance at him, turned away.

Leaving her to her call, he went to look out the window above the sink.

The backyard trees drooped tiredly, sodden with last night's rain, and the grass—mostly weeds— looked like swamp moss. The cedar hedge separating Mayday from St. Ivan's sorely needed a shave and a haircut, and a couple of rundown sheds, one of them with its side falling in, fought a losing battle with the blackberry bushes crawling halfway over their roofs. But the sun had come out and the yard steamed under it.

For the first time, he noticed the lumpy old sandbox in the back corner, the rusted swing beside it. A few feet from the sandbox a long abandoned garden lay choked by weeds and thistle.

He sipped his coffee, thought about Keeley playing there as a kid, imagined her mop of copper hair under a summer sun. Like a small bonfire. Like the woman herself. He let his gaze travel over the big grassy yard. Without the weeds and the bumps and hollows that had come with the years, it must have been damn fine in its day. A good safe place for a kid.

April always wanted a swing. He'd even tried to build one for her once, in the alley behind the last dump they'd lived in, but the rope he'd found in the dumpster was rotten, and there'd been no place to string it anyway, so she'd had to settle for a skipping rope. It broke, too, but it lasted for three days, and she'd spent them skipping her little-girl heart out in that miserable alley.

"I'll *be* there, Duke."

The voice, irritated, rose behind him, and caught his attention. He turned. When Christiana glanced up to see him watching her, she reddened. "Noon. Yes, darling. I know. I said I'll be there, and I will. See you then." She clicked off.

"My manager," she said—a little too quickly— then set the phone back on the table.

Gus sipped some coffee. "More than a manager, I'd say."

When it looked as though she was going to deny it, he raised a brow.

She cleared her throat. "You're right."

"Does he know what you're doing here?"

She shook her head. "No. And he wouldn't like it."

Keeley burst into the kitchen, her brow furrowed, holding what looked like a small piece of paper in her hand. "Look at this. I found it in one of Mary's miscellaneous boxes, marked nineteen sixty-eight, but the back of it says nineteen seventy."

From what Gus had seen so far, all of Mary's boxes were miscellaneous, and all of them were a mess of paperwork and memories that laid waste to any concept of organization. The efficient, leave-no-string-untied Cassie could easily make Mayday's paperwork her life's work.

"What is it?" he asked.

She held out a photo. "Me. And someone else."

She came to stand beside him, and they both rested their hips against the counter edge. He held out his hand, and she put the picture in it. Colored, faded a bit, but clear enough.

She pointed to the woman in the picture. "That's my mother. And that"—she pointed to one of the two babies her mother was holding up to the camera—"is me."

Gus, his attention derailed by the brush of Keeley's bare arm against his, forced his concentration on the photograph. *Damn!* That shot of distraction, what it meant, pissed him off. *If there was ever a lousy time to be attracted to a woman, Hammond, this is it. Especially one like Farrell. Be like robbing a goddamn church.*

Holding the babies was a pretty, dark-haired woman, but to him both babies looked the same. Christiana came to stand with them.

"How do you know it's you?" he asked.

"It says it's me"—Keeley turned the picture over—"on the back. Right here." She pointed. "See? 'Left, Keeley Aileen, two months. Right, Baby C.'" She glanced toward Christiana. "Maybe baby C is you."

Christiana took the picture. "God, it *is* me." She sounded stunned, put a hand to her mouth.

"Jesus, those babies"—he gestured at the picture—"look like matched bookends. How can you be sure?"

Christiana seemed unable to take her eyes from the picture. "Because of this." She swept her long blond hair back from her left temple to expose a pale birthmark. Gus had to strain to see it. "I had it lightened in my early twenties, but look"—she dropped her hair and pointed to baby C in the photo—"it's plain as day."

Keeley frowned again, then headed for the door. "I just thought of something. I'll be right back."

She came back into the room carrying a red and gold photo album the size of a generational Bible. She set it on the table and flipped through its heavy black pages.

The album was in good condition, and all the photos were held securely in place by gilt corner grips. Keeley turned the pages steadily until she reached the middle, stopped abruptly. "Odd," she said. "There are no pictures missing from that time. Which means the picture I found was never in here, and I certainly don't remember ever seeing it before."

"I'm not following you," Gus said.

"Mary might have been the scourge of filing systems everywhere, but she was meticulous about her photographs. She took pictures of everyone who ever came to Mayday—especially the mothers and babies. When I was a kid, I remember going through the albums with her, and she'd tell me everyone's name, when they were here, and what, if anything, she knew about their lives at the time. A lot of the women kept in contact with her for years after leaving Mayday." Keeley again nodded at the picture, which Christiana was still studying intently, and added, "I wonder why she didn't put this one in the album."

"Maybe she couldn't resist keeping the photo, probably because you're in it, Keeley, but because I'm in it, too, she was afraid to." Christiana handed the photo back to Keeley.

"Because she couldn't talk about you," Gus said. "Or your mother."

Christiana nodded. "And if one part of her story is true, Keeley, it makes the other part a strong possibility."

Keeley straightened her shoulders. "You mean her killing your father."

It wasn't phrased as a question and Christiana didn't answer her. Her expression grim, she said, "Look, I have to get back to Seattle. My manager's waiting for me, and I've got two interviews lined up for this afternoon." A newspaper lay open on the table in front of her; she pulled it forward and scribbled her name and number on it. "This is my cell." She wrote down another number, then looked at Keeley directly. "I know this is hard for you, and I know how you feel about Mary, but, please, *please*, call me when you find out more. I need to know. I *have to* know."

Keeley dropped the hand holding the picture to her side. "I'm not sure I will find anything more. If Mary deliberately misfiled the picture, why would she keep any other records?"

Gus figured he knew damn well why Weaver had kept records. If she hadn't held on to her proof, she'd have had nothing to hold over Dinah. This thing was making more sense by the second. There was a better than even chance Christiana *was* Dinah's daughter. But until he knew for sure, he'd keep his mouth shut.

"She kept the picture, remember, she just misfiled it," Christiana said.

"Mary misfiled most things out of plain bad habit. The idea of her doing it on purpose is *really* scary." Keeley knotted her hands on the table. He sensed she was hedging, that the enormity of Christiana's revelation was only now settling into some corner of her mind.

"Just keep looking. There has to be something."
Christiana placed her hand over Keeley's. "I'd *need*
to know who my mother is—and exactly what happened here."

Keeley glanced at Gus, and he knew she was thinking about Dinah; then she turned to face Christiana. "I know this is awful for you, but I won't
promise anything, because I can't believe—"

Christiana shook her head, compressed her lips.
"You don't have to believe anything. Not yet, at
least. But not knowing what happened to my father
won't do either of us any good."

Gus watched the two women, fascinated. They'd
known each other for less than twenty-four hours,
yet they talked to each other as if it had been years.
His mind shifted gears. Down. To Dinah Marsden—
self-absorbed, self-protective Dinah. Damn.

With a half dozen words, she could clear this mess up.

Chances of his getting her to say those words were
slim to none, but it sure as hell wouldn't hurt to try.

Fifteen minutes later Keeley and Gus stood on the
porch and watched Christiana Fordham drive out of
Mayday's rutted driveway. Keeley's heart was a ball
of thorns in her chest, her eyes thick with the pressure of tears.

Gus took a step toward her and lifted her face to
his with a knuckle. "What's this?" He wiped the
moisture from her cheek with his thumb.

She brushed his hand away, frustrated with herself,
her growing penchant for tears. "Nothing. It's just
sad. And confusing. Christiana's story, Mary . . .

Mayday House. It's a bit overwhelming, I guess. Not exactly what I . . . expected."

"What did you expect?"

She walked over to the creaky porch swing and sat down, bracing her hands on the edge to keep it from swinging. "Quiet. Peace." *Absolution.* She brushed at her traitorous weepy eyes. "A place to get my bearings." She paused. "Do something good and decent with my life."

"Your life getting any more 'good and decent' doesn't seem possible."

Her eyes shot to his—so dark, fixed on hers as if she were a puzzle with a piece missing. "Is that how you see me, Gus? All virtue and righteousness, like some do-gooder frontier church lady?" The image irritated her, probably because it was so far from the truth.

He rested his hip on the rail and crossed his arms. "The description 'good woman' seems to fit. Convent, nursing, missions, all that."

"What about the marriage? You left that out."

"What about it?"

"I broke my vows to marry Marc. Solemn vows. I didn't keep my word to—"

"God?"

His Name sounded odd coming from him. "Yes."

"You made a contract. Contracts are negotiable. Things change."

"If it were only that simple." She shook her head.

"You think your husband—stepping on that land mine—was some kind of punishment, don't you?"

Keeley, uncertain how to answer, pressed a hand on her heart, tried to still it—and tried to understand why she was talking to a man like Gus about Marc, her broken vows . . . when she hadn't knelt in a confessional for years. Because she couldn't sit still any longer, she stood and walked to the railing Gus had propped himself against.

When she didn't say anything, he said, "It wasn't, you know." He stopped. "You didn't plant the mine, some conscienceless asshole with his own axe to grind did, and he didn't give a damn who stepped on it—a wandering animal, an innocent kid . . . a doctor. All he wanted to do was kill someone. Anyone. It wasn't punishment. It was bad luck. Chaos. Life's good at that."

"Part of me knows what you're saying is true, but another part—"

"Feels guilty as hell?"

"Mm-hm."

He ran a finger across her cheek, then turned her face to his. "I'll bet you're good at the guilt thing."

Too personal, Keeley, you're getting far too personal.

"Expert, I'm afraid," she said, lightening her tone and trying unsuccessfully to dredge up a smile. "But I'm working on downgrading my standing. It's why I came home." She looked up at him, determined to change the subject; instead, she couldn't stop her gaze from sliding to his angular jaw, his mouth, straight, relaxed, seductive. His clean-shaven skin was darkly clear, his scar accented by the sunlight now drifting onto the wide front porch. Inhaling, she took in the scent of him. Indescribable.

Her heart pounding, she moistened her lips and dropped her gaze to what she mistakenly thought was safer territory, the soft white cotton shirt covering his broad chest, cotton that pulled tight over hard muscles when he drew in a deep breath.

This was crazy!

CHAPTER 12

Keeley raised her eyes—certain they looked startled and wild—and met his. His calm gaze focused on her, intense and probing, before he slowly dropped it to her mouth.

"I think I'm about to acquire some guilt of my own," he murmured and, bending his dark head, he brushed his lips over hers. More whisper than kiss, achingly soft.

Before their mouths met, there was the chatter of birds, the rustle of leaves, now only silence.

Before . . . the flutter of a morning breeze, cool on her face, now only warmth.

Before . . . the light of morning, bright on pearl gray clouds, now only hot, swirling darkness.

Her breath a silk storm in her lungs, she ran her hands up and along the taut muscles of his arms, grasped his shoulders. His mouth was so light on hers it was dreamlike, surreal, yet every one of her senses shifted to white-hot and knife-sharp.

He pulled back, held her shoulders, and looked into her eyes. "Should I apologize?"

Keeley blinked, allowing reality and the edge of truth to cut through the sexual glitter in her head. "No," she said, stepping back. "But maybe I should."

He cocked his head, waited.

"For acting like an overwhelmed, under-brained woman." She added, "I don't usually talk so much about private things. I suppose it made me seem needy."

"Which would make my kiss what? An act of kindness?" He let out a disbelieving gust of breath and shook his head.

"Not exactly, but—"

"Farrell, you're the least needy woman I've ever met." He came near to smiling, but quickly displaced it with a darker, unreadable look. "And kissing you had more to do with my need than yours. I've wanted to . . . touch you since the first day I stepped into your kitchen."

Keeley wasn't sure she heard right and was too confused, both by his actions and hers, to pursue this uneasy conversation. Besides, she wasn't sure how she felt about the discomfort his admission obviously caused him.

"I think I'll go back to the boxes," she said, deciding retreat was her best option. "See if I can find anything else about Christiana." She'd think about what had happened between her and Gus later, when she could make sense of it. It certainly didn't make sense to stand here, with Gus Hammond looking as cool as the autumn morning that embraced them, while she couldn't put two rational thoughts together.

He watched her calmly, but his serious eyes told her he sensed her unease. "I'm going into town, but I won't be long. When I get back, I'll help." He paused. "Keep the doors locked while I'm gone." He went in the house, retrieved his jacket, and came out scribbling on a piece of paper. "My cell number." He handed the paper to her. "The door," he repeated, his tone stern. "Lock it."

"It's a gorgeous morning in small-town America, Gus. I think we're safe enough."

"Humor me," he said, without a trace of humor in his tone.

"Okay, okay." She lifted her hands in surrender. "And after the doors are locked, I'll pull up the drawbridge." When her lame attempt at a joke fell flat, and he said nothing, she turned to go back into the house.

"Keeley?"

She looked back, met his solemn face, eyes now holding a touch of awe.

"There's something you should know." He hesitated, but his gaze didn't waver from hers. "I haven't wanted to kiss a woman that much since I was seventeen."

He obviously didn't expect an answer because he started down the stairs, settling into his jacket as he went.

Keeley waited until he got in his car and reversed out of the driveway, then touched her mouth and let out a long breath. If he had waited for an answer, and she'd given him an honest one, it would have surprised him as much as it surprised her.

That on some deeply complex and unnerving level, she was exceedingly glad she was that woman.

* * *

Gus didn't intend to go far or be gone long, but he needed to calm down. Think. Make some calls.

Hell, he was acting like a randy teenager. When his breath eased in his lungs, and he figured there was a chance his brain had backtracked from lust to logic, he pulled into a roadside park. He leaned his head back against the seat and closed his eyes.

Jesus, the woman should have slugged him.

He'd told her what he was—exactly what Hagan Marsden had said, a male whore, a man who'd made a living looking good and bedding women. He hadn't planned it that way, but that's how it turned out. No way around it, and no way to justify it. He'd taken what life offered him and Josh, and he'd learned to live with it—but it left him with no right to mess with Keeley Farrell.

He'd never admit it to her—or anyone else—but she was too goddamned good for him.

Even if she had felt like heaven in his arms.

He opened the car door, got out, and took in some fresh air.

He'd let his control slip. It wouldn't happen again. Keeley didn't need an overused, practiced lover— she needed protection. Letting sex mess with his head would endanger her.

And ruin his chance of finding April.

That thought firm in his mind, he went to the Jag's trunk and unlocked it. He pulled an aluminum briefcase toward him and opened it. Inside were three cell phones, two sets of all-steel throwing knives, and his new PDA—yet to be figured out. He took out one of the phones, decided to bypass Cassie, and dialed Dinah's private line. He got her voice mail.

"Dinah, it's Gus. We need to meet. Call me." He left the number of the cell phone he was using and hung up.

His next call was to Hagan. He walked toward the park's guardrail as he keyed in the number. Beyond the rail a stream, rain-flushed and bright, ran over a bed of rocks like liquid glass. He straddled the guardrail and sat on one of the posts.

Voice mail again. "Hagan. Gus. It looks as though you were right. Our mutual friend definitely has a secret. When I know more, I'll call." He clicked off. If nothing else, the message would keep Hagan off his back for a few more days.

His phone rang immediately. He answered it, his gaze again attracted to the crystal clarity of the fast-moving stream.

"Well, well, well, if it isn't the mystery man himself. I've been trying to get in touch with you for days." Dinah's voice was hard, angry. "You know I'm in Seattle. I left a message. Why didn't you call?"

"I'm calling now."

"Where are you?"

"It doesn't matter where I am. We need to meet."

"Just like that," she said, her tone brittle. "Gus snaps his fingers and Dinah jumps?"

Shit! Not one of Dinah's better moods. He settled himself on the post. "I didn't ask you to jump, baby. I asked you to meet me. If you don't want to . . ." He waited.

"What I should do, '*baby*,' is tell you to fuck off."

"In case you haven't noticed, I've already done that."

"Oh, I noticed, all right. I've also noticed you're working for my ex."

Zebra Contemporary Romance

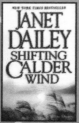
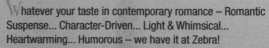
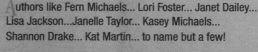

To start your membership, simply complete and return the Free Book Certificate. You'll receive your Introductory Shipment of FREE Zebra Contemporary Romances, you only pay $1.99 for shipping and handling. Then, each month you will receive the 4 newest Zebra Contemporary Romances. Each shipment will be yours to examine FREE for 10 days. If you decide to keep the books, you'll pay the preferred subscriber price (a savings of up to 30% off the cover price), plus shipping and handling. If you want us to stop sending books, just say the word... it's that simple.

FREE BOOK CERTIFICATE

Yes! Please send me FREE Zebra Contemporary romance novels. I only pay $1.99 for shipping and handling. I understand that each month thereafter I will be able to preview 4 brand-new Contemporary Romances FREE for 10 days. Then, if I should decide to keep them, I will pay the money-saving preferred subscriber's price (that's a savings of up to 30% off the retail price), plus shipping and handling. I understand I am under no obligation to purchase any books, as explained on this card.

NAME _____

ADDRESS _____ APT. _____

CITY _____ STATE _____ ZIP _____

TELEPHONE (_____) _____

E-MAIL _____

SIGNATURE _____

(If under 18, parent or guardian must sign)

Offer limited to one per household and not to current subscribers. Terms, offer and prices subject to change. Orders subject to acceptance by Zebra Contemporary Book Club. Offer Valid in the U.S. only.

Thank You!

CN125A

ll..l.lll..ll.l.l.l.l.l.l.l.l.l.l.l.l.l.l.l.l.ll..l

Zebra Contemporary Romance Book Club
Zebra Home Subscription Service, Inc.
P.O. Box 5214
Clifton NJ 07015-5214

PLACE
STAMP
HERE

"Hagan called you." It might have been logical for the bastard to keep his mouth shut until Gus delivered the goods, but nothing in the war between Hagan and Dinah was ever logical. Obviously he couldn't resist the chance to set in a screw and turn it.

"How could you, Gus? After all I did for you, all we had together."

"The way I saw it? Better me than some sleazy private eye." He shifted the phone to his other ear. "Hagan's out to get you, Dinah, and he thinks he's found a way to do it."

"Hagan is an idiot," she said, but her tone had lost its edge, turned toward interested.

"I agree. He hired me, didn't he?" As did you, as did Keeley. Hell, he was the most hired guy between here and Texas. There were times when the chameleon business got damned complicated.

Some silence came down the line, then a short laugh. "I guess I won't tell you to fuck off after all."

"I didn't think you would. Unless you've lost interest in saving that perfect ass of yours."

"Whatever he's paying you, I'll double it."

Gus sucked in some air and think time. If he didn't go for the cash, Dinah would get suspicious. "I kind of figured you would." He named a sum large enough to satisfy a third-world despot, knowing he'd never collect. He was done with Dinah, and done with her money, which didn't make him any more comfortable playing the role of Hagan's lackey—or lying to Farrell. For now he'd take one step at a time, because he wasn't about to lose his sister again.

"Done," she said immediately. "When can we

meet?" Then, irritably, "Where exactly are you, anyway?"

"Erinville. I'm staying at Mayday House." He didn't miss her quick intake of breath.

"Staying there . . . Jesus, Gus, I told you to close the place, not live in it."

"I'm here because Hagan wants me here. He said the Farrell woman needed protection—from you."

After a moment of silence, she said, "That's absurd."

"That's what I told him," he said. "I'll be in Seattle tomorrow morning, Dinah. I'll call when I get there." He snapped the phone closed.

Now all he had to do was make sure Keeley was covered for the day, and he knew exactly how to do it.

He headed into town.

The next morning Keeley opened the door at eight o'clock to three men in clean but splotchy white coveralls. The words Paynters, Inc., and a brush in the shape of a torch were embroidered on their chest pockets.

"Miss Farrell?" the tallest of the trio asked, smiling.

"That's me, but the big question is who are you?" She looked past them to see a truck bearing the same red logo parked in the Mayday House driveway.

He touched the lettering on his chest. "Painters. We were told to start this morning."

"Start what?"

The man was starting to look as confused as she was until a voice came from behind her. "Morning. Get your stuff and come on in. After the lady's had her second cup of coffee, she'll tell you what to do."

The men headed back to the truck and Keeley turned to see Gus. His black hair was still glistening from the shower, his face was closely shaven, and he smelled . . . delicious. Standing tall with his hands on his hips, he looked as if he were preparing for an armored tank invasion—and he took her breath away. And her words.

"They're painters," he said, repeating the obvious. "I hired them. They'll be here until you have done whatever it is you want done." He waited, defensive, and as still as . . . one of her many yet-to-be-opened paint cans.

She found her voice and her missing brain cells. "Dear God, you look as if you think I'm going to say no."

"I never know what you're going to do."

Painters! Her back and right arm would sing hymns if backs and arms did such things. "This is a big house, Gus. It will cost a fortune."

He shrugged. "Then I can consider my rent paid."

She smiled, couldn't help herself. "What you're doing is more like a long-term lease." She took a step toward him, hesitated only a moment, then gave him a quick hug and a maiden-aunt cheek-kiss. His black sweater was kitten soft, the body under it anything but, and she stepped back quickly. "I thank you, Mr. Hammond. Mayday thanks you."

He nodded. "The men will be here until four. I'll be back before they leave."

"You're leaving?" She mentally kicked herself for letting her question come out as if she were a wife being deserted for a barmaid.

He gave her that strangely guarded half smile he was so good at, again making her wonder what a full smile would do to his handsome face—to her. "I don't do paint, remember?"

"Right." She brushed a leftover bed-head curl from her eyes. "Can I ask where you're going?"

"Seattle," he said. "To see Dinah Marsden."

Keeley's heart quickened. "Do you think she'll tell you anything about Christiana?"

"Knowing Dinah"—he shook his head—"I can't say. I'll do what I can."

Keeley had only a moment to wonder what that might be, before two more men showed up at her still-open door. "This Mayday House?" one asked.

She nodded.

"We've got your dishwasher."

Keeley shot a surprised look toward Gus, having no doubt at all who was behind all this charity.

"I don't do dishes, either." He grabbed his leather jacket from the coat stand. "See you later." With that he was gone.

When Gus arrived at Dinah's door, it was after eleven. Cassie stood on the other side, her bag and coat in hand. She gave him a quick, tight embrace. "We've missed you." She gestured with her head toward Dinah, who was a couple of feet behind her. "Both of us."

He leaned down and kissed her on the cheek.

"How come you always smell so good?" she asked, smiling.

"You flirting with me, Cassie?"

"As if it would do me any good—not to mention cost me my job."

"Damn right it would. Now for God's sake, Cassie, get going, will you? Gus and I need to talk."

Cassie grimaced, winked at Gus, and started to put on her coat. He took it from her and helped her into it. Then, gripping her shoulders, he whispered close to her ear, "It's Hagan who'll cost you your job, Cassie. If you're smart, you'll realign your loyalties."

She gasped and spun, her mouth slack with shock.

"Go," he said quietly.

She went and Gus faced Dinah. No embrace this time, just a cold censure.

"You screwing the nun?"

"She's not a nun. Not anymore. And if I did get that lucky, you'd be the last to know." He took off his jacket and tossed it on the sofa. "So how about we start over? How are you, Dinah?"

She walked to him, put her hands on his chest, and looked up at him. "I'd be better if you'd take me to bed." She started to open his belt buckle. "I've been wet since you called me yesterday."

"Not going to happen." He stopped her hand, raised it to his mouth. "What brings me here is strictly business." He kissed her knuckles, then released her hand. "You look beautiful, by the way."

She stared at him a moment, then laughed. "You should give lessons in how to say no, Gus. You do it so well."

He sat on the couch, leaned back, and slid his eyes over her perfect figure, shining skin—her work in progress. "You don't make it easy."

"And you're a good liar." She turned her back on him. "Want a drink?"

"It's barely eleven. I'll pass."

She poured herself something made of champagne

and orange juice and joined him, taking a place at the opposite end of the long sofa. She sipped from her drink and set it on the table. "Tell me about the nun—excuse me—ex-nun."

"She's Mary Weaver's godchild. She was born in Mayday and grew up there. She has no intention of leaving."

"Born there?" She raised her brows. "You're sure?"

"So she says."

Her gaze flickered as if something registered. "That's it. That's all you know."

"Yeah, which is a lot less than you do, obviously."

"I don't know what you mean."

"Tell me why you've supported that place all these years." Gus watched her carefully and caught the quick drop of her eyes, the rally.

"I told you," she said. "Mary Weaver was a friend."

"You've given millions over the years. Hell of an expensive friend."

She picked up her spiked orange juice and sipped. "You've been digging where I haven't asked you to dig, Gus."

"I'm a curious guy." He took the glass from her hand, set it back on the table. "What's going on here, Dinah? What the hell is Hagan after?"

After a long pause, she let out an irritated breath and got up. "You want to know about Mary and me, I'll tell you. But it's a damn boring story." She eyed him. "I was born in Erinville."

He shot up a brow. "You told me you were born in New York. That you hated the West Coast."

"The last part's true." She looked out the suite's window at the stunning autumn day and shuddered. "Bloody rain forest."

"Go on."

"I met Mary when I was . . . I don't know, maybe eleven or twelve. I guess she would have been mid-twenties. Her Dad had died the year before, and she'd just lost her mother." She stopped, then smiled without mirth.

"Something funny?"

"No, I'm just getting to the dysfunctional child-hood part and wondering how boring to make it. I think I'll go for the condensed version." She dropped the smile. "I was an only child who'd come late into my parents' lives. Looking back, I don't think they knew what to do with me, and I didn't help." Her shrug was casual, her expression pained. "I was the kind of kid who did what I wanted, when I wanted. Not easy. All of which"—she looked at him with a challenging smile—"probably comes as no surprise to you."

She was right, but he let it go. Waited.

"By the time I met Mary, I was drifting around Erinville on my own. Happy enough to be left alone and get the hell away from that stupid farm my parents ran. Chickens and pigs. Can you believe it? God, what an awful place!" Her brows knit, and for a moment she was lost in her own thoughts. "As a family, we were like three sick people forced to-gether in a hospital ward."

"How did you meet Mary Weaver?"

"In church. Or, to be more accurate, the St. Ivan's church front yard. They were having some kind of sale, old things, home baking, things like that. Fund-raising crap." She smiled at him, as if the memory amused her. "I stole a pie."

When she didn't go on, he urged, "And?"

"It was Mary's pie. She saw me take it, and she followed me. Found me eating it behind the church in the old graveyard." She paused. "I thought she'd be mad—and before she could say anything, I swore at her and threw the pie at her shoes." She winced, then smiled. "Made a hell of a mess."

"What did she do?"

"Nothing." Dinah picked up her glass and went to the bar to refill it, this time with straight orange juice. She returned to her seat on the couch. "Then she invited me to dinner." She again looked amused. "She thought I was hungry."

"Weren't you?"

"No, the pie looked good, and I wanted it." She smiled. "Like I wanted you when I saw you trying to hustle yesterday's prepackaged sandwiches from that gas attendant." Her gaze raked him.

"I *was* hungry."

"And so was Josh." She took in a breath. "I'll never forget that night, taking you home. . . . You were so gorgeous, you took my breath away."

"I didn't come here to talk about me or Josh. I came to talk about Mary." He hated thinking about those days. The gas guy had said no to the sandwich deal, so Gus had said yes to Dinah's sex-for-money deal and gotten into her dark blue Mercedes. He wasn't the first of Dinah's young men, but it turned out he was her last. The next day that same Mercedes took him, and Josh, to something resembling security—and protected him from a bogus murder charge that had hung over him like stink.

He shoved the past aside. "If you don't talk to me, Dinah, you'll be talking to Hagan, or some PI he's hired to make mincemeat out of your life. Take your choice."

"What I've told you is about it. I had dinner with Mary that night. And after that, I started to hang out at that big old empty house of hers." She shook her head. "Weird, too, because Mary was such a prig. And I was—well, let's say I was anything but. But we got along. She was like a big sister in some ways. She might have been a pain in the ass a lot of the time—especially when she got preachy on me, but I liked her. And she liked me." Her expression touched on wistful. "About the time she started taking in unwed mothers, battered wives, and the like and warning me about the perils of"—she made quote marks in the air—"'immoral behavior and the sins of the flesh,' I took off to somewhere I could find exactly that."

"How old were you?"

"Fourteen. Maybe fifteen." She shuddered dramatically, then got up from the sofa. "God, I couldn't wait to get out of that awful town." She looked down at him, her eyes curious. "A story not unlike your own, I'm guessing?"

He'd never told Dinah about his life before their gas station meeting, and he didn't intend to. But it was nothing at all like hers. Hell, he and April would have traded for hers in a heartbeat. "Did you keep in touch?"

"Off and on. I'd call, she'd try to talk me into coming back, I'd say 'no way.' Gradually I stopped calling."

"And the money. When did you start sending the money?"

"When I had some. My first husband was both old

and generous." She walked back to the bar but didn't pour herself another drink. "I figured I owed her."

"You owed her?" he repeated. "That's it? Somewhere in your twenties, years after leaving Erinville, you up and decide to start sending Mary Weaver money—lots of money. That's what you want me to believe? What you expect Hagan to believe?"

"Believe whatever you like. I do." Dinah shrugged her cashmere-covered shoulders. "But that's it, lover. No big conspiracy, no under-the-table dealings, nothing—"

"No illegitimate daughter."

She stared at him as if he'd spilled maggots from his mouth. "I don't know what you're talking about."

Gus rose from the sofa, walked toward her. "Dinah, you were young, you made a mistake. It happens. Your best bet is to level with me—before Hagan finds out."

"Hagan!" She spit out the name. "So that's his game, is it? Concoct some miserable story to get back at me, for taking his goddamn money." She raised her chin and glared at him. "And if I did have a daughter, what of it? It won't change anything except to give a few people something to chatter about. In a couple of months it will go away." Wrapping her arms around herself, her eyes going hard and dark, she said, "Hagan can go to hell."

"He probably will," Gus said.

"Besides, if I did have a daughter, which I'm not admit—"

"Dinah, for Christ's sake, cut the crap, will you?"

"*If I did have a daughter,*" she repeated, "she'll never be found. Never."

Gus stared at the arrogant, stubborn woman in

front of him and took a shot to the gut, equal parts guilt and sympathy. Who the hell was he to poke at someone's else's façade when his own was tinted glass? For Dinah, image, saving face, meant everything. It defined her. He'd always known that behind her beautiful face, beneath the luxury homes and lavish lifestyle, lay the soggy ground of the path she'd taken to get them.

Dinah was one big con.

It took one to know one. He'd trodden some damn soggy ground himself, and he wasn't her judge but, like it or not, Dinah was the route to his sister. He needed to know what she knew—and he needed to know it now.

"Well, baby, the thing is that daughter you 'don't have' has been found—and she's found Mayday House." He ran a finger along his scar, took a moment. "And she's looking to find out about her mother—"

Dinah's eyes, stark and shot with fear, met his.

"—and why Mary Weaver killed her birth father."

CHAPTER 13

Mace pulled the truck to the shoulder about a hundred yards up the road from Mayday, got out of the car, and propped the hood open. He made a show of studying the motor.

He glanced around at the flat farmland surrounding Erinville. Gusting out a breath, he cursed. He was fresh out of patience. The blond had left—at least that was one down, but that Erica bitch hadn't shown her face all day. And it was her ass he was after.

Damn country, gave him no cover at all. He'd have no more than half an hour to tinker under this hood before either some do-gooder insisted on helping him, or got suspicious. He didn't want either. He'd already had two rentals, spent hours risking his ass, watching for Stark.

This time he'd been smart enough to rent an open pickup, the most innocent car on the road, but even that would hold them off only so long. For one thing, country people were born nosy.

He checked his watch. Three forty-five.

He watched Mayday from under the protection of

the hood. A silver Jag came from the opposite direction and turned in the driveway. Hammond. He didn't knock, Mace noticed, just walked right on in. Right at home. Not for long.

The door was barely closed before it opened again and three guys came out and piled into the white van that had been there all day. When it lumbered out of the driveway, the door opened again.

Bingo!

Mace stood back from the hood, wiped his hands idly on a white cotton cloth, and watched Erica Stark ease her bulk into a platinum Altima. Damn woman was big as a house. A looker, though.

She headed back the way Hammond had come. Mace slammed the hood down, tossed the towel onto the passenger seat, and followed.

Erica was hot, exhausted, and irritated. She hadn't intended to come back to the Jasper Inn so soon, but to add to her stress, Paul was second-guessing every damn thing. Going on about how they'd find the money some other way—maybe get out of the business entirely. He'd flipped to negative, a bad place to be.

Jesus, so they had made some crummy films, the internet was cutting their market . . . yada, yada. So what? All they needed was one hot film, some solid foreign sales—which she'd already lined up, thank you very much—and they were back in business. She was going to make another *Getting A Long*, rake in a bundle. Hell, she'd even signed up Silky Blue, aka Glenda Phisterman, to star.

All Paul had to do was sit in his office and count

the cash. Was that asking too much? She didn't think so.

At the Jasper, she parked in front of Paul's room and turned off the car. For a second or two she rested her head back and did some easy breathing. God, she was tired. She felt like a slug, a gigantic Alice-in-Wonderland kind of slug—with lead weights on its back.

She pulled herself out of the car.

Paul would come around. She'd make sure of it. Maybe the porn business was more competitive, maybe the margins weren't what they used to be, but they were better than most businesses. She'd remind him of that, calm him down, and be back to Mayday in time for dinner. Tonight she'd check out the cellar. Thinking about the night ahead, the drain on her limited energy, a wave of weariness washed over her. There were days when all she wanted to do was sleep, but whenever she did lie down, the babies took up hip-hop, and she couldn't sleep anyway.

She stopped at number eleven and glanced around. God, what a sleepy hollow this place was. How the hell they stayed in business was a miracle. A pickup pulled in next to her and she watched a man get out.

Whoa . . . not bad. Not bad at all. Longish brown hair jutted out from a baseball cap, but clean, thick hair, not the straggly kind that signaled Balding-In-Process. He wore jeans, good ones, and a gray sweat jacket, both tight enough to accent a body designed more for show than clothes.

When he noticed her scrutiny, he smiled at her, slow and direct, the kind of smile she'd expect from a man who looked good and knew it, the kind of smile that said, if you like this, you should see me without my clothes on.

Erica's kind of man.

She smiled back, rapped a couple of times on Paul's door, and followed Mr. Should-be-naked's tight butt as it headed to the motel office.

"Erica," Paul said, opening the door, then poking his head out and looking around. "I thought we agreed you weren't going to come here anymore."

"And I wouldn't, if you weren't sitting in this room worrying yourself into a frenzy."

After another furtive scan of the motel parking lot, he pulled her into the room, closed the door, and scowled at her. "I never liked this crazy idea of yours in the first place, but I am *not* worrying. All I'm doing is examining our other options." He walked to the window and closed the blinds.

Erica rolled her eyes and sat on the edge of the bed. "We don't have 'other' options, brother mine. And we've been over this—and over this." She tried to sound soothing instead of pissed off. "We come up with the cash in three weeks, or Starrier—and the Starks along with it—are loan-shark meat." She sat up straighter and planted her palms near the small of her back. "They won't even give us an extension."

Paul stop looking preoccupied and gave her a sharp look. "You called Lester?"

"I called Lester *again*." She reined in her impatience—barely. "And I got the same answer. Have the money to them before November or else. The 'or else' bit I leave to your imagination, but I hear cement shoes are still a popular choice." She lifted a shoulder, tired of going over this, then got to her feet. "We've got one chance, Paul, and that's Mayday House. Once we find out exactly who was involved, we—"

A knock on the door interrupted. They both stared at it. Erica frowned. "You expecting company?"

"No." Paul made for the door. "Probably the room cleaners. I'll get rid of them."

He opened the door.

A split second later, Erica's parking lot fantasy man was in the room, with a gun jammed in Paul's ribs. He kicked the door closed behind him.

"What the hell—" Paul started.

"Shut up and step back. Near the woman."

Paul did as he was told, gripped Erica's hand, and urged her to stand behind him. The man scanned the meager room, visibly relaxed when he confirmed they were the only ones there.

When he waved the gun, Erica noticed it had a silencer on it, at least what she thought was a silencer; the barrel looked overly long and thick. Terrifying. She tried to swallow what felt like a tennis ball in her throat, couldn't take her eyes off the gun or the man holding it.

He looked at her and smiled.

Erica moved from shock to a forced wariness. "If it's money you want—"

"We'll get to what I want soon enough. Sit. Both of you"—he gestured with the gun to the two chairs settled against the Formica-covered table near the window—"and flatten your hands, palms down, on the table." When neither of them moved, he lowered his voice and pointed the gun in Paul's face. "Now."

They sat and placed their hands as instructed. Erica told herself to get a grip, stay calm, when what she felt like doing was throwing up. "What do you want?" she asked.

He studied her. "Maybe just to meet the famous Starks. Erica and Paul, right? Starrier Productions." The smile dropped from his face. "Then again maybe I'm interested in what they're doin' hanging around a crappy burg like this." He jerked his head toward the town outside the covered window.

Erica forced herself to think, not easy when someone had a gun barrel pointed at your brother and your elephant-sized stomach made a better-than-average target. She sucked in some courage. "So you know us. Who the hell are you?"

"Mace"—he flattened his lips—"your new best friend."

"Yeah, well, we've got all the friends we need. So you can get the hell out of here, before I scream down the house."

Mace took one step forward, grabbed Paul's wrist, pressed his hand flat on the table, and shot off his little finger. The whoosh of the silencer made less noise than a popped champagne cork. He stepped back, looked down at her. "You were saying?"

Flash frozen, Erica gaped, registering a gush of blood, absolute silence, an odd burning smell, and one of the babies giving her a hard kick to the left of her belly button.

Paul's mouth opened but not a sound came out; his face chalked to a gray-white slate. Expressionless. In a slow-motion gesture, his eyes wide, he clasped his bloodied hand and pulled it to his chest. Rivers of red spilled over his knuckles and down the front of his white shirt.

When she found her voice, she cried, "Paul, oh my God." She looked at Mace. "I've got to help him."

"Sit," he snarled.

"Erica, don't—the babies," Paul gasped, clutching his hand. "Just do what he says."

"Good suggestion." He glanced at Paul, looking amused. "They say a guy can bleed out from a finger shot. Never seen it myself, though. Probably damn slow, but it might be interesting." He sat on the edge of the bed, the same spot Erica had been in just moments ago, and appeared perfectly relaxed— perfectly dangerous. "Be a good girl and I'll let you get him a towel. If you're not a good girl, I'll make you a matched set."

Erica glanced at the bathroom, then back at the animal on the bed. She took a couple of breaths. "What do you want?"

"Like I said, I want to know what the hell you're doing here."

Erica looked at Paul. "In case you haven't noticed, I'm pregnant—with twins. I came to Mayday to get some help—with my decision about the babies." She hesitated. "I thought Mayday House could help me arrange an adoption—a private adoption."

His eyes skimmed over her, and his tongue slid from one side of his lower lip to the other. The gesture left the lips glistening under the room's harsh overhead light. Without a word, he pointed the gun at her belly. "You want to get rid of the kids"—he lifted a brow—"I can help you with that."

Her blood frozen in her veins, Erica stared into his eyes, glassy, ruthless eyes set in grim purpose. He would kill her, kill her babies . . . babies until this split second she hadn't even been sure she'd wanted. She heard Paul gasp, but her own voice had congealed somewhere low in her throat and was as paralyzed as the rest of her. She dropped her eyes to the gun, tried to swallow, to think.

"Jesus, Erica, tell him!" Paul roared. "Nothing's worth those babies."

"We're trying to, uh, find a . . . sister." The words bumped into one another, like rocks in a tumbler.

Her answer didn't make him happy. He lowered the gun and drew a circle with it—around her stomach. "Want to try again?"

"It's the truth," Paul said. "She's telling the truth." He was still clutching his hand, still obviously in pain, but he was looking at the man on the bed without flinching. "We got a call—"

"What kind of call?" His gaze sharpened.

"From the woman who used to run the house. She said we had a sister. That she'd been adopted out." He stopped, his face a ghastly white. Covered in blood from his chest to his waist, he held his damaged hand to his heart.

"The woman who called. What was her name?"

"Weaver," Erica said. "Mary Weaver."

He nodded his head slowly, as if agreeing with himself. But even though he looked lost in thought, he didn't relax his grip on the gun.

Erica found her voice and another shred of courage—and considering it was all she had, she decided to use them. "Now if it's all the same to you, I'd like to get my brother a towel." Amazingly her voice was steady.

Using the gun he gestured distractedly toward the bathroom. "Don't do anything stupid, or Pauly here will lose the rest of his hand."

Erica was back in seconds. Busying herself with tending to Paul, she glared at the man on the bed. "Now you know our story; what's yours?" She wrapped the towel securely around Paul's hand, tucked the edge in to form as tight a bandage as she could, and set his elbow on the table, bending it to ensure he held the bleeding finger up. Not good enough, but it had to do until she could get them out of here. It wasn't the blood loss that scared her—it was the chance of infection.

"Well, now, it looks like me and you are after the exact same thing."

She didn't get it. "You're looking for a sister?"

"Maybe." His amused expression soured. "The thing is, my *sister* is worth a lot of money, and I'm betting yours is, too." His foxy eyes fixed on her face. "I wouldn't try to shit me, if I were you, feed me crap about a family reunion. I know all about the red ink your company's drowning in." He sneered. "You're here for cash. The question is how much."

Erica ran a hand over the lives in her body, her own flesh enfolding them, and knew she couldn't risk a lie. Then she glanced at her brother, saw the blood coloring the cheap white towel. Paul looked ready to faint, his anxious eyes flitting between Mace and her. "You're right," she said. "It's the red ink. We owe people. And if we can find out who this sister is, get a line on her mother, the ink turns to black."

"So the mommy's got money, huh?" He grinned, as if enjoying himself, his shitty rhyme.

"Plenty of it." She stopped, her heart crazy in her chest. Okay, she was guessing, a guess based on Mary's slurred description of the mother as "a special someone who did many good things and was famous." Where there was fame, there was money—that was Erica's take on things.

"So why the hell should she give any of it to you?" His gaze coiled around her.

Erica swore she heard a damn cash register clanging in his empty skull. "She owes us."

"How's that?"

Erica took a breath, prepared to answer.

Paul answered for her. "How about because she destroyed our family, maybe murdered our father? And we figure it's time she paid for it. All of it."

Erica's gaze shot from Paul to Mace. She watched as he blinked, then blinked again, as if he had trouble understanding his own thoughts. Then he got up, stuffed the gun in the waistband of his slacks, and smiled.

"I like the last part," he said. "The bit about getting paid?" His cold eyes made his smile a sham when he looked at her and Paul in turn. "Meet your new partner."

"Dinah must have said *something*," Keeley said to Gus. Fed up with the paper overload she'd been buried in for hours, she opened the office file cabinet and stuffed in the files she'd just gone through. She left the next stack on her desk.

She turned then to face Gus. He sat on the settee that had sagged under Mary's office window for as long as Keeley could remember—always stacked high with magazines, flyers, and her to-be-filed files. Keeley had cleared it earlier this afternoon, while the blessed painters had been busy bringing the hall and kitchen colors into the twenty-first century.

"Not only did she not say anything, she asked me to leave." His mouth shifted toward a smile, then shifted away. "Practically threw me out the door." He put an ankle on one knee and grasped it with his hand.

Keeley walked over and sat beside him. "I assume that's a new experience for you—being asked to leave?"

He slanted her a gaze, his serious eyes—as usual—a curious mix of somber and heat. "Dinah just needs time to think things over. Make up her own mind about what to do."

"Do you think she'll tell the truth?"

"I think she'll do what she thinks is right for Dinah."

"That's not an answer."

"It's the best I've got." He let go of the ankle he was holding and put both feet on the floor. "She'll call. Eventually. If she doesn't, I'll call her. We'll take it from there."

Keeley rested her arm along the back of the settee and shifted so she could face him directly. She had to get what was bothering her out in the open, because if she didn't, either her brain would burst or her heart would break. It was a lose/lose situation either way. "About Mary . . ."

His gaze met hers, quiet and waiting.

"If what she told Christiana was true—and I'm not saying it was—and there was some kind of, uh, situation and she did *accidentally* . . . kill Christiana's father . . ." She rubbed her cheek, hesitated, swam in her own guilt, then pushed forward. "The thing is, Mary wasn't a big woman. She'd have needed help to, uh, get rid of the body." Lord, she sounded like a third-rate detective.

"Yes, I think she would have."

"And that would mean someone else was involved."

"Yes, it would."

Keeley's heart did an odd, irregular thump in her chest. She attributed it to disloyalty, the discomfort of assuming aloud Mary had done something wrong. Or maybe it was nervousness about how Gus would react if she were honest about her thoughts. It felt most like an bad omen, a jungle drum warning of more trouble ahead. "Dinah, maybe? That would make sense of her denying she had a daughter—and her support of Mayday House all these years."

"Possibly, but not necessarily." Gus studied her, and she swore he saw her heart pounding behind her ribs. His face impassive, he said, "There were other people in the house at the time."

The blood drained from Keeley's face, turned leaden in her chest. "You're not—you can't be implying—" She shot to her feet. "You think my mother was involved?"

He stood. "I'm not implying anything. And I'm not accusing. I'm saying she was here. Period."

"My mother had nothing to do with this. Whatever went on here was between Mary and Dinah. If you don't believe that, you can. get out of this house. Now." Her voice rose on the last word and more bubbled up under it. "I won't listen to you malign my mother. I won't!"

"Settle down, it's not—"

"I will not settle down. My mother was a good—very holy—woman. Understand? She made one mistake.

An error in judgment. She got involved with the wrong man, and he left her—pregnant and alone in a strange country. She spent her life making up for what she considered her *sin*. She prayed, took care of me—loved me!—and went to Mass every day. She lived in grace and she died in grace." She looked away, her face hot, her mind now so alive with heat and sparks, she couldn't form any more words.

How dare he . . . How dare he . . .

The silence in the room hung thick and heavy, suspended perilously between her closed mind and Gus's tightly closed mouth.

"Then you were lucky," he said in a low voice. "My mother was a crackhead who sold her daughter to her drug dealer."

His flat statement entered the room like the eye of a hurricane—bringing an instant, numbing calm.

Keeley, still hot with temper, her mind still tumbling over her defense of her mother, didn't immediately grasp his horrifyingly raw admission. If there were words to be said, she couldn't find them.

She watched Gus draw in a long breath and run a hand along his scar, as he always did when he was thinking. "Look, I wasn't accusing your mother of anything," he said. "Nor am I accusing Mary or Dinah. I don't know what happened here. Neither do you. But we won't find out unless we face the facts. *All the facts.*"

She heard what he said, but it was the words that came before that made her legs rubbery and unreliable. She sat back down on the settee and looked up at him. "Tell me," she said, "about your sister."

"I don't talk about it."

"You just did."

His mouth tightened to form a rigid line, as fixed on his face as the uneven scar running along his jaw.

She waited, her breath unmoving in her throat.

"April was nine," he said. "I was twelve. I didn't know it happened—how it happened—until it was too late. Connie—"

"Connie?"

"Our mother."

"Oh." Using her given name instead of the mother honorific was understandable, she thought, giving him a necessary degree of separation. From what she'd come to know of August Hammond, separation— apartness—was important to him. He wore solitude like a shroud.

"She told me April had gone to stay with a girl-friend of hers." His lips twisted. "Aunty Rosa." He glanced away. "I bought it." He stood over her, per-fect in his stillness, his face set in the guarded con-centration demanded when calling on ugly memories. "I found out what happened when I learned I was the next to go. I heard Connie whin-ing to her latest boyfriend. Not about what she'd done with April, but that she was getting less money for me." He stopped. "The guy she was with told her she shouldn't be surprised because, not only was I too old, which was risky, but"—his face, though it didn't seem possible, tightened even more—"'girls always brought more.'"

"Dear God."

He looked at her, his expression savage. "Appar-ently God had other business, because I was due to be picked up that night."

"What about your father? Where was he?"

"Steve had died of an overdose six months before.

He was no screaming hell as a dad, but looking back, I guess he was the watered-down glue that held our fine little family together. Occasionally working, occasionally straight and sober. When he died, Connie skidded downhill fast, drugging out twenty-four/seven." He looked at her with eyes bleakly ironic. "Addiction has no bottom, you know. Except getting dead."

"What did you do? Where did you go?"

"I grabbed what I thought April and I would need, and took off. I knew the dealer. I'd seen him often enough. I figured I'd find him, get April back, and head out," he said and shook his head. "Had no idea where."

"And?"

"I found the guy, all right, but all I got for my trouble was a matched set of black eyes and assorted contusions." He paused. "He told me to get lost, then helped me along by throwing me down two flights of stairs.

"I went back twice more. Got more of the same. The last time I paid him a visit, he was dead. Had a hole in his chest the size of a dinner plate."

Again silence claimed the office. Keeley was lost in the images of a boy in a desperate and futile search for his sister. The silence was broken by the sound of the hall clock chiming eleven. When it stopped its chime, she said, "You never found her, did you?"

"No."

"And you never stopped looking."

"No." He raked his fingers through his hair, looked angry, then dropped his gaze from hers. "Sidetracked along the way, but no, I never stopped looking."

She hesitated before adding, "And you're not . . .

concerned—after all these years—about what you might find?" Keeley didn't want to think about what might happen to a girl taken under those circumstances.

His eyes sparked, much as she expected her own had when he'd mentioned the possibility of her mother's involvement in Mayday's dreadful secret.

"No. Whatever happened, she's my sister."

Keeley frowned when her next thought came, but she didn't think about not verbalizing it. "Is that why you stayed with Dinah? So you could search for April?"

Her question chilled the room, and Gus didn't look inclined to answer it. Finally he shook his head. "No. I stayed with Dinah for other reasons."

Not enough. "Such as?"

"You really want to know?"

In for a penny . . . She nodded.

"I stayed with Dinah for money, for sex, and to get off the goddamned street. That woman saved my sorry ass." His eyes were unflinching when they met hers, challenging. "Dinah is rich and generous. I took advantage of both."

"I don't believe that."

"Most people believe what they want to believe. Especially when the truth isn't pretty."

Keeley knew he was back to her mother, the ugliness at Mayday House.

"It's late." He headed for the door. "I'm going to check the house and go to bed." His cold eyes met hers. "If you're smart, you'll leave this"—he gestured at the files on her desk—"and do the same."

End of conversation.

Keeley watched him go. The idea of Dinah, or

anyone else, saving August Hammond refused to play through, although one thing was clear, in Gus's mind he owed Dinah Marsden. He might not like it, but something in him wouldn't let him escape it, which made it unbelievable he'd come here on behalf of her ex-husband. It didn't make sense, because there wasn't a chance Gus would turn on Dinah, for Hagan . . . or her.

Yet, she trusted him.

She'd always thought herself a realist, pragmatic to a fault, but maybe Gus was right. Maybe she was one of those people who believed what they wanted to believe, when the truth was too frightening to contemplate.

She walked to her desk, sat down, and pulled the stack of files toward her, determined to work, but her mind refused to leave the enigma that was Gus.

Keeley didn't know much about men, but she had a sense for souls, and she sensed his was a good one; torn and tattered, perhaps, but whose wasn't?

She tapped her chin with a pen she'd picked up.

Then again, maybe she was seeing what she wanted to see, because she was starting to feel something for him—which wouldn't do either of them any good, of course. No future in it.

She sat back in her chair, wooden and oddly regretful. Women thoughts, she decided, invading along with attraction and the insecurities that came with it. On the attraction issue, she was definitely pragmatic.

Gus moved in a different female-sphere than the one she inhabited, a sphere populated with beautiful, sophisticated, confident women—women who wore designer clothes, drank five-dollar cups of coffee, and knew exactly what they wanted.

Confident, Keeley was. But sophisticated? She wasn't sure what the word meant, but she'd bet it was the polar opposite to a woman who'd gone from a nun's habit to the khaki and cotton fashion of Africa. A woman dedicated to a rundown women's refuge in a small town.

Okay, so she liked the man, liked the way his mouth felt on hers, liked the way his kiss took her breath away. It was irrelevant. All of it.

They were mismatched, out of sync, and psychically incompatible. All the kisses in the world wouldn't change that—because, like it or not, she'd have to watch those shifting loyalties of his.

They were too much like her own for comfort.

She opened a file and set to work.

CHAPTER 14

Gus walked the perimeter of Mayday House three times. Still edgy, he went through the hedge to St. Ivan's graveyard. It was a fairly decent night, no rain, just the ever-present threat of it embedded in the scudding clouds overhead. But tonight they were thin clouds, and few, so the moon had some say in the night's lighting, giving it a pewter tone with lots of murky shadow. A horror-meister's delight.

Looking at the haphazard headstones and grave markers, all of them slate dull under the moon's scant light, he had a flash of envy for the people resting under them. Out of reach of their demons and their anger. Their lust.

Fuck!

He should have kept his mouth shut, damn it!

He'd talked more about his life in the last hour than he had in his whole rotten life. Rubbing the back of his neck, he stared down sightlessly at the grave at his feet and found an unsettling truth.

He wanted Keeley Farrell. More than he'd ever wanted a woman in his life before, and it wasn't about sex—that he'd handle. It was more—and it scared the crap out of him.

He was losing it, and at the worst possible time. He had a chance, a real chance, of finding April, and he was screwing it up by spilling his guts to the last woman on earth he should be talking to about it. What had Hagan called her? The keeper of the keys. Yeah. She was that all right. The keys to finding April.

He had to get the information he needed. If it implicated Dinah, and after her reactions today, he was damn sure it would, he'd figure a way to handle it. Dinah was sure as hell guilty of something; he just didn't know what. The proof was buried in Mayday House—either in those endless files, or six feet under those weeds in the backyard.

His gut constricted, and he walked a few paces along the path between the graves. Keeley was right about one thing; it would take more than one woman to deal with the dead weight of a man's body. There had to be an accomplice. Keeley's mother? Maybe, but a real long shot; she had no stake in the game.

For now his money was on Dinah.

Why else would she have adopted Christiana out illegally? Paid off Mary Weaver all these years? And why did she still lie about having a kid? He shook his head. Hell, she'd even lied about where she was born. And in his experience lies didn't sleep alone.

All speculation, Hammond. You've got no damn proof, and no way are you going to hang the woman before you do.

The trouble was, no matter how it turned out, Keeley got hurt.

His chest loaded up with lead, and he rolled his head to ease the tension in his neck. Too damn late to develop a conscience. And a damned inconvenient time to go juvenile, get some weird goddamn crush on a nun.

Light exploded against his eyes.

He squinted against it.

"I'll assume the best, that you're not here to dig up the blessed dead for some nefarious scientific purpose." The voice came from behind the light. "But may I inquire as to your purpose here?"

The light didn't move; neither did the state of Gus's blindness in the face of it. "Your graves are safe from me. I'm staying at Mayday House." He lifted a hand to shade his eyes. "Gus Hammond."

"Ah, yes, Keeley mentioned you."

That surprised him, and while he was curious enough to wonder what she'd said, he didn't ask. "You are?"

The pierce of the light hit the ground, swept the grass on the grave between them. "Father Glen Barton. I run this show," he said. "Although it doesn't generally draw a crowd after midnight."

Gus shook his hand, then scanned the dreary yard, the tilting gravestones. "I can understand why."

His remark brought a brief chuckle. "Now that we've ascertained you're not a grave robber, what brings you here at this—pardon the expression—ungodly hour of the night?"

"A late-night walk. I'll be moving along."

"Fine woman, Keeley Farrell."

"Excuse me?"

The voice, as Gus's eyes adjusted, now had a tall, dark shape surrounding it. It went on, "She was a fine nun, too. Or so I'm told."

"I'm sure."

"Good to think someone of her caliber will be running Mayday again. The world needs havens like that—and this graveyard. Good reminders."

Gus bit on the last one. "Reminders of what?"

He turned his light on the gravestone between them. "That no matter what route we take, we all end up in the same place. Like the fine lady resting here."

The name on the gravestone was Aileen Farrell. In the dark he hadn't noticed. Or had he?

"On that upbeat thought," Gus said, "I'm out of here." He turned to go; talking to priests in the black of midnight graveyards wasn't his idea of fun. Plus he had a cellar full of records waiting for him. Keeley was probably already down there. He sure as hell didn't expect her to take his advice and go to bed.

"Son?"

Gus turned back. Being called *son* was a new experience.

"Keeley may not be a nun anymore, but she's an exceptional woman," Barton said, his voice low but firm. "She deserves every respect—has earned it. It would be wise to remember that and to treat her accordingly. Which means none of this modern-day sleep-and-run stuff."

"By sleep you mean—"

"Sex," he said without missing a beat. "And now, my fatherly admonishment done, it's bed for me. Come over sometime. I serve a remarkable brandy." With the last he was gone, leaving Gus in the graveyard to think on an exceptional woman and the alternatives to sleep-and-run.

By the time Gus got back to the house, it sat in darkness. He cursed when he noticed Keeley had left the back door open for him. She knew he had keys. Damn it, the woman refused to take the security of Mayday seriously.

Back in his room he took a quick shower, then pulled on some sweats. His plan was to head back down to the paper trove in the cellar and restack a few more boxes. His mistake was stretching out on the bed after his shower, because when he next looked at his watch, it was after two. He debated going back to sleep, leaving the cellar until the morning, but his body refused to cooperate. It was awake and edgy.

Ignoring his shoes and not owning slippers, he pulled on some white sport socks and let himself out his bedroom door and into the darkened hall as quietly as possible. He paused outside Keeley's bedroom, then moved on.

There'd be no more fantasies tonight. The sooner he got what he wanted, the sooner he'd get out of here. Best for both of them if he hit the road sooner, rather than later. Like the priest said, the woman was exceptional—definitely the commitment type.

He was a few steps from the cellar door when he heard it—a shuffling, scraping sound. Something being shoved across a hard floor.

Gus stopped dead. If it were Keeley, there'd be constant light spilling from under the cellar door. Instead there was only the occasional slash of yellow. A flashlight.

He considered his advantage. Whoever was down there was trapped. Maybe armed. Trapped and armed did not make a winning combination.

He padded back to his room, got what he needed.

A minute later he was at the cellar door, easing it open. He heard someone crying.

He flipped on the light, and the ancient cellar came into the whitewashed view provided by the new and much brighter light bulb he'd put in a couple of days ago.

"What the hell . . ." He sheathed the knife, felt it slide safely home over his wrist.

Erica Stark was sitting on a box, clutching her stomach and weeping like a child. Her eyes, when they shot to his, were red rimmed, hot but dead looking, like zombie eyes in a horror movie. She got to her feet, scrambling upward awkwardly, one hand pushing from behind.

She looked flat-out terrified.

"What are you doing down here?" he asked, keeping his voice low. He put his hands on his hips.

"I, uh, couldn't sleep." She brushed at her cheeks, her eyes. "I was just . . . looking around." She was in silk pajamas and wearing a dark blue velvet robe, tied high over her belly.

"It's two in the morning. Hell of a time to be 'looking around' a crappy old basement."

She didn't answer, but her rapid, harsh breathing was clearly audible in the silence of the cellar. When she straightened as if to confront him, he spied the mess of papers she'd obviously been sorting through strewn across the top of the boxes.

He looked at the files. "What are you looking for?"

"Good question." Keeley's voice came from behind him. He turned to see her take the last step, then come to stand beside him.

She wore exactly the kind of nightgown he'd expect her to wear, flowered pink flannel, on the big

side of large, and ugly as hell. A man could make a
life's work out of figuring out what was under it. It
maddened him that it wouldn't be his job. His eyes
dropped to her feet. Bare. With bright pink nail
polish. That jolted him. He felt like a kid who'd
found a silver dollar surprise in a birthday cake.

Dollar or not, she shouldn't be here; for what it
was worth, Mayday Security was his job. Annoyed
now—or maybe frustrated—he glared down at her.
"Don't you ever nod off?"

She ignored him. Her attention fixed on Erica, she
took some steps to get closer. "What *are* you doing
down here, Erica?" she said, tilting her head. "Are
you all right? Are the babies all right?"

Stark was right as rain as far as Gus could see, and
nosing around for a reason. At Keeley's question, the
woman's eyes darted to the stairway, gauging the possibility of escape. Her face was drained, rigid with
confused tension.

Gus took a step back and sat on the stairs, making
flight impossible. Might as well get to the bottom of
this now, rather than later.

Keeley touched Erica's hair, then stroked it. "It's all
right. Whatever it is, you can tell us." She stroked
again.

Erica shook her head and stepped away from
Keeley. When the tears started flowing again, she
reached into her robe pocket—and pulled out a gun.

Keeley stumbled backward.

Gus shot to his feet. *Jesus!*

"Stay away from me. Both of you." She ran the back
of her free hand over her cheek, her mouth. "I
didn't want this to happen, but I don't—I don't
have a choice."

Keeley, whose face had gone gray the second the gun came out, looked at her openmouthed for a moment. "You've got a gun," she said, stating the obvious.

Erica swallowed. "And I'll use it. Don't think I won't."

Gus stepped forward and pulled Keeley away from the muzzle of the gun. She moved awkwardly as if mesmerized by the cold steel in Erica's hand. When he had her tucked at least halfway behind him, he put out his hand. "Give me the gun before you hurt someone—and that includes yourself." He didn't expect she'd hand it over. No one ever did. But he needed think time. How the hell did a man defend himself and the woman he lov—

Gus's blood surged. Everything stopped. For a lifelong split second his brain was more paralyzed by the word forming in his mind than by the Glock pointed at his chest. His thinking stumbled.

He righted it, called back his current problem; how to defend himself and Keeley against a pregnant woman—without hurting her. He had no fucking idea. Erica's condition might be delicate, but the 9mm in her hand wasn't. He had to do something and he had to do it fast.

"I'll give you the gun when she"—she wagged the gun in Keeley's direction and Gus's heart stopped a second time—"tells me what I need to know." Her voice had steadied somewhat, as had the gun she now held with both hands.

Gus felt the brush of Keeley's shoulder against his arm when she stepped from behind him to face Stark.

Her face might be gray as smoke, but her back was straight, and her eyes possessed a serene calm when she rested them on Stark. Drummed-up courage. He recognized it. "Give Gus the gun, and do it now. There's no place for violence in Mayday House. Do you understand?"

The cool authority in Keeley's voice seemed to get Erica's attention; then she laughed. "Now who's lying, sister?" she said. "Mary Weaver killed my father in this fucking house. That's as violent as it gets."

Gus stared at her. This was sure as hell breaking news, because either two men were killed in Mayday House, or this flash meant Erica and Christiana were sisters.

"And you know this how?" Gus asked, even though he'd guessed the answer.

"The old bat called my brother." Her lips twisted. "She wanted his *abandoned children* to forgive her. Said she didn't want to die with us thinking our father had deserted us. I guess she thought it was better we know she killed the bastard."

Keeley's face went even whiter, but she let the shock pass, didn't falter. "I don't understand. Why didn't you just say so when you came here? Why didn't you call the police?"

"Because the police don't pay. Our father didn't do a hell of a lot for us while he was alive, so if there's a silver lining in his death, we intend to find it." She looked distressed when she added, "*I* intend to find it."

"You want someone to pay you . . . for your father's death?" Keeley said, sounding confused. Not getting it.

Gus got it, all right, but then he was more familiar with greed than Keeley. More familiar with sin.

Erica focused on Gus. "Weaver said we had a sister born here, at Mayday. And where there's a sister, there's a mother—a mother who likely was involved in the murder. Someone who'll pay to keep that ugly little fact from anyone who might give a damn. Like the cops."

Keeley glared at her. "You're talking about blackmail."

"And who is this mysterious mother?" Gus asked.

"The million-dollar question and the one you"—she swung the gun toward Keeley, desperate again—"are going to answer. I want the 1970 records, and I want them now."

Gus's stomach clenched, and he released the blade back into his hand, palmed it, his gut a hard coil.

Keeley looked down at the gun, then up into Erica's face. "Death doesn't scare me, Erica, so threatening me with it won't do you any good. And I won't be party to blackmail." She stopped. "So put the gun away and we'll talk things out."

"Talk things?—" She looked wild now, as if she were the one trapped, the one staring down the muzzle of a loaded gun. "You don't understand—"

Keeley took a step forward. "I understand you're not a killer, that you're a pregnant woman with lives other than her own at stake. I understand you're not going to fire that gun. That if you do, whatever plans you've made for your life and"—she looked pointedly at Erica's distended stomach—"for your children's lives will end when you pull the trigger."

Erica rested one hand on her pregnancy, and the tears started again. Gus knew she couldn't see clearly, that this was his moment.

"You don't understand," she said again. "He has my brother. He has Paul! I can't let him hurt Paul. I can't!"

"What are you talking about? Who has Paul?" Gus

asked, aware of her rising panic, a panic making her dangerously volatile.

"Mace. Some guy named Mace. He knows about the sister, told me to get the information on the mother or he'd kill him. Two days"—Gus saw her throat close over a deep breath—"he said two days, or he'll kill Paul." Her voice turned shrill, her eyes darting and frantic; then she leveled them on Keeley. Wide, crazed eyes. "You have to tell me. You have to." She raised the gun, aimed it at Keeley's face.

Gus threw the knife.

CHAPTER 15

The sounds . . .

The whir of steel slicing through air, the sharp clink of metal on metal, the even sharper intake of Erica's breath.

The soundless . . .

The splatter of blood against a rounded tummy, the movement of bare feet over cement floor, flannel shifting against her legs as Keeley rushed toward Erica.

"My God! What did you do?" Her gaze shot to Gus as she reached for Erica's hand.

"What I had to." He walked to where his knife had fallen and picked it up—the gun, too. The six-inch throwing blade he slipped back into his wrist grip. Wearing sweats, he had no place to put the Glock, so he dangled it at his side.

Erica looked at him, her eyes stunned wide. "You could have killed me. Killed my . . . babies."

"No. I couldn't."

Keeley shot him an unreadable glance, then turned her attention to Erica's bleeding hand. He heard her exhale loudly. "It's just a small cut. Some antiseptic and a Band-Aid should take care of it."

Erica continued to stare at Gus with a look of utter incomprehension. Keeley touched her face, then tugged her chin, forcing their eyes to meet. "Are you all right? No pains?" She rested her hand on Erica's stomach. "Quiet?"

Erica closed her eyes, nodded. But she didn't look fine. She looked as though she'd keel over any minute. Gus looked warily at her stomach. He didn't know much about pregnant women, but he knew enough to know shock could bring on labor. Hell!

"Let's get you upstairs, take care of that cut." Keeley urged her toward the stairs, while looking at Gus as if he were an axe murderer.

"No." Erica shook her head. "I can't. Paul needs me. You don't understand, he's all . . . I have." She pulled away from Keeley, damn near toppled over.

Gus steadied her until Keeley could get a better hold. "You want to help your brother," he said. "You do what the lady says."

"Paul will be okay," Keeley said, shooting another glance toward Gus, this one less hostile. "We'll figure something out, won't we, Gus?"

Gus didn't give a rat's ass about Erica's brother, but he agreed anyway.

With one arm around a visibly trembling Erica, Keeley gestured angrily toward the Glock in his hand. "Get rid of that filthy thing."

He'd get rid of it, all right, when this mess around Mayday House was over—a mess with the pattern of a dropped egg. He'd thought the Dinah, Christiana, Hagan trio was bad enough, but now . . .

According to Erica, there was a new player in the

game, another vulture circling Mayday House, a man named Mace. And Gus intended to make his acquaintance at the first opportunity.

But for now, all he could do was follow Keeley's pink toenailed feet up the basement stairs.

Keeley's mouth was dry and she was cold, shivering as though she were naked in the January Arctic. Half an hour of listening to Erica, crazed with worry about her brother and the 'family business,' while trying to keep her own nerves from jumping out of her skin, had exhausted her.

God, Erica Stark was a pornographer!

Keeley didn't want to judge, but—

Knowing the *but* was the lead into the judgment she was trying to avoid, she put it on hold. She'd think about Erica later, tomorrow when her head was clear, and she could make sense of things. Right now she had to get out of here.

She looked at the sleeping woman. Her brow was deeply furrowed, and one arm rested outside the covers, its hand fisted. Keeley hoped she hadn't made a mistake, assuring her again and again that she—and Gus—would keep her brother safe.

Certain that Erica was in a deep sleep, Keeley lifted her fisted hand and tucked it under the quilt. She stood on her unreliable legs and briefly leaned against the bed for support.

She had to get to her room. Fast. Needed to be alone.

She made her way to the door, stopped when her hand closed over the knob, and shut her eyes against the smothering feeling creeping over her like a dank fog. Her heart quivering in her breast, she tightened her grip on the latch, ignored the palpitations, the tingling in her arms, and opened her door.

Damn it to hell! She wasn't a weak-kneed, useless fool. She could control this. She could. It might have got the better of her a few times in Africa, but not here. Not at home.

God, all I have to do is get down a few stairs. Can you lend a hand?

Erica was in pain and Keeley ached with it, had absorbed it, then trembled with it. Damn it! She didn't have time for a bout of self-indulgent, quivering panic. Whether she liked Erica or not, she needed her, and her babies needed her. She had to be strong, face the evil encroaching on Mayday House. Tonight that evil had lurked in the black shaft of Erica's gun, disabling her, pushing her mind into the blank white of fear.

Like before.

She closed the door on Erica's room and stepped into the hall, rested there a moment, getting her bearings.

When she saw Gus standing at the top of the stairs, she knew he'd been waiting for her, and the heat of embarrassment warmed her neck, made her try to straighten. She didn't want to be seen like this, weak-kneed and wobbly.

Without a word, Gus had helped her get Erica up the stairs and into bed; then just as wordlessly he'd left her to calm the distraught woman, soothe her as best she could, and make promises she wasn't at all sure she could keep.

Now he stood in front of her, stone still, his shadowed gaze sliding over her, smooth and intense—

as if he were a doctor studying a complex X-ray. "You okay?"

Her throat was so tight she couldn't speak, but she managed a nod. He'd think she was crazy.

She pushed away from the door, took a couple of steps, then stopped, focused on clearing her head and fighting her body's weak-muscled urge to let go and crumple to the floor.

"I don't think you are okay." Gus walked to where she stood, leaning like an understuffed doll against the wall. "Put your arm around my waist." He pulled her to his side. Too busy battling back her panic demons, she didn't fight him. Didn't want to fight him.

He was strong, and solid, and with each step down the stairs, their bodies shifted and rubbed against each other, the friction warm and reassuring.

She didn't know whether to be angry at him for throwing a knife, or grateful he'd saved her life. Whether or not Erica would have pulled the trigger, she'd never know, and wasn't sure she wanted to. In this moment, she was just grateful for Gus's strength, the heat of him seeping into her cold bones.

She stumbled on the last stair and leaned into Gus to keep from falling, her fingers curling around his belt.

"Easy, I've got you." He pulled her closer.

Keeley tried not to tremble and quake, to fight the dizziness, but she was losing the battle. She had to lie down. Curl into a ball. Hold herself together until it passed. She hoped it wouldn't be days—like the last time.

"Here we go." He opened the door to her room and helped her into her bed with the same deft movements he'd used with Erica earlier. "This happen often?" He reached over her for a second pillow and put it under her head.

Keeley tugged the ancient quilt up to her neck and shivered. "Not lately," she murmured, still cold despite the heavy quilt. "And it's not nearly as bad."

He turned on the bedside lamp. "Delayed stress. It's not every day you stare down a gun barrel." He picked up the glass on her bedside table, took it to the bathroom, and filled it with water. "Here." He placed his hand at the back of her head, lifted it, and held the glass to her mouth.

She sipped, then sagged back against the pillow and snuggled deep under the covers. God, she was a wimp. She couldn't stop the shakes. He went back to the bathroom, returned with a damp facecloth. When he touched her cheek with the coolness of it, she took it from his hand—or tried to. "I can do it. Thanks."

For a second both of them held onto the cloth; then Gus let go. He sat on the edge of the bed, and she felt his hip against her thigh. "Can I get you anything else?"

"No. You can go now." She sounded ungrateful, dismissive, but couldn't help it. Her heart pounded scarily in her chest, and unless she wanted him to literally see her sweat—it always came with these attacks— she'd best get him gone. "And thanks . . . again." With that she covered her whole face with the cloth and closed her eyes, intent on breathing slowly instead of pumping air through her lungs as if she were tuning a pipe organ. Most times it worked, the breathing business.

"I'm not going anywhere."

His words filtered through the damp facecloth.

"Until you're asleep," he added.

"Sleep will be a long time coming," she said from behind the cloth. "I'm okay. Really," she added.

Breathe, Keeley, breathe. You'll be fine. Everything will be fine. She took another breath, and except for her throat constricting as though it were in a noose, and the prickling sensation in her arms, she felt a little better.

Gus took the terry cloth from her face and gave her a serious scan. "You're a mess. *Really.*"

The light hurt, and she pulled the cloth back over her eyes. "Mayday House is a mess. Me, I'm all right. So go."

He put his hand on her forehead, smoothed her hair back, and then said, "Roll over."

"What?"

"Get on your stomach. Either you do it, or I do it for you." He tugged the cloth from her hand.

"I don't think I—" Actually she didn't know what she thought. Her stupid panic episode was swamped by her body's unexpected—and currently indecipherable—reaction to the man looming over her bed in the middle of the night telling her what to do, as if it were an normal occurrence.

"Just do it. I know what I'm doing." His tone was softer, more cajoling, but no less determined. "I won't hurt you, and I won't touch anything you don't want touched."

She set her eyes on his, and he didn't blink. Neither did she. What she did was roll over.

The next second the quilt was down to her hips, exposing nothing but her thick flannel nightgown. "Shift closer to me." Using both hands, he gripped her waist and moved her toward the edge of the bed.

"Concentrate on your breathing," he instructed.

"Relax your arms." He positioned her arms at her sides, inches from her body, then returned his hands to her waist, sliding them up her back to her shoulders in one long, firm glide. Gripping and kneading her shoulders with strong fingers, he pulled down, released, pulled down and released, before sliding his hands again to her lower back. This time when he started back up, he used more force, probing her spine with his thumbs and applying pressure to her sides and back with strong, expert fingers. Then the neck again, easy, rhythmic . . . Her eyes drifted closed.

Dear God, it was heaven.

It had been so long since she'd been touched.

"The breathing, remember? Deep. As deep as you can. In. Out. Concentrate. Good."

Keeley did what she was told, matched her breathing to the rhythm in his hands. His amazing hands.

"You're doing great. Keep it up."

Why was he whispering? She tried to open her eyes, but they felt too heavy to bother with.

She felt his hand stroke her hair, his fingers run along her cheek. He said something else, something about real massage needing skin; then she was gone.

Keeley woke with a start, sitting abruptly upright and looking at the clock. Past four-thirty. She'd slept an hour, maybe more.

"Feeling better?" Gus's voice came from the darkness beside her bed.

"You're still here," she said, the words as unnecessary as her hand flying to her throat and closing the open collar of her gown. He was only a shadow in the chair he'd pulled up to the bedside—a very still shadow. She couldn't see his face, but she knew his eyes were on her. "We should talk to Erica, decide what to do," she said, then added, "Did you know that Erica and her brother make . . . adult films?"

"Uh-huh."

"You checked on her?" She guessed it made sense he would, given that he was in the security business. "You didn't tell me."

"Would it have mattered? Didn't make her less pregnant."

"No, I suppose not. But I should call Christiana, let her know she has . . . family." Although Keeley knew she'd be underwhelmed by her new relatives—or at least the business they were in.

"Erica can wait. So can Christiana. Tomorrow's soon enough."

"It is tomorrow." She let go of her collar and swung her body to sit on the bed, facing him. The bed was an old four-poster, too high for her to sit and have her feet touch the floor. She let them dangle, shoving her hair off her face. "I should go check on her."

"I already did. She's sleeping sound enough. All you'll do is wake her up."

Her eyes, losing the last of sleep, grew accustomed to the dim light provided by a watery moon seeping through the clouds, and the room came into focus. A less shadowy Gus emerged, sitting comfortably in her wicker chair, his long legs stretched out in from of him. He was staring at her feet.

"Pink nail polish," he said. "You surprised me."

"That knife from nowhere surprised me. Where did you learn to do that? Better yet, why?"

"Survival. My father gave me my first knife, taught me how to use it. I was seven."

"You could have hurt Erica."

"No, I couldn't, but she could've hurt you."

"She's pregnant, for heaven's sake."

"She had a gun pointed at your face."

"I don't want weapons in Mayday House. Knives or guns." She gave him a pointed look. "I don't want anyone hurt."

"Neither do I," he said. "Now if we're done agreeing with each other, I'll ask again. How are you feeling?"

As agreements went, his had the solidity of smoke, but Keeley knew the end of a subject when she saw one. No point in pressing her point right now, but if he thought she was going to let this go, he was dead wrong. What she'd do was wait until her wits were less scattered, her mind less cottoned with sleep.

"I'm fine." She paused. "Your massage did the trick. You're good with your hands."

His mouth twitched. "So I've been told."

Keeley felt herself redden, but knew he wouldn't see it in the dimness of the room. "I meant in a professional sense."

Another twitch of his lips.

She blushed deeper. "You're enjoying this, aren't you?"

"You mean your discomfort with my past career choice?"

"Yes."

"No. I'm more caught up in my own confusion when I think of yours."

"My being a nun," she stated, unable to say he wasn't alone with his confusion. Despite the years she had tried, she'd never fit the mold. Mary Weaver had been right all along. *Your calling is to do good in this world, girl, but you? A nun? Won't suit you at all.* Turned out she was right, even though Keeley's decision to leave her order left her feeling a miserable failure. "I thought it was the right choice for me. It wasn't."

"Marc? Was he right for you?"

"Yes, he was." His question made her hesitate. "But the truth is things weren't feeling right for me even before Marc. I wasn't cut for the cloth." A cloth woven of poverty, chastity, and obedience. The poverty was okay, and she'd coped with the chastity issue all right—until Marc, but the obedience? There she had messed up.

"What cloth are you cut for?"

She eyed him. "What makes you so nosy all of a sudden?"

"Interested, not 'nosy,'" he said. "And it comes with the job," he said, adding, "The panic attacks. When did they start?"

She slid off the bed, slipped on the thick terry robe she'd draped over one of its posts. Pulling the sash tight to her waist, she turned back to him. "First off, it's none of your business, and second, they're not panic attacks—at least not like they were."

"How were they?"

Lord, she'd never known a man so still—so relentless. "You're not going to let this go, are you?"

"No."

CHAPTER 16

Keeley wasn't afraid to face her weakness, just reluctant. Yet there was something in her wanting to get her story out. Whether Gus Hammond was the person to hear it, she didn't know. While she wasn't sure he would understand, something in her told her he wouldn't judge. It was enough.

"The last six months in the Sudan were tough." She closed her eyes a moment. "So much death. When the militia stormed into the villages, they didn't care who they killed—or how. People were . . . butchered. Men, women, children, it didn't matter to them. It was like a frenzy. Everyone was afraid, no one felt safe—and no one knew when or if their village would be hit next." She took a few steps away from him, then back. "Our camp, close to the Chad border, had been lucky. But the luck didn't last."

She rubbed her upper chest, her heart. "They came at sunup. The first thing we heard was the sound of horses, then the yelling. Gunfire . . ." She licked her suddenly dry lips. "They started shooting, first into the air, then . . . everything, the villagers, their homes, their animals . . . just shooting."

Keeley massaged her temples. She'd never forget the din. The wailing and screams. The glare of sunlight on the bridles of the horses. The shiny rifles spilling red death into the already-miserable refugee camp.

More bullets in the guns than stars in the sky.

She took a breath and went on, "Our hospital and sleeping tents were on the edge of the village. That gave us a little time, but in the end there was nothing to do but run and hide wherever you could. There were five patients in the hospital, an old man, a young girl who'd just given birth, her newborn, and two children. We, myself and two of the aid workers attached to Medics-At-Large, gathered them up, and along with the people streaming out of the village, ran—as my mother would have said, as if the devil himself was on our heels." She stopped. "Which in this case he was."

"You made it."

"Ashai, the new mother, died of hemorrhage, and over half the village was killed." She looked away, unable to stop the pain, the powerlessness, from washing over her. "But, yes, I made it."

"And came home."

"I stayed on for a while after the raid, but I couldn't sleep. Then the panic attacks started."

"How long had you been in Africa?"

"Not always Sudan, but on and off, almost seven years."

He whistled softly.

"When the directive came for me to come home, I didn't fight it." She looked at him directly, wanting him to understand. "Sudan didn't need another walking wounded," she said. "They were right to bring me home. The shape I was in, I was no use to anyone."

"That's what counts with you, isn't it? Being of use?"

If he looked at her with any more intensity, she'd turn to a heap of ash or a wash of tears. She didn't intend that to happen. "If you're asking if I aspire to change the world, right every injustice, and banish all sickness and evil from the face of the earth"—she swept her hand in a wide, purposely careless arc, anxious to lighten the mood, change the subject—"or if you're thinking my heroine of choice is Wonder Woman, she of the narrow waist and magic belt, you'd be wrong. I'm not that good, not that pious, and not that dedicated."

"That's how you see it." He shook his head.

"All I want to do is work in my little corner of the universe—Mayday House. If I can make it a decent, safe haven for women who need one, I'll be content."

"No plans to go back?"

"To Africa?" Her thoughts stumbled, then righted themselves. "No plans, but someday? Maybe. You don't walk away from Africa—it won't let you." She felt the sharp clutch in her chest, the ache there when she remembered the desperate suffering people of Darfur, her work there. "I left part of my heart there. With Marc . . . and others."

Gus looked at her a long time, but he didn't appear inclined to speak.

Curious and increasingly uncomfortable, she asked, "What are you thinking?"

He stood and walked up to her. "Not thinking exactly. More like wondering."

"About what?"

"About whether or not the part of your heart you brought home has room for something new. If it's up to another risk."

Suddenly wary, she asked, "Like what?"

He lifted her chin, forcing their gazes to meet. "Like me."

"I don't know what you're saying," Keeley said, too aware of his warm hand on her face, his dark eyes looking down at her. She couldn't move. It was as if someone had stolen into her dimly lit bedroom and nailed her feet to the floor.

"Not sure I know myself." He moved his thumb along her jaw, the gesture idle, his expression thoughtful. "We're the last two people on this earth who should come together. An ex-nun and an ex . . . gigolo, for want of a better word." He stopped, both his words and the movement of his thumb, then added, "But there's a sense of inevitability to it. To us." It didn't look as if the idea made him happy.

Keeley knew he was right, knew it was what she'd been feeling and fighting since she'd seen him that first day, standing in Mayday's front yard. Like a gift.

"Definitely inevitable." He whispered the last, his tone smoky when he bent to brush his mouth over hers. "But it ends with this."

When his lips met hers fully, they came softly, questioningly, as if he were tasting woman for the first time. As if he couldn't stop himself.

As if he were waiting for her to stop him, giving her time to say no.

The word refused to come.

Instead Keeley's breath surged and swirled in her lungs, even as her mind softened to a warm gray light.

She wanted to close her eyes, but it would mean
taking them from his, and she couldn't, too mesmerized watching the fire in his gaze deepen, from the
glow of rich brown to the darkness of desire.

Inevitable. Another word for fate.

She'd never believed in fate, things happening
under their own momentum. She believed in God's
hand and making things happen by hard work and
commitment. Good things didn't simply come to
you, you had to earn them.

But Gus had come to her, unplanned, unan-
nounced. And since that day, she'd known a growing tension she could neither identify nor still—as
if his presence had short-circuited her internal
wiring—and her will. He was too big, too beautiful,
too . . . dazzling for her.

Yet she leaned into him, drawn to his strong body,
the strength of his arms, his hard length warming her
deepest reaches. Making her want. Making her need.

Their gazes locked, and he slid his hands from her
face, down her neck, over her shoulders, and
grasped her waist, pulled her flush against him. He
stared down at her, silent, then kissed her forehead,
her cheeks, her ears, her throat. His every movement
fluid, insistent.

Finally he came back to her mouth, this time
boldly.

Keeley's neck curved backward, and she shifted
her body to get closer to him. Closer yet, desperate
to feel the hardness of him against her belly. She
knew this feeling, the power in it, what it could
mean, but she was unafraid—oddly serene. If that
was a word you could use in the middle of a sexual
maelstrom.

Gus pulled back, slowly, carefully, until he again held her face in his hands. Using his thumbs, he rubbed her cheeks. "Definitely stops here," he repeated, and she heard the rasp and harshness in his breathing.

His jaw tensed when he drew in another hard breath, looked heavenward. Dropping his hands from her face, he said, "I should have listened to Barton."

"Father Barton?"

"He told me to leave you alone."

"He said that?"

"Close to it." A wry smile briefly turned up his lips. "He said no 'sleep-and-runs.'"

"You talked to Father Barton about us?" The word *us* slipped into her surprise of its own free will. She had no desire to call it back, even if confusion at having Father Barton's name bandied around in her bedroom had set her brain on spin cycle.

"More like he talked to me."

"Too bad he didn't talk to me, I'd have talked back." She stopped, a clear thought rising from her mental disorder. "Is that what you want, Gus? A sleep-and-run?" A slice of her earlier panic came back.

He rubbed his scar, seemingly locked in his own thoughts and not happy with them. He walked a few paces away from her, then turned to look at her directly. "The answer to your question is no." He stopped. "When it comes to you, I'm not sure what I want." His lips turned grim. "Other than to toss you on that bed and make love to you until neither of us can breathe."

Her chest loosened, made room for her heart to pound.

He paced again; then, with a careful few feet between, he slid his hand to the back of his neck, kept it there. "And that's just for starters."

"And after the starter, what then?"

He took his hand from his neck, put both hands on his hips, and cursed to himself. "I don't believe we're having this conversation."

"You started it. I repeat, 'what then?'"

A fog of silence fell over the room.

"The 'then' part is having breakfast with you, *then* lunch, *then* dinner, *then* starting all over again." He paused. "The trouble with you, Farrell, is you're not the kind of woman a smart man walks away from. You're what's called a keeper."

"And that's a bad thing?"

"It is when you're not one of those 'smart' guys I mentioned." His voice firmed. "I was a paid escort, Keeley, paid for services in bed and out. Before that I was running from a murder charge. Before that I lived on the streets, under the name Gus Vanelleto, among others, doing whatever it took to survive. I've spent a lifetime getting by and getting laid. A woman like you isn't in my cards."

She let the last go. "A murder charge?" she said. "Tell me about it." When he didn't answer, she urged, "I want to know."

"It's ugly."

"Life can be that way," she countered.

"Okay." He paused, seemed to gather his thoughts. "When I was a kid, for a short time, I was in the care of Washington State. Specifically a woman called Belle Bliss, part-time prostitute, full-time child abuser. She made her living scamming Child Services. Alcoholic and stone mean, that woman. I owe her this."

He touched his scar, shook his head. "When she got herself shot in the head, and very dead as a result, the cops pegged me and a couple of other kids in the house as the murderers. We spent fifteen years running before they got the guy who did it."

"Where is he now?"

"In the room they'd reserved for me. Behind bars." He gave her a straight-on look. "That's not all of it. I took Josh."

"Who's Josh?"

His eyes settled on hers. "Josh is my . . . brother, or as close to it as you can get. They put him with Belle the day she was murdered. When he was dropped off, she parked him in a broken-down crib and left him there to soak his pants and scream for hours. He was a baby, for Christ's sake. Not even two years old. Hell, Belle was dead, lying in a pool of her own blood. It was too dangerous to leave him there— alone, crying in that damn crib, his face so hot . . . So I took him and left the state. Raised him."

"You raised a child?" She couldn't imagine it. "Why didn't you drop him off at a hospital, some place safe?"

"He'd already been '*dropped off,*'" he said, his tone hard, his face implacable. "At Belle's house of horrors."

"But you were a kid yourself, the risk . . ."

"The risk was me going to jail and Josh being dumped on someone else who didn't give a damn. Understand, I didn't exactly have a rosy experience with family life. What I knew was the streets. I figured I'd do as good a job looking out for him as anyone else. Make sure nobody messed with him." The last was said fiercely and with total conviction.

She had no response to it. "Where is Josh now?"

"When things finally got settled in Bliss's killing, I found out his mother had died of an overdose, that he had a grandmother and would never have been at Belle's place if she'd known about him. But she didn't know he even existed until weeks after the murder. By then Josh and I were on our way east. I didn't know anyone was looking for him. If I had—" He shrugged and left the thought unfinished. "Anyway, he's with her now. Staying with her and going to college. Straight As. A good kid."

Keeley heard the pride in his voice—and the love. "A lucky boy," she said. "All we need in this life is one person in our corner, one person to care. You gave that to Josh."

He stared at her. "Josh was the one good thing in a damned selfish life. It doesn't make up for the rest."

"Like being paid for sex? And not finding April."

His handsome, ravaged face hardened, and she sensed him pulling away from her. "That's a couple of them, yes."

"I see," she said, although she couldn't see at all. It would take years to unravel the mystery of Gus Hammond. She decided to start now. "What's your real name, Gus?"

He studied her for what seemed forever, then said, "Hanlon. August John Hanlon."

"Thank you," she said. "For that truth and the others." She fidgeted with the tie on her robe, sure of her heart, but not what it was telling her to do. She took a moment and steadied her breathing. "Father Barton was right—about the sleep-and-run thing. I wouldn't like it. But I like you. And the getting-tossed-on-the-bed-making-love scenario"—she closed her eyes—"I like that, too." She walked toward him, straightening her shoulders. "And while I'm not absolutely sure about the inevitability thing you talked about, I'd like to investigate the possibility."

"Jesus, Keeley, didn't you hear anything I said?" He touched his scar, but didn't take his eyes off her. "You have no idea what you're saying."

"I know exactly what I'm saying, and I know what I'm feeling"—she glanced out the window, still dark but with the glimmer of morning coming from the east—"and I know we're running out of time."

"This could go very wrong," he said, his voice low. He left a long silence before adding, "I could fall in love with you." He said the words ominously, as if he were foretelling the worst of disasters.

Keeley thought about his kiss, the intimate and dangerous truths he'd shared with her, and she smiled. "I think you already have, August John Hanlon. I think you already have."

Gus's heart hammered, and his neck went cold, then hot.

The man who thought he'd learned all there was to know about pleasuring women—even before the experienced, demanding, and highly sexed Dinah decided to make their arrangement exclusive—stood stalled in his tracks. Whatever degree of cool, of restraint, he'd ever possessed burned away, leaving the sorry equivalent of the inflamed mind of a teenaged boy who'd spotted his first naked breast. And so far Gus had only imagined that.

I can't do this. It's not right.

Keeley dropped her robe and once again the ugly pink flannel came into view. It might as well have been a thousand-dollar black negligee. Christ, hadn't he seen a thousand of them in his time? Always the trigger to strip off his clothes and get to work.

Not that it had been all that bad, all the time. He was young, he liked women, and he liked sex. Was damn good at it. And more often than not, the women were beautiful. And Dinah, for a time, incredible.

But nothing in his experience prepared him for Keeley Farrel with her pink toenails and her flannel nightgown.

He watched her walk to the bed and jump up to sit on its edge. When she saw he hadn't moved, she sat for a time, dangling her feet, then said, "You're not the only one who might fall in love here, you know. And I'm okay with that." Her voice was soft, and he heard her take a deep breath. "Truth is, I'm halfway there already, and I have been since the day you wanted to kick me out of my house."

He strode over to her, pulled her from the bed, and held her away from him, wanting to see her eyes. "You don't know what you're in for. I'll let you down."

"I'll take my chances." She touched his face. "The question is, will you?"

Gus looked at her, his gut drum-taut, and considered the chance she offered, the trust she offered— the hot want of her low in his groin.

She didn't know him, what he was capable of. Any way he looked at it, taking Keeley to bed now would be making love on a bed of nails.

Like Barton said, a sleep-and-run.

He could do that. Hell, it was a major part of his MO. What he didn't know was whether or not he could walk away. If he'd want to.

* * *

Christiana lay on her back, unmoving, on the king-sized bed, her naked body damp, slowly cooling from the fire of morning lovemaking.

The hotel room, lit only by the lamp on Duke's side of the bed, its window drapes drawn, was shadowed. The table was still weighted with the waste of last night's meal: scrap-laden plates, smudged coffee cups, and empty wine glasses.

The floor was a scatter of discarded clothes.

When she heard Duke turn on the shower, she sat up and plumped the pillows behind her head. When thoughts of Keeley's early-morning call intruded, she pushed them aside. Those thoughts were too cold and hard to take hold in the afterglow of lovemaking.

She touched her tender, sensitized vulva, ran her finger along its engorged, sex-slicked folds, and closed her eyes. Always a good lover, last night and this morning Duke had been extraordinary, taking her to a sexual peak she'd never experienced before. She could still hear his murmur in her ear.

"You like this, baby, don't you?" His fingers sliding deep inside her, opening her. His teeth tugging her earlobe. "You want more? You open up for me. Wide. Wider. Ah . . ." His breath a hot wind against her throat. "Yes, that's it, spread 'em, baby. I'm going to fuck you good."

She adored/despised it when he spoke to her that way, but it excited her. Sex excited her.

She loved Duke, and the ache of it wouldn't stop, no matter how many times she told herself he was wrong for her.

He had entanglements, yes, but he'd had them from the beginning. He hadn't tried to hide them, hadn't lied to her about his wife. It was wrong of her

to push, to nag him about a situation she'd so readily accepted at the beginning of their affair.

She loved him, and like the stone face of a steep
mountain, that love would endure.

*Jesus! Listen to yourself, Christiana, rationalizing, ex-
cusing, prating on about love and some damn mountain.
Give me a break! This isn't about* love. *It's about sex. He'll
never leave his wife and you know it.*

*What you're doing is settling, for second place in his life,
and for second best in yours.*

Cold now, she leaned to pick up her silk gown
from beside the bed. One strap was torn, a casualty
of sexual impatience. She slipped the sheer knee-
length garment over her head and glanced at her
empty wine glass on the bedside table, suddenly
wishing it were full.

With the sweat and distraction of sex worn off, she
could use some alcohol courage. She owed Duke the
truth about her birth circumstances.

Keeley hadn't told her much, other than she had
a sister and a brother in an 'unsavory business.'
When she'd pressed for Keeley's definition of *unsavory*, it turned out it fit with her own—and didn't fit
at all with her career plans. Keeley said the rest was
best left to a time when she could hear it firsthand,
and asked her to come to Mayday House as soon as
she could.

Christiana caught herself viewing the nightmare
that had become her life as if from a distance. A spec-
tator without a ticket. But not a nightmare, a farce,
a ludicrous, uncontrollable, ruinous farce.

But, like it or not, aside from his being her lover,
Duke was her manager, and no matter how messy
and upsetting the situation was, he didn't deserve to

be blindsided, didn't deserve to read about her new family, murdered father, and no-name mother in the checkout stand at his local supermarket. He needed to be prepared. He couldn't fix it, of course, but she knew he'd try.

"How about some coffee?" Duke stood in the open door of the bathroom, naked, toweling his hair. When he started toward the bedside phone, his every step accented the soft sway of his penis. He saw where her attention was and stopped beside her, smiling. "You keep looking at me like that, and we won't see coffee until the end of next month."

She smiled back, even though it felt like someone was loosening her jaws with a wrench, and said, "Order the coffee, Duke. I'll take a shower." When she was out of bed, she faced him. "I have something I need to talk to you about. I meant to earlier but—"

He touched his genitals. "Something came up?"

She couldn't find a second smile, but she managed a nod. "Yes, it certainly did."

He grinned and picked up the phone; she headed for the shower.

By the time she came out of the bathroom, wrapped in the hotel's terry robe, last night's dishes were gone, and the table was set with coffee and croissants. She took a seat, sipped a coffee, and attempted a bite of the warm, buttery pastry, but her throat felt as though it were lined with lead. She set down the roll and daubed her mouth with the napkin.

Duke, who'd donned jeans and a dark blue shirt, didn't seem to notice, attacking breakfast with a man's easy hunger.

"Duke," she opened. "There's something you

should know." She took a breath. "You're not going to like it."

He raised his eyes to hers, his expression relaxed, and took another bite of his roll. "What I don't like is the interview we have scheduled today. This Harper character is one cynical hard-ass. You're going to have to be careful. Your best bet is to say as little as possible. Don't let him get you on that 'cult of self-help, useless do-gooder' track he goes on about. How 'all you people live in glass houses.'" He put down his coffee. "What you have to do is rise above that, stand out from the crowd. Here's what I think you should—"

She held up a hand, palm out, then stood. "I think you should listen to me, Duke. Because we could be in serious trouble."

"What are you talking about?"

Now or never, Christiana. "I've recently discovered I was adopted."

"What?" The roll he had in his hand stopped on its way to his mouth, and his eyes narrowed. "Go on."

"The adoption was, uh, unrecorded, and—"

"You mean illegal."

She nodded.

"Okay," he said the word slowly, frowning as he did so. Christiana got the sense he was already working on the press release. "Not a problem we can't handle. This kind of thing happens all the time. Anything else?" He asked brusquely, sounding like a chairperson about to close a business meeting. Not a word of understanding or concern about what impact this finding had on her. Hurtful enough, but what bothered her more was she hadn't expected it.

She'd started this conversation nervous and confused, but now she was irritated. She rubbed at the knot in her throat and stared down at him. "Let me see . . . 'Anything else?'" She tapped her chin. "How about this? The woman who delivered me killed my birth father."

"Jesus!"

"It gets worse." Some twisted part of her was starting to enjoy this.

"Jesus," he said again, this time shaking his head. It was as if he hadn't, or couldn't, assimilate what she'd said.

Christiana realized that for the first time in months she had his full attention. Outside of bed. Most of the time it was Duke doing the talking, the telling, the controlling. Organizing what she did, how she did it. Right now he looked as if he couldn't organize room service. He stood, then started to pace.

"Oh, and I have some new relatives I can't wait to meet." She couldn't stop the smile, the mad chuckle burbling upward in her throat. She tried to stifle it. She was crazy. Her life was going down the tubes, and she was greasing the skid with mirth.

Duke stared down at her as if she were mad. "Relatives. What relatives?"

"You might have trouble putting a spin on this, Duke. It seems they're"—she choked up again, and this time her eyes started to water—"they're . . . pornographers." Barely getting the last word out, she clutched her stomach and doubled over, not to be sick but to stop herself from giving in to a full and inane laughter breakdown.

She failed.

Choking, air-sucking, throat-closing, eye-streaming

hilarity cramped her belly and shut down her brain—like a swath of bright light, a clean ocean tide.

Sweeping in and sweeping out. Taking all the debris.

The debris . . .

She struggled for a lung-filling inhalation, but instead logic drizzled the stickiness of common sense onto her laughter-thickened brain and provided a searing moment of calm—of absolute truth. She had indeed been crazy. Life was absurd, she thought, sending clarity along during an attack of belly-clenching giggles.

Her face wet from the wash of tears, her skin hot, her stomach muscles tight and aching, she straightened her back, her mind clear for the first time since Mary Weaver's midnight call.

An aghast Duke said, "Get hold of yourself, Christiana. For God's sake. We've got work to do and you go hysterical on me. I can't believe you think having a family of pornographers is funny."

She drew in some air and with it some calm. "I think it's *my truth*, and something I have to deal with." That and finding the secret behind her father's death, who her real mother was.

He twisted his lips, the way he did when he was thinking hard. "Maybe you're right," he said, warming to a new spin. "There's got to be a way to turn this to our advantage. Hell, the public loves a good underdog." He looked away from her, walked a few steps. "That's it. That's the tack to take. Make a great first show. We'll do a big reveal thing. The beautiful, smart, and ultra-successful Christiana Fordham, broadsided by life, taking on the task of redeeming her sick family, turning their lives around. Maybe do a kind of reality thing."

"There is no 'tack to take.' Because I'm not doing the show."

"You're not—"

"Doing the show," she repeated. "And I'm not *doing you* anymore, either. I want you to get out of my life, Duke, both personal and business—and I want you to get out right now."

CHAPTER 17

"Morning," Bridget said, coming into the kitchen wearing a short cotton sleep shirt and the ugliest lime-colored mules Gus had ever seen.

"Morning." He turned back to his coffee and to beating himself up over last night's episode with Keeley. Damn, he was a fool . . .

Yawning, Bridget put some bread in the toaster and pulled out a battered tray from a cupboard above the new dishwasher. She made the noise of a dozen kitchen flunkies working a mess hall.

"You got a plan for that?" He nodded at the tray and dragged his mind back to Mayday business and away from a bedroom where he didn't belong.

"It's for Erica. She's getting dressed, but she says she's not feeling well."

I'll bet. Ransacking a house in the middle of the night, when you're a hundred months pregnant, takes it out of a woman. He didn't like Erica, but they had unfinished business, and he had said he'd help her—even if it was to further his own ends. No better time to start than right now, because her getting dressed signaled the possibility she'd split, maybe do something stupid like lead that Mace character back to Mayday. Not going to happen.

He got up from the table and went to the counter. "I'll take it." He gestured at the tray.

"Oh, no. Thanks, I'm—"

"You're what?" He watched her tighten her hold on the tray, gripping it as if it were a lifeline.

"I want to help her out. A couple of days ago, she, uh, said something about maybe giving me a job. Acting in some movie she's making." Her blush told Gus she knew exactly what kind of movie. "I could use the money, and Erica said I was pretty enough." She said the last defensively, as if she didn't believe herself and feared being called a liar.

He scanned her sad, delicate face, too young to have pain lines for love and loss. *Jesus, women had it tough sometimes.* "You're beautiful." He stroked her cheek lightly. "Much too beautiful to work for Erica Stark. If I were you, I'd hold off on that. Aim higher."

She blushed. "You think so? That I'm pretty, I mean."

"Yes, I think so." He lifted her chin, smiled down at her. "But I still want to take Erica her tray. I need to talk to her."

"Okay." She hesitated, then nodded. "Tell her I'll come get it when she's done."

"Will do."

Two minutes later he rapped on Erica's door and walked in. She was already dressed, on her cell phone, and agitated.

"Is he all right?" she said into the phone, her eyes going wide at the sight of Gus. "You're sure?" She looked at Gus again, this time with a hint of nervousness.

"Yes, I'm definitely getting closer . . . No, uh, no one's onto me." Again her gaze shot to Gus; then her tone sharpened. "Of course, I won't do anything stupid . . . Now let me talk to my brother, so I can—" She clicked off, threw the phone on the bed, cursed, then glared at Gus. "What the hell do you want?"

She was angry enough for him to assume her telephone call would have taken a different turn if he hadn't shown up.

"Settle down." He set the tray on the bedside table. "Aren't pregnant women supposed to stay calm?"

"As if a guy like you would know what the hell a pregnant woman needs." She snorted. "I repeat, what do you want? I've got business."

"I want you to tell me exactly where your brother is and everything you know about Mace."

She looked at him as if he were crazy, then shook her head and cursed. "So that's what the nun meant about you and her taking care of things. You running off and playing hero, guns blazing." She glared at him. "No fucking way."

"You got a better idea?" He knew she didn't, recognized she was panicked, waffling between flight or fight. Best she let off some steam.

"You don't get it, do you?" she said. "The son of a bitch has already shot off my brother's finger. He'll kill him if I don't do things his way, get him what he wants." The distraught woman of last night was gone, replaced by a hard-faced woman in crisp black slacks and a power red sweater. This morning Erica Stark was all business. Her eyes were knife sharp when she added, "You're security around here, right?"

"That's right."

Her look was speculative when she said, "Whatever she's paying you, I'll double it."

"Sorry. I'm not in the market for a new boss."

"I'll make it worth your while. Just get me what I need . . . please."

Her lame attempt at getting to him by tacking on a *please* carried the weight of the dry toast he'd picked up from her tray. "Which is?"

"The names of my long-lost sister and her mother." She planted her hands on her hips. He noticed she still had the Band-Aid on her right index finger.

Gus took a bite of the toast and studied the aggressive woman in front of him. She was ambitious, bitchy, goddamn mean—and scared shitless about her brother. Whoever Mace was, he had her terrified.

"Not sure that long-lost sister is going to be too happy to make your acquaintance," he said.

Her mouth slackened. "You already know who the bitch is?"

"Uh-huh." He left the room to silence.

"And the mother. You know her name, too?"

Gus chewed on the dry toast, said nothing.

"Tell me," she demanded. "I'll triple the deal."

"We don't have a deal to triple."

He heard the door close, then Keeley's voice. "Gus can't be bought, Erica," she said. "You'll meet your sister when the time is right. In the meantime, you can tell us about your father—and his connection to this house."

Keeley came up beside him, and with her came the scent of roses and lemon. She slipped her hand in his, and while her hand tightened around his fingers, her trust tightened around his heart.

Erica shot a knowing, impatient look at their

joined hands. "I figured there was something going on with you two."

Keeley glanced up at Gus, her face sober. "Not yet, but I'm working on it."

Gus met her gaze: it was steady enough, but as perplexed now as it had been earlier, when he'd walked out of her bedroom and taken his messed-up feelings with him. He'd spent what was left of the night trying to tidy them up, and still wasn't sure how, or if, this new idea of his would play out, an idea that shot his nerves more effectively than Erica's damn Glock could ever do.

When he squeezed Keeley's hand, she closed her eyes briefly as if to block him out, then turned to again look at Erica. Good idea, Keeley, he thought, concentrate on the matter at hand. Time enough for their . . . thing when this was over. "Now about your father, Erica," she said. "Tell us about him. Everything. Maybe between us we can put the pieces together and do something for your brother—and sister." She let go of Gus's hand and gave him a get-on-board look. Not a problem.

"Sounds like a plan to me," he said. He picked up Erica's phone from the bed, hit redial, listened, and clicked off. He tossed the phone back on the bed. "They're at the Jasper." He looked at Erica. "And now that's settled, we've got time to hear your side of things. You either help get your brother out of there, or I do it my way. Your choice."

"Shit!" She finger-combed her long dark hair off her temples, sighed noisily, then sat on the edge of the bed. "You know about the call from the Weaver woman?"

They both nodded.

"At first it didn't make any sense," she said. "All her yammering about forgiveness, us having a sister, her killing our 'daddy,' but then we got to thinking about it, because the dates matched. Fall, nineteen seventy. That's when my father, the late, great Jimmy Stark, took off and the last time any of us ever saw him. I was ten or so; Paul was thirteen. To be honest, I never missed the son of a bitch, because as fathers went, he wasn't much. Always busy with the business."

"He made those movies, too, then," Keeley said.

Erica shot her a hard look. "Yeah, *Sister* Keeley, he made 'those movies.' Damn good at it, too. The movies weren't the problem. The problem was he couldn't keep his hands off the hired help." She got up and went to the window. "Paul knew he was fucking one of the actresses, a newcomer named Icy Cream. We figured they'd run off together. End of story."

"Icy Cream. That would be a stage name." Keeley again.

"Unless she had an ice cream wagon for a mother, yes, I'd say it was a stage name," Erica said, her voice dripping scorn. "Most porn actors use a pseudonym. They're not exactly panting to let the folks back home know they make their livings off their . . . genitalia."

"No, I don't suppose they would," Keeley said.

"You judging me?" Erica's eyes were flame hot.

"Do you see a robe and gavel?"

"No, what I see is a goddamn halo."

Keeley waved a hand through the empty air above her head. "Darn thing, follows me everywhere." She gave Erica a steely look. "Now stop being defensive, and tell us about Icy Cream. Everything you know."

Erica's stubborn expression didn't soften. "I'm not defensive, just not sure you can handle it. Maybe I should just talk to your boyfriend here."

Keeley ignored her. "Surely an actress had to give her real name somewhere along the line, payroll, taxes, that kind of thing."

Erica rolled her eyes and took on a long-suffering look. As irritating, abrasive women went, Gus put her in the top ten. "Talk," he said.

"Okay, okay. The thing is back then, nobody did 'payroll, or that kind of thing.' Dad ran his business on cash. Actors, crew, suppliers. All of it. He played it safe. Most actors were paid the day they did their work. A lot of them made one film and you never saw them again. Some came back for more. From what we can figure—and you can bet we scoured the archives—Icy Cream was a one-film wonder. I guess she decided it was more lucrative to spend her time banging the producer than bouncing on bedsprings with a bunch of unknown hard-ons every day." She glanced at Keeley and raised a brow, as if waiting for a reaction. She got none.

"And your mother?" Gus said. "She never looked for Jimmy, never wondered what happened to him?"

Erica rubbed her rounded stomach, then shook her head. "The bastard broke my mother's heart, but the answer to your question is no. She just snorted more coke. The day he left, he put a sizable chunk of cash in her account, said he wouldn't be back. That was good enough for her."

"Do you have the film?" he asked. "The one starring Icy Cream?"

"Yeah, the woman had some good moves, but it's a shitty film. The master's in Seattle, but I had Paul make up a disk. It's at the Jasper with him." Mentioning the Jasper turned her edgy again.

"Does anyone else know about the movie?" he asked. "Anyone associated with Starrier?"

"No."

"The man holding your brother?"

"No. Why the hell would we tell him? First off, the guy has a habit of shooting people's fingers off, and second—"

"It might ruin your blackmail scheme," Keeley said calmly, adding, "Anyone ever tell you you're not a very nice human being?"

"There's the halo again," Erica sniped.

"What you've done, you've done, and whether I approve or disapprove doesn't matter," she said. "But your children deserve someone better than a blackmailer and a pornographer for a mother, Erica. You're not stupid, you have to know that."

"Christ, you sound exactly like Paul." She looked as if she might explode.

"How about we get back to the business of saving your brother's life?" Gus interjected. "You make him sound as if he's worth the effort." Gus rubbed his scar. "We need that disk." And if it proved Icy Cream was who he thought she was, he needed to make sure Hagan never got his oily hands on it. "Call the Jasper. Tell Mace you've found what he's looking for and that you'll bring it to the Jasper as soon as you can get away."

"You're crazy!" Erica's eyes, heavy with dread and concern, shot to his. "Mace catches me lying, he'll kill Paul. He'll kill all of us."

"Nobody's going to get killed." *I hope.*

"You can't risk the babies," Keeley said firmly. "No way."

"I don't plan to," Gus said. "Those babies are staying right here with you, at Mayday House."

"Then how in hell are you going to get in the motel room?" Erica asked.

"With a short recording." He held up his PDA. "And your key."

"You're crazy."

Gus figured she was right, but getting Paul Stark out of that motel room wouldn't be made easier by wasting time. "No time like the present."

"I'm going with you," Keeley said. "I am a nurse, remember. I can help Paul."

"Not a chance." He shook his head for emphasis. "If Paul's made it this far, he can make it here on his own. So forget the heroics. This is a one *man* operation. You're staying here."

The look she shot him was lethal. "Then we should call in the police."

Erica shot to her feet. "No cops! All they'd do is fuck things up. A whiff of blue and Mace'll kill Paul in a heartbeat. I'll eat my goddamn key first. You got that?"

Erica stopped, jerked, and scrunched her face in pain. "Goddamn it!" She clutched her back and straightened.

Keeley rushed to her. "Sit down. Now."

Gus looked at Keeley. "She's right about the cops, but I need the key and I need it now. And a short tape recording."

Gus parked on the street behind the Jasper a block away, got out of the car, pulled his jacket collar up against the rain, and started to walk. Less than five minutes later he was across the street from the brightly painted but badly aging motel. He studied its two-floor structure closely.

Room eleven, where Mace was holed up with Paul, yielded a lucky break. It was at the far end of the lower floor near the stairwell, and only one room, ten, bordered it.

Other advantages: none of the doors on the rooms had peepholes, the day was dark, and it was raining like a bitch, which kept people indoors and sound muted.

If his luck held, room ten was vacant. He clicked on his cell phone, called the Jasper, and asked to be connected to ten. When a man's voice grumped a hello into his ear, he hung up.

Not lucky.

He shrugged deeper into his jacket and crossed the street. He had one chance, but he'd have to be fast. Very fast.

He came up on the room's door from its blind side, the stairwell leading to the second floor. Positioning himself tight to the door, to avoid detection from the windows on the other side, he rapped sharply three times.

"Who is it?" a tired voice said. He figured it for Paul.

He inserted Erica's key in the lock and put the miniature tape recorder against the door. "It's Erica." Pause. "I've got it. I've got it, Paul." Erica was good. She sounded both nervous and excited. Perfect.

Slipping the recorder into his pocket, he turned the key and shoved into the room, Erica's gun in his left hand.

"Everybody easy," he ordered, and kicked the door closed behind him.

"What the—"

Gus scanned the room in one sweep. Same as the one he'd been in. Long and narrow, bathroom in the back, two beds. TV on.

One man lying on the bed closest to the bathroom, hand wrapped in a towel. Tall, thin, and sheet white. *Paul.*

Second man, Mace, on the bed nearest the door, big, overly muscled—and lightning fast.

On the bed one second, off it the next, Mace rolled to the floor. Gun in hand. A split second from surprise to armed and dangerous.

Shit!

Gus leveled his gun at the bed, the point closest to where he thought Mace would be, and slipped some cold steel insurance from his wrist sheath into his right palm. "Get rid of the gun, Mace," he ordered. "Or I'll get rid of you."

"Sure, buddy, anything you say." A muffled voice came from behind the bed.

Next came a gun barrel. "Your turn to drop it, asshole." The gun barrel came further into view, as did Mace's head, his eyes, like the gun, aimed at Gus's gut.

Then came a goddamn pillow swung fast and hard to the back of Mace's head. Mace's neck jerked and the gun wobbled.

Paul swung again. "You son of a bitch! Threatening my sister. You son of a bitch!" He kept swinging.

A blizzard of feathers exploded into the room. Mace turned his head.

Gus took his chance and threw. Blood spurted from Mace's ear. Gus switched the gun from his left to his right hand, but with Paul cursing and bashing at Mace with what was left of the pillow, he couldn't get a clear shot.

It was nuts. While Paul unleashed his wild, one-armed assault, someone on the TV talked about bad breath, the guy next door banged on the wall, and Mace growled like a rabid dog.

Through the swirl of dusty feathers, and holding his hand to his bloodied ear, Mace roared up and off his knees. In a blur of motion, he slammed Paul against the headboard, put his head down, and tackled Gus in the mid-section.

Gus went down hard, his breath leaving him in a harsh, abrupt rush. He started to get up, and Mace went for him again, intent on ramming his gun into Gus's head. Gus shifted in time, but caught a grazing blow over his right ear. He didn't black out, but the stars and pulsing lights in his skull stopped him long enough for Mace to make the door, fling it open, and take off.

By the time Gus lurched to his feet and got to the door, the bastard was gone. *Shit!*

There was a thump on the wall, and a man's voice yelled, "Put a lid on it in there or I'll call the fuckin' manager."

Gus stumbled to the nearest bed and sat down. Holding his head between his hands to mute the kaleidoscope of colors his brain was mired in, he caught his breath. Then he cursed.

"You all right?"

Gus lifted his head, the movement making him wince. "You're Paul Stark?" *He damn well better be!*

He nodded. "I'll get you a towel." When he came back two seconds later, he said, "Erica hire you?"

"In a way." Burying his face in the damp towel, he decided to leave explanations for later. When he took the towel away from his face, it had a splotch of red. He looked at Paul's bandaged hand, the thin motel terry heavily encrusted with dried blood. The guy had done a lot of bleeding. "Get the Icy Cream disk, and whatever else you need," he said. "We're getting the hell out of here."

"Where are we going?"

"Mayday House."

"Erica?"

"She's there. She's okay."

"Good." Paul went back to his bed, slid his good hand under the mattress, and took out a disk. "Let's go."

"Not much of a hiding place." Gus gestured with the Glock to the bed.

"Good enough when no one thinks you're hiding anything."

Gus grunted. When he got to his feet, unsteadily, Stark gave him his good hand, then a shoulder to help him out the door.

"Thanks," Gus said. "And thanks for the help back there. You swing a mean pillow."

By the time they'd walked to Gus's car, his head thumped like hell, but other than that he was okay. A headache he could handle. What really pissed him off was Mace getting away.

He'd be back. Gus was sure of it.

Keeley was a lean, mean nursing machine. Within minutes, she had Paul's finger cleaned, stitched, and bandaged. "We're lucky, no sign of infection," she announced. "But we'll need to keep an eye on it."

She wouldn't look at Gus and replied in grunts to any questions he put to her. Inelegant grunts, non-committal grunts, angry grunts. He gave up.

After she'd heard the bones of what had happened at the Jasper, she insisted Paul get settled into the second-floor bedroom next to Erica and get some rest. Any more talking could wait. She told Erica to stay with him, enlisted Bridget for kitchen duty, and made a mid-afternoon meal. Bridget took the Starks theirs on an overladen tray and disappeared into her own room.

Then Keeley disappeared, didn't come back until well after six. The house, except for the rain slashing at the windows, was quiet as a tomb. Gus met her kicking off her boots at the back door.

"You should have told me where you were going." Anger replaced relief the second he set eyes on her wet hair and dripping face. He'd covered half the miserable, muddy roads in the neighborhood looking for her until he'd knocked on the priest's door and the housekeeper had told him she was there.

She brushed some strands of hair from her face.

He lifted his chin and took in some air, a trace of control, when what he wanted to do was throttle her. *Hold her.* "I can't protect you if I don't know where you are."

She rounded on him then, her eyes curiously bright, as if she'd been crying. "If you must know, I went to visit my mother, then . . . Father Barton. We had tea." She shot him a challenging look.

"I know that. What pisses me off is I had to find out the hard way. Stalk around like a second-rate gumshoe."

Her face tightened. "And while we're on the subject

of your '*protecting me*,' that was your idea, and by the
looks of it a bad one." She glared at him, frowned
deeply. "You're bleeding again." She stomped to the
table and picked up the medical kit she'd left there
earlier, when she'd slapped a bandage on him and
patched up Paul.

"Sit." She jerked her head in the direction of a
kitchen chair. "Your bandage is soaked with rain—
and blood."

"It's fine." Hell, it was barely a scrape.

"Sit," she said again.

When he didn't move, she added, "Paul's not the
only one at risk of infection, you know." She waited.

He sat, winced when she dabbed some kind of
germ-killing hot sauce on his head.

"Baby," she whispered under breath, then dabbed
some more.

He grabbed her hand. "Care to tell me why you were
Florence Nightingale with him"—he gestured with his
sore head to the upper floor—"and you morph into
Nurse Ratched the minute you touch me?"

She pulled her hand free, dabbed again. Harder
this time. "Because I'm angry." She tugged out a
square bandage and pasted it on with the same lack
of finesse she'd used earlier.

"Who'd have guessed?" Gus touched the bandage
gingerly, got up, and took himself a safe distance
away.

"What you did was stupid. You could have been"—
her mouth tightened—"And I told you to get rid of
the gun. You didn't."

"Might as well have, for all the good it did." He
wished to hell he had got a piece of the guy, slowed
him down long enough to ask him what game he was

playing—and who he was playing it with. Maybe when Keeley gave him a chance to think of something besides her, and where the hell she was, he'd be clear-headed enough to figure it out, but for now at least, with everyone snug in their beds, the not-so-quietly-fuming woman in front of him had his full attention.

She didn't know it—yet—but looking down the barrel of a gun had reorganized his priorities.

"Give it to me," she said, her voice crisp, her hand out, palm up.

"It's in a safe place." He walked toward her. He had no intention of getting rid of the gun until this mess was resolved. He lifted her chin and looked into her face, all tight with anger—and concern. "It's not the gun that's bothering you."

She gave him a scathing look and jerked her face from his hand.

"You're angry because I didn't make love to you last night."

She rolled her eyes. "The ego speaks."

"You're irritating me, Farrell. Talk to me."

"I'm irritating you! Dear God!" She put her face inches from his, her eyes shot with fire. "You don't want to make love with me. Fine. I'll cope. But you roaring off to play hero with guns, knives, and assorted artillery? That doesn't play with me, Gus. You could have been—"

He kissed her to shut her up, kissed her because he wanted to, and because that gun Mace had pointed at his gut had changed everything. But before things went further, he had to sort a few things out. He set her away from him.

"I need to tell you why I'm here," he said and paused. "Hagan Marsden hired me—"

"You told me that." She touched her just-kissed mouth.

"I didn't tell you everything."

"Have you ever?" She looked as if she were mad all over again.

"No. But I had my reasons."

"I'm sure you did."

"Hagan knows where April is." He took a couple of steps away from her. "He said he'd tell me if I got him something to use against Dinah."

"Oh, Gus . . ." She closed her eyes and shook her head.

He couldn't read her reaction, but it was either pity or disappointment. He didn't like either choice. After a moment, she added, "And, of course, you agreed."

"Yes."

"You really were going to sell Dinah out. You never were working for me, were you?" The last came out softly as if there were pain attached.

"Yes. And no."

"You lied to me."

"Yes," he said.

"I see." She took a step back. "And you're telling me this now, why?" She studied him, her expression unreadable.

"Because the lies are over," he said.

She looked wary. "Another change of allegiance, Gus—or a change of heart?"

Gus couldn't think of a better choice of words. "The latter—and I need you to believe me." The admission had him feeling raw, exposed. He didn't like it. And he didn't like the way his breath snarled in his throat or the way his heart pounded. Yet he stood stone still waiting for her answer.

She nodded her head, slowly, thoughtfully, then turned her back on him and walked to the kitchen window where she stared out into the darkness for what seemed goddamn hours. When she turned back to him, he expected questions, a demand for promises. He was half right.

"What will happen now?" she asked. "How will we find April?"

We . . .

He swallowed hard. "Did you hear what I said? I lied to you."

"I heard." She let out a long breath. "Is that the last of them? The lies?"

"Yes."

"Absolutely the end? Not even a small white one lying around waiting to pounce?"

He shook his head.

"Okay, then." She pushed at her hair and nodded as if agreeing with herself.

"That's it?" He took her head in his hands, forced her to look in his eyes. He had to be sure about this, absolutely sure. "You're not angry?"

"Of course, I'm angry. But you did ask me to forgive you, so——" She stopped and her brow furrowed. "Didn't you? Ask me?"

"In my own roundabout way."

"Then I do. Forgive you, I mean." She paused. "Although I'll never, never understand you."

"You don't have to. All you have to do right now, is trust me—and let me kiss you." He brushed his lips over hers. "Sound okay to you?"

She nodded.

He kissed her deeply, pulled her flush to his body, to where he burned for her. He loved this woman. He loved her hair, her baggy jeans, her ugly shoes, and her even uglier nightgown. Lifting his head, he smiled against her mouth.

"You're smiling." She touched his mouth with her finger. "You don't paint. You don't do dishes— and you don't smile. Ever."

"It's been known to happen." He smoothed her hair back. "There is one other thing."

"What?" She looked wary again.

"I was thinking how much I hate that pink nightgown. Any chance you'll burn it?"

When she started to protest, he put his finger on her moist, just-kissed lips. "And there's something else I want."

"You want to talk at the strangest times. We've got people upstairs, all kinds of unanswered—"

"I want you to think about the long term. I want you to think about us waking up together—morning after morning. I want you to think about the future. Our future." He kissed her before she had a chance to answer, selfishly taking advantage of her surprise at his question, the soft slackness in her mouth. "Because if you want more than this, you're going to have to make an honest man out of me."

Chapter 18

At his words silence invaded the room, so deep it was impenetrable, a solid where air should be.

The word *shock* didn't describe Keeley's wide eyes and slack mouth. She looked as if he'd stunned her with a laser.

He set her away from him. "Well?"

She took a couple of steps back, looked dazed.

"Well?" he said again, bending his head to catch her eyes.

"You'll have to cut me some slack here. Getting from you walking out of my room less than twenty-four hours ago to the, uh, *ever after* thing is a stretch. I need a little time."

"Take all the time you want, as long as it's less than sixty seconds."

"First off . . ." She took a breath. "What you said, mornings, future, all of that. It sounds suspiciously like a proposal of . . . marriage."

Gus thought about that. What he knew about marriage he'd viewed from an outside window, and looking in he'd seen cheating wives—and husbands, alimony fights, and drug-inspired violence. As institutions went, it was easier to see himself standing in a cell block than at an altar, but if that's what it took to have Keeley . . . "That would be . . . okay with me."

"Okay?" She frowned.

She wasn't getting it and it was his fault. He'd never tried to get more from a woman than an orgasm and a call back. *Shit!* "What I'm trying to say is I . . . don't want one of those sleep-and-run things your priest—"

"He's not my priest, he's my friend."

He ground his teeth, started again. "I want more than . . ." He stopped to sort through the clutter of words in his head, the mess of feelings in his gut. "I want more from you than I've ever wanted from a woman. And I want you to want more from me. To expect more. I want the sleep part of Barton's equation, but not the run part." He looked at the ceiling. "And I'm sounding more like a goddamn fool with every word I say."

Silence. So heavy it damn near sank him.

She moved closer and touched his face. "I think you sound wonderful, but . . ."

Jesus, the lady said but!

"As you said before, we're all wrong for each other. You with your cool silences, your detachment. Me with my involvement—which is neither cool nor silent." She sounded a little breathless. "You with all your—and don't hate me for saying this—experience with women. Me with . . . none of that."

It didn't sound as if she expected a response, so he opted for the cool silence again. The experience thing stung, but it was what it was. So he waited, and gained a full understanding of the heart-in-throat phenomenon.

"Which means we'd have to work hard to make it work, be seriously committed."

He nodded. No problem there.

"And I won't leave my work here. You'd have to live at Mayday House."

His chest lightened, his throat loosened; another nod. Hell, he'd live in an igloo in Alaska if she were in it.

Silence again, then, her face sober, she said, "You're talking about a possible life sentence here, Gus. And I'm not an . . . easy person. Never will be. Are you absolutely sure this"—she straightened, met his gaze directly—"*I* am what you want?"

"Never more sure of anything in my life."

"And this isn't something you feel obliged to say because I was a nun, or because of Glen Barton?" Her tone had an edge of nerves, and she grasped both his hands, held them tight to her chest.

He thought about that. "Partly," he said. "Then there's the other part, the one that won't let me imagine my life without you in it."

She studied him with those lie-detector eyes of hers, but he couldn't read her face, couldn't figure what she was thinking. What she'd say. Suddenly, she let go of his hands, shook her head, and took a step back.

He braced himself.

"The thing is . . ." Her expression softened, turned wry. "That's a perfectly good nightgown—"

Ignoring the flood of relief that nearly took him to his knees, he stood his ground and smiled. "A man has his limits, Keeley."

"Oh, well," she said, sighing dramatically. "Two out of three ain't bad." She moved back to him, into his arms. "My answer is yes, August John Hanlon. For the foreseeable future there'll be no running. I'll stay right here, until the day after forever."

Whatever chill was left in Gus's sleet-covered heart thawed; he held her fiercely. He'd given her his life, and he would die to protect hers. She was his. "I want to make love to you, Keeley," he whispered into her hair and felt her arms tighten around his waist.

"I want that, too," she answered.

"My place or yours?"

"Yours . . . it's closer." She touched his scar, kissed him softly, then smiled into his eyes.

In his room, they fell on the bed together, breathless. When they were side to side, staring into each other's eyes, Keeley kissed him again, then put her head back on the pillow and continued to look at him. "I love you, Gus," she said. The words were simple, but the expression on her face was a complex mixture of honesty, fear, determination, passion. "And I will love you forever."

He pushed some red curls off her forehead, couldn't take his eyes off her face. He wanted to say something profound but came up empty. Hell, he'd never been much for words at the best of times.

He kissed her hair, her forehead, her eyelids, breathed her scent deep into his lungs. His heart.

In the end the most profound words came on their own, just marched front and center. Potent, life-altering words he couldn't hold back, didn't want to hold back. "And I love you, Keeley."

They were new to him, these words. Not the word *love*; he'd used that often enough, but always in the heat of lovemaking, then it was, I love this, I love that . . . but never *you.* The word that changed everything. The word filled him with warmth in places long deadened by cold and loneliness. It occurred to him he'd never thought himself lonely; until the gray of it lifted from him, he hadn't known it was there.

She kissed him then, deeply, her tongue circling his mouth making her wishes clear. Then she moved her lips to his ear and whispered, "I want to make love with you, Gus. I want to make love with you forever."

Something in him settled, rested in a way it never had. "You're big into the forever stuff, aren't you?" He nuzzled her hair, soaked up the fragrance of it. The fragrance of her. "Trouble is, it isn't long enough."

He undid the buttons on her shirt, slipped his hand in, and cupped her small firm breast. "You're perfect." He touched her nipple, already hardening, drew a circle around it, listened to her sharp intake of breath.

She kissed his jagged scar. "So are you."

They undressed in slow motion.

Gus taking off her shirt, undoing the clasp of her bra. Taking time to taste her skin, caress her exposed nipple.

Keeley slipping his belt from its loops, undoing his zipper. Taking time to enfold him in her hand, run her finger along his hard length, until he jerked and pulsed in her hand.

Until he couldn't think.

They didn't get to naked before he was kissing his way down her stomach, savoring her wet heat, savoring her. But if he were going to stop, it had to be now. He kissed her thigh, then shifted off the bed.

"Where are you going?" she asked, hot and disheveled in his bed. And confused.

"Protection." He turned toward the bathroom.

She grasped his hand, pulled him back. "Are you okay?"

"I'm healthy, if that's what you're asking." When it came to STDs, Dinah said he was phobic. He always used protection, always had checkups, and insisted she do the same. Hell, he had a kid to raise. He wasn't about to leave Josh by being stupid.

"Me, too. And I'm on the pill."

He was surprised, and it probably showed, because she looked faintly embarrassed.

"Rough menstrual cycle," she added. "The pill helps."

He got back into bed. "I hate to be the beneficiary of that, but—"

She smiled. "You'll make do, right?"

Gus stretched out beside her, propped his head in his hand, and looked down at her. "I'll definitely make do."

She hesitated then and he cocked his head.

"You should know I'm a little nervous." She gave him one of her direct looks, the one with a hint of stubborn.

He gave it right back. "The me-being-experienced-and-you-not thing?"

She averted her eyes briefly, then ran her hand down his bicep. "Yes."

He quivered, then smiled. "You should be nervous."

The look she gave him was wary.

"Because I've never made love to a woman I've loved. Who knows what might happen?" He tilted her chin, lifting her face to his. "This is my first time, Keeley. My very first time."

She nodded slowly, then clasped his hand and kissed it. "Good," she said and took a breath. "Now where exactly did we leave off?"

Gus slid down the bed, kissed his way down her stomach, and lifted her to his mouth. "Right about here."

She groaned, opened for him, and Gus, lost in the scent and softness of the woman he loved, did what he'd learned to be expert at—for the very first time.

Two hours later, Gus dragged himself from sleep, his head pounding. No. The pounding was on his door. As he tried to clear his head, he glanced at the bedside table clock. Not quite eight.

He'd been dreaming . . .

"What is it?" a sleepy voice said from near his shoulder.

Not a dream. Thank God!

"Someone's at the door." He leaned over, kissed her forehead. "I'll get it." Get rid of them.

Keeley smiled at him, then dove under the quilt.

He pulled on his jeans, ran his hand over her hip, then headed to the door.

It was Bridget. "I'm going into town, but that woman's come back. She's downstairs."

Gus shoved his hair back. "What woman?"

"She's looking for Keeley, but I can't find her anywhere." She tried to look around him and he blocked her.

"What woman?" he said again.

"Christiana something." She took a step to his

left and looked past him to his rumpled bed. "She was here a few days ago."

"Tell her Keeley will be right down."

She was still looking at his bed when he closed the door, maybe a bit too firmly, in her face.

Keeley's head emerged from the covers.

"Christiana's here. She wants to see you."

"I heard," she said, but made no move to get up. "We'll have to tell everyone. About us. Right away. I'm the world's worst sneaker-arounder."

"Fair enough, but who's everybody and why should we sneak?"

She slid to the edge of the bed, gathered up her clothes, and started to get dressed, then stopped. "You're right." She looked at him, her jeans zipper still open, no shirt on. "But I'd feel better all the same."

Gus sat on the bed she'd just left, his attention snagged by her naked breasts. "We'll take out an ad if you want." His breathing quickened. "You've got a fantastic body. I could sit here and look at you all day. On second thought"—he reached for her— "I'd rather touch, and taste." He held her by the waist, curling his fingers into her firm flesh, and buried his face between her breasts, shifting to blow on a nipple, take it in his mouth.

Keeley gasped and plunged her hands into his hair. Her breathing shifted to ragged. "What a . . . way to . . . start . . . the day."

He looked up at her. "And end it." Reluctantly releasing her, he said, "You better go. Fordham's waiting." Along with her arrival, the Starks and their dirty secrets also came to mind, and he felt the warmth of the night slip away. Mayday was still at risk. His home was in danger. He glanced out the window.

Still raining. When he looked back, Keeley was dressed and looking down at him.

She brushed his hair back from his forehead and leaned to kiss it. "You look grim," she said. "You're thinking about Christiana, the Starks. You're worried about their meeting."

He considered glib assurances, rejected them. "No. It's not them. Hell, tangled family ties are nothing new. They'll work it out, if they want to."

"It won't happen without Dinah Marsden." She stepped away from him. "You have to get her here, Gus. It's essential."

She made it sound easy, but Gus knew Dinah wouldn't do anything it wasn't in her interest to do. "I'll do what I can." He stood. "Now you better go downstairs. I'll be down in a few minutes."

When she was gone, Gus hit the shower. Standing under the rush of water, he braced his hands against the shower wall, dropped his head, and waited for the water to clear his sex-crazed mind.

Keeley was right, he did feel grim. He might not give a damn about the mess of a family about to gather downstairs, but he sure as hell gave a damn about a man called Mace.

Still out there. Still a risk.

Chances were the bastard was on Hagan Marsden's payroll. Insurance in case Gus screwed up or didn't come through.

Mace would be back, all right, and this time it would take more than a feather pillow to take him out.

He turned off the shower, slicked his hair back.

This mess had to come to a head, and to make it

happen, Keeley was dead right, he needed Dinah's highly toned ass at Mayday House.

He decided to pay a quick visit to Paul Stark.

Keeley met Bridget in the hall outside her bedroom. The look in her eyes was censorious and Keeley's stomach fluttered. For a moment she felt awkward, even defensive—until she reordered her thoughts, remembered the happiness, the ecstasy, of last night in Gus's arms.

She leaned on her door and looked at Bridget's sullen face. "Okay, out with it."

Her gaze slid away. "Out with what?"

"I was with Gus. You're shocked."

"I didn't know, uh, nuns did that kind of thing."

"What kind of 'thing' are you talking about?" God, she was so tired of the darn nun thing.

"You know. Have sex." Her gaze shot to Keeley's, then slid away again.

Keeley let out a breath. "For the millionth and absolutely last time, I am *not* a nun, Bridget. I haven't been for a lot of years now."

"I know, but—"

"And Gus and I—" She stopped. She didn't need to explain. Besides, how could she expect anyone to understand what was between her and Gus when she wasn't sure she understood it herself? "Get used to Gus, Bridget, he'll be around for a long time." She smiled. *Forever.* "Now would you please go and tell Christiana I'll be right down? I need to change."

"Sure." Bridget nodded, started down the hall, then stopped and said, "Keeley?"

"Uh-huh." Keeley was opening the door when she heard her. She turned.

"I felt like you once. I know what it's like to, uh, want somebody. Real bad like." She looked as if she were going to cry, ran a hand under her nose. "With me, it didn't work like I wanted." She sniffed and squared her bony shoulders. "Gus is nice, super . . . hot, but you'll be careful, won't you?"

"I'll be careful, Bridget. Thanks."

Bridget nodded and headed for the stairs, leaving Keeley with a lump in her throat and a dose of morning-after reality.

When she'd closed the bedroom door behind her, she leaned against it. Bridget was right. About Gus being . . . hot—she smiled—and about the need to be careful. She should be smart about this, not rash or impulsive. She should be logical and cautious. Sober as a nun. Maybe the least bit guilty . . .

But she wasn't any of those things. She was in love, and last night she'd given Gus her body—and more important—her heart. She had no intention of taking either back.

Keeley brought the thermos coffeepot to the table, set it down between her and Christiana, and took a seat. "Erica and Paul are upstairs now."

Christiana instantly got to her feet, looked around the kitchen as if to pinpoint an escape route. "God, I don't know if I'm ready for this. For them."

"You can always cut and run." Keeley's response was facetious and accompanied by a smile. She didn't peg Christiana for a runner—from anything, but she empathized with the tense woman now pacing her kitchen. It had to be emotionally tricky to stay calm when you were about to meet a brother and sister you didn't even know you had until a few days ago.

"I think you know I won't do that. I want to meet them. Need to. But my . . . mother? Have you found out anything about her?"

Keeley didn't know what to say, and she wasn't ready to tell this elegant and proper woman her first sight of her mother might be in a triple-X-rated film. She was glad when Gus came into the room and answered for her.

"We're working on it." He took a mug from the cupboard, strolled to the table, and poured himself a coffee. He glanced at Keeley. "Where are they?"

Keeley knew he meant the Starks, but before she could tell him they'd be right down, Erica strode into the room. She looked tired and irritable. But then Erica always looked irritable. Paul, his hand securely bandaged, followed her in. Both were dressed casually, but expensively, in jeans and shirts, Paul's neatly tucked in, Erica's flowing over her pregnancy.

Erica stopped in her tracks when she spotted Christiana. For a few seconds, the two women stared at each other. Christiana looked calm enough, but Keeley saw her knuckles whiten.

"Jesus," Erica finally said, "You're her." If she was feeling anything, it didn't show through her obvious shock.

"If by 'her' you mean your half-sister, you'd be right." Christiana held out her hand; Erica ignored it and continued to stare.

Paul stepped toward the two women and took Christiana's hand just as she was pulling it back.

"Paul Stark," he said. "You'll have to excuse Erica. We weren't expecting you. Not yet, at least."

"Neither were we," Keeley said. "Christiana's visit was unexpected, but now she's here, I thought you should meet."

Erica shook her head as if to clear it. "I need a coffee." She followed Gus's path to the cupboard and retrieved two mugs, poured for herself and Paul, and sat down heavily at the table.

"You're pregnant," Christiana said, stating the obvious and clearly no more able to start a dialogue than Erica.

Erica rolled her eyes, said nothing.

Given Erica's nonanswer, Christiana looked at Paul's bandaged hand. "And you're hurt."

"Another astute observation," Erica said, rising from her chair. "Now can we get down to business?" She eyed Christiana, then tilted her head. "You look a lot like her. Same bland blondeness men seem to like so much."

"Excuse me?" Christiana looked confused.

Erica ignored her. "Wouldn't you say, Paul? Especially from an angle. Long neck, too." She smiled. "Of course we'd have to see her naked to know for sure."

"Jesus, Erica." Paul gave her a disgusted look.

"Nice," Gus said, shaking his head. He was standing, hip propped against the kitchen counter, as far away from the tableau at the table as the kitchen allowed.

Keeley got to her feet and faced Erica. "If you're going to be crude and cruel, Erica, pack your bag and get out of here. Otherwise—and I quote—if you can't say something nice, keep your ugly mouth shut." She leaned closer. "Have I made myself clear?"

Erica's face filled with heat and anger. "I don't have to—"

Keeley raised a brow. Her own temper barely restrained, she sealed her lips into a tight line.

"Erica," Paul said. "For God's sake, shut up." He looked at Christiana, who appeared frozen to her chair. "I apologize for my sister. This whole . . . experience is difficult."

Christiana was holding her breath, had been since Erica's words had filtered through her shock and reached her brain. Not only were these two strange people her brother and sister, it was obvious they knew who her birth mother was—or thought they did. She didn't warm to Erica, nor Erica to her. So much for sisterly affections. She quelled the tiny shaft of disappointment, putting it down to some romanticized idea of what having a sister might mean. She'd actually hoped to like this angry woman.

"I'd like to say I understand," she said to Paul, who was at least attempting to be pleasant. "But I don't." She looked at the taut-faced, sullen Erica. Paul had put his coffee down and was massaging her shoulders. "And you have the advantage over me," she added, "because I have no clue who my mother is."

"Lucky you," Erica murmured.

"And all we have is a '*clue*,'" Keeley said calmly. She stood beside Gus across the kitchen. "We think we know who she is, Christiana. We're not certain."

Gus folded his arms across his chest but said nothing.

"Speak for yourself, *sister*." Erica looked up at Paul. "Get the disk." She leered at Christiana. "One look at Icy Cream and this little mystery is solved."

"Icy Cream," Christiana said. "What are you talking

about?" Something with a thousand legs skittered across her nape.

"We're talking about a sex tape, a third-rate porn movie with your mommy's naked ass—along with everything else—in the starring role." Erica spat the words.

Christiana swallowed her response as Erica's words sank in. Her mother wasn't an actress, she was, she was . . . God, she didn't want to think about what she was. Again, she had the insane urge to laugh.

Paul didn't move. "I don't think we have to deal with that right now, Erica." He sounded stern, but looked uncertain.

Gus said, "Watching the movie will prove nothing. All you know is your father—allegedly—took off with the woman who was in it. That might make her the *evil* other woman in your books, but it doesn't make her Christiana's mother."

"Bull. She's a dead ringer."

"So you say," Gus said.

"So will you when you've seen the movie," Erica said.

"He already has," Paul said.

"When?"

"This morning. Couldn't think of a reason not to show him." He glanced at Gus. "Persuasive guy."

Erica knit her brows and seemed to think on what Paul had said, then nodded her head. "Doesn't matter, we can still use it."

"No, Erica, we can't," he said, his tone hard. "Give it up, would you? It's over. I should never have let your ridiculous plan get as far as it did. Mace could have killed you and the babies. Nothing's worth that. Certainly not a failing pornography business."

"It's not failing, all we need is—"

"Stop!" Christiana slapped a hand on the table, then stood. She'd had enough, and she refused to be drawn into the Stark family disagreements. "I don't care about your business. If you have a tape of my mother, I want to see it. And I want to see it now."

All eyes turned to her. Keeley looked alarmed.

Gus's gaze came last, his amazingly vivid eyes sliding over her as if taking her measure. "I don't think you do," he said, his tone soft.

"If there's a chance this Icy Cream person is my mother, I want to know." She wondered if that were a lie even as she said it, because right now, she wanted to run until she couldn't breathe anymore, get as far from these people as her legs would take her. She'd already had enough of her new *family*, and by the sound of things, the worst was yet to come. Her mother.

But she needed the truth, then to deal with it the best way she could.

Keeley coughed. "It's an adult film, Christiana. And even if you're okay with that, seeing someone who could be your mother starring in it will be painful." She looked at Gus, who stood as still as steel beside her. "Don't you agree, Gus?"

"Whether I agree or disagree won't change anything."

His nonanswer seemed to disturb Keeley, and she turned back to Christiana. "Why not give us time to confirm things? Then—if you still want to—you can watch it."

"Where? On the Internet after my new sister plasters it up on a Web site?" Christiana shook her head while looking pointedly at Erica. "No. I'll watch it now."

Erica smiled. "Get the disk, Paul, and your laptop. It's got a bigger screen than the DVD player." She looked at Christiana, and her smile changed to a smirk. "Shall I make some popcorn?"

Paul put his hands in his pockets and cast a nervous glance at his sister, then a questioning one at Gus, who responded with a raised brow and a noncommittal twist of his lips.

Keeley was angry and didn't try to hide it. "If you're intent on being self-serving, unfeeling idiots, I'm taking a walk." She glowered at Erica. "I need some fresh air."

Christiana watched Keeley take a yellow rain slicker from a peg near the kitchen door and walk out. Everything in her wanted to go with her. Instead she sat down and waited for Paul to go and get his laptop, her heart racing in her chest.

CHAPTER 19

Keeley pushed through the rain-washed hedge to St. Ivan's and went to the bench that sat against the back stone wall of the church overlooking the graveyard. There was some protection from the rain here, depending on which way the wind blew.

Two minutes later, Gus sat down beside her, zipped up his windbreaker, stuck his hands in his pockets, and stretched his legs out in front of him.

Where his shoulder touched hers a nice heat grew.

"You're mad," he said, not looking at her.

"I'm always mad," she said. "You might as well get used to it. It comes with the hair."

He slid her a glance, one she felt rather than saw, because her eyes were straight ahead, trying to pierce the soft sheets of rain falling on the graves, while her mind sorted through the clamor and tangles haunting Mayday House.

"Care to tell me what's got you stoked this time around?" he asked.

"You didn't tell me you'd seen the video."

"I didn't get a chance. Too many people."

Keeley turned to him. "It was Dinah, wasn't it?"

"Yup, and money in the bank for Hagan, because knowing Dinah, she'd do anything—pay anything—to stop that movie being seen. By anyone." He rubbed his forehead. "As graphic sex goes, I'd say all her body parts got their fifteen minutes of fame."

Keeley's stomach tightened. "Now I'm sad. I like Christiana. It's terrible to think she'll meet her mother that way."

"She won't."

Keeley gave him a questioning look, which he ignored. When he continued to sit there like one of those life-sized bronze statues you see sitting on park benches, she finally asked, "What did you do, Gus?"

He held up a disk. "I borrowed this."

"That's the Icy Cream movie?"

He nodded. "It'll hold them off for a time."

"Why not just destroy it?"

"I think you know why."

She sighed. "It's only a copy, and the Starks probably have a warehouse full of them—plus the original."

"You got it." He stuffed the disk back inside his leather jacket. "And if you've still got room at the Inn, I'd suggest you make up another room."

They were staring at each other, and when Keeley could get past the stunning fact she was in love with this enigmatic man, and he with her, she said, "She's coming, then? Dinah Marsden is coming to Mayday House?"

He nodded. "I called her after I saw the video. Figured she should be the first to know. She'll be here tonight. So we might as well go back in and let everyone know." He stood up, offering her his hand. "As family reunions go, this one should be a beaut."

Mace had driven to the next town, dropped into a doc's office, and gotten himself patched up. Thank God, that bastard back at the Jasper had used a knife. Gunshot wounds weren't so easy to lie about.

Turned out the cut was clean, more blood than anything else, but he'd lost the tip of his ear.

Now he was holed up in some place called the Homespun Motel. Both the town and the motel were even crummier than Erinville, and his head was pounding like a son of a bitch.

He should have blown the fucker away. Him and Stark. Would have, too, but a double homicide tended to attract a cop or two—and there was too much at stake.

He'd get them both when the time was right.

His gut was on fire and it wasn't heartburn. It was white-hot fury. Who'd have thought the skinny, sad-assed Stark had it in him? If either of the Starks had balls, he'd have put his money on Erica.

He'd been taken out by a fuckin' feather pillow!

That twisted in his craw like a dull blade. His neck heated and he looked at the phone again.

Dolan was expecting him to call, tell him his sister had died an accidental death. He wouldn't be happy, knowing the job wasn't done. Add to that he was an unpredictable asshole and damned full of himself.

Which meant, for Mace, the smart thing to do was keep his little fuck-up to himself.

No way did he want Dolan hauling his ass down here and getting in the middle of things.

Mace took a couple more painkillers, put his hand to his bandaged ear, held it lightly, and got to his feet. Goddamn head felt as if his brains were ready to burst from his skull, but he had to move, had to plan his next step—and figure out what spin to put on things.

Telling Dolan he'd been neutralized by a feather pillow and sliced up by some guy who'd walked into his own hotel room wouldn't do much for his rep. Finding out Mace had gone through with his milk-the-Starks plan wouldn't help, either, considering Dolan had been against it in the first place. If he got wind of it, figured in the risks to the main operation, he'd freak on him.

Maybe dredge up enough guts to hire another guy. *One to take him out.*

Mace pulled down a few slats on the blind, peered out into the rain-slicked parking lot, and for a few seconds watched the blur and splash of traffic on the busy street beyond that. Lousy day. If this kept up, there'd be one black night ahead. Good cover.

He let the blind slats clatter closed, put his hands on his lean hips, and stared at nothing.

He did not want Dolan James to freak.

Time to visit that crappy old house, get things done. He touched his aching ear again and growled. "Get this fuckin' job over with."

As the day wore on, Erica couldn't settle down, so she paced. If she didn't weigh a thousand pounds, and wasn't so burned out worrying about the business, she'd . . . hell, she didn't know what she'd do, and that was the problem. They were going down—

Paul, her, Starrier Productions, all of them—and she had no idea what to do about it.

Damned Internet, damned banks, damn loan sharks . . .

And damn Gus Hammond for being an arrogant son of a bitch. He might be hot to look at, but he was ruining her life. He had no right to take the disk, none at all, but she guessed when you were sleeping with the boss, you got to do whatever the hell you wanted.

Like bringing in the whore who'd messed up their lives in the first place and shoving her in Paul's and her faces.

Paul didn't seem to mind Gus taking the disk, or arranging for that hag to come here, seemed relieved, in fact. He'd muttered some crap about finally getting everything out in the open, then went to his bedroom, complaining his hand hurt. She hadn't seen him all day.

Her stomach knotted when she thought again how near she'd come to losing him. *Thank God, he was okay. She didn't know what she'd do without him.*

Not that he wasn't as soppy as ever, even about the bitch Christiana. "Kind of neat," he'd said, "having a new relative."

Erica didn't think so. She didn't need more family; she needed cold, hard cash. Not a sister who looked as soft as her brother. Miss Christiana Fordham. Jesus, what a la-te-dah name!

"Can we talk?"

Erica turned toward the door—think of the devil. At the sight of Christiana, she was instantly angry all over again. "Can't imagine what about."

Christiana walked in and joined her where she stood at the second-floor window. Together they looked down at the yard and driveway, dominated by the wet gleam of Gus's Jag and Keeley's rusted pickup truck. "We're sisters, Erica. Nothing will change that."

"Half-sisters," Erica corrected with a snap. "And who the hell knows *that* for sure? Your mother was a whore, a second-rate porn star who knew how to give good head. She probably slept with a hundred guys. Hell, there's three of them on the damn disk Hammond stole from us." She watched the woman's face, waiting for her to cut and run.

What she did was swallow and say, "I'm sorry you're so . . . upset. But I'm glad Gus took the disk. When I thought about it more, I decided I don't need to see it as much as I need to meet my mother, get the truth of things. As for whether or not we're sisters, if it comes down to it, any good medical lab will settle that question. But for now based on what Mary Weaver said—"

Erica snorted. She didn't want to hear any more about Weaver and her idiotic phone calls.

Christiana ignored her and went on doggedly. "Based on what Mary said, and your own evidence, my gut tells me a lab will only confirm what we already know."

Erica turned away. She was probably right, but damned if she was going to admit it.

"Look, I don't want to interfere in your life—but I am curious about . . ."

The way her words trailed off caught Erica's attention, and she turned to look at her. God, she was going to ask about their father, the no good son of—

"When are you due?"

Erica blinked, too surprised to speak.

"I know it's none of my business, but in the last few weeks, I've gone from having no family—my adoptive parents died a few years ago—to discovering a sister, a brother"—she shrugged as if to lend a casual tone to her words—"and apparently a mother who's due on the scene any moment." Her gaze lingered on Erica's breadbasket of a stomach. "And now either a niece or nephew."

Erica twisted her lips in lieu of words. She didn't want to talk to this woman, and her pregnancy was none of her business. She should tell her to get lost; instead she heard herself say, "One of each." She patted her tummy. "Twins." *Okay, so a little brag felt good.*

To say Christiana's eyes lit up would have been the understatement of the millennium. They shone. Jesus, it looked as if she were going to cry. Erica couldn't think what to say, didn't know why she'd told her in the first place. She sure as hell wasn't looking for prenatal girly talk. Erica didn't go in for that, never had the chance. Paul did his best, better than most men, but he was still a man.

"That's wonderful," Christiana said. "You must be thrilled." She said the last so softly, so reverently, you'd have thought they were at a church funeral.

Erica said nothing. If she said anything else, the woman would probably never leave.

"When?" she asked, her gaze riveted on what Erica and Paul had come to call *the babies.*

"Seven, eight weeks, maybe."

"Twins often come early, don't they?"

"So I'm told."

When she didn't add anything further, Christiana smiled and let out a breath. "I'll leave you alone now." She gestured with her chin to the babies. "Good luck."

When she was almost out the door, Erica—for God knew what reason—said, "What about you?"

"Me?" She stopped in the middle of the doorway.

"Yes, you. Do you have any kids?"

For a time it looked as if she weren't going to answer. "No," she finally said. "No kids in the past and none in my future. Not my own, anyway. I can't have any."

Erica looked at her, knew she should say something, but had no idea what, and it didn't seem the time to get into a discussion of medical advances in fertility—which she didn't know shit about, anyway. "Tough," was the best she could do.

"Yeah," she said, adding, "I had a hard time with it when I found out for sure, a few years back, but I'm reconciled, I guess you'd say. And there are a lot of kids out there who need parents. I'd have adopted by now if—"

"The right man had come along?"

A ghost of a smile crossed her face, then disappeared. "That's how I figured it at first. I always thought a child needed two parents, so I'd planned on establishing myself in my work, meeting the right man—" She paused. "I'd have leveled with him about my not being able to have kids, of course." She stopped again, as if uncertain what to say next, then added, "I thought I was being all grown up, terribly smart and rational about the whole thing, but now I think naïve is a better description. I've wasted a lot of time."

"Things didn't go as you planned."

This time her smile was wry. "Do they ever?"

Erica tapped her chin. "Let me guess which part didn't work out . . . the 'meet the right man' part?"

"You got it in one." She glanced away, then back, looking a bit embarrassed. "Relationships with men are where I make my finest mistakes."

Erica nodded, taken aback by her honesty. "Me, too." She again patted her tummy. "The last time I saw the babies' father was the day I found out I was pregnant. Not that I told him that."

"Why not?"

"Because it was also the day I found out he was married." Her stomach curled. "Bastard."

"Ouch. What did you do?"

"Showed him the door. What do you think? No way was I playing second fiddle to another woman, especially some apron-wearing suburbanite." Erica didn't like to remember that day, the hole he'd left in her heart—and her pride. It was the same day the Starrier loan was called. She couldn't do anything about losing her man, so she'd turned all her efforts to saving the company.

Christiana nodded, but she had an odd look on her face, when she said, "Men. Who can figure them?"

"You can't figure them. All you can do is manipulate them with whatever tools you have." The voice came from behind them, and Erica and Christiana turned in unison to see a blond woman standing casually in the open doorway.

There'd been enough close-ups on the disk for Erica to recognize her instantly. "How'd you get in without Keeley sounding a trumpet?" Erica said, more inclined to sneer than smile.

"Some girl let me in." She glanced around. "There's no one downstairs, so I decided on a trip down memory lane." She shuddered theatrically. "Though Nightmare Alley is a more appropriate description, I think."

Erica glanced at Christiana. "Meet your mother, Fordham. The great Icy Cream herself." She turned her attention back to Dinah Marsden and gave her the once-over.

The woman was tall, beautiful, and seriously stacked. The years and the surgeon's knife had kept all front-line body parts sag free, clear, and smooth. She didn't look much different from the twenty-something girl in the movie. She was also as icy as her stage name implied, because Erica's using it had no visible effect on her composure.

"In the flesh," she said, then moved her gaze, studying one woman, then the other. It stopped on Christiana, who looked as though someone had inserted an iron rod in her back. "I sure hope you're Christiana, because if that one"—she gestured at Erica—"was my daughter, I'd have to drown myself in my own gene pool."

"I'm Christiana," she said, sounding stiff and formal. "Which gives you the advantage. You know my name."

Erica was fascinated, but her back hurt as much as her feet, so she lowered herself into a chair near the window. A front-row seat.

"Dinah Marsden," the woman said. "Now we're even."

Erica put a hand on her heart in case it suddenly stopped beating.

Dinah Marsden . . .

It took less than a nanosecond for her to place the name. Huge, extremely ugly divorce. Maybe twelve or so years ago. Front-page tabloid fodder. Big, big money on the line, with most of it going to the poor abused wife. Shit! She knew there was money, she knew it!

Dinah turned cold eyes on Erica. "That makes you Jimmy Stark's daughter, the owner of a bad porn movie and, according to Gus, a wannabe blackmailer."

"Seemed like a good idea at the time." Erica met her gaze with one equally as cold. "Maybe still is. We still have the master."

"No. It's a bad idea—a very bad idea. There's only one thing I value more than my good name"— she half smiled, but it was as chilly and hard as her eyes—"and that's my money." She walked deeper into the bedroom. "If you had managed to get your little plan off the ground, believe me, sweetheart, you'd have lost."

She glanced again at Christiana, and this time her expression turned wary. "You'll want to talk, I presume."

Christiana, who hadn't taken her eyes off Dinah since she'd shown up at the door, said, "Yes, but not right now. I need to catch my breath." She took a step toward the door and stopped abreast of Dinah. "Before we talk, there's the matter of Mary Weaver's confession."

"Confession. What confession?"

"She said she killed Erica and Paul's father— and apparently my own. We'll want to know your part in that."

"Hear, hear," Erica said. Hell, it turned out Christiana wasn't such a softie after all.

"My part?" Dinah ignored Erica and fixed a brittle stare on Christiana. "I don't know what you're talking about."

"Cut the crap, Dinah." Gus stepped into the open doorway.

"Just because you dragged me here, Gus, it doesn't mean—"

He cut her off. "Something happened here, and someone named Jimmy Stark dropped off the face of the earth because of it. We'll start there." He gestured with his head to the hallway behind him. "Keeley's downstairs waiting." He looked at Erica. "Get Paul, would you? And Christiana, your 'catching your breath' time will have to wait."

Christiana nodded and strode out of the room without looking back.

Gus gave Dinah a steely look. "Dinah is going to tell us everything she knows about what happened. When that's done, you"—he transferred his attention to Erica—"will make arrangements to transfer every reel, frame, copy, or still taken from the movie into Dinah's hands." He stopped. "If none of that happens, we call in the boys in blue."

"Not too bad at the blackmail yourself, Hammond," Erica said, but she knew when she was beaten.

Apparently so did Marsden, because after giving Hammond a look both hurt and angry, she nodded abruptly.

Erica remained sitting and glanced between Dinah and Gus. "You two know each other."

Gus didn't answer; his full attention was on Dinah. "I'll get your bags," he said. "Show you to your room."

When Gus left, Marsden followed. No doubt about it, the woman had the hots for him. Erica wasn't surprised, couldn't imagine a woman not hot for a guy put together like Hammond. The guy might as well have a tattoo on his forehead: *Fabulous in Bed.* If she were in fighting trim, she'd have a go at him herself.

Erica decided to do what she was told for a change and get Paul. She hefted herself out of the chair. Starrier might be going broke, but at least they'd been given free tickets to a good show.

Marsden, Gus, and Keeley in the same room promised interesting staging. Because unless the Marsden woman was deaf, dumb, and blind, no way could she miss what was going on between Gus and the nun.

Erica was certain she wouldn't like what she saw. A small vengeance, but all she had.

Keeley waited for Gus and her odd collection of houseguests to assemble in the kitchen, but she couldn't sit still, could barely breathe. She went out onto the back porch, a cup of rapidly cooling coffee in her hands, and stared into the raw dampness of the night. Rain hovered; she could sense it. She shivered, brought the tepid coffee to her mouth, and tried to make sense of the events that had overtaken her since her return to Mayday House.

She couldn't. All she could think about was Mary, murder, mothers . . . and lost sisters. The jumble of thoughts about each of them refused to line up.

"What are you doing out here?" Christiana stepped up beside her, rubbing her upper arms against the cold. "It's freezing."

Keeley looked at the sky. "It's going to rain." She finished the last of her coffee and poured the dregs outside the porch rail. "In more ways than one."

"You're thinking about Dinah Marsden."

"Yes, and I'll bet you're doing the same." Keeley gave her a sidelong glance. "She's nothing like you expected, is she?"

"No. She's beautiful, but—"

"Not exactly a milk-and-cookies mama."

Christiana laughed softly. "No, so it's a good thing I'm long past the milk and cookies stage." She stopped. "I didn't get the impression Dinah's in the market for a daughter, so I'm not going to push myself on her."

Keeley took her hand and squeezed it. "Are you going to be okay?"

"Yes. I'll be okay. Confused, but okay. I want to know everything, but I don't. It doesn't make sense."

"It makes perfect sense. I feel the same way." She paused. "It's not easy having your history rewritten."

"No. It isn't."

The thread of the conversation dropped, Keeley and Christiana each lost in their own thoughts. Keeley listened as the first drops of rain hit the roof. In the dim yellow of the porch light, she watched the drops slowly paint the steps a wet-dark, the arrhythmic drops, coming faster now, closing in on each other, merging to form a solid brackish black.

"Do you think she did it?" Christiana finally asked, her tone hushed, and still hugging herself against the cold. "Mary, I mean. Do you think she killed Jimmy Stark?"

"I don't want to, but two confessions? One to you and one to Paul Stark?" She let the hand holding the empty mug drop to her side, then shook her head. "I don't know . . ." Her throat constricted against her suspicion and disloyalty.

Silence.

Keeley gave herself a mental shake, fed up with her broody mood and the non-conversation she was having with Christiana. The truth would come out and she'd deal with it; they'd all deal with it. And they'd be better for it . . . she hoped. Then she'd get on with running Mayday House and seeing where these new feelings surrounding Gus would take her. Would take them. It was the only warm thought on a frigid night.

She turned to Christiana. "Where is everyone, anyway?"

"I left them in Erica's room. Gus is getting Dinah's bags, getting her settled. Erica was going to get Paul. They should all be down soon."

"How did it go with Erica?"

"You mean other than her hating me and wanting to push me off the nearest bridge?"

"Other than that." Keeley pulled her old sweater around her.

Christiana looked past her and into the rain, now falling steadily. "The weird thing is, while I'm not too crazy about the, uh, business she's in, I . . . don't mind her. She's tough, says what she means, and stands up for herself." She paused. "I think she's also overwhelmed right now. Afraid."

"Afraid?" Keeley had trouble accepting that one.

"Of the changes in her life, the"—she rolled her eyes—"business, the babies. All of it. The ground is shifting under her feet and she's scared."

"Not the best excuse I've ever heard for hatching a blackmail scheme, but I suspect you're right." Keeley stopped, then added, half in jest, half seriously, "Maybe you two can get together, and you can soften some of those hard edges of hers."

Christiana smiled. "I think you've already forgotten the 'she hates me' part."

"She'll get over it."

Christiana eyed her. "Will you get over it, Keeley? The blackmail? The killing of Jimmy Stark? What it all might mean for Mayday House?"

"I honestly don't know. They say there's always some good to be found in the worst situations"—she thought of Gus—"but for now I think I'll let the universe, and Dinah Marsden, unfold as it will. Take it from there." She stopped, her hand on the old metal knob. "Erica's not the only one who's on shifting ground. Mary's forgiveness calls have made the earth heave under all of us. I can't help wondering if she'd have made the calls if she'd known the trouble they'd cause."

"It was her way, her time, to set things right. She can't be blamed for that."

"I know." Keeley studied her new friend, one she was certain she would value forever. "So tell me, what made you so darn smart, Miss Fordham?"

Christiana's answering smile held a touch of irony, or maybe sadness. "Considering the mistakes I've made in my life," she replied, "I have no answer for that."

"You don't have to." She peered through the window in the door. "I see Gus, Erica and Paul." She took a deep breath. "I think the show is about to begin."

CHAPTER 20

Keeley and Christiana stepped into the kitchen at the same instant Dinah Marsden entered from the hall.

She was exactly how Keeley had pictured her, cool, beautiful, and with a model's air of self-possession. Her jeans fit as if they were tailored, and she wore a soft, dark green sweater and one immense diamond that glittered sharply under the overhead light.

So this was Gus's . . . what?

Keeley settled on the word *ex*. She pictured them together, these two, both of them so charmed, blessed with physical perfection and the deep inner assurance that came with it. They must have been a match for one another, she thought—except for their one disconnect—the secrets and pain they held from one another, their fear of sharing their souls.

Keeley's stomach did a low roll, and she flattened a hand against it, took a seat, and went back to taking a good look. Dinah's wide-set eyes and stature were much like Christiana's, she decided, but it was there the resemblance ended. Both women were beautiful but in different ways. One warm. One cool.

"You're Keeley Farrell." Dinah eyed her speculatively. "Mary's goddaughter."

"Yes." Keeley's courtesy reflex prompted her to add the usual nice-to-meet-you phrase, but it wouldn't come out.

Without another word, Dinah took a seat at the head of the long kitchen table, putting her between Keeley and Christiana. She gave Christiana a quick nod but said nothing.

Gus strolled in. Keeley expected he'd stand by her, but he walked past her without a glance and took up his usual post—as far away from everyone else in the room as he could get—and leaned against the counter.

Dinah's eyes followed his every movement. Hungry eyes. Carnal eyes. Possessive eyes.

When Keeley looked up at Gus and frowned, he acknowledged her with the barest shake of his head, his expression remote, his face impassive.

When Dinah stopped staring at Gus, she turned to Erica and Paul Stark, both of whom were now sitting, Erica tensely, Paul somberly, at the opposite end of the table from her. Her gaze skipped over Erica. "You're Paul Stark."

He nodded.

"You look like your father."

From what Keeley could see, her remark didn't make either of them happy.

She eyed the kitchen then. "This place hasn't changed a bit. Except for the color."

"We're not here to critique Mayday's décor, Dinah. Just start," Gus said.

She shot Gus a look, then stared down the table at the Starks. "Where is the master?" she demanded.

"Seattle. In a safe place," Paul said. His expression, flat since he'd arrived in the kitchen, seemed to go flatter.

"You'll give me all the copies."

"Yes."

She looked up at Gus and raised a questioning brow.

"You'll get them," Gus said, not moving a muscle. "I'll make sure of it."

At his cold, assured tone, Keeley's stomach rolled again. There was a dark power in Gus and it frightened her at the same time as it drew her to him. She knew enough about his life to understand where the darkness and determination came from. He'd needed both to survive.

Keeley watched Dinah nod her head, spread her hands on the table in front of her, and breathe deeply. "Okay," she finally said, to everyone and no one, "here goes. What Mary Weaver told you was true. She did kill Jimmy . . . your father"—she glanced at the Starks and Christiana—"but it was an accident. She would have admitted to it then, but I wouldn't let her, because I didn't see the point."

"Jesus," Erica said, shaking her head and looking away.

"Go on," Paul said, his tone clipped.

Dinah glanced at them both, unperturbed. "Look, if I could sugarcoat this story, I would. But I can't. I met your dad in a bar, we hit it off. He offered me a decent amount of money to make the film, I was broke, so I agreed. Figured there wasn't much difference between doing it behind closed doors, or in front of a camera."

She rubbed her forehead, looking as if she'd discovered there was a difference after all. "It happened fast. All of it. I was on the set the next day. I worked for maybe a week making something called . . . can't remember the name of it—"

"Bedtime Blonde," Erica offered. "Cute, huh?"

Dinah ignored her. "I was twenty-one, maybe twenty-two. Jimmy was quite a bit older. He had some charm then—and money. When he came on to me, I thought that was okay. When he didn't want me to make any more films, that was okay, too. We had a thing for a few months, then I—like a zillion stupid women before me—got pregnant."

Erica shifted in her chair, her face tight as timber.

Dinah got up from the table and went to stand beside Gus at the counter, shoulder to shoulder. "Frankly, I was too damn scared to abort, and just about then is when things between Jimmy and me got ugly. Which made me even more sure I didn't want any kind of long-term relationship with him." She glanced at the Starks. "Your daddy was a mean little bastard, kiddies. But I'm guessing you already know that."

Neither of the Starks leaped to their father's defense. Paul's jaw was locked so hard it looked paralyzed; Erica's gaze dropped to the table.

"Funny," Dinah went on, "it started out he couldn't keep his hands off me, then he couldn't keep his fists off me. It got worse when he found out I was pregnant. After a bad bout, I called Mary. When I told her about Jimmy, and my, uh, delicate condition, she told me to come home. Just get on the first bus to Erinville, she said."

"Erinville is your home?" Keeley said. This was news to her.

"I grew up just a few miles from this house. When I left, I never intended to come back, but there I was broke, pregnant, with a couple of puce-colored eyes, and nowhere to go. Mary saved my life," she said, this time quietly.

Christiana spoke up. "He found you, didn't he? And he came here to get you."

Dinah's gaze, which for a time had seemed hazy and unfocused, zeroed in on Christiana. "Yes. He showed up at Mayday a few days before I was due—close to midnight." She stood, wrapped her arms around herself as her daughter had done a few minutes earlier while on the back porch with Keeley. "Mary tried to head him off at the door, but he brushed past her and found me in the room next to hers."

The one Gus is in now, Keeley thought.

"He didn't waste any time, went on about me leaving him, taking his kid. After he'd called me every name in the book, he said he wanted me back. I told him to"—she looked at Keeley, shrugged—"I told him to fuck off. After that, it got ugly fast. He hit me, and I hit him back—with a book, cut his lip." She looked annoyed. "It didn't hurt him, of course, but it sure as hell enraged him. He lost it, came at me with both fists, yelling about how no 'fucking porn slut' was going to raise a kid of his." She stopped. "He hit me in the belly." She put a hand on her stomach and glanced at Christiana. "That's when Mary and Aileen showed up."

Keeley's blood backed up in her veins, and words she might have said turned to sharp stones in her mouth.

Her mother had been involved . . .

The idea wouldn't gel in her mind. She knew Gus was looking at her, but she fixed dry eyes on Dinah, desperate to hear the complete story—not to think until she had all the facts.

"They both came at him from behind, screaming, pulling, shoving . . . Whatever they could do, they did. They managed to get him off me—or at least distract him—but then he turned on them. First, he hit Aileen, who was only slightly less pregnant than I was. She went down hard, hit her forehead on a table, and was out cold in seconds. From that point, it got even crazier. He got hold of me again, started choking . . ."

When her words trailed off, the only sounds left in the room were the rain splattering against the kitchen window and the humph of the old furnace in the cellar below.

Dinah twisted her lips, and glanced away, then back again to look at them all. "That's when Mary hit him with the lamp."

"A lamp?" Gus echoed. They were the first words he'd spoken since Dinah started speaking.

"One of those brass ones. They used to be in the bedrooms here. Heavy old things. Mary got rid of them after . . ."

"I get the picture," Gus said. "Go on."

"Jimmy dropped like a stone. Went down right on top of Aileen. I remember that, because we had to pull him off. At first we thought he was just knocked out. Unconscious." She pushed away from the counter, went to the back door, and stared into the black, wet night. "He was dead. I guess Mary's lamp attack landed just right, somewhere near the base of the skull. There wasn't even a lot of blood." She stopped. So far she'd been cool, unmoved. Now she shivered. "It all happened so fast."

Gus said, "What happened then?"

"Aileen started moaning, trying to get up, so we did what we could for her. I remember the cut on her head was quite deep."

And Keeley remembered the pale one-inch scar on her mother's forehead, remembered asking her about it, remembered her touching it, then looking away. *"From a fall, my dear one," she'd said, "a clumsy fall."*

". . . So we dealt with Aileen, bandaged her head," Dinah said, and Keeley was drawn back to that horrific night. "Anything so we didn't have to think about the dead man lying on my bedroom floor. Then, just about the time we were trying to figure out what to do next"—she smiled grimly—"with my usual perfect timing, I went into labor."

Christiana's eyes, fixed intently on her mother, silvered with tears.

"Mary made me lie down," Dinah said. "Told me to calm down and breathe. She might as well have told me to visualize a Polynesian beach while I was naked in a blizzard." She walked back to the table and took the seat she'd vacated between Keeley and Christiana. Her gaze went to her daughter directly, defensively. "You were born not long after."

Christiana brushed at her tears, nodded, but said nothing.

"With our father lying dead on the floor," Erica said, her face a mask of disgust.

"Not the prettiest image in the world, is it?" Dinah laced her fingers together and put her joined hands on the table. She looked around the group, all trace of emotion wiped from her face. "And now I'll take questions from the floor."

"Why didn't you call the police?" Keeley asked, determined to wring every bit of information she could from the untouchable woman sitting beside her.

"Good question," she said. "And totally expected. For an hour or so, Mary and Aileen were busy delivering a baby"—another quick glance at Christiana—"and when that was done, I wouldn't let them call anyone."

"Did they want to?" Keeley asked.

"Oh, yeah, they wanted to, all right."

"How did you stop them?"

"A lot of hysteria, a lot of begging—and a big dose of common sense. Mary had killed a man, for God's sake. Jesus, the whole thing was too messy for words!" Her expression turned angry, frustrated. "We were all scared out of our minds. Me, because if the police got involved, Jimmy's dirty little film business would be exposed—and my part in it. Hell, the papers would love the porn angle. It would have been seriously ugly. I'd have been in every paper from here to Mexico." She stopped. "And so would Mary— and her precious Mayday House. There was no point in letting a scumbag like Jimmy ruin all our lives."

Gus moved away from the counter to stand by the table and loom over Dinah's shoulder. "And you sold that crap to Mary Weaver."

Her eyes shot to his. "It was easier to get rid of the body. Pretend it never happened. Everyone saw that."

"Even my mother?" Keeley asked, her stomach filled with snakes, her mind alive with warring images.

"Your mother would have jumped into a live volcano for Mary," Dinah said. "She didn't want to see her hurt—possibly go to jail. Plus she had her own reasons. Something about not wanting the publicity. At least that's what she said. Actually, she was easier to convince than Mary." She gave Keeley a direct look. "As I said, she had her reasons. She didn't tell me what they were, and I didn't ask." She shrugged. "It was Mayday House. Everybody had a past, everybody had a secret."

"Speaking of secrets, where's the body?" Paul interjected, the same inscrutable expression on his face at the end of Dinah's confession as there had been at the beginning.

"I have no idea."

Again the room went quiet, and Dinah rose from the table. She was tired, Keeley saw, and trying hard not to let it show. Probably knew it wouldn't garner any sympathy from this room. "I'd just had a baby. I was exhausted. The last thing I remember before falling asleep was Mary telling me 'not to worry.' She and Aileen would take care of things, she said. When I woke up, the body was gone. She didn't tell me what they'd done with it, and I never asked." Dinah headed for the door, stopped when she got there, and surveyed the gathering with a frigid calm before settling her gaze on Paul. "I've told you everything I know, which means I've kept my part of the bargain. Now you keep yours. Get me that film." She walked out.

Erica spat out the word, "Bitch!" and glared at Dinah's back, then watched her disappear through the doorway.

Christiana squared her arms on the table and

rested her head on them, her blond hair making a curtain to shield her obvious distress.

All of them looked as stunned as Keeley felt, and none of them seemed capable of offering up more than silence.

Keeley reached across the table and stroked Christiana's head. At the same time Gus put his big warm hand on Keeley's nape, squeezed, then leaned down to whisper in her ear, "I'm going to talk to Dinah."

His breath still warming her ear, Dinah's words still chilling her heart, Keeley watched him leave.

Question period was over.

A half hour later, her hood pulled snug to her head against the intermittent splatters of rain and the threat of more, Keeley was on her own and grateful for it. Mayday House seethed with tension and personal confusions, and with everyone caught up in their own reactions to Dinah's story, no one had figured out a way to ease them. Least of all herself.

Everyone agreed on one thing: Jimmy Stark's body had to be found, even if it meant leveling Mayday House to do it.

Keeley, a good couple of miles from Mayday House, trudged along the muddy country road and tried to make sense of things. Like her mind, the night was murky and dark, but her eyes were accustomed to it, and she knew the lumpy, puddle-studded farmer's road well enough to watch her step.

What she could not do was ease her heart, organize her disoriented thinking, or shake the feeling she'd been washed up on a strange shore, where the trees were blue and the sky was green.

Before Dinah told her story, the mystery had centered on Mayday House and Mary Weaver. Now the mystery swirled around her own dear mother.

The idea of her shy, deeply religious mother having secrets was as difficult to accept as her part in covering up the death of Stark, or the shocking visual of Mary Weaver swinging a bedside lamp and killing Stark.

"Everyone has a darkness in them," she remembered Mary telling her. "Sometimes they put it there themselves, and sometimes it arrives on its own. People come in shades of gray, darlin'." She hadn't thought back then that Mary was referring to herself— or to Aileen.

Keeley knew her mother's story, or thought she did. Aileen had come over from Ireland with an American college student. She was eighteen when she became pregnant with Keeley. The boy, for "certain reasons," was compelled to leave her.

When Keeley was ten, a year before her mother died, she'd asked about those "certain reasons" and she'd been told, her "*da* was a good man, but a melancholy one. One with his own calling."

When she'd asked where he was, the answer was vague. "A place too far away to find."

When Aileen died, whatever clues there were to Keeley's father's past or whereabouts went with her to her grave. There were no photos, no letters, no young girl's diary in which to dig. Eventually, Keeley stopped wondering about her mother's ill-fated love, and accepted it as a painful part of her life she was unwilling to talk about.

Keeley hadn't thought about it for a long time.

She thought about it now, both the story she'd grown up with and about her mother who, if Dinah's story was true, had kept quiet about a lot more than Keeley's father. She'd been silent about a killing . . .

According to Dinah, she hadn't wanted "publicity." The word loomed large in her mind, as if it were an elephant at Sunday Mass; the idea of her mother concerned with such a thing was at odds with her every childhood memory of her. Yet Aileen had involved herself in covering up a killing and a secret burial because of it.

A burial that meant there was a body, Jimmy Stark's body, deep in Mayday's past—and future.

Numb and unsettled, Keeley stopped walking and stared unseeing into the mist-shrouded night. The first pelting of serious rain slapped at her face, and with it came the terrible, stomach-turning sense she may be the only one to know where the body was.

The only one to ever know *if I keep it to myself, leave Stark where he is and honor the secret my mother and grandmother spent their lives protecting.*

A clap of distant thunder made her look up. Her wet feet made her look down, and she turned and started walking slowly back to the house.

Tomorrow at first light she'd find Jimmy Stark. Then she'd make her decision.

Dolan put down his cell phone, took a breath so deep it was painful, then shot a stream of vile curses into his luxurious hotel suite.

Still alive. The bitch was still alive!

"Goddamn you, Mace."

After another couple of breaths, he walked to the hotel phone on the desk under the window and picked it up.

"I'd like a map. Southern Washington. And a rental car, doesn't matter what as long as they can deliver within the hour. . . . No, I'm not checking out, just a small emergency. . . . Call me when the car's here. If you can do it in less than an hour, I'll make it worth your while." He put down the phone.

For the first time since this fiasco started, he felt in control. Maybe there was something to this clean and sober shit, after all. Maybe he'd finally found the brain he'd buried under a ton of booze and cocaine for ten years.

Not that he couldn't use a little blow right now, help him cope with the hot poker embedded in his brain.

I should never have relied on Mace, never have trusted him.

All this time—wasted—and she was still breathing.

Just like that antique, William, still hanging on to life. Jesus—he shook his head—you'd think the bastard had something to live for, while Dolan had nothing at all, until he got what was due him—the miserable son of a bitch's money. It seemed like forever he'd been waiting for it, playing his stupid son-that-gives-a-shit game. Maybe he should rethink himself on that score when he got home, too. After he'd done Farrell.

He tossed some clothes in his bag, and on top of them he placed his brand-new toy, a Smith and Wesson Sigma 9mm automatic. He'd bought it the day after Mace's and his last meeting. It wouldn't drop a charging rhino, but it would take care of his problems.

"Say your prayers, *sister*. You're about to meet the man upstairs." Not that he believed there was one.

He zipped up the bag, his mind racing. While he was taking care of family matters, he'd take care of Mace, too, end what he called their 'partnership' permanently.

The idea of that warmed him. In the next few hours his life was about to change for the better. He grinned.

Maybe he was a chip off the dying geezer's block after all. The old man always said if you wanted something done right, you had to do it yourself.

His plan exactly.

CHAPTER 21

Close to midnight, Gus, his leather jacket sodden, his jeans the same, walked the graveyard, went through the hole in the hedge, and crossed the backyard. He'd come back to get his car, because wherever Keeley had gone, this time it wasn't anywhere near the church. He'd started with the priest's house, thinking it would be her first stop, but instead of Barton he'd wakened his ancient housekeeper who'd told him "the father was away," visiting his brother in the next town.

This time she'd eluded him.

He'd circled out from Mayday and walked until the heat of his anger at her for leaving the house alone turned to cold dread in his chest.

Sidestepping the lumpy sandbox, he crossed the grid of weeds and high grass, now rooted in a series of rain ponds dotting Mayday's back lawn, and headed for the house. Nearing it, Gus shook the rain from his hair and glanced up in time to see the kitchen light go on.

He slammed through the back door. "Where in

hell have you been?" The heat boiled up again. He wanted to shake her until her teeth rattled, but for that he'd need muscle, and his had gone soft with relief on sight of her.

She was heading toward the stove with a kettle in her hand; she stopped and frowned at him, then said, "Tea?"

"Jesus . . ." He forked his fingers through his wet hair, shoved it roughly off his forehead. "No, I don't want any goddamn tea. I want to know where you were."

"Quit cursing." She put the kettle on the stove and turned on the element. "It was either go for a walk or have one of my shake-and-quake episodes, so I decided on the former."

"You should have—"

"I should have told you?" She walked toward him and touched his face. "I thought about it, but I needed to be alone. I had some thoughts to sort through. And the way I saw it, all the bogeymen were sound asleep at Mayday."

"Not Mace."

"The chance of that man having any interest in me is less than zero." She gave him a direct look. "Even if he was, I was careful. Unless he was hiding in the backyard and knew the farm roads as well as I do, I knew there'd be no problem. There wasn't." Her jaw firmed. "Plus I took that." She pointed to a can of pepper spray on the kitchen table. "I'm not careless, Gus, and I'm not stupid, and I won't live in fear."

He took her by the shoulders. "Well, I do—at least when it comes to you—and I want you to promise me you won't do that again."

"No. I don't make promises I won't keep."

He let his hands drop, afraid this time he would throttle her, and said, "Fair enough. We both understand the rules." And if she thought he was going to let her out of his sight until this business with Mace was cleared up, she was dead wrong. But it wasn't worth arguing about. Most things weren't. You meet an immovable object, you don't butt heads with it. You watch, keep your mouth shut, and wait it out. Maybe she didn't get it yet, but she was his and he'd protect her; he wasn't asking her permission. "This relationship of ours grows more interesting every day," he said.

She lifted her chin, and he saw the tension in her face. "If you're worried about it, you can always leave and—"

He touched her mouth with his fingers to shut her up and lowered his head to ensure he met her eyes. "The only thing I'm worried about is you and this damn place. I want you safe, because I don't want to lose you. Ever. Leaving is not an option. You got that?"

She nodded, but her tension didn't appear to ease.

The whistle of the kettle cut through the kitchen with the pitched whine of an emergency siren. Keeley set it aside, then turned off the stove. "How did you make out with Dinah?" she asked, her back still to him. "Do you believe her about not knowing where Jimmy Stark is buried?"

Gus shrugged out of his wet jacket and went to hang it on one of the hooks beside the back door. "Yes, I believe her. All she did was repeat what she said. She fell asleep, and when she woke up, the body was gone. Mary didn't volunteer the information about what they did with it, and Dinah didn't ask. It looks as if they all played the game of let's-pretend-it-never-happened and went on with their lives." He stopped. "Except—"

"Except what?" She poured the boiling water into a brown teapot.

"Stark's death was the reason Dinah gave up Christiana. When she left Seattle for Mayday House, no one knew she was carrying Stark's kid, and after what happened, she decided to leave it that way. For her sake and Mary's, so she says. The way Dinah saw it, as links to a dead man go, a kid is as strong as they get. She didn't want the link. To Stark. The porn movie. Any of it."

"So the adoption was done under the radar."

"Apparently the women"—he watched her face, saw it close up at his use of the plural—"talked it over, decided it would be best."

"I see." She carried the teapot to the table, where she'd set out a mug and poured herself some tea—with only a slight tremor.

Tense, Gus thought, seriously tense. "After the baby was born, Dinah left. Went back east. She hasn't been back here since—until now."

Keeley didn't seem to be listening. Her mug cradled between her hands, she stared into nowhere. He sat down in the chair opposite her across the table. "You all right?"

"As well as can be expected for a daughter who's just found out her mother was involved in covering up a killing."

"We screw up. It's what people do. Then they're stuck with it." He knew all about being in that hellish place. He'd spent half a life there, living with a

bogus murder charge, certain no one would believe a street kid.

"It was a clear case of self-defense. They should
have called the police. The priest at St. Ivan's.
Anyone. They shouldn't have lied." She closed her
eyes a moment, then slowly opened them as if it hurt
to do so.

He wanted to tell her people lied all the time, but
knew his hard-earned cynicism wouldn't help. But
a change in direction might. "There's one other
thing."

"Uh-huh."

"It was Dinah who sent the books. Or more accu-
rately arranged they be sent." Good old Cassie, Gus
thought, a true-blue gofer until the end.

Her eyes lifted to his, still tired, only dimly interested. "Why?"

"Her way of helping the cause. She figured a good
scare and you'd do what I wanted you to do. Sell
out." He lifted her chin, smiled into her eyes. "She
had no idea she was dealing with a warrior woman."

The smile she gave him in return looked fragile.

"It's late," he said. "And you're tired. The smart
thing to do is go to bed. Think about it tomorrow."

She drank her tea, and as if she hadn't heard
him, stared out the window. "That's what they should
have done," she murmured. "They should have
called Father Randall." It was as if she were slipping into a dream state, as if her thoughts were
smothering her.

Gus had no idea who Father Randall was and at
this point didn't much care. Second-guessing a
thirty-five-year-old mind-set was a waste of time. Best
to deal with reality. And reality right now was getting

this woman to rest. He walked around the table and pulled out her chair. "Come on. You need sleep. Tomorrow's going to be rough."

"By rough, you mean Christiana and Paul, don't you?"

"They want to organize the next step."

"Finding the body." Her voice was flat, lifeless.

"Has to happen, Keeley."

"You're right," she said in the same dry tone. "Tomorrow will be rough."

Gus put his arm around her, and they walked down the hall to her door. When he turned to go to his own room, she grasped his hand and drew him inside. "Don't go."

"I thought with everyone in the house, you'd be uncomfortable." He gestured with his head to the room beyond her door. "Me, being there."

"If I were uncomfortable, it would mean I'm ashamed," she said, her voice cool, warming when she added, "I'm not."

He brushed her damp hair behind her ears and cupped her face. "And that's the biggest compliment I've ever had. Plus there's an added bonus."

She looked at him.

"I can hold you in my arms instead of doing guard duty outside your door."

Her eyes looked weary when she said, "You can't protect everyone, Gus. Not from themselves, anyway." She stood on her toes and kissed him. "Now, let's go to bed." She smiled, but he sensed it was forced. "As you said, tomorrow's going to be a rough day."

* * *

Mace drove around the abandoned property he'd checked out earlier in the day. Only a mile or two from Farrell's place. It'd work.

Empty for years. Had to be. The barn was damn near rubble; the windows in the house, most of them broken, were dark. Some rusted-out farm equipment, or what was left of it, was settled hard into deep grass beside the rutted road leading to the house.

He pulled in behind the barn. He'd come at Mayday from the back, where the Farrell woman's bedroom was. At least he'd got that much out of the Erica bitch before things went sideways. He touched his bandaged ear, got fuckin' mad all over again, then told himself to calm down.

Main floor, rear of the house, that's what she said. This whole thing should be a snap. Get in, get her dead as quietly as possible, and get out.

Simple plans were always the best.

The grin faded. The unknown factor was the asshole with the knife who, according to Erica, was in the next room to the nun. With luck he'd get the job done before one of the bastard's eyelids so much as twitched, but if not . . .

But first the woman. He had to get the woman.

Peering through the rain slashing at his windshield, he let out a frustrated breath. Not a chance it was going to let up tonight. Mace pulled on the rubber boots he'd bought at the local Wal-Mart. Looking out the car window, he wished he'd bought goddamn hip-waders. This job would give him pneumonia for sure.

He briefly switched on the overhead light to check his watch. Two-fifty A.M. Figuring somewhere between twenty and thirty minutes to cross the field, he'd be there before four, no sweat.

He got out of the car, out of habit locked it, and pulled his jacket collar up around his ears. Butting his head against a rain turned into bullets by the punishing wind, he started across the field.

Keeley, lying on her back, stared into the darkness above her head. She knew it was nearly three, had to be, because she'd heard the two o'clock chime from the old wall clock in the dining room, and she'd been awake for what seemed forever.

When she wasn't thinking about the lean hard body in bed with her—and wondering how deeply Gus slept—she was thinking about another body. Jimmy Stark's.

Doing what she had to do wasn't something she could do in the daylight with the cast of thousands currently in Mayday House peering over her shoulder— and the police in the wings. No. To confirm where they'd buried him, and decide what to do if she was right, was best done alone and in the dark.

She had two or three hours at most.

Carefully, oh-so-carefully, she shifted to the edge of the bed.

"Where are you going?" Gus said, his voice heavy with sleep.

Damn! "Bathroom. Go back to sleep." Only a half lie, because it was her first stop. She put her feet on the floor, but before she could stand, his hand shackled her wrist.

"And after that?" No more sleep in his voice, only a terse coolness. Suspicion.

She took a deep breath, couldn't find another lie, and didn't want to. "Out."

"Jesus." He let go of her wrist, sat up, and turned on the bedside lamp. Its light cast him in pale yellow, turning his bare chest to gold and leaving his face in darkness. "Talk to me, Keeley. Tell me what the hell is going on with you."

She knew those dangerous probing eyes of his were settled on her. And she knew there was no escaping them, and the chances of her getting away from him now were zero to nil.

She stood and took a couple of steps away from the bed, wishing she could be honest, but she was too cowardly, too ashamed for him to know her thoughts. If she was right about where Stark's body was, no one but she would ever find it. If she held her silence, she'd keep the faith with her mother and grandmother. Mayday House would go on as before.

As a house of lies, a house of deceit, a house of shame.
Leaden silence filled the room.

And when he'd had enough of it, Gus threw the covers off and got out of bed. He pulled on his jeans, took his shirt from the chair, and said, "We go together."

"No. What I have to do, I have to do alone." She wouldn't involve Gus in this, ask him to be dishonest. She couldn't.

He took the few steps separating them, studied her for what seemed forever, then narrowed his eyes and nodded his head slowly. "I get it."

He cupped her chin and pulled her face to his. "You know where the body is." He didn't ask; he stated it, looking absolutely sure of himself.

Keeley pulled away from his grip, wrapped her

arms around herself against the room's chill, and said nothing.

"You're a lousy liar, Keeley, so why even think about trying?"

"I'm not lying—about anything. I'm just not absolutely sure yet, and I don't want to tell the others—"

"And you consider me one of the '*others*.'"

"No, it's just that . . ." How could she tell him she was considering telling the biggest lie of all, a sin of omission, by denying Erica, Paul, and Christiana access to their father's body, proof of what had happened to him. God, even she hadn't processed that yet.

"Get dressed." He walked back toward the bed to retrieve his shoes. "We'll go together." He looked up at her from where he sat on the edge of the bed. "And if you don't want to tell the others you know where he is, that's fine by me." He paused, his hands still on the laces of his shoes. "Although I doubt it'll make you happy."

Keeley gasped. *How could he—*

"What is *not* fine by me," he went on, "is you putting yourself in the sights of Mace's gun."

He finished tying his shoes, stood. Keeley hadn't yet moved a inch, her mind too busy trying to figure out how her planned one-woman reconnaissance had turned into a team effort. She studied the irritated man in front of her, and her mouth went dry. Love, she thought. "Flashlights," she said. "We'll need flashlights."

"What about shovels?" he asked, his face set with grim purpose.

Keeley shuddered. "No. No shovels . . . yet."

* * *

When Mace's cell phone rang, its tone was barely audible over the wind and rain. He fumbled in his pocket for it and raised it to his ear.

"Where are you?"

Shit! Dolan. Mace took a deep breath of cool. "Working the night shift."

There was a slight pause. "Tonight's the night, then?"

"Uh-huh." Mace stopped near a copse of trees to get his breath and get out of the weather. He rubbed the dampness off his cheeks. "Almost there. So how's about you leave me to it. I'll call you when the job's done. We can plan a little celebration." Might as well start making nice-nice to idiot boy, considering payday was at hand.

"Where exactly is 'there'?" Dolan asked.

"Weaver's place."

"What's your plan?"

Mace let out a breath and with it some of his cool. "Jesus, Dolan, I'm handling it. Let me do my job, will ya?"

"Seems to me that's what I have been doing and the bitch is still alive. I repeat, what's your plan?"

This time Mace held his curses to himself. Dolan was doing his thing, making like he was the boss. Easy to be tough from the other end of a phone line. Shit, he'd have to humor the jerk, if only to get him off the goddamn phone. "Going in from the back. That's where Farrell's room is. I take her out and I'm gone."

"Mace."

"Yeah."

"Do not fuck this up."

Mace clicked off. "Yes, boss-man. Anything you say,

boss-man." He stuffed the phone in his pocket and headed out across the empty windswept field.

In the kitchen, cast in the dim gray of the kitchen's nightlight, Gus watched Keeley disappear into the shadow of the mud room. When she came out she was wearing overalls over her jeans, a woolen cap on her head pulled low over her ears, and a hooded rain jacket. She retrieved two flashlights from a shelf in the kitchen and handed one of them to Gus. "Ready?" she whispered, intent on not waking the second-floor sleepers.

In the lousy light, Gus eyed her from top to toe; she vaguely reminded him of an Inuit on a seal hunt. "I take it Stark isn't in the cellar."

"You take it right."

"Where, then?"

She put her fingers to her lips. "Shush." She closed the Velcro fastener at her neck, her face disappearing behind a hood that encompassed her head and left no peripheral vision. "Let's go."

Gus claimed his still-wet leather jacket from the hook by the door, and they went out the back door where the weather waited to attack them.

Keeley paused on the top step and grimaced. "I hope the rain and wind will save us from waking Father Barton. The man would hear a pin drop on a cloud."

"He's not there, but his housekeeper is."

"Mrs. Rankin." She nodded and thought a minute. "She shouldn't be a problem. She's a little bit deaf and with the storm . . ." She grabbed his hand. "Let's go."

"Whoa." When she started to step off the porch,

he tugged her back. "You're telling me Stark's buried in the graveyard?"

"Yes. That's where I *think* he is."

"Keeley, there must be three hundred graves over there." The wind lashed at his hair; the craziness of what they were doing did the same in his head. This was nuts.

"Three hundred and twenty-two, to be exact. My mother"—she paused a moment and glanced away, then back—"was among the last to be buried there. But we won't have to check them all." Her voice came out of the hood. "The older graves are nearest the church, the newer ones fan out from there. I think the one we're looking for, a seventies grave, will be close to the Mayday House hedge." She paused. "I know the graveyard layout. I spent a lot of time in there when I was a kid. I used to sit there for hours." She paused. "Praying for the dead."

"Strange kid." He tried to visualize his energetic redhead slowing down enough to kneel in an old graveyard.

"Maybe, but you know what *they* say, the dead don't bother you; it's the living you have to watch out for."

Gus couldn't argue with that. "And you think Mary and your mother buried Stark in a church graveyard."

"Yes, I do. I know it sounds crazy, but I can see them doing it . . . for a lot of reasons."

"You think it might have been their way of making things right," he said. "Burying Stark in the churchyard."

Her shrug was uncertain. "It's possible."

He thought about it. Possible. Yes, and aside from the hallowed ground, religious aspect of things, damn smart. Especially if there happened to be a grave already dug and waiting for its occupant. Dig a little deeper, put the body in, cover it with dirt. Yeah. It'd work, although he kept his more pragmatic view to himself. "Even if they did, how will you find it? All the graves look pretty much the same."

"They're not." She pulled his hand. "Can we go? It'll lighten up soon, and I'd rather do what I have to do while everyone's still asleep."

They walked across Mayday's huge backyard and pushed through the dripping hedge. The night lamp attached under the peak of St. Ivan's steep roof cast a foggy wash of gray light on the graves nearest the church, and bleak shadows over those beyond it. Gus turned on his flashlight.

Once on the other side, Keeley waved her light along the hedge and the graves closest to it, walked about thirty feet, and dropped to her knees. She set her flashlight beside her to illuminate a grave and ran her hands slowly over its surface.

Gus, standing over her, said, "If you tell me what you're looking for, I can help." He pulled his wet collar up against the rain-laden wind.

Still on her knees, she moved to the next grave. "Stones. I'm looking for a series of stones embedded on the surface of the grave." She looked down the uneven row of tilted headstones and mossy plaques bearing the names of the dead and records of their time on earth. All of them black with rain, the plots themselves were buried inches deep in leaves driven to earth by the wind and rain.

Gus didn't bother asking why he was looking for stones. He followed her lead, sank to his knees, and started probing the surface of the nearest grave.

The heavy rain soaked the rest of the way through his jacket; then, with the suddenness common to a Pacific Northwest storm, it stopped. Gus knew the reprieve was temporary.

Keeley shoved the hood from her head, mumbling, "Thank God." But she carried on with her grim task.

He felt a hard lump under his palm, shifted his hand back, and pressed harder. A stone, then another. "There's something here."

Keeley crawled to his side. "Where?"

He took her hand and pressed it against the stones. She moved her own hands in a circle, her face tight with purpose; then she shook her head. "No. That's not it. There should be a pattern." She went back to the grave she'd abandoned, but after running her hands over it, she rested on her heels. When her flashlight dimmed, she picked it up, and pointed it down the row of graves. "Maybe you should start there," she said, circling her light on a headstone about fifty feet away. "I'll go there." She swung it in the opposite direction. "We'll work toward each other instead of away." She paused. "The pattern might be hard to find. It's been a lot of years."

"We'll take it slow." He gave her his much brighter flashlight and took hers.

She took his hand, squeezed it, and let it go. "Thanks, Gus," she said, her tone low. "For coming with me. I know you think this is crazy."

He crouched down and stroked her face. Wet from tears or wet from the rain, he couldn't tell. "Not so crazy, and from now on—just to be sure we understand each other—where you go, I go. No thanks are necessary."

She nodded but said nothing, then got up and walked along the path between the graves where she dropped to her knees, morphing into a gray ghost, a kneeling shadow in his peripheral vision.

As they worked, the beam of her flashlight splayed across the ground, grass, and leaves, blanketing the long-departed souls of St. Ivan's, and the wind, flicking at the trees overhead and swirling along the hedge behind them, was the only break in the deadness of the silence.

For a few minutes, they searched quietly, Gus's flashlight growing dimmer by the second, finally going out completely. He shook it a couple of times, but other than one quick flash, nothing. He looked up at the sky, lighter now that some of the rain clouds had scudded off, took another reading on Keeley's light, and went back to working toward it, pressing his hands, deeply and palm flat, into the wet earth over the graves leading to Keeley's light.

They were maybe forty feet apart when he heard Keeley shout, "I've found it. Dear God, Gus, I think I found it."

She waved the brilliant beam of the flashlight in his direction, temporarily blinding him.

He started to get up. The action abruptly aborted when something as hard and solid as a St. Ivan's gravestone connected with his head.

Gus's jolted senses registered two things: the dense odor of sodden leaves shooting up his nose and the chill of dead earth against his cheek.

His brain, amidst an array of wildly shooting colors, registered rage—and one name.

Keeley.

CHAPTER 22

Keeley sat back on her knees, lifted her hand from the grave, and wiped it slowly on her jean-covered thigh. Her mind was a jumble, her heart incoherent with emotion.

Everything Dinah and Mary had said was true. She'd found the grave. The grave she'd prayed wouldn't be there.

Until a stone daisy said otherwise.

Mary Weaver had killed Jimmy Stark and her mother had helped her bury him.

Keeley tried to imagine carrying the weight of Mary and her mother's guilt, to understand the reasons for their years of secrecy, their terrible silence.

How had they lived with the sin of it?

So many questions, and the biggest one of all what she would do now. Expose Mary and her mother or take on the mantle of that silence?

She knew she wouldn't decide here, with her knees, cold and wet, bent over forgotten bones, an unknown soul. No, she'd go back to Mayday, talk to Gus—then talk to God.

On one knee now, she called out again, "Gus, did you hear me? I've found him."

A hand came from behind, grabbed her hair, and yanked her the rest of the way to her feet.

"No, he doesn't hear you," a low harsh voice said in her ear. "And he probably won't . . . ever again."

Keeley, pulled hard against the body behind hers, couldn't get a breath, and her heart pumped so hard, she couldn't think. The arm around her waist formed a vise tight enough to crack her ribs—push air out of her lungs.

The flashlight fell from her hand, spilling light on the daisy-marked grave before rolling across the path and into the base of the hedge.

He dragged her backward, roughly. "Who are you?" She choked out the words at the second he grabbed her shoulder and spun her to face him.

"Who are—"

"Shut the fuck up." He used the palm of his hand against her chin to shove her backward into the dense hedge. With his other hand, he jammed a gun into her stomach.

Shock blurred her brain.

A wave of nausea threatened to take her to her knees.

He stepped back, and the pressure of the gun left her stomach, but he stayed close enough that she could see his night-dark face.

A stranger.

"It don't matter who I am. So long as you're Farrell."

When she didn't say anything—still too paralyzed by shock to access her brain—he reached over and touched her hair, pulled some strands, rolled them between his fingers, the gesture eerily gentle. He let her hair go, then ran his hand down her throat and across her breast. "You're her, all right. Even in this shit weather I can make out that red hair."

Keeley, shuddering under his touch, couldn't make sense of any of it, but something told her it wasn't a good idea to be "*her*" right now. She took in a couple of breaths, took time before saying, "And if I'm not?"

He casually lifted the gun in the direction of Mayday House. "Then I'll just head on over there and start shootin' until I find her." His tone chilled. "Your call, *sister.*"

"I'm Farrell." She forced her shoulders to straighten, her mind to stifle her panic. "And I'd like to know why my name has you pointing a gun at me. I don't even know you." She tried to stare him down, keep her eyes off the gun, turn her fear into something more useful than the shakes and a dry mouth.

"Well, now let's us straighten things out for you. The name's Mace and I'm pointing a gun at you because I aim to send you to your Maker."

"My Maker," she echoed stupidly. Afraid her knees would give way, she put her hands behind her, buried them in the thorny brush of the hedge, and held tight.

Think, Keeley, think!

Time, she needed time.

"Why? I've never seen you before in my life." She glanced at the light near her feet. *The flashlight.*

"The why don't matter, sweetheart. Dead's dead. And that's the way your brother wants you."

"You've made a mistake. I don't have a brother."

He laughed. "Not one you're gonna meet, anyway.

Now about the dead part"—he lifted the gun—"best we get to it . . . just as soon as I'm done with you."

For a second, her mind stuck on the *brother* word, the fact she was going to die because of a mistake. A stupid, stupid mistake. Then her mind landed on his last words, and it wasn't fear firing along her veins, it was a sudden white-hot anger. She let go of the hedge growth. "By 'done with,' I take it you plan to rape me," she said, the words as crisp and cool as those of a fourth-grade teacher. She inched away, her hands at her sides, her back brushing the hedge behind her, her focus on the flashlight maybe a foot or two from her feet.

"Don't see why we shouldn't have ourselves a little fun." He touched her hair again. "Your dead boyfriend sure as hell ain't gonna be giving you any."

At the reference to Gus, Keeley went sleet cold. Gus wasn't dead. She might not know why, but she was absolutely certain of it. And equally as certain she needed to get to him—quickly.

"The priest who lives in that house might," she said, jerking her head in the direction of the rectory. When Mace glanced up, she gained another few inches. "And if I scream loud enough, they'll hear me all the way to Mayday House."

"Well, then you'll just have to be quiet, won't you?" He looked at her, as if sizing her up, ran his tongue over his lower lip. "And ya know what, missy? I don't think I'll be needing this." He shoved the gun in his belt and lunged.

Keeley dropped to her knees, closed her fingers around the flashlight. She raised it, brought it down hard, but managed only a grazing blow to his shoulder. Enough to anger him.

"Bitch!" He grabbed her hair, and she hit him again, this time ramming the flashlight into his stomach. A slight whoosh of his breath crossed her cheek and he swore again, yanking her hair until her face was inches from his. She saw mean, ugly eyes, a cold sneer. "I didn't expect this much fun, you being a nun and all."

When she rammed him again, he hit her, his first blow glancing off her ear, his second connecting with her jaw. Her head ringing, she stumbled and fell to the ground. When he came toward her, she beamed the flashlight into his eyes and scuttled backward along the path.

She didn't get far.

He fell on her, broad and heavy, like a giant tree sawn at the base. The gun he'd stuffed in his belt bore hard into her hipbone. She pounded his back with the light, kicked, clawed, then screamed as long and loud as she could, but he was too big, too heavy. Nothing moved him.

Nothing moved.

"You dumb son of a bitch!"

The body on top of her rolled away in a slow sliding motion, leaving her chest clear, but their legs entangled, and her hand, with its death grip on the flashlight, mashed under the weight of his torso.

To work herself free of the body, Keeley let go of the light. Breathing heavy and unable to comprehend what had just happened, she looked up.

Another man, smaller than the first, stared down at her, a gun held loosely in the hand at his side. While he stared at her, she glanced at the inert body beside her—the man called Mace—and saw the dark wash of blood staining his neck.

He was dead.

She couldn't breathe, couldn't find power enough to get to her feet. Panic closed her throat and she scampered backward and looked up.

The man staring down at her seemed to be chewing on something, because his mouth kept moving, even as his eyes never left her face.

Nerves. Excitement. She registered both but still couldn't move, couldn't speak.

The gun still dangled from his hand. "You're her, aren't you?" he finally said, his tone ripe with disgust. "Aileen Farrell's daughter? That stupid piece of shit got that right, didn't he?"

What was he saying . . .

Keeley stared dumbly, eyes wide, mouth dry. It was as if a tidal wave had crested in her brain, then receded, leaving a dulling amorphous calm, an inability to think, to fear.

I should get up.

Instead she closed her eyes, forced herself to calm, to think. When she opened her eyes, she asked, "Who are you?" Her voice was weak, but okay. She swallowed. "And how do you know my mother?"

"I don't, but my father sure as hell did, looked for that Irish whore for years. Never said a goddamn word about you, though. I wouldn't have known you existed if it weren't for the old woman."

Another forgiveness call. "Mary called you."

"She called my old man, William, that's who she called. But she got me. She wanted him to know he had a daughter, how she should have told him about you, what a freakin' saint you were. How you two should get together. Shit about being sorry, said it was all her fault because Aileen and her kept some secret about a dead guy." His mouth worked even harder, lips jerking and twitching. He was all nerves and they were all snapping. "Total bullshit," he spit out. "The hag knew he was dying, knew he was fuckin' loaded. All she wanted was the money—for you. My money!"

"You're my . . . brother." Some of his words trickled through her addled mind, but they didn't line up, refused to make sense. *Brother . . .*

"Yeah. I'm your brother, all right. The name's Dolan and I'm your brother from hell. And you? You're my dead sister."

He raised the gun, and Keeley stared at it dumbly, shook her head when she lost focus and its edges blurred. "I don't have a—"

He kicked her in the thigh. "Get up."

She resisted standing, couldn't see the logic in assisting in her own murder. She rubbed her leg, stayed where she was, and started to pray. From the corner of her eye a black shape moved through the darkness, low and fast, coming from behind the man holding the revolver.

Keeley shifted her gaze back to the man in front of her. Determined to hold his attention, she scrambled to get up.

The man, as if smelling danger, spun around. Too late.

Gus tackled him at knee level and brought him down hard. Keeley heard a bone crack.

The gun flew out of Dolan's hand, and Keeley, hesitating only a second, picked it up. Her hand, numb with cold, and shaking, was barely able to grip it.

The next second Gus took it from her. Holding the gun, he nudged the prostrate man with the toe of his wet, dirty sneaker. He rolled over and clasped his arm. "You broke my fuckin' arm."

Gus ignored him and reached for Keeley, his dark eyes seeming to cover all of her at a glance. "Are you all right?"

"I'm okay . . ." She focused on him. His face was black with mud, and blood oozed down the side of his face. The bandage she'd applied earlier hung by a piece of tape over his ear. His hair was matted. "But you're not." She wanted to touch his face, but was afraid to hurt him, so she took his arm. "We need to stop the bleeding."

"It can wait." He tore off the dangling bandage. "Go back to the house, Keeley. Call the police. Tell them they'll need an ambulance." He gestured with his chin to the dead Mace and the shivering, moaning Dolan curled up in a ball at their feet clutching his arm. "And that there's a mess here that needs cleaning up."

Gus was right she should go, but her body felt dull, incapable of motion—in a dream state. Looking down at Dolan, she wondered aloud, "He says he's my brother. That my father's still alive." It was painful to say, impossible to understand. "If it's true, why would he want to kill me? It doesn't make sense."

"Greed never makes sense, and from what I heard, there's money involved. He was afraid you'd stake a claim."

"Money." She said the word slowly, carefully, as if it were a foreign phrase, but it didn't help her understanding. Tomorrow, it would all make sense tomorrow.

Gus used the back of his free hand to wipe some

blood and grime from his face. "He might be your
brother, but blood doesn't make a family."

Dolan moaned, but when she made a move to go
to him, Gus put his hand on her shoulder, stopped
her. "Leave him. He's all right, and the quicker you
get that ambulance here, the quicker he'll get his
arm set. He's not going anywhere. You can sort
things out with him tomorrow." He lowered his
voice and urged softly, "Call the cops, Keeley. That's
what you have to do."

She turned toward the hedge, her muddy thinking beginning to clear. It was time to get moving, do
something useful—about everything. She'd come to
St. Ivan's to find a body, and she had. She'd also
found her right path.

She took a few faltering steps to Mayday House,
then turned to look back. "Do you know what does
make a family, Gus?"

Silence came out of the darkness, then the shadow
that was Gus said, "Yeah, I do."

"And?"

Silence.

"You plan on bringing the cynical, hot-stuff gigolo
to his knees, don't you?"

She lifted her face to the rain and smiled weakly.
"That would be good."

More silence, then, "Love, Keeley. Love makes a
family."

She nodded and headed to Mayday House.

The following afternoon, Gus, steaming coffee
in hand, stood on the back porch, waiting for
Keeley to come through the hole in the hedge.

She'd already explained everything to Father Barton—she and one of the cops, but after that, she'd wanted some "quiet time" with her mother.

Her eye nearly swollen shut, and her jaw about two sizes bigger than normal, she looked like hell, and he'd suggested she take things easy. But no way could he stop her, and no way would she rest. They were damn near a matched set: his face was cut, and the lump on his head, added to the one Mace had given him earlier, was the size of a baseball. But a couple of painkillers had reduced the ache to a dull throb.

He was settled enough. For now.

He glanced up. The weather had cleared, not to the gold of autumn sunshine, but to a light silver and a sky thick with clouds. Thanks to the storm, the world was scrubbed and polished, and the air moist from last night's rain. The scent of it was clean, sharp, and fresh with promise.

"Doesn't it smell like a brand-new promise, Gussy, like yesterday never happened?"

Gus started when the words jumped into his mind, followed by an image of his grandmother standing on a rickety fire escape landing with him and April. She was urging them to look up at the blue lane of sky running between the tall, dirty buildings—April beside him, nodding solemnly, saying, "I can smell it, Gramma, I really can."

A month later his grandmother was dead, and he and April went back to live with their parents. Two hellish years after that, April was gone. Sold like a trinket to fill a crack pipe.

Gus drew in a deep breath, willed the painful memory aside.

Yesterday *did* happen; he knew that for a fact, and because of it, he had business with Hagan Marsden. He didn't figure it would take long, and it would be easier now he knew Mayday House and Keeley were safe.

The police were gone—for now. Probably already doing the paperwork required to start digging up St. Ivan's. The Starks had left an hour ago, and Dinah was upstairs packing. Christiana, at Keeley's insistence, was staying on a few days. He'd just passed her and Bridget in the kitchen on their way out for a walk.

That was good, Gus thought, better that Bridget attach herself to someone like Christiana than Erica Stark. Paul was okay, but Erica . . . he'd take a pass. He'd see both of them soon enough, when they came back for the exhumation and to claim the body—or bones, to be dead accurate. The way he saw it, Erica was damn lucky because Keeley adamantly refused to tell the police about the cellar incident when Stark had trained her Glock on Keeley's chest— or the blackmail attempt. For the babies' sake, she said, not for Erica. His opinion? Those babies had losing tickets in the motherhood lottery.

Although Erica had exchanged telephone numbers with Christiana. Hell, they'd come damn close to hugging before they'd shaken hands and Erica stomped out the door. Probably wouldn't hurt the Stark kids to have an aunt like Christiana in the background.

"Gus." Dinah came up from behind, and stepped up beside him at the rail.

"How you doing?" he asked, turning to touch her cheek.

"I'm perfect. What else would you expect?" The words were pure Dinah, but the tone wasn't.

"Somehow I doubt that." He set his coffee down and crossed his arms. "It was rough on you. And maybe not over yet?" He raised a brow.

She shrugged. "I'm stopping at the"—she adopted a sarcastic tone—"local constabulary before I leave town. They want to go over my story—again—but no one's said anything about my not leaving, so I'm heading home today."

"No charges then."

She shook her head. "One cop muttered about my being an accessory after the fact for keeping my mouth shut, but the other one said that because of Mary's confession and after all this time, they probably wouldn't charge. I talked to my lawyer a few minutes ago, and he said the second cop was probably on the money." She looked out over the backyard. "If that changes, they know where to find me—and my lawyer. I'm leaving. Can't wait to get out of here." She looked around with distaste. "God, I hate this place!"

At that point Keeley's head came through the hedge. Dinah watched her unfold from the tangled bush and head for the house. After a moment she said, "It's you and her, isn't it?"

"It is."

She nodded and he saw her swallow. "I kind of figured that out from the first day in the kitchen. You were working so goddamned hard at ignoring her. There had to be a reason. What did you think I'd do, put a knife in her back?"

"Something like that."

"You underestimate me. I'd have been much more shrewd and creative."

"Yes. I guess you would."

A breeze drifted between them, bringing a riff of silence. She moved into him, put a hand on his face, and covered his jaw with her palm. "You know I love you, don't you?"

He took her hand from his face and kissed her palm. "You'll get over it. Over me. You and I both know that."

She looked at him a long time, then took her hand from his and shook her head. She smiled, but Gus didn't miss the sheen of tears in her eyes. "There's always shopping," she said as Keeley took the first stair.

Gus nodded, pulled her close, and kissed her forehead. "Take care of yourself, Dinah."

She straightened away from him. "Now there's something I do know how to do." She turned and walked back into the kitchen.

Keeley took the top step, watched her go, then switched her attention to him, or as much of her attention as she could give from an eye that grew more vivid by the hour. "Complicated, huh?"

"Yeah."

"You okay with it?"

He took the two steps separating them and stood in front of her. "I'm okay with you. Only you."

She wrapped her arms around his waist and for a few moments they held each other. Finally, Keeley said, "When are you leaving?"

"Tomorrow. I've set up a meeting with Hagan for late afternoon in Seattle."

"What if he won't tell you where April is? After

everything that's gone on, he's not going to be happy."

"Hagan's never happy, but I'll work it out," he said. *And I'll get what I want from him, or he'll be one sorry bastard.* He kept his last thoughts to himself. "What about you? When are you going?"

"They plan to exhume the body the day after tomorrow, I'll leave right after that. I don't see any reason to wait. His, uh, son said William doesn't have much time left. And I want to visit Dolan—if he'll see me." She shrugged.

"Complicated," Gus said, using her description of his relationship with Dinah.

She stepped back. "Definitely complicated. But I have to go. No matter what, he's my father."

"I know." He smoothed her hair. "How long will you be gone?"

"Two or three days, maybe. I don't really know, because I'm not sure what to expect. It isn't every day I meet a father I didn't know I had."

"I'll be waiting."

CHAPTER 23

It was more than a week, and as Gus had promised, he was waiting for her. After a couple of days of flight delays due to bad weather, Sea-Tac was jammed. There was barely enough time for a hurried embrace before they joined the throngs waiting for luggage at the carousel. Serious talk would have to wait.

"Did Christiana get hold of you? She left a message at the house. Something about a service for Stark," Gus asked, his eyes on the passing luggage.

"Yes, I saw her there. She and Paul arranged it. It was small, just a few people." And one of the most uncomfortable days of her life.

He looked surprised, then shook his head. "You went."

"I think Mary and my mother would have wanted it"

"Mm-hm."

He glanced down at her. "Then you know Bridget went with Chris." He checked on a look-alike bag to Keeley's, then stepped back.

"Yes. She's given her a job, not sure what, exactly.

Something like an assistant to her assistant. Christiana has a large measure of do-gooder in her, I think." She settled her shoulder bag more comfortably. "Oh, and she's going to New York—Christiana, I mean. To meet her brother, Perry. God, I hope she's luckier in the brother department than me." She grimaced, stifled her hurt and disappointment. Dolan still refused to talk to her, so she'd decided to give him some time before trying again. What she wouldn't do was give up on him.

"Perry's okay. They'll like each other."

"Good." Keeley prayed that out of all the tragedy and chaos of the past, some good would come out of it for Christiana. As it had for her. She stole a glance at the tall, purposeful man at her side. Definitely good.

"Here it is." Gus retrieved her case. "Let's go."

When they got to the car, he dropped the bag and pulled her into his arms. "Now, let's say hello again. Properly." He made up for the hurried part of their reunion by kissing her breathless. "God, I've missed you." He put his forehead to hers when he ended the kiss. Then he kissed her again, this time until her knees went weak.

"I think . . ." She managed to get some air in her lungs. "We'd better move along before we get arrested for public indecency." Which at the moment didn't bother her a bit. It had been a hard week emotionally, and she couldn't think of a softer place for it to end than in Gus's arms.

"Indecent, huh? Sounds good to me." Gus touched her hair and smiled down at her. Like his kisses, his rare smiles captivated her, turning his handsome, sharp-angled face to mesmerizing and lightening his brown eyes to a deep amber. When joy touched his face, all the wariness and cool remoteness disappeared, leaving it clearer and more beautiful than ever.

Keeley tightened her grip on his waist, overwhelmed with her feelings for him—the fierceness of them. "Me, too, but if it's all the same to you, I'd like the indecent part behind closed doors."

He laughed and opened the car door. "Get in," he said. "I want to hear all about your week, your time with your father."

And I want to hear about April.

During their telephone calls, whenever she'd asked, he'd sidestepped her questions, saying vague things about how he was still working on it. Gus would tell her when he was ready, but she couldn't squelch the fear that Hagan had been too angry to be cooperative, that Gus had lost his only lead to his sister because of her.

When he settled in beside her, he said, "Okay, shoot. From what you told me, you and he hit if off well enough." He started the car, checked the car's mirrors, and reversed out of the parking spot.

"My father is—" She tried to think of the right words. "A very rich, very lonely, very bitter man."

Gus slanted her a gaze. "I'd be bitter, too, if I had Dolan for a son. Finding out he's up on murder charges can't be easy."

"The odd thing is that didn't seem to upset him—or surprise him. He muttered something about Dolan being a 'bad seed' and never said his name again." Keeley's heart weighed heavy in her chest. "Something's so awfully wrong between them. If there was ever any love there, it was lost long ago. It's so sad."

"Dolan's mother around?"

Keeley shook her head. "Dead. Years ago. She was William's third wife. And last, so he said."

When she didn't add anything else, he prompted her, "Will you see him again? William, I mean."

"Yes. And soon, I think." She needed to know him better, this man with the faded red hair and the gloomy soul. In the few days she'd spent with him, a tenuous link was formed, and soon that link would be broken. Her father was much too ill to last much longer, a fact her years of nursing made obvious, and his doctor confirmed.

"What happened? Between him and your mother?"

"She walked out on him—which isn't the story I heard. Apparently, my father's family was . . . prestigious, for want of a better word, and had a lot of money—which I gather he's spent most of his life adding to. When his father found out about the 'young Irish girl' he was involved with, he threatened to disinherit him. William says he was prepared for that, that he loved my mother and wanted to marry her, but in the heat of things she wrote a note, saying something about not wanting to ruin his family, and walked away."

"Did he know about you?"

"No. He thought it was a possibility, he said, but my mother never told him she was pregnant."

Gus whistled. "That must have been something. His meeting a daughter he didn't know existed."

"Yes." And strange, because William had accepted Keeley immediately, with very few questions asked. Although several times, as she'd smoothed his bedding or sat with him while he ate, she'd caught him staring at her, once with tears in his eyes. "He said I had his hair and my mother's smile."

"And that was that?"

"He said he looked for my mother, but never found a trace of her. He thought she'd gone back to Ireland. He's finding it hard to believe she was here all these years." She paused. "An old story, isn't it? Love gone wrong."

"And you believe him."

The comment, so cautious and guarded, was so . . . Gus, that she smiled. "Yes, I believe him." She stopped smiling. "Maybe because it makes my mother's secrecy about Jimmy Stark's death make a crazy kind of sense. She must have been afraid if there was publicity of any kind, William would find her." She looked out the car window, puzzled. They were heading north, not south. "Where are we going?"

"You'll see."

Fifteen minutes later, Gus pulled into the parking lot of the Marriott Waterfront Hotel; ten minutes after that, they were in a suite looking out over Seattle's waterfront.

"This is decadent," Keeley whispered, standing at the window and looking in awe at the glimmer of lights across Elliott Bay.

Gus came up behind her, wrapped his arms around her, and rested his chin on her head. "I figured you could handle a taste of 'decadent' for one night." When he nuzzled her ear, she closed her eyes. "I ordered room service," he said, "but I can cancel if you prefer to go out."

"What do you think?"

He tightened his grip on her, and she felt his smile in her hair. "You're my kind of woman, Farrell. I think I'll keep you. Forever."

"I love that word."

"I know."

"But—" She turned in his arms and faced him. "Before forever begins, I need to know about April."

Tension tightened his mouth, and he dropped his hands from her shoulders, took a few steps back. His face was so closed, it looked as if—if he were going to speak—it wouldn't be until the next millennium.

Keeley didn't intend to wait. "During our calls, every time I asked, all you said was 'things looked good,' and you were working on it."

He put his hands on his hips. "Still am."

"Hagan didn't tell, Hagan lied . . . what?"

"Hagan came through all right." He rubbed an eyebrow. "He took some persuading, but, yeah, he came through."

Silence. She didn't want to know.

"*And?*" Keeley decided if she was going to spend her life drawing information from this man, she'd better hone her interrogational skills. She had visions of Chinese water torture, or maybe one of those medieval racks.

"I was too late. By about two weeks." He let out a heavy breath. "Two lousy weeks. She'd been living in some kind of low-rent apartment in Portland. The building manager said she left in the middle of the night. Skipped out on the rent."

"No forwarding address, then."

"No."

Keeley wrapped her arms around him. She wanted to absorb his disappointment, and though easy words of sympathy weren't nearly enough, she said, "I'm so sorry, Gus."

He ran his hands down her back, squeezed her waist. "It wasn't a total loss. I talked to a neighbor. She said April told her she was going south. San Diego, maybe. Or San Francisco. As leads go, it's not much. But I'll see where it takes me. The thing is—"

"Go on."

"She's alive," he said, his voice tight. "All these years, looking for her, never a trace—I could never be sure. But knowing she's alive . . . I'll find her. Sooner or later, I'll find her." He stopped again. "Her and her girl."

Keeley's head came up. "She has a child?"

"A young teenager, the woman said. She was vague on the age."

"And all these years on her own." Keeley, afraid she'd cry, went back to the window overlooking the bay where she stood and watched the evening darken into night.

She thought about April, a woman on her own with a young daughter, both of them running in the middle of the night—from God knows what or who. No money to pay the rent, nowhere to go. There was pain there—and fear. She rubbed her chest where her heart rested uneasily.

Such women were the women of Mayday House. Women Mary and her mother had spent their lives trying to help. Women for whom she would do the same. Mayday House would be a place to mend lives like April's, a soft place to fall.

She said a silent prayer that wherever April was, she would find just such a place.

Gus came up behind her and took her in his arms.

"We'll find her, Gus," she said. "We won't stop looking until we do."

He kissed he hair. "Yes, we will."

"Let's go home." She spun in his arms, suddenly excited, eager to get started . . . on everything. "Let's eat the wonderful dinner you've ordered, then drive to Mayday House. I want to be there." *I need to be there—with you.*

Gus smiled, raised a brow at the king-sized bed dominating the luxurious room.

"We've got one just like it at home," she coaxed.

He kissed her. "Damned if we don't," he said. "Mayday House, it is."

BOOK YOUR PLACE ON OUR WEBSITE AND MAKE THE READING CONNECTION!

We've created a customized website just for our very special readers, where you can get the inside scoop on everything that's going on with Zebra, Pinnacle and Kensington books.

When you come online, you'll have the exciting opportunity to:

- View covers of upcoming books
- Read sample chapters
- Learn about our future publishing schedule (listed by publication month *and author*)
- Find out when your favorite authors will be visiting a city near you
- Search for and order backlist books from our online catalog
- Check out author bios and background information
- Send e-mail to your favorite authors
- Meet the Kensington staff online
- Join us in weekly chats with authors, readers and other guests
- Get writing guidelines
- AND MUCH MORE!

**Visit our website at
http://www.kensingtonbooks.com**